Beautiful Beautiful

BRANDON REID

Beautiful Beautiful

NIGHTWOOD EDITIONS

2023

Nightwood Editions
P.O. Box 1779
Gibsons, BC VON 1V0
Canada
www.nightwoodeditions.com

COVER DESIGN: Carleton Wilson
TYPOGRAPHY: Carleton Wilson
COVER IMAGE: Vector Tradition / creativemarket.com

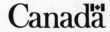 Canada Council   Conseil des Arts
for the Arts   du Canada

Nightwood Editions acknowledges the support of the Canada Council for the Arts, the Government of Canada, and the Province of British Columbia through the BC Arts Council.

This book has been printed on 100% post-consumer recycled paper.

Printed and bound in Canada.

LIBRARY AND ARCHIVES CANADA CATALOGUING IN PUBLICATION

Title: Beautiful beautiful / Brandon Reid.
Names: Reid, Brandon, author.
Identifiers: Canadiana (print) 20230444024 | Canadiana (ebook) 20230444032 |
    ISBN 9780889714540 (softcover) | ISBN 9780889714557 (EPUB)
Subjects: LCGFT: Novels.
Classification: LCC PS8635.E39595 B43 2023 | DDC C813/.6—dc23

To my grandparents,
I love you all.

PART ONE

...a couple of old people
went hand-lining codfish
you know, codfish in the pass here,
and the first steamboat travelled through this pass
—no steamboat before that—
the first big steamboat travelling through,
and they seen as it was coming,
that big thing on top,
and they were just paralyzed, the two of them.
And the captain went on the side of the canoe
—picked him off,
picked her off—
set them at the table and feed them,
feed them just like you feed kids...

—Gordon Reid

1. Egg Island

Derik pops the Canada Dry as he's feeling queasy. It's not the waves, nor the weight of the moon, but George's marked intensity about taking them to the homeland, reliving his glory days as a fisherman. Twelve-year-old Derik takes a seat by Raven at the booth, watching his dad with trepidation.

"Do you think Aunt Lizzy will be at the funeral?" Derik asks.

"Probably," says George, eyes steady on the way ahead.

"How does that make you feel?"

"I don't want to talk about it. I hope I don't see her there. She'll probably just make a scene."

"What did she do that made you hate her so much?"

"She was just an evil person—the way she manipulated Grandpa into giving her money and then blew it on drugs, saying it was for her kids. She showed up to Sam's funeral high as can be on cocaine and was yelling at everyone." Sam was George's sister. She died when Derik was a baby. "I was holding you in my arms when she came up to us, and she said, 'I hope he never makes it to five.'"

This makes Derik think of Candace, his older sister, and her row over who used the computer. She had scowled from the peek in the door as he quickly closed the browser. "I know what you're doing."

"Really?" he continues now with George. "She said that to me when I was a baby?"

"Yeah, total psycho. Then she proceeded to make an ass of herself by taking the pamphlets off the table and throwing them around," he mimics her stupidly, albeit quite accurately. "She was yelling too, 'I'm glad she's dead. Stupid…' Well, she kept swearing and getting in people's faces, *her own* relatives. God it was embarrassing. We haven't seen her since; Mom can't stand her."

"Why would she wish that upon me, my own aunt?"

"'Cause she's a mean, spiteful person who probably wanted it to happen to you 'cause you're my son. She always resented our parents having me, she said that's what killed our mom, having me. So anything to get back at me, she'd do."

"That's messed up, to wish that upon a kid."

"Yeah, it is."

"How did Auntie Sammy die again?"

"She had lymphoma—probably from all those chemicals she used to spray on her lawn. I told her it was a bad idea, but she always said, 'Look how green my backyard is.' She couldn't water it 'cause of water restrictions, so she resorted to using chemicals."

Derik drinks his soda while gauging Raven. *What does he see?*

He has Entei's eyes.

Do you think he knows who Entei is?

Maybe. He used to collect Pokémon cards.

I wish I had dark circles below my eyes like he does.

"It sucks, because so many Indigenous families were torn apart by intergenerational trauma and addiction," says Raven. "It continues to plague reserves, how to adapt to the Western way... not that they need to."

"What do you mean by that?" says Derik.

"Well, some First Nations are taking the initiative to self-govern, or to *decolonize*, which means to break down what it means to be a settler, and not do it; they do things *their* way."

"Wouldn't they have to not use plumbing and stop speaking English then?"

"It's not quite that extreme. It's more like letting First Nations decide what they teach, or how to use their natural resources, rather than forcing them to vote NDP, you know. I'm all for it; it makes sense to me. But I try to merge Western and Indigenous beliefs, so it's difficult for me to grapple with sometimes, as I see them as similar more often than not. I'm sure many would disagree, say that I'm not defining it properly, or that I'm for the other side, but the fact that I'm controversial just goes to show I've hit a nerve, and that's what it takes for change to happen—for reconciliation to start."

"I know what you mean: my dad's Native, but my mom's white. I can't win. They tried to pull me out of class to make a drum with the Indigenous teacher but I didn't want to be singled out over my race so I refused and stayed in class with everyone else."

"Well, there's no harm in exploring your heritage... but I can see why you wouldn't want to be treated differently."

"I just want to be normal, with my friends."

"Hey." Raven smiles. "What's *normal*, anyway? Everyone sees the world through their own eyes, 'cause everyone sees through their own eyes... except if you're blind, but *vision* is what I'm talking about; everyone has their own world they experience."

"That's true." Derik takes another sip of his pop.

Port Hardy is now far behind them, to starboard nothing but wild shore, adorned with its lush green and ranges arching into forgotten, remote lands. Only the birds flock these parts—many a friend of mine.

They enter a new world, a world of spirit (sure enough) but also that of true Earth, where Nature has her course, where the living gods breathe through her and the deeds of evil men are absorbed, taken apart and reassembled for the greater good; like the radiation of fallen reactors, their heavy water dispersed into the ocean whence it came; though the stars melt and the night falls, nature returns just the same; like Jesus nailed to the cross, a brighter day, the resurrection, arrives in time; and seeds grow from the mindless passing of men into a rich crop until the man in black reaps it with his scythe.

"I remember," George says, "when I was younger and my mom was still alive, we'd go looking for gulls' eggs. We'd take the boat up to these giant cliffs that would just tower above us; and I was little too, so they just went on forever. Dad would leave us there as he scaled the cliffs, me with my sisters and mom; and this one time, the waves were crashing, pushing us closer to the rocks where it was really dangerous, you know, 'cause the boat could've easily capsized."

"What kind of boat was it?"

"This was just our punt, really shallow." He shows Derik with his hands the height, just past his knees. "I thought for sure this time we were going to flip over, the boat was rocking that much. But my mom was jigging for halibut, calm as could be. And I was screaming, crying, 'Mom, Mom, we're going to flip, we're going to flip!' She didn't care, though, she just kept jigging. And then she caught one: a great big halibut, about this big!" George gestures, arms wide. "She pulled it up and threw it on board. I'd never seen a halibut that big before. My sisters were laughing, saying, 'What a crybaby.' Then Grandpa came down with a bucket full of gulls' eggs. He lowered them down with a rope to us and we took them in and went back and boiled them up, they were so good. We had them with the halibut. I'll never forget how good they were." No doubt, risk added precedence to the reward. George continues staring ahead, reminiscing, the story resonating through him.

Raven searches for life. "Look!" He jumps, pointing to port. "I saw a spout!"

Derik jumps up too, not wanting to disappoint. "Where, where? I didn't see it."

Raven scans, discerning spout from the myriad other patterns before and after, but it fades. "You didn't see it?"

Derik desperately seeks. "...No."

"Dang." He returns to the booth while Derik keeps searching, hoping to spot the next.

On this day of their journey, the first place of geographical interest our three encounter is the Egg Island Lighthouse, situated on a tiny island with all the wrath of the Pacific clamouring against it; the great horses of Neptune clash at the gates, threatening to raze the lonely lighthouse. The former keeper claimed he heard whispers, and then his wife went insane. The very first lighthouse was destroyed by waves during a particularly harsh storm, so they made the second one of concrete and put it on the highest point of the island. One day a distress call went out, and none other than Henry Mormin himself answered the call, saving the keeper and his wife while the storm lashed their ankles. They'd finally had enough.

"They had to take shelter in their chicken coop at the top of the island, surviving off eggs. Then Grandpa picked them up and took them to the hospital in Bella Bella," says George.

"That's cool. He was a hero then, wasn't he?" says Derik.

"He sure did them a favour by picking them up off that island. I wouldn't want to be there during a storm."

Raven admires it as they pass. "I wouldn't mind living there by myself, to be honest."

"You wouldn't, would you?" says George.

"Nope, that'd be dope. I've always entertained the idea of living somewhere remote, like Kerouac in *Desolation Angels*. He was a fire watcher—you know those guys who live in the middle of a forest on a mountain looking for fires caused by lightning? Apparently lightning causes a lot of fires."

"I wouldn't want to live alone. To think of all the nights I spent alone in my dad's house while he was out fishing and partying—that great big lonely house—wishing for some company. I hated it."

"That would suck as a kid. I'd take that job, though—I'd be stoked if all I had to do was change a light bulb. Yup, that'd be the perfect life for me, just meditating, playing music or making art."

"Sounds like a nightmare to me," says George.

"You know shamans used to do that: they would go away and live alone for long periods of time, seeking some sort of vision or enlightenment. The prophets, too—Jesus, Buddha, Moses—they each ventured into the wilderness, lived alone, then returned enlightened, preaching the *word*."

"Really?" says Derik.

"So you think you're a prophet?" George asks Raven.

"All I'm saying is there's a clear link between shamanism and what the prophets did for Buddhism, Christianity and Islam. You ever just sit in the dark and listen to music or white noise? Or lay in one of those deprivation tanks? When your mind isn't distracted by what the eye sees, or what the ears hear, it begins to wander inward and focus on itself. The further you go within, the further you go without. That's why I like sitting in the dark and staring at the wall—it helps me think."

"That's weird man. I like having people around." George laughs dismissively. "I think maybe you should see someone about that, if you can't stand being around people."

"There's nothing more interesting or more distracting than people," says Raven. "Like, I find it hard to write around people without making it about them in some abstract manner. I would always write in my cabin in Bella Bella for my thesis after interviewing people, like your dad. All I would hear was the lapping of waves, which was perfect! White noise helps me focus."

"I had to write a thesis for school," says Derik. "What was yours on?"

"The Cannibal Dance... which was difficult to research, as it was traditionally kept secret. Your grandpa was the only one who would talk to me about it."

"Really?" says Derik. "What would he say?"

"His eyes would light up and he'd go into great detail about how he saw one, but never actually danced. He said they dug up the head of a woman who'd recently died, then they started eating it, scaring everyone in attendance. It was meant to be horrifying, and, well, I can't think of anything scarier than that. I gave up on writing my thesis though, 'cause I realized some things are better kept secret. Like, what's the point of me going there to try and write about something no one wants me to write about as an outsider? Pointless, if you ask me."

George clears his throat.

"At least I get to go back and pay my respects to a truly great storyteller. Gosh, for hours Henry and I would talk, sometimes till the sun came up. I can give you the tapes if you like. I have them in storage."

EGG ISLAND

"That'd be amazing," says Derik. "I don't really have anything to remember my grandpa by. He was never really in my life."

George sucks his vape.

"Why'd they consider you an outsider though?" asks Derik. "Aren't you Heiltsuk?"

"Far back on my mom's side I am, but not enough to have status," replies Raven. "I'm from all over: white, Haisla, Sioux, even Choctaw—a total mut." Sun beams around his head.

"I wish I wasn't half-Indian and half-white sometimes. Would be easier to belong to one group instead of two."

"Yeah, I had to pay out of my own pocket to go to university (like a real white person)—another reason why I stopped trying to earn my doctorate."

"...Aren't shamans doctors though?" asks Derik.

"I think that's fair to say: they heal people and help them better understand themselves."

"So you're already a doctor. Why do you need a school to tell you you are?"

"*Exactly.*" He searches for spouts or otters. "I'm much more effective in my lot."

Derik, on the other hand, thinking of isolation, seeks some, venturing to the top deck, exposed to the elements. But as he does so, the sun tucks behind cloud, and for the first time on their journey the sky is overcast.

I wish I could play Heroes of the Storm *with my friends. No one can heal like I can.*

I hope texting isn't long distance.

He gets no reception, so lays back, staring to sky, letting phone slide to deck, recalling the one that got away.

2. The One That Got Away

Two days ago it happened, near Texada Island. The sun beat down and sparkled upon the water.

"Why'd we stop?" I asked. "What are you doing?"

Dad went for the rods. "Let's try some fishing. This looks like a good spot."

"Nice!" I was excited, I really was.

He brought out the tackle and sat with legs splayed on the front deck, beginning the intricate work of attaching lures.

"How do you know which ones to use?" I asked him.

"The goal is to make it appetizing for the fish; it should look like what they normally eat. We're fishing for rock cod 'cause I don't think there'll be many salmon around. They're not that picky, so we'll try a jig."

"How do you know they're around here?"

"'Cause it shows them on the fish finder, and I can sense where they are. I used to tell my dad when we went out for herring season, 'They're here—there are fish here—I can feel it,' and we'd put out the net and you wouldn't *believe* how many we'd catch. I can think like a fish."

No way. He can't actually sense where the fish are.

Why not? You talk to birds when no one's looking. You talk to me.

"Fish aren't that smart, though," I said.

"You calling me stupid?"

"No." I chuckled.

Look at the water. If I fell in, no one would find me.

Maybe the fish *are* speaking to us, and we just don't listen.

Nah, that's stupid. Imagine it with a top hat and monocle.

That's funny. Scratch neck.

Dad attached the jigs. ("Do the jig," he used to say when I was a toddler, holding me under my arms until I danced). He gave me the rod. "You're good to go!"

"Cool! ...What do I do now?" So stupid. Can't believe I didn't know.

"Cast it off the bow, toward those rocks there," he said.

You noob.

"Then what? Do I jig?"

"Yeah."

"What's that, again?"

"I told you, let it sink, then pull up—repeat. Let it sink, pull up, repeat. Keep doing that till you get a bite, then reel it in."

"Got it." I approached the bow, inspecting the rod. It was light. I thought maybe I could catch a salmon (if there were any).

It was a trap!

No, the lure was attached tight. I wanted to make him proud, to show I was a real man who could catch a fish and provide for his family.

You're twelve; why think of such things?

I don't know, have to grow up at some point. Everyone says I'm a mama's boy. Probably why Dad makes me work for him, to snap me out of it. My sword rested on my shoulder.

I looked to where all forces converged, just like sparring; you sense when a punch is coming and when to counter. I drew back, cocked the rod, then cast, but the goddamn stupid rigged piece of shit didn't cast.

You didn't release the bail arm!

Well how was I suppose to know?! He didn't tell me.

Didn't ask.

He was waiting for it to happen so he could correct me and look like a hero. He always does that. Always putting me down so he feels great.

Don't say that.

It's true!

No it's not, you're exaggerating (Mom would say). Maybe he forgot to tell you, maybe he wanted you to mess up so you learned on your own and thus never forgot.

Whatever, he didn't warn me.

"You bozo!" Dad said. "You have to release the bail arm!"

I was so pissed. "Well you didn't tell me that!"

"I thought you knew!" He kept on attaching jigs like it wasn't his fault. "Here Raven. You're all set."

"Thank you." Raven sauntered to port like a deer. Is there anything he can't do? He cast, then within seconds, he already had his first bite. Jealousy—shove away. He was quiet so as to not spoil the catch. The rod slightly bent. He made it look easy, until that orange flame breached the water—then we knew it was a rock cod. No point in letting it run, fish was as good as sunk, already filleting itself on the table.

"Is this good?" it said.

Raven pulled it aboard by hand. It flipped and flopped on deck, spritzing us like a sprinkler. Filling water balloons to throw at the bus.

"Wow," I said. "You're lucky."

He said, "All skill, baby!"

"Nice catch," said Dad.

"Thanks. I used to fish every Sunday. It's like riding a bike. Now where's the club?"

"Over there."

He grabbed the club and brought it high before whacking the fish on the head. It seized, postured, indicating severe head trauma. I saw that happen to someone at karate when they got knocked out by a head kick. Vacant eyes.

"Is it dead?" I asked.

"Pretty much," said Raven. He held it up, proud as can be. "Fine rock cod, that."

I asked if we could eat it, and he said yeah, 'cause it's not poisonous, though its spines are slightly venomous. "You wouldn't want to step on one of those spines," he said. "That'd hurt."

I was so eager to catch one. I went right back to the bow to cast again, making sure this time the bail arm was released. I cast, and it worked! I was only a few metres off. I had improved. I was jigging, just like they showed me. I was too impatient, though—I kept reeling in; you have to let the buzz bomb sink, that's what makes it buzz. I kept thinking I saw a fish, but it was just the jig, then I had to start all over again. Got a little better each time.

That's good. Gotta keep practising, that's all.

Kept thinking I had a bite.

Then I saw a salmon pass. I wondered what it was doing there—Dad said there weren't any.

He was wrong. What does he know? He's only been a fisherman his whole life. "Hey!" I shouted. "I just saw a salmon."

"There might be some around," Dad said. He approached the gunwale. Cannons fire in the distance. He stood right beside me, like jocks at the urinal. He cast, reeled in his years. I prayed he wouldn't get one before me.

It was fun (for a while), us three fishing. Sometimes you catch something, sometimes you don't. It's an excuse to look at nature, which I don't mind.

Raven got another bite.

"You got another one?" said Dad.

"Yup," said he. Reeled in another rock cod. "It's a bit bigger." He dropped it on deck. It flipped, then flopped. "You have pliers, right?" He searched the tackle.

"They're in there."

Then Dad got a bite and everything went to hell. I just want to catch a fish.

"*Woo-ee*," he hollered. "I got a bite!" He tugged the line to make sure. It ran. "Yup! I got something." Rod bent heavily. I approached, thinking it was a rock cod.

"What are you doing? Why don't you reel it in?" I said.

"I'm letting it tire itself out." The reel spun. Could tell it was big by the way it tugged.

"The rod won't break, will it?"

"It'll be fine." The reel kept spinning. I thought it'd run out of line. The fish pulled left, then right, right, then left, round in circles, swimming close, then far. Then it swam beneath the boat, causing Dad to lean over the gunwale. He was trying to yank it back, but it was stubborn. Stubborn little bugger. Meanwhile, Raven clubbed his catch behind us. He pried the hook free with the pliers. "They're easier to net when you tire them out, but this is a feisty one. Get the net! It's right over there."

I grabbed the net. I leaned over the gunwale and positioned it underwater, ready to scoop. Then we saw it: the telltale silver of a salmon.

"There he is!" said George. Reel reel reel; run run run.

It was tired, but it still put up a fight. It *looked* upset, as if it had been hooked before. "What do you want with me?" It kept diving and flipping out of the water. Years seemed to pass; progress was slow. Then, finally, it gave up.

Dad reeled it in close. I was so ready, I had the net in perfect position, but as soon as it touched the net, zap! It took off again, zigzagging away.

Dad said his arms were getting tired. You and me both, brother. He managed to tire it again, and it swam close, but soon as it sensed the net, it fled. They're smarter than people give them credit for.

"Sure has a lot of fight in it," I said.

"Yup. Here he comes! Get ready."

It came in for another pass. I figured it would flee again, so I was just holding the net still. "OK, go!" Dad yelled. "Get it!"

I *knew* it wasn't close enough, I *knew* it would flee again. I did my best to anticipate where it was headed, but it was still *way* too far.

"Go! What are you doing?" he kept saying, that idiot. I knew what I was doing. You can't just swing the net up at the fish, you have to guide it into the net, or else it reacts as if a predator is coming at it, 'cause we are predators; we're catching them.

"It's too far still!" I told him, but he didn't care. He pulled hard on the rod, pulling the fish's head from the water. "You're gonna lose it! Go go go."

I knew it was too far—I should've trusted my instincts. He should've trusted me. But he told me to scoop, so I scooped, and it did exactly what I thought it would do: it jolted to the left, half in the net, as I raised it from the water, and flipped right out, going *splat* against the water, which knocked the hook free and it swam off, free—that was the one that got away. I was so mad.

"What the hell did you do that for?" said Dad. "You had it! You had it, then you let it go."

"You said *grab it*!" I stomped in frustration. I wanted to throw him overboard. "You should've pulled it in closer."

All the while, Raven cast quietly, pretending not to hear us. I felt so embarrassed, him hearing us argue like that, 'cause we would've caught it if Dad had just let me do what I was going to do, but nope! He had to butt in and give me horrible advice, like he always does.

Don't say that. It was my fault.

"I can't believe you messed that up. You *had* it. It was so close," he said.

"How was I supposed to know it would jolt like that?" I said.

He reeled in the fruitless line. "Next time, make sure it's in the net before you pull up." He was disappointed, but it was his fault too! I couldn't believe it, it was right there, then it was gone.

He changed the lure for salmon instead of rock cod. "It was right there. I can't believe that."

God, I just wanted to go home. He was acting crazy ever since we left, talking about drugs and sasquatches, and sabotaging my first fishing experience. He was never actually a captain. Grandpa was always the captain.

Yeah, well, he's dead.

I was so set on proving Dad wrong. I *had* to catch the first salmon. I returned to the bow and channelled all my energy, all my rage and frustration at that one mark, and cast. I made sure to not reel in too much; I jigged. But for some reason I thought it would be a good idea to let it sink all the way down. When I tried to reel in, I couldn't, 'cause it was snagged. What are you supposed to do but yank and pray it comes loose? I tried everything! It wouldn't come free. Most frustrating thing in the world. I contemplated diving in and choking the rock that held my hook. I wished I could part the sea and see everything on the bottom.

You should've asked Dad for help.

There was no way I was asking him for help after what happened—he would've just yelled at me. I pulled up on the rod. Nothing. I tried to grab the line with both my hands but it just cut into my fingers, so I wrapped it around my right then yanked. Still, nothing. So I yanked harder and harder, as hard as I could, until finally it came free.

But it *didn't* come free. The line went limp because the tip of the rod broke; it slunk limp down the line, dangling like a Christmas ornament. I wanted to die. I wanted to lay down and never get up. Then, of course! (Of *course!*) The hook came free... I threw down the rod and stormed inside, saying, "Stupid half-breed can't catch a fish."

"Hey! Don't be like that," said Dad. But the damage was already done.

3. Storm and Dreams

OK, your turn.

Hello, friends. I guess it's time I introduce myself. My name is Redbird Anon, and I'm here to guide you. Think of me as Derik's guardian: I know what he thinks. I take many forms. I will tell you all the things that you'll know, because I'm magic, you see. You may notice both the environment and I change according to Derik's attitude, because I connect Derik to his environment; what he perceives is through my aid, as he's only twelve, so needs a wing.

You are wondering, I can tell: Why is this strange bird talking to me? The truth is, Derik wants me to tell you this story because he gets in trouble for running his mouth. *Not always true.* He's in the background, but he's also occasionally the narrator, as demonstrated in the previous chapter. It's unclear who's in charge, thus no one can be blamed for any liberties taken. If he wants me to tell you his story, I'm going to tell it the way it *should* be told.

So let us begin. We find our crew approaching Calvert Island on the third day of their voyage, en route to attend the celebration of life for Henry Mormin, Derik's grandfather. At the helm of *Wild Thing* and weighing in at two hundred pounds, we have George, Derik's dad, and for a deckhand, we have Raven, the eternal trickster. Join us, and be not ashamed.

Derik opens his eyes. *I'm still here, on this boat?* The sky is charcoal with cloud. A few drops of rain sprinkle the deck and his legs. The trees sway manically on the coast, letting all know where the winds and spirits move. Derik hurries down the ladder to warn his dad of the approaching storm.

"I got my first job from a Freemason," George tells Raven over the roar of engine and waves. "Don Beausoleil was his name. When I was eleven, he came up to me right after we docked in the yard there at Steveston, and he said, 'George, I'm a friend of your dad's, we used to work together. I was hoping you'd like to come up to my office. I have an offer for you.' So we went up to his office, which was this great big room with lots of bookshelves and books, like a professor's office. He told me to have a seat. 'Your dad is a great fisherman; I've known him for many years. The amount of work he has done for me is truly astounding. But I remember some years were difficult, and we couldn't always pay him a fair wage. It was the same for everyone. But he kept working for me, as hard as can be. He never asked for anything in return. I offered to repay him as soon as I could, but he refused. The only thing he asked for, was for you to have a job when you were old enough. So here I am, keeping the promise I made him. If you're willing, I guarantee you a wage and position with our fleets or in the cannery.' I never had to go searching for work until BC Packers shut down. He gave me my first *real* job."

"That's pretty cool," says Raven. "How did you know he was a Freemason though?"

"He gave me the handshake."

Raven nods.

"What handshake? Like the salmon?" says Derik. George looks ahead.

"What's the salmon?" asks Raven.

"Hold out your arm." Derik pats his forearm like a salmon slapping its tail. Raven catches on, and does the same—two fish flapping. "Do you know the trout?"

"What's that?"

Derik pats Raven's wrist instead, because it's a shorter fish, you see.

"Nice." They giggle. "Yeah, that's interesting." Raven says, returning to his conversation with George. "A lot of the early explorers were Freemasons."

"Well, look at the founding fathers—they were all masons. And they have the All-Seeing Eye on the dollar bill."

"What's a Freemason?" says Derik, grabbing a seat at the booth.

"It's a group of people who perform rituals together and have ceremonies for certain occasions, ceremonies that aren't usually celebrated by the general public," says Raven.

"Like when Homer Simpson joins the Stonecutters and they paddle him on the butt and then send him back in reverse but give it a different name even though it's basically the same ritual but he can't tell 'cause he's blindfolded?"

"Yeah, sort of," says Raven. "That was a parody of the Freemasons."

"Are you a Freemason?"

"No." Raven chuckles. "I couldn't tell you if I was, though."

"How come?"

"'Cause you're supposed to keep it a secret; it's a secret society… No, I'm more into Thelema and the O.T.O. than Freemasonry."

"What are those?"

"Just groups of loving people. *Thelema* is Greek for divine will."

"What do *they* believe in?" says George Suspicious.

"Basically, love everyone and everything 'cause love unites all. It was a group started by Aleister Crowley, so they follow his maxim: 'Do what thou wilt shall be the whole of the law—love under will.'"

"Oh, I remember that," says Derik. "It was written in that weird book you brought into the pawnshop."

"Right!" says Raven. "He was an exciting, imaginative writer."

"I've heard of him," says George. "He was nothing but a satanist and a pedophile."

"Not quite, no. He wasn't a satanist. He never worshiped Satan (well, at least not any more than any other angel or god or spirit); he would write about and *research* anything theological, philosophical or magical; he wasn't scared to delve into the darker parts of belief and of the mind. People think because he wrote about the Devil, or Satan, or Lucifer (especially), that he was a satanist, which isn't really true."

"He was evil, man. I watched a documentary on him once. He was having sex with little boys and sacrificing animals and summoning demons. The guy was a total freak."

"A lot of that was made up or taken out of context. He was a renaissance man: he travelled to Mecca disguised as a Muslim, he studied Buddhism, he climbed K2—one of the highest mountains in the world—without oxygen tanks, he was an occultist, a writer, a poet, a painter—he did it all! Some think he was even a spy during World War II. You have to read his actual writings to understand what he was about. He was a shaman insofar as he'd say things to make people think and perceive differently to better understand themselves."

"I don't want no part in that shit, that's bad energy coming your way if you start dabbling with black magic."

Raven thinks about what to say, as George isn't giving him the benefit of the doubt but, as he does, arguing for the sake of arguing. "Crowley brought forth a new age of spiritualism while it was dying in the West. Christianity's still dying—look at all the hate they generated with residential schooling."

"The guy was a pedophile," George says. "You know that I was sexually molested myself? You have any idea what it's like to go through that? No one should ever have to experience that! Anyone who does that to a kid should be killed. They should have their head cut off."

"But plenty of great minds did weird stuff like that, you know? Pederasty was common in some ancient societies. Uh—" He hesitates, with Derik's virgin ears present. "And then look at van Gogh, or Picasso: van Gogh cut off his ear and gave it to a prostitute and Picasso was a womanizer."

"Really?" says Derik, ears perked. "I didn't know they did that."

"That doesn't make it right," Raven continues, "yet we still can appreciate their work."

"I've had family and friends go insane 'cause of the sexual abuse they experienced. Some killed themselves. It's completely unacceptable."

"Of course it is. That doesn't mean we can't appreciate the work these people did. People get cancelled these days for far less, sometimes for something they did twenty years ago, back when it was actually somewhat acceptable. Look at Trudeau getting all kinds of flak for wearing brownface, when I bet his friends *encouraged* him to do it! Should we cancel him, our own prime minister? I don't think so. My point is, Crowley wrote some amazing things which I continue to identify with. When I read them, it was like hearing from a long-lost friend, or a voice I had always longed to hear. He did some horrible things, yeah, but his writings taught me how to love, how to be and how to find truth!"

George shakes his head. "I think he was a freak." And he keeps on piloting, the windows fogging and the rain falling.

"I think we're heading into the storm," says Derik, looking over the bow, the rain fragmenting his view. *Those clouds sure do look mean.* "Do you think we'll be safe?" he asks his dad.

"Pfft, yeah. This is nothing. I've been in forty-foot waves before."

"I don't want to go into forty-foot waves."

"That won't happen here. That was closer to Alaska. We'll have the islands to protect us soon, then we'll have nothing to worry about."

Derik looks out the back of the ship— Friends, I know, I know this isn't a ship. Derik knows it too. It's a boat. But on an adventure, anything can become something else. Anyways, from my vantage, the sky, they all look the same—specs on water. Derik looks out the back of the ship at the rolling grey swells from Japan and Raven pacing back and forth, the ship bobbing up and down. The Zodiac attached to stern jolts violently each time it crashes down. Derik imagines it detaching and falling into the water; part of him wills disaster so that it never happens. Unfortunately, it's only worse ahead—yea, verily— as they head into the storm. Night approaches early, with her pallid clouds giving way to black. "I feel like we're going into a tunnel, it's so dark ahead. You sure we're going to be all right?"

"Positive. We're about halfway to Bella Bella now. Might as well go all the way."

"OK," says Derik, rife with doubt.

To the right are the rolling toes of the mountains, saturated with trees, the occasional grey bluff. This is the rainforest, rich with flora. You may think rainforests only exist in South America, with anacondas and jaguars, but no, this part of BC is technically rainforest—the largest coastal temperate rainforest in the world. .There are thousands of islands along the coast, cresting from the water like the plates of a stegosaurus, overgrown with leaf and vine—so much so that without a road, they are often impossible to penetrate. Then there are the granite cliffs and perpendicular layers of rock, black or swirled with iron, with all mixes of striation, in the fjords where the glaciers of the last age slid slowly down to the sea. There's a theory that the First Peoples to populate the Americas migrated from Asia via canoe, following the abundance of kelp along the West Coast, feeding off all the fish that did feast there too, as fish tend to mingle with kelp, along with seals and probably dolphins. This theory persists because one look at the inhospitality of the mountains and rainforest—with their lack of edibles, abundance of predators like bears and wolves, and indomitable terrain—combined with the once-present mile-thick ice and snow that covered them, would tell you: "Yeah, it would be better living off clams and fish than trying to survive anywhere near that."

Our three travellers hear a crash and turn to see the Zodiac loose from its chains, its stern smacking against the water.

"The Zodiac! The Zodiac!" cries Derik. He runs to help Raven who's trying to grab hold.

"Fuck!" says George, swivelling his head to gauge the situation while still steering the boat. He can either let the boat drift and run back to help (which could quickly get out of hand, like an inverted pendulum), keep on steering forward, or pull to port and take cover by Calvert Island, out of the wind. He chooses the third, quickly turning to.

"Dad! Stop the boat! What are you doing?"

George is focused on getting to safety.

"Dad!"

"I *can't*! We'll run aground!" He goes berserk when stressed.

Raven waits for *Wild Thing*'s stern to sink with the trough of wave, when the Zodiac collides with the water and is pushed up violently into its hold, chains rattling. He times it just right so his arm isn't crushed; he grabs hold of the loose end. "Hook the chain back on!" he calls to Derik.

Derik struggles to see where to attach the chain as he's never dealt with the Zodiac before.

"Here, here!" shouts Raven, wrestling to keep hold.

Derik manages to reattach it just as a wave slams back. "I got it, I got it!"

Raven lets go. It holds! He checks to make sure it's secure. Relief washes over them. They head back inside as it starts to pour.

"We got the Zodiac back on," Raven tells George.

"Dad this is crazy, we gotta find a harbour or something."

"I know!" shouts George Chokeslam. "I'm heading for that cove there."

They all gaze to the cove, to the spot he'll call safe. But friends, the prospects are not great. Many a bluffed cove, many a rock, yet the waves bombard the isle from all angles, refracting from the deep, swaying in and coursing all waters uneasy. Nowhere is safe. All night they will be tossed to and fro like a ball. Derik stands between the men—the hopeful Raven, the fuming George. Dare anyone or anything stop the son of Sir Henry Mormin from going where he will? Not until the blood runs dry from his veins.

They take shelter on the east coast of Calvert Island, with the waves still reaching them—but, luckily, no swells. They drop anchor. "We'll wait out the storm here overnight," says George.

"Is it safe though?" Derik asks. "Look at these waves!"

"We'll be fine. It's going to be a bumpy night, but this is our best bet. Since you cowards don't want to keep going."

"I'll keep going," says Raven. "I don't care… Probably better we stop, though."

"Dad, we almost lost the Zodiac! This is a storm, we shouldn't be out in this."

"This is nothing! I've been in way worse."

"You keep saying that, but what would Mom say? What do you think she would say about you bringing us out into this in your new expensive boat?"

George would never win that fight. Betty would get so mad, he'd have no choice but to sleep on the couch. "Quit being a mama's boy," he mumbles.

"Sure looks like a heavy storm," says Raven. "I don't see it letting up anywhere."

"There's a 10 percent chance it'll let up," says George. "I checked this morning before we left."

"So you knowingly brought us out into this?" says Derik.

"You're talking to me like I don't know what I'm doing."

"I'm not sure you do."

George glares at the boy. "Watch it. This is the 'wet' coast; it's usually bad weather here. It'll clear by morning, just watch. Stupid Gino said she'd go twelve knots against the wind—I was barely making eight. What a scumbag." He gets himself a bag of chips. *Crunch crunch crunch.*

"So you think Gino scammed us?"

"No I don't think Gino scammed us; he just doesn't know anything about boats. He has his minions take care of them."

Wild Thing pivots around its anchor, rising and dipping with the waves like a newborn on your chest with every breath.

"I sure hope that anchor holds," says George.

Derik perspires, in a panic. —*And then the dog thrashed my arm as I tried to scream, but nothing came out, and*—

"That probably won't happen though," George continues. "We'll be fine; I know this route like the back of my hand."

"Why don't you take us to a harbour, then, where it's safe?"

"This is a harbour. Like I said, it's our best bet. Why don't you try and get some sleep? You sound cranky. Maybe you need to rest."

"Now? It's not even seven." You wouldn't think it by looking outside, the clouds low and dark in the summertime. I take to the sky.

"Try and rest up for the morning. I figure we'll get up by five and get out of here."

"There's no way I'm sleeping through this."

"Quit being such a wuss. You have any idea what I had to sleep through on the *Marge Valence*? My bunk room was right next to the engine, and I had a whole bunch of noisy sailors shouting and partying all night with the lights on. You think I ever stopped to complain to my dad, the captain? I would've been kicked off the boat if I did." A glass rolls in the cabinet, knocking over the others, shattering one. "Goddammit." Raven attends to it, disposing of the shards with care. George gives him praise.

"I understand that Grandpa was strict, but we're not aboard the *Marge Valence*. I'm used to sleeping at home in my own bed, not on a cramped boat during a storm. There's got to be a town nearby we can stop in for the night."

"There isn't, Derik, we're in the middle of the pass here. The waves are a bit rough 'cause all the water and the currents from the rivers and other passes flow through here. You're just going to have to toughen up. Man, kids nowadays—they expect everything to be easy."

"That's not true, we're just practical."

"There is the Hiroshi Institute on the other side of the island," says Raven. "I stayed there for a bit while writing my thesis. We should be able to dock there for the night to get out of these waves."

"Sounds good to me," says Derik.

"No, I'm not staying there. Those Japanese are racist toward our people."

Derik throws his arms in the air. The ebon worm crawls down the screen and buries itself in the mud, lit faint by the moon. *Nothing is ever good enough.*

"Why do you think they're racist?" says Raven. "I'm pretty sure they're not even Japanese, beyond the name."

"Because I remember we showed up there one time during herring season when we were all out of food, shivering and starving. The heat wasn't working on the boat and we needed someone to fix it. So we showed up and asked them for a couple rooms, just a couple rooms for a crew of about seven or eight. And they turned us away! They said, 'We don't want you here.' We knew they had rooms; there was hardly anyone docked there, those bastards. Also, when they did their research about those old footprints they found, they never consulted our people about it. They just ignored our Elders and kept digging on *our* land. They pretended they discovered them all by themselves when our people *knew* they were there. That's *local* knowledge."

He is of course referring to the footprints discovered on Calvert Island dating back thirteen thousand years, which were the oldest known footprints in North America upon discovery. You see, they're special because that was well before the end of the last ice age, which means people were living on the coast then, and probably enjoyed kelp—lots of kombu. Once upon a time, Calvert Island was taken from the Heiltsuk by British explorers aboard the *Princess Royal*. The *Princess Royal* was captured a year later and brought to Nootka Sound, which pissed off the Brits, who bollocked the Spaniards. They eventually reached an agreement—once Spain pawned their lot due to finding no Northwest Passage, a fabled waterway through North America that all sailors and metropoles desired—continuing to ignore the Heiltsuk.

"I don't think they're racist," continues Raven. "The researchers from the University of Victoria consulted the locals; they asked them where to look for any evidence of migration or settlement in the area. They were constantly in communication with Elders and people in the know, you know?"

"Yeah, and what did the Heiltsuk get for it? Nothing."

"Well, I mean neither did the scientists, really. They probably got some funding for further research, but I'm pretty sure they're leaving the rest of the footprints until they have better technology to study them. There's probably lots of buried evidence of people in the region and probably all up the coast—we just need the technology to see it."

"Good, well they should stay away if they know what's good for them."

"I think the Heiltsuk benefit from having people work with them to study their culture and land, then we all get to know about their history."

"You don't get it. We already *knew* we travelled and lived in this region long before anyone else was here—we have stories of doing so. We don't need them to tell us we did."

"Why are you being so racist?" says Derik. "What if I said Indians are all a bunch of drunks?"

"Don't say that about our people."

He's being such a hypocrite. Choked me at dinner when I mentioned the same thing.

No, just grabbed you by the collar.

"Then quit being racist!"

"They deserve it for what they did to our people!" George shouts over the idle engines. "You have no idea the amount of abuse I suffered because I was Indigenous *and* because I was Heiltsuk. So quit talking to me like you know what I've been through, nothing gives you that right." A wave rocks *Wild Thing*, forcing them brace. I feel the electricity in my wings. "You're really starting to piss me off now. Where did you get the idea that you could talk to me like that, your own father? You think I don't know anything, like I haven't seen the things I've seen? I know these people; I know they're racist. I've experienced it myself. So don't tell me I don't know what I'm talking about."

Don't say anything, you'll just make him angrier.

The waves continue to crash against the boat, crash against each other, crash against the shore, crash against the rocks. Palpable is the static. Derik leaves for his cabin below deck, leaving George to deal with the boat. *Raven probably thinks I'm a wimp.*

They ride out the storm, with the liquid chrome that rolls beneath them tossing *Wild Thing* to and fro, and the rain shelling, going *drip-a-dap-dum*. Night surrounds them. Derik lays atop his sheets, striped navy and white, staring at the ceiling, discerning the patterns over and over, reflecting on the day, projecting the past, contemplating the future. He tries to feel settled but the waves distract him; he tries to predict when they'll dip, so he can brace for impact, and when they'll rise, so he can relax for that brief period of weightlessness—but the waves keep shifting their rhythm slightly, this time slightly ahead, this time way behind, so instead of being lulled to rest, he's shook in a can. *Please let it stop. Please let me have some peace.* Expectations shred against coral. You can't predict when turbulence will stop; it goes on and on, becoming quite humorous, really—the acceptance that it can only get worse.

How can Dad sleep in this? It's impossible. Impossible! Listen to all this noise and rocking. How could he have gotten any sleep? How can I get any sleep?

Well, you like some noise when you sleep. Remember how you used to flush the toilet before bed, then run back to your room so you could hear the water run down the pipes? It never lasted long enough for you to fall asleep, though. You used to only face the right, toward the pipes, because you thought a monster was on the left. You also used to hop away from the bed because you thought It would slash your ankles, hiding underneath. That's pretty much what this is—just a bunch of white noise. It should help you sleep.

Derik refuses to cave to the idea that his dad was right about the boat providing some comfort for sleeping.

"I used to like the sound of the engine," George had said, looking up from the engine room with the trap door open. "It's like being in a crib." For years, Derik struggled to sleep, second-guessing whether the room were breathing, or UFOs were humming outside his window, whether he was hearing footsteps of a ghost by his feet or just Shadow returning to sleep on the edge of the bed.

—Until I kicked him off. He probably threw himself down the stairs 'cause I kicked him off. All he wanted to do was sleep on the edge of the bed 'cause he knew I had nightmares after the dog attack, and I kicked him off. I disowned him when he wanted nothing more than to protect and love me. Derik retraces Shadow's death vividly, as it happened only last summer: remaking it, reliving it, crafting different outcomes—everything that could've been, and everything that went wrong—until the sandman casts his spell and Derik lets his mind slip, forgetting himself. *That's the feeling. I almost fell asleep. I'm falling asleep.*

Don't think about it or else it'll never happen.

Derik gets used to the turbulence, discerning music from the slosh of waves. A tear slides down his cheek. He turns to his side, resting on his outstretched arm as if he were being cradled, and falls asleep.

Derik steps to sand, stooping to admire footprints. Raven caws, his long beak clacking, smirking, eloquent but hoarse, "These are the footprints of your ancestors. They have been here since before any of us have, and the ones before that, and the ones before them, and the ones before, and the ones before even, and the ones before—" His voices fades as Derik follows the footprints along the beach. The grey sand, the purple night, the moon surrounded by stars and the evergreens standing firm, with the dark green earth encompassing the grey path through. The grass is wet with dew, each drop mirroring the whole world. All blurs past as shadows and streams of silver.

The way is dank and dark. The white light shines through, imprisoned, barred by the arches and pillars of the ancient West, the time when the West (the blanket stitches to cloth of Egypt, cloth of Greece, cloth of Rome) was Indigenous, heir to the land, its buildings made of shade. Derik attends the spectacle, with thousands of eyes bobbing, shifting, the crowds streaming in through the many entrances like termites to a stump.

I must get a seat for the games, I gotta find my seat.

Derik joins the crowd—once in, there is no getting out. They push him along, just another current to the stream. Push and shove to the front, to the edge of the ring of dirt and scarlet walls, a dodecagon, with an entrance way off to the right, black, where the presence seethes—a tortured presence, a presence oppressed, contrived and allowed to mould until it clings to air, residing in the breath of the spectators. Swirl back to Derik. He stammers about, looking for his seat. He asks the usher, who points him to 243 where someone is already sitting.

"Excuse me, but you're in my seat."

"No way."

"Yes, look!" Derik shows his ticket, but the ticket melts and warps away from the eyes of the seated man, who turns into a snake that stretches up, but then Derik realizes he has shrunk. "Oh, sorry," he says. "The usher said my seat was here." *The usher said my seat was here.*

Everything returns to the way it was (and wasn't).

Where is my seat? I can't find my seat. I can't check my ticket. Derik roams around, searching for his seat, but the information on the ticket keeps changing; he keeps going to where it says, until he checks once more to find it has changed again. *Where is my seat? I can't find my seat.* Finally, deterred, scared and cold in the rain that pours only over him from his own personal cloud, he sits at the bottom of the aisle, on the stone step there.

Without sound, out charges a bull made of swirling lavender cloud and white horns bright as starlight upon its own cloud hovering above the ground, the camera locked, angled up slightly, the bull filling the frame.

The matador waves the red cape before the bull, the crowd cheering, but the bull does not move. Again, the matador waves the cape but the bull does not move. The matador's face fills with shadow, grows angry. He stomps and waves harder the cape, but the bull is not interested. He sits on his butt in the shade, slouching over, no motivation to charge. The matador grows darker. Swords stab from all directions with a pale blue wind, piercing the shadowed pincushion, which writhes, posturing its neck back; the bull collapses with vacant eyes and limp tongue. The crowd roars, but fades as Derik moves on: *Where is my seat? I can't find it. I gotta find my seat.*

I don't know where I'm supposed to be; I don't know where I am. Derik searches through the woods, the dark, murky woods, with the purple night behind them and the white crescent and stars overhead. He comes to a crossroads with two torches, one on the far left and the other on the far right. He looks all ways around, not sure where to go. He goes straight. Through another set of woods he goes, until he comes to another crossroads. This time both torches are closer, but still left and right. Again, he goes straight. Through the woods. To another crossroads, the same as the first. *I just want to get home. I was supposed to be home for dinner a long time ago.* He goes left this time. The crossroads are the same as the first. So he goes left, and the crossroads are the same as the second. *Am I going around in circles?* With realization comes a new scene. He runs on the clouds. He runs through the smoky forest. He makes no progress at all. He looks down, then up, and finally the village, his *home*, is in view.

The village is quiet. There is no one in the streets. Totem poles stand outside the longhouses telling the family stories, the entrances to their lives. Here is Derik's family totem: the Thunderbird on top, then the whale, then three people—one with knife, one with hook, one in the middle with open hands, gesturing welcome—then the beaver and frog and intricate carvings at the bottom, leading to the ground. Derik looks up at the protruding beak and wings at the top, the rest closely contained like the natural pattern of bark around cedar. He looks up proud; he looks up happy to have found what he was searching for. Happiness fades, as the air is thick with death. The smell of hot, rotting flesh stings his nostrils. It floods his nose and senses and brain. Not a soul has moved through the streets. There are no crossroads here.

"Mom, I'm home," he says, entering like mist. "Mom? Where are you?" He looks to his bed, but there's only an old man there, sleeping with his back to Derik. "Hey," says Derik. "Why are you in my bed?"

And the blanket turns to dust and hairs that disperse, and the pox of the man's pale-pink back shows itself, its pattern grave, and he rolls with shallow breath, gazing with yellow eyes and murky pupils—cataracts—and coughs, casting water droplets into the air, which frightens Derik; he falls back against the dresser, then scrambles to his feet and flees, flees to the barren street where the ghosts walk, and the sky is midnight blue, and all the stars are visible, as the spirits leave freely the Earth for other planets and galaxies, and the air is cold, cold as winter. The silence roars in Derik's ears, his mouth agape.

Through the forest he runs, far from that place, like his great grandfather before him, running through the woods, running away from the disease that claimed his village—the invisible serpent that sapped them of life. He runs through the woods and leaps off the hill, landing in the fallen leaves, then leaps again, bounding over roots, descending the slope's winding trail. He reaches level ground and stumbles, sliding on his chest into the leaves. He scurries up—*They're right behind me, they're right behind*—and races through the trees, leaving death behind him, back there over his shoulder.

He plunges into the water. The marsh is blue, dull silver and pale green, all cold and void of life except for a brilliant blue light that glows beneath. *I have to find her. Where is my sister? Where is Candace?* The frogs croak, their bulbous sacs expand; their eggs drift apart. "Ack!" Derik starts at a snake brushing against him. It slithers across the water, parting the iridescent slick, changing colour with the angle, just like the armour of the knock-off Batman toy Aunt Lizzy bought him for Christmas the last time the Mormins were together. The fog hangs dense over the rushes and reeds.

Then Candace shows herself, rising tall in her white dress. Derik is excited to see her; he was searching all over. She towers over him. She stoops, saying, "I'm going to eat you alive," and soon begins to suck on his face. It feels very good to Derik. She sucks in his head like an anaconda, then his shoulders, arms, stomach and hips. She lifts Derik up, his legs kicking about.

Friends, this dream is filled with all sorts of erotic episodes that won't be detailed here—just know it is common to dream of such acts unfeasible in waking life. Perhaps they symbolize the desire for a closer bond; maybe they are simply the products of a mind transmuting its immediate environment. Either way, you perverts, Derik awakens before climax, as Candace splits into three, speaking white light, each replete with Liberty's crown.

That feels good. That's right.

Hey, where did she go? Derik looks around, startled to find himself in his bed. One by one the realizations come: *Oh, I'm on the boat. It was just a dream. What day is it? Where are we now, at sea?* He feels under the covers. *Thank God. Man, that was weird.* He hears a cluck, then the whistling of birds, his perception hazy. *I have to find my seat. I have to get home.* "Phew," he says for no one, "I was only dreaming." *I don't have to do any of that.* He is ashamed, but relieved, to be awake, having dreamt what he has dreamt. He recollects before it all fades from memory.

Hey, the storm has passed. Out the porthole he sees the blue sky over the green trees. The boat rocks gently.

I often dream that I've fallen out of the nest and can't for the life of me fly back up. Can you believe birds dream? Nothing is provable outside one's own mind; you can't be sure what anyone else is thinking, or whether anything is real outside your own perception. You see through your eyes, colours are rendered by the brain, and the words you hear are vibrations within your ears. The mind is the only thing you can prove for certain exists; as the great philosopher Billie Eilish once said, "I think, therefore I am." Dreams are as convincing as perceptions while awake, and, while awake, one is constantly dreaming—reliving past experiences, imagining the future. Are dreams and imagination not part of reality? If you'll believe in me, I'll believe in you.

Our crew eats breakfast at the booth in the calm morning, *Wild Thing* rocking gentle as a cradle. "What do you think it all means?" asks Derik, having just told them what was appropriate to tell of his dream.

"I'm not sure. Maybe you shouldn't eat so much before going to sleep," George responds.

"I didn't have anything for dinner last night! I went straight to my room once we anchored." Derik of course omits their arguing as he doesn't want to stir the pot. Although he yearns for resolution, he'd sooner hold a grudge than relent to opposition.

Let's be honest: many dreams are best left untold. You may confess to a priest, or to a seagull, but even then, could you articulate your wildest dreams?

"Maybe it's 'cause I don't have my dream catcher," he jokes, half-sincere. Every night at home, Derik would bring in his dream catcher attached to the latch of his window, the web now a tangle of loose strands. To some, he is like a monk: devoted to his spiritual ritual, tending to his paraphernalia, having faith; while modern educators would print him a label, as he's a counterculturalist who exhibits repetitive behaviours. (Lock him up!) He doesn't mind, though; he understands his actions generate faith, and faith is confidence, and confidence is power, and power hones the will, garnering success.

"Maybe you were out in the sun too long. How's your head? You don't have a fever, do you?" George motions to feel his son's forehead. Derik pulls away.

"I don't have a fever. I was inside most of the day."

"You know dream catchers aren't really part of our tradition. That was more of an Ojibwe thing."

"Well, what is ours? I can't figure out what is actually Heiltsuk and what isn't." Derik bites the dry toast slathered with raspberry jam. Sun sparkles through fog. "And who cares anyway? Dream catchers are cool. They're interesting. I don't care where they *really* came from—that's not my concern."

"I told you what our people were known for," says George. "We made great bentwood boxes and war canoes. We were revered as the only ones who could stand up to the Haida, who used to raid everyone else's village. You don't remember any of that?"

Derik, as usual, says, "Not really," playing dumb for more information.

"Man, I can't get over how bad your memory is."

"He's got a magical memory, there, old Georgie boy," Raven says. "He just vividly recalled his dream. No point in memorizing things a computer can tell us."

"I guess so," says George. They finish eating breakfast.

The voyage resumes. The bird flies over Calvert Island. North of here is Hecate Island where an old woman in black robes casts lightning into the sky; you won't see her—you'll just have to trust she's there.

"Is this the place you said gets really rough?" Derik asks.

"No," George answers. "It doesn't usually get that rough around here. You're thinking of the Hecate Strait—that's farther up, near Haida Gwaii. That place gets rough. The Haida used to use that to their advantage: they would time their raids so that when they fled back across the water, the waves and tide would come up, and anyone chasing them wouldn't be able to follow."

Raven nods, looking to his left out a window.

"How come?" Derik asks. "What would happen?"

"Well, their boats would sink because the waves were so unpredictable. It's very shallow, so they have lots of storms and bad weather there."

And friends, George is right. Once, the Hecate Strait was a coastal plane, exposed land, until the great deluge—the Biblical Flood Noah rode, the great flood that swallowed coast around the globe—sunk it down, isolating Haida Gwaii. That's why it's so shallow today, as is Atlantis.

"That's probably why they named it the Hecate Strait: Hecate is the Greek goddess of witchcraft and magic," says Raven. "They probably thought the frequent storms and waves were caused by witchcraft."

"Did they actually?" says Derik.

"I wouldn't doubt it. The waves are deceptive you see, like magic." Raven's voice climbs an octave, which Derik notices, as his own voice would crack if he did the same, which would bring him great humiliation. "Like, you have magic tricks which are usually acts of deception, causing the viewer to think something is one way when it's really another. Also, magic and witchcraft and things like these aren't usually what they appear to be—that's why most people don't take them seriously. They think it's all casting spells with instant results, or they don't know how to gauge their results: they think it's one way, when it's really another—or both ways at once! Love is losing yourself in union with another." Raven rubs his chin. "Or maybe they named it Hecate just because they were superstitious and figured all the Natives were witches. I don't know."

"Do you think that's true?"

"Could be. They certainly were scared of some Indigenous people, with their fearsome countenances, mischief and long hair full of lice. That's outside looking in, of course. You have to keep in mind, these aren't like stereotypical witches who wear pointy hats and ride brooms. Hecate was the original goddess of magic and often worshipped by witches."

"What did these witches do then, if they weren't riding brooms?" Derik chuckles to himself.

"They used to have strange rituals on mountaintops (almost like astronomers) so they could get the best view of the sky at night. They particularly liked full moons, which they're still associated with today. But the original witches of Thessaly? They used to be able to make the moon disappear, they say, which, if you're looking for a physical explanation, probably means they could predict lunar eclipses."

"What is magic, though? I remember me and my friends got a rain spell from some website, and we performed it in the field during recess. The sky was blue, but when we called on the spirits to make it rain, within minutes, clouds formed and it started to pour."

"I've heard all sorts of explanations for what magic is; it's always abstract or invisible. The best definition I know is: magic is causing change to occur according to will. So aligning anything with your true will and causing it to happen is considered magic, which is basically any act, anything you do."

"Huh... So what's so special about magic if it happens all the time?"

"Well, that's it: life is full of magic. Life *is* magic." Raven smiles, eyes sparkling. "Most people tend not to realize that. That's why it's secretive; it's so simple people overthink it."

"Don't be messing around with witches," says George, steady at the wheel. "I saw a witch try to cast a spell on my friend Terry once. I went to the bar to get some drinks, and when I came back she was casting a spell on him." He extends his arms, making subtle sweeps and swirls with his hands. "Like that. And I could tell if I didn't grab him right then, she would've seduced him. So I yanked him out of his chair and took him outside. He was hitting me, shouting, 'Let me go! She was hot!' And I said, 'Didn't you see? She was casting a *spell* on you. She's a witch!' Then he said, 'I don't believe in *witches*. Let me go talk to her!' But I told him, 'If you go back in there, I promise you, you'll regret it.' He didn't listen. She ended up taking him back to her place, and when he woke up he was on the curb, naked, without his wallet or any way to get home. He thought I did it! He didn't remember what happened."

"Maybe he was just really drunk," says Derik.

"No, he just didn't listen; she cast a spell on him. He got off easy, too. She could've used him in one of their rituals or sacrificed him and we never would've seen him again."

Derik smiles. "So, we got devil worshippers on Vancouver Island, we got witches in bars, and we're going to a place with cannibals—is there anything else I should know before we get there? Are there dragons there, too?"

"I was watching a show on the History Channel where they said dragons might've existed. They could've had gases in their stomachs that they could blow out their mouths and ignite with a special organ in their throat that made a spark. That explains how they could breathe fire."

"No," says Derik, pointing. "Get out."

"They even found their bones in China."

"All right, I've heard enough."

George continues relaying what he might have heard once, while Derik heads outside to admire the clear skies.

4. Beautiful Beautiful

Boy, are my wings tired. Those were some strong winds, let me tell ya. But here we are: a bastion of light amid land murky. You turn the bend, passing island after island, then see the homes—a haven from chaos. The first thing you notice is the size of the birds, all well fed on the abundance of seafood caught or scavenged. The most lordly, the bald eagles, are aplenty here, singing their shrill song—a much higher register than their size would have you believe—cackling treble, or calling above a lonely lake while gliding on thermal currents; then there are the gulls, pecking the guts of fish, murking the water pink, understanding the ancient processing of fish and *there* for it, there whole-heartedly, gathering in flocks, calling like sirens. But let's not sleep on those ravens—hell knows no mockery like that of the raven—with their clucking and screeching like a man gone insane, throwing himself at the padded walls; for together, are they not called a *conspiracy*? Then there's the loon, alone on the waves, calling, yearning for their lover, the most beautiful sound you've ever heard. There are also, of course, crows, who thrive just about anywhere, rural or urban. Indeed, many of my colleagues are here. I don't discriminate: sometimes I'm a robin, tomorrow I'm a sparrow, for lunch I'm the Thunderbird, and yesterday I'm not what you thought.

Air only gets better the farther north you go (this being most evident upon deboarding a plane after fleeing the smoggy city and burning churches—taking that first breath free of the exhaust of industry, swept clean by the briny sea). As does the water, for the most part. No ambiguous Fraser here, friends, sure to make your teeth fall out. Here it's clean and full of life.

Everyone has a boat here, or at least access to one. In other words, boats are cars in Bella Bella. This is even more pronounced by the prevalence of trucks, favoured for the rocky outskirts of town—no orange-tanned men interrupting your commute or strung-out breakfast here, friends. You might spy a spare yacht or two passing by, but they'll dock at Shearwater where all the tourists go, as there ain't no place for them among noble fishing vessels. Yes, here, even the whiteys are foreign. Everyone breathes a sigh of relief.

"Wow," says Derik. "Look at all these birds! They're huge, too! Are those ravens, Dad?"

"They sure are," George responds.

"I don't think I've ever seen one before."

"All right, go put the fenders down! We're docking now."

"Oh, sorry," Derik repents. He and Raven drop the fenders, bracing the gunwale as George slowly manoeuvres *Wild Thing*, looking over his shoulder with subtle turns of the wheel.

Once close, Raven steps one foot over and pushes the boat back from collision with the dock. He helps guide her into berth. "All right, we're good!" He gives George a thumbs-up.

"Perfect," George says. He takes off his mariner's cap and rubs his sweaty head. His eyes are wide with the spirit now flaming within him, fuelled by the coming-home, rising with the past.

The call of an eagle coils through Derik's one ear and out the other, resonating within him, bringing him to joy. *I've never heard that before. It was beautiful.* He bathes in the melodies of the happy, healthy, thriving birds, unlike those scavengers down south fighting over refuse and hand-outs. Here, they are mighty. Here, they are worthy.

"There's Louis," says George. He waves to his brother-in-law of the Tanner clan. They have similar jowly faces. Louis waves back with his trademark smirk, but doesn't betray his stoic discipline not to smile, kind of like a salmon. "All right, let's get everything packed that we're going to take to Auntie Rena's. You're gonna want some clothes to change into tomorrow morning when we go fishing."

"Why?" says Derik. "You said we were staying on the boat." He doesn't remember the last time he saw Auntie Rena or Uncle Louis; it would've been at Sam's funeral when he was just a baby.

"No, they said we could stay with them. Auntie Rena said she'll make us breakfast and we'll have a proper bed to sleep in," George says, knowing full well he promised Derik otherwise and is now trying to convince him other-otherwise even though it's all already been settled. "You remember Uncle Louis don't you? He's here to pick us up."

"Why do we have to stay with them, though, and bother them? Wouldn't it be easier to stay on the boat?"

"No I already told them we'd stay with them—they're excited to have us as guests. We'll have an actual shower. Besides, I don't want to have to fill the water tank again, and you can sleep without having to worry about the ship rocking."

"But I just got used to sleeping on the boat—it's comforting now. I just wanna stay on the ship, Dad, come on." Derik enjoys the privacy of his own room, but is wary to offend family. He sighs, knowing he won't change George's mind, quickly throwing some shirts in a bag with his toothbrush.

Louis's steps knock the wood. "Good to see ya, George!" he says.

"Hey, Louis," George adopts his rez accent. "It's been a while." They hug like titans, a couple of tough guys.

"Hey, I'm Raven." They shake hands.

"So this is your new boat, huh?" asks Louis.

"Yup. Ain't she a beaut? I got her for real cheap. She got us here in under ten hours."

"No it didn't," says Derik. "It took us three days to get here."

George ignores the correction because he's not a man of correctness, no, no; he speaks to *engage*. "Yup, thirty-three-foot, twin-Cummins-diesel Bayliner. We were going about fourteen knots against the wind."

Louis soaks it all in, slowly perceiving the dynamic between the three new arrivals.

"Hey."

"And this is Derik," George adds. As usual, Derik has waited for his father to introduce him.

Did you know orcas wait for their mom to introduce them to strangers? "Hey."

"Hey." They too shake hands.

Even though Derik is young, the others feel the spirit of vengeance upon him—they see it in his eyes, where light rarely escapes.

"Me and Louis were shipmates aboard the *Marge Valence*," says George.

"Nice," says Raven.

"Those were the days, eh?" Louis adds.

"He and I used to share a room."

"Yup, me and George 'That's Not My Job' Mormin. Your old man read more than he worked."

"You used to like reading?" asks Derik.

"I used to read the biggest books I could find. There was nothing else to do."

"'Cause *we* were busy doing all the work," says Louis.

"That's not true. I had to stay up all night at the wheel while my dad caught some sleep."

"I know, I know. I'm just messing."

"I was probably a lot more sober than you guys too."

"Now, I don't know about that. You just got away with it 'cause your dad was captain."

Lots of chuckles.

"Yeah," says George. "Hey, do you know if anyone's selling any downriggers? We're looking to snag a few. We've been using these rods, but they're more for trout fishing than salmon. I was telling the boy how easy it is to use them but he still doesn't believe me."

Derik pouts, absorbing the deprecation.

"Yeah … You should be able to pick some up in Shearwater. We'll go there tomorrow."

"Awesome. We can get some lunch while we're there, too, then try fishing for sockeye, show the boy how real fishermen do it."

Louis chuckles. "All right."

My stomach hurts. I just want to stay on the boat.

But you gotta go.

George passes his luggage over, then steps to the pier. They move to the truck.

"So where's Rena?" asks George. "How's she doing these days?"

"Good... She's working her usual job at the hatchery. I'll give you a tour so you can see how everything's changed."

"I'm sure not much has changed. I was here back in 2015, the last time I went out for herring season."

"Oh yeah. I remember that. Why the hell did you stop coming out?"

"I had a falling out with the old man. He promised to give me the herring licence, but he gave it to Lizzy's kids instead. It's also not worth coming out here anymore with so much foreign competition and the fish numbers being the way they are. Back in the day, we were taking home twenty grand a season. Now we'd be lucky to break even."

"Some people still make a profit, but I know what you mean. It's not as viable as it once was. Might as well become a carpenter." Louis laughs ('cause they say the carpenters in Bella Bella are incompetent, you see). "Rich, Sophie's boyfriend, still does pretty good. He still goes out for herring season."

"Right."

And they talk, fading from Derik's attention. *I remember Dad always used to leave in the summer to work for Grandpa. That's why Dad made me start working for him at the pawnshop so young, while my friends praised the sun, 'cause it was done to him by his dad. We used to pick him up at the little domestic terminal at YVR. He looked like a soldier, with his green duffle bag and weird beard. "Gross!" Candace snickered once. "You have a beard!" His immersion was shattered.*

"I remember you always came back with a beard," Derik says now to his dad.

"Natives can't really grow beards, you know," says Beetle Brows.

"It's true," says Raven. "It's always scraggly or grows in patches... I still try though, sometimes."

Louis puts the last of their luggage in the truck's cargo bed, then takes them on a tour around town, George shotgun, Derik and Raven in the back seat of the cab.

They go by the general store, they go by the hospital, they go past the school, past the main roads and houses, to the winding backways, riddled with potholes and grey rocks, with wild hills on both sides, until they reach trees with broad leaves next to the river where the hatchery is—a series of tanks and a small house. Derik had seen something similar on a field trip once, learning the life cycle of salmon from eggs to fry to adults. They get out.

"So are these farmed salmon?" asks Derik.

"No, they're not farmed," says Louis, leaning over the tank to look down at the school of alevin. "It's a hatchery. We breed the salmon, then release them once they're ready."

"Farmed salmon spend their whole lives in pens," says George. "That's why they get diseases, and their fins turn to bloody stumps 'cause they're bumping into walls all the time instead of swimming in open water."

"Do you eat farmed salmon?" Derik asks Louis. "He won't." Thumb to George.

Louis smirks, looks at George. "Could you imagine one of us buying farmed salmon?" They both laugh at Derik's naïveté.

"See? Nobody eats farmed fish here, they're all against it. Everyone goes out and catches their own."

"But what happens when it's not in season? Then what do you eat?"

"You freeze or can it! Then you have it year-round."

"Well, what happens when there's no more wild salmon left?"

George and Louis look at each other dumbfounded. Louis shakes his head and says, "That won't ever happen. Not as long as Rena keeps care of the stocks."

And here she comes in green rubber boots. "Hey George," says Rena. "Good to see you. How ya been?" They hug. She introduces herself to everyone, stopping at Derik. She holds both his shoulders and stares at him with a smirk. He drops his gaze, then looks back, wondering why she's so imposing. "Oh my gosh, you've *grown*! You're so big now."

Derik looks at his legs. "Have I? I'm still pretty short."

"You don't remember me, do you? Last time I saw you, you were just a baby. Now look at you!"

"I wish I c-could remember."

She pinches his cheeks. "He looks just like his mom."

"Yup. He's a mama's boy all right," George confirms.

He's insulting you.

Who cares? I love my mom. Is there anything wrong with that?

Yeah, it means you're feminine. Sylvia said you have woman fingers.

I don't have women's fingers, I got these from climbing trees and breaking boards—nothing feminine about that... right?

I don't know, you tell me, mama's boy. That's why you haven't hit puberty—you're still half inside the womb.

Rena walks to the small house, waving hither. "Come on. I'll show you around a bit. Come see where the bears tried to get in."

They follow to a stream that runs into the forest, enchanted with the mist that grazes round it. Wherever concrete does not smother, wherever humans have not tampered, the forest thrives, entangled in its passion for flowing water. And the river is packed with salmon, literally jam-packed, friends, like sardines in a tin, their red-and-green bodies poking above the water. So much so that one could walk across their backs.

"Wow! I've never seen so many salmon all at once before," says Derik. He runs down the rocks, to the wood ledge inches above the water. On his knees, he leans over, looking at them looking up at him. He reaches down slowly and strokes one. "Wow, it hardly moved when I pet it. It's like a pet salmon. I guess that's why they call them pets, 'cause you pet them," he rambles his thoughts aloud.

"They're starting to swim upstream now," says Rena. "The water levels are so low though. Never seen it like that. It'll only get worse the further into summer we head."

"Can you eat them when they're like that?"

"I wouldn't want to."

"Why not? Do they taste bad?"

"I don't know anyone who eats spawning salmon."

"You don't want to eat them like that," says George. "They're basically turning into zombies at this point. They lose all their fat, their organs shut down and they begin rotting in the water. Bears will, but we don't eat them like that."

Derik notices a few with chunks taken out of their sides—baseball-sized pink wounds. Then he sees the casualties: dozens stranded on the rocks or in drying pools, rotting in the sun, peeking through the canopy of leaves and buzzing flies, dead eyes and fangs protruding.

"So no one comes down here and grabs them by hand and brings them home to eat?"

"The royals might have," laughs Rena. "This walkway was built for them when they came to visit." Indeed, Prince William and the Duchess of Cambridge herself came to visit in 2016. (Long live the King… I guess.) They'd probably eat the children first, as George would say.

I could reach down right now, grab one, fling it to shore and end the ordeal.

Would have to be quick. It'll probably slip right out of your hands, they're so slippy. That's a slippy salmon right there.

Don't mess it up like you did the one that got away.

That was Dad's fault, though—he told me to lift the net!

Netting's the easy part. More embarrassing messing that up.

Whatever, he messed up too, netting the one in Port Hardy. I had it hooked, tired and everything. Gotta catch one on my own. Gotta catch 'em all.

What better way to prove one's manhood than by catching a salmon? *Dare I?* Derik contemplates ending the trial to finally be initiated into the league of fishermen, or waiting, pondering day and night how to apply expertise, all technique demonstrated, taught and detailed, until the moment comes to hook a salmon using a fishing rod, to tire it, to reel it in, then, finally, to bring it aboard with the net. He has already done everything else—the netting, the hooking, the tiring, the gutting, the cleaning and the cooking—but not from start to finish. He still has to perform the sequence without aid until he catches that salmon without cheating, 'cause, friends, Derik is a lad of principles; he can't let someone beat his game for him and call himself the winner. No, he must do it all on his own or he'll live with regret all his days. He stands. "Nah. I'm gonna wait till we hit the water, then I can catch one for real," he affirms himself.

"We're going fishing for salmon tomorrow," says George. "Just wait and maybe you can catch a sockeye."

"I also got a longline we could set—see if we can catch some halibut."

"Oh, you'll like that, Derik—longlining."

"What's that?"

And George looks incredulously upon his son. "I just *told* you. You really don't remember?"

"Nope." He only half remembers, which isn't a full remember.

"Forget it. You'll see once we go out. Geez, everything I tell him goes right over his head."

"It's basically fishing, but you use many hooks instead of one," says Raven.

"Oh," says Derik, staring at the fish. He's amazed how many there are, as the rivers and streams he's known were dirty, polluted, filled with mud and void of life (certainly void of fish). Here, salmon still thrive, and for that, he is grateful—too much so! For even the locals take it a little for granted, it being their birthright.

"Derik." Raven calls him to a shrub. "Come look."

Derik steps forth. "What are they?" he asks.

"Good eating, that's what they are," says Raven. "They're thimbleberries. You just slide them off and pop 'em in your mouth."

Derik tries a few. "Mm. They're not bad... They kind of taste like raspberries." They pick away.

Rena stares to where the river ends. "Let's go back to the house," she says. "Then you can drop off your luggage and see where you'll be sleeping. I'll whip you up some lunch, too."

They head back to the truck amid the myriad eagle calls and raven clucks there for the salmon buffet. As they drive back to town, every passerby stares into the cab to see who's inside. Louis drives slow, waving to everyone, saying hello, as one does in a small town. He stops the truck often for a chat.

As they're pulling into the driveway, the music stops and the news begins: "We begin with breaking news out of Ottawa this afternoon, where Prime Minister Justin Trudeau is asking Pope Francis for an official apology for the Catholic Church's involvement with the residential school system in Canada, after another seven hundred unmarked graves were discovered yesterday at a former residential school in Saskatchewan."

"I have spoken personally, directly, with His Holiness Pope Francis, uh, to impress upon him how important it is, not just that he makes an apology, but that he makes an apology to Indigenous Canadians, on Canadian soil."

"I like how he hesitated, unsure whether to call it *Canadian* soil," says Raven.

"He's a fucking crook," says George. "Him and his long hair."

"Yeah? You really gonna do our prime minister dirty like that?"

"What has he done for our people? They've done nothing but steal our water and give away our land to build pipelines on."

"I didn't vote for him," says Louis. "I could see right through his BS."

"Who did you vote for then? Scheer?" says Raven. "Conservatives are way worse for Indigenous people than Liberals are. At least Trudeau has progressed relations *somewhat*. He's asking for an apology from the pope on Canadian soil—that's unheard of! Think about it, the Vatican never does anything like that."

"I voted NDP, like most of us did," clarifies Louis.

"We'll always be Indians in their eyes," says George. "Always have been, always will be."

"Yeah."

"I like Trudeau," says Derik.

"Oh yeah? What do you like about him?" says George.

"I like that he's standing up to the Church, who committed all those crimes and killed all those Natives."

"We can't just blame the *Church*," says Raven. "The Canadian government knew exactly what was going on."

"You're saying the government helped kill all those kids?"

"Yeah, basically. They ran the education system. Education system ran the residential schools. Residential schools killed children. What will be really interesting is whether the Pope apologizes on Canadian soil or not. I know he's progressive, using YouTube and all, but what he needs to do is visit the First Nations and apologize on *their* land. You can't just apologize from Rome. What kind of message does that send, if you don't even visit the First Nations you helped destroy?"

"Do you think he'll do it?"

"Well, I doubt it. 'Cause then he's admitting blame on behalf of the Catholic Church, and they'll be sued up the wazoo. Legally, it's suicidal. Also, the United Church ran most of the residential schools and Indian day schools out here, so it wasn't just the Vatican's fault, which is just another reason why they won't admit guilt."

George says, "They're all a bunch of pedophiles as far as I'm concerned. You have no idea what they did to us at that day school." Louis begins visibly shaking. He hides his startled blue eyes. Derik doesn't dare ask what occurred.

No more is said. The group gets out of the truck and starts moving luggage into the house. And a beautiful house it is, friends— well, relatively speaking, coming from Vancouver where they start at a million solid. Indeed, it is more well kept than most. It also cost Rena and Louis nothing, as it was passed down to them. No junk in the yard, no dilapidated deck, just a rancher with white panelling and dark-green roof. There's a stack of home-canned pinks in the corner by the fridge. A trail winds into the wilderness out back.

It smells like Grandma's. Derik's thinking of his mom's mom, of course, as he never met Grandma Julia, who died when George and Rena were children. Both grandmas instilled tidiness as a moral imperative: the former by inheritance, the latter by strangulation (aw yes: "Wipe your toes, you filthy savage, before the agent takes you away!"). There are lace curtains, glass containers of stale candy, brass picture frames and stained-hardwood shelves. The brown tiles of the foyer, dining room and kitchen mix with the grey plush carpet of the living room like an estuary. Two sofas face a flat-screen over the mantel of a fireplace they no longer use.

"You three can decide who gets to stay in the guest room and who gets to sleep on one of the couches," says Rena. "I got as many blankets and pillows as you'd like."

Oh nice—maybe I do get my own room. Derik looks around, shameful enough not to claim the room right away, but shameless enough not to refuse it.

"I get real bad back pain," says George. "Maybe me and the boy can share the room. Otherwise my back's really gonna start hurting, sleeping on one of those."

"Okay. Sounds fine to me," says Raven. "You two can be like Queequeg and Ishmael, sleeping side by side. Though I'm not sure who the head-hunting savage is."

"That's me." George points to himself, proud. He slurps and licks his lips. "Don't get on my bad side," he says to Derik.

Derik furrows his brow. He inspects a picture of a man wearing a raven frontlet and a yellow blanket decorated with formline faces over his shoulders. "Who's that?" he asks.

Rena says with pleasure, "That's your grandpa."

"*That's* Grandpa?"

"You bet. That was him during one of the dances."

Grandpa used to dance? "Wow. Do you remember what dance it was?"

She shakes her head. "No, I forget. That was years ago, well before you were born."

Derik stares, mesmerized by the man he thought he knew. Huh. *He actually looks kinda… cool?* He doesn't notice much resemblance beyond the signature Mormin brow.

"Derik, come check out our room!" calls George. Derik follows, stowing their luggage. It's a spare room with pale-yellow paint, oak bed frame, two nightstands and a window to the backyard, with its patio and shed lined with rusty tools and scraps of various projects that (Who knows?) might be needed someday. There's a framed painting of a rose on the wall, with a quote in script: *Flowers never bend to the rain.*

"Happy?" says George. "Now you get a nice bed to sleep in."

"Yup," says Derik, though he doesn't sound like it. "I was scared we were gonna have to sleep with like seventeen other relatives… That'd be weird."

They return to the living room to find Raven sitting on the sofa. They sit at the dinner table. Rena is busy at the stove preparing lunch.

"Man, it's hot," says George. He flaps his shirt with his hands. "It's always so cold in the morning, then it gets so hot in the afternoon."

"Were there any forest fires here this year?" asks Derik.

Louis chuckles. "We don't get forest fires here, that was mostly in the Interior. Can't have forest fires on a small island like this."

"What about Richmond? They had one in the middle of the city, in that bog there."

"It sure was smoky though." He glosses over the fact. "The worst I've ever seen. The sun was red, there was so much smoke blocking it."

"It was terrible back home. I don't get it: we were all supposed to stay inside during school, to avoid the smoke, but then go outside and get fresh air 'cause of COVID?"

"Quite the paradox," says Raven.

It takes Derik a few seconds to comprehend. "Yeah! I hope it doesn't get that hot again."

"It's supposed to be thirty-six degrees tomorrow! I heard in the Interior it's gonna get up to forty," says Louis.

"Wow. That's crazy."

Rena abates their male pessimism with a pitcher of iced tea and glasses stacked with ice, all on a brown tray. She pours them each a glass. The ice cubes crack and rattle, bumping into each other, bumping into sides of glass.

"To global warming," says George in salute.

"To global warming," seconds Raven. Louis smiles. They sip their iced tea; George chugs his. Rena brings out a platter of salmon sandwiches: white bread with a spread of canned salmon, mayo and green onions, soft and supple.

"Reminds me of something you would make," Derik tells his dad.

"It's good, huh?"

"It's canned salmon, isn't it?"

"Mhm," says Rena.

"Did you can it yourself?"

"We sure did."

"Wow. I've never heard of someone canning it themself."

"It's a batch of pinks we caught last year."

"What are pinks?"

"They're a type of salmon," says George. "Really great for canning."

"I thought sockeye was the best."

"Sockeye is better fresh. Pinks are better canned."

"Remember that soup you used to make for Candace and me when we were sick, with udon noodles, seaweed and canned salmon? You always used to make us eat the bones."

"You have to eat the bones," says George, full steam ahead. "How do you think I got such strong bones? It was all the salmon I ate, bones and all. That's how our people got calcium; we never drank milk. You know, I've never broken a bone? I've been thrown off cliffs, been in car accidents, had crab pots crush my arms, but not *once* did I break a bone. It's 'cause of all the salmon I ate, bones and all."

Derik munches away. "This is so much better than your soup."

George conveys without looking or speaking, *When it's just us, that's OK. But here, you're undermining my authority and reputation.*

Derik registers this as if it were said aloud. The others eat on, intrigued by their interplay.

"So what are we going to do till tomorrow when we go fishing?" Derik says.

"We'll unpack and get settled. Then I want to head into town and catch up with some old friends and relatives," says George. "If you want you can stay here and hang out."

"You can watch TV, or we got some board games you can play," says Rena.

Derik looks at the flat-screen, all covered in glare, and is instantly depressed. *I came all this way to watch TV? There's probably nothing on. Do they even have cable?* "I'll come with you into town," he tells his dad.

"OK. Well you better get ready then."

"Maybe they have Pokémon cards in the band store."

"I doubt they will—it's a small town, remember."

"You never know where you might find them. Maybe they got a shipment in and no one wants to buy them"

"Don't get your hopes up."

They finish eating—chasing down those salmon sandwiches with iced tea—then tidy. George gets ready while Derik pretend sword-fights in the backyard—*And then I'll slash them like that, and stab them through the heart!*—while Raven searches for more berries.

"Aah!" Derik hears, causing him to laugh.

"What was that?" he asks Raven.

"Must've been a raven."

"Aah!" There it is again!

Derik laughs even harder, holding his stomach. "Why, does it sound so *funny*?" he stammers.

"'Cause ravens are funny. They mock people and make funny noises—true comedians of the sky."

And friends, he's right. "Aah!" Ravens are the comedians of the sky, mocking the voices they hear. "Aah!" This one sounds like a man who withdrew his life savings, fanning the bills for a selfie on the dock—only for the wind to rip them to sea, laying them on the water—and screamed, "Aah!" as he pulled out his hair, letting the last bills fall as he dove, grasping for each soggy dollar, screaming louder and louder, "Aah! Aah!" No, he never made it all the way back, as he remains, snug in his straitjacket in his padded room, to this very day, murmuring "Aah! ... Aah ..." That's what this raven sounds like to me.

"*Aah!*" mimics Derik. He manoeuvres around the backyard, searching for the raven on neighbouring roofs or utility posts. He spots it on the neighbours' roof. It gives him a side glance. "*Aah!*" Derik attempts conversation, but the raven just stares with black eyes, shifting its head this way, then that, unimpressed. "Come on, do it again!"

"They're on their own time," Raven says.

It clucks, as ravens do, way back in the throat, elongating its neck. Derik observes, fascinated. It clucks again. Derik tries to replicate the sound, but only induces a fit of coughs. "I can't do it," he says hoarsely. The raven purrs like a cat.

🜂 🜂 🜂

George, Derik and Raven head out the front door.

"All right, I'll see you guys in a bit," says Raven. "I promised I'd meet someone I haven't seen in a long time."

"Who's that?" asks Derik. "Do we know them?"

"I doubt it. Levi McMurtry—ring any bells?"

George says, "Nope."

"Oh yeah," Rena says with disapproval. "He lives on the edge of town."

"He's an old friend of mine. Bit of a recluse, but he's into all that occult business I was telling you guys about."

"Mm," says Rena, suspicious.

"Anyway, I'll catch ya later."

"OK," says Derik, sorry to see him go. *Occult business? Are they sacrificing goats? Probably worshipping Pan.*

"Bye!" Raven heads the other way.

"Buh-bye!"

Here we go: Mormins out on the town, looking for old faces, some new. Everywhere they tread, every corner they take, Derik is captivated by the new view—the unique town, its values and culture. The sky is blue, the fog fully banished by sun.

"You should be more respectful around family," says George abruptly. "You know, when you mentioned the canned salmon and my cooking… A lot of our people, that's all they have. Sometimes, that's all they can afford."

"I wasn't trying to be rude! I was just wondering whether she used canned salmon or not."

"You sounded like you were making fun of the food she gave you."

Did I? I was just asking. Her face, downcast in shade. Was she sad? I thought that's just how people look around here. "I liked her sandwiches, though. They tasted good. They reminded me of home. Why, do you think she was upset?"

"You just appeared ungrateful. You need to show more respect to your culture and your hosts, 'cause they're doing all this for you, Derik. This whole trip is for you. And you don't seem appreciative of what others are doing for you."

For me? I thought this was for Grandpa. "It's always like that: people ask me if I'm sad, or *all right*, when I'm perfectly fine. They think I'm sad when it's them asking that makes me sad." He resents being misinterpreted.

"Well, you could smile more. It's not easy for people to tell if you're having a good time or not."

Derik suddenly doubts his reality. *I was happy, I was smiling. Do they want me to smile all the time, like a psychopath?* He hangs his head, frowning, accepting the universal sorrow. This pleases his father, because he finally has something to work on. Derik is too content with his own existence, too proud of his life for the average simpleton to abide by, which causes them to chip away at him, bring him down to their level so they can relax and not work so hard. He's probably right: people tend to take the *complementary* attitude, like red to green. He's still learning to curb his idealism as, let's face it, society runs on prejudice. *If they want me to be sad, I'll be sad. It's not difficult for me to feel sad.* He says, "Sorry."

"Just watch what you say, 'cause you really come off as … not rude, but … too *serious*. People just want to have a good time. Maybe you're too smart for them, but you should dumb it down a little so they can like you."

They approach a pack of dogs in the middle of the street. The alpha, a golden-haired Tibetan mastiff (its predominant breed, as they're all mutts) with a thick mane trots forth. It barks thrice. George walks right past, chest high. Derik tries the same, but the dog detects his nervous energy, and so he is challenged.

"Dad wait—the dog won't let me past."

"Just ignore it. It won't hurt you."

Derik tries to do so, but he can't help but focus on the dog as it postures, just like the dog that mauled him a few years back while he waited for its owner, his neighbour and friend, to fetch his Pokémon cards. The beast had appeared in the doorway, its hairs bristling, teeth bared, snarling, legs taut, rage radiating, taking one tense step at a time from its lair, like Cerberus. Derik had slowly stepped back, then realized that wasn't enough; he knew there was no escaping. He adopted his boxing stance, resting most weight on his back leg, the right, and putting up his guard out of instinct, like he did so many times against his peers once the mouth guards were in, like he did so many times before the punching bag while George reminded him sternly to tuck his chin. All his training had risen up in him, the young lad, to prepare him for the inevitable. The dog lunged, chomping at his neck. Derik threw forth a block with his left and sacrificed his arm, feeding it into the beast's mouth. It gnawed to the bone, rent vein and ripped flesh as blood rained upon the lawn, knocking Derik to his back with its initial charge. And the dog shook its fortress of a head back and forth, grinding its teeth in deeper, tearing to the bone, severing nerve, severing all feeling, while Derik tried to cry for help; yet nothing came out, nothing but a faint high-pitched whine like a distant alarm, as his neighbour, his *friend*, stood motionless in the doorway. But somehow he was heard: an angel with flowing blonde hair staved off the beast with a side panel from a plastic wagon, sending the dog flying back. His saviour, a neighbour, stood over him as the dog circled, cowering with its tail between its legs. She took Derik to safety, to his parents, as one by one the neighbours came out to judge the commotion, as Derik, at last perceiving his wounds, fainted in her arms.

Derik gathers his nerves, then skirts past, not turning his back to the dog. It barks a couple more times, follows him to the edge of its territory, then returns to its pack.

5. Shearwater

Hey friends, still me—interdimensional apparition, Redbird. Let me take you across the water from Bella Bella to Shearwater, where all the whiteys are. Here we find a resort, a restaurant, a couple shops and a shipyard. Yes, they come from far and wide to stay at the lodge—between episodes of sport fishing and taking what isn't theirs—to drink domestic beer, get hammered in the restaurant, which has served a good burger ever since the Heiltsuk took over. Nowadays it's all Heiltsuk territory which, anti-colonial sentiments aside, is the way it was before the settlers arrived and told them, "You can have the nest, but we get the tree."

Shearwater was built by the military to launch antisubmarine reconnaissance ships during World War II. Yes, Canada contributed something to the Pacific Ocean theatre (not much, but something). The most striking relic is the aircraft hangar, about the size of a school gymnasium. Here, on the remote West Coast, they launched planes from the now-defunct airstrip. There's little indication of the military history, besides a former bunker, presently nothing more than a concrete tube tucked into the forest with dicks spray-painted inside. Everything was abandoned before the war's end in 1944, until some-one had the bright idea of repurposing the place as a resort. Today you can buy Mr. Noodles and park your RV up the hill (though how one gets an RV here is a mystery to me). Here, titans once forged the green girders of the cosmos—now, no longer.

They take Louis's boat because it's smaller, faster and more fuel-efficient. They dock at the Shearwater pier among the fancy sailboats from Oregon. Derik admires the rusty barrels beneath the white-plumed anemones and occasional jellyfish from the bobbing dock.

They inspect the marina shop, get themselves some T-shirts of formline wolves—which Derik vows never to wear to school on account of being mocked the last time he wore a wolf shirt, though these are actually in vogue—and two downriggers, sure to fit *Wild Thing*. Then they hit up the restaurant across the street for some burgers. Raven orders a beer.

"You guys don't drink, do you?" he asks Louis and George.

"No," Louis shakes his head.

"No. I quit years ago," says George. "Just after I had the kids."

"That's good. I still like a good spirit every now and then—though beer technically isn't a spirit, I suppose."

"I thought you're in AA though?" says Derik. "That's what Dad told me."

"Is that right? Oh... Yeah... Well, I mostly just help set up. I have a drink every now and then."

The waiter places the frosty ale on the table. Raven takes a gulp. "*Ah... Tasty.*"

"Can I try some?" says Derik.

"No," says George before Raven can answer.

"Why not? 'Cause it's illegal?"

"*Yes.*"

"What's so good about alcohol, though? What does it do?"

"It's poison, if you ask me," says Louis.

"It takes over your brain, so you can relax a bit. If you drink too much, then you lose your brain—that's when the troubles start," says George.

"How come you don't drink, Dad?"

"'Cause I'm an alcoholic; I can't control my drinking, so it's best I stay away from it."

"How can you be an alcoholic if you don't drink?"

"Once an alcoholic, *always* an alcoholic."

"So, say you haven't had a beer for fifty years—you'd still be considered an alcoholic?"

"Yes," he says tensely. The burgers are brought to the table with a ketchup squeeze bottle.

"Crazy. Thank you!"

"Thanks."

They tuck into their juicy burgers, fat and sauce dripping down their chins onto their plates, onto their fries.

"My daughter Sophie and her boyfriend should be coming home from the Island this afternoon," says Louis. He considers Bella Bella the *true* home, as do many.

"Oh. Are they staying at the house too?" asks George.

"No, she said they're staying with Richard's parents. Don't mention you're staying in her old room, if she asks. You know how girls get."

"Will she get mad?" asks Derik.

"She'd probably get upset, but it's not her room anymore. She's the one who decided to move out. We turned it into a guest room."

"Yeah, my daughter's like that: she makes a scene if she doesn't get her way," says George. God forbid there are no vegan meals prepared when Candace gets home from the club at four a.m. (she's still in high school). For Candace, even the mundane is fraught with argument.

"She's so lucky," continues Louis. "All the work we had to do to get where we are now. Kids these days don't know what real work is."

Is he talking about me?

"Every generation says that about the younger ones," says Raven. "Each has its difficulties, while certain things become easier. Mine has to deal with climate change, school shootings, inflation, the pandemic, unaffordable housing, the threat of nuclear war. And to top it all off, the Pentagon is entertaining the idea of aliens. You guys have already got houses; I don't think I'll ever own a house… Well, not a typical one at least."

Louis looks at his messy plate. George smirks.

"I had to work for everything I have," Raven adds. "I went to school. I worked sixteen hours a day as a cook and janitor; I had to sweep up needles from under stairs. Nothing was handed to me on a silver platter except what I *earned.*"

"Yeah, well, you're an exception," says George. "I heard most young people live with their parents until they're thirty. When I started working for *my* dad, he docked my pay for rent. As soon as I had enough saved, I was out of there—I found my own place."

"Rent was a lot cheaper back then. Costs me eighteen hundred dollars a month for a hole in the wall."

"That's true."

"Everything is so goddamn expensive nowadays: gotta pay for Netflix, gotta pay for funeral flowers, gotta pay him, gotta pay her. Everyone takes a piece, and everyone needs a piece."

They finish their burgers. They wipe their greasy chins.

George covers the bill and leaves a nice tip, then they drain their bladders before hitting the open water (peeing off the side of a boat is difficult in the best of times). The restaurant has a small stage, piano and dance floor. Raven can't help but rattle out some blues on the piano before they head out.

"You're gonna love me, like nobody's loved me, come rain or come shine," he sings. "Happy together. Unhappy together. And wouldn't it be fine?" Derik follows his hands. "Days may be cloudy or sunny. We're in or we're out of the money. But I'm with you always. I'm with you rain or shine." He twinkles the final few notes. "Can you play?" he asks Derik.

"A little... Not really." Derik rolls out some chords and scales— really angular, uneducated. By feel he goes, striding across sonic land-scapes, raising cities from sand, then letting them fall from his hands. Their sketches fade in resonance; the end alters the start.

"Wow, that was pretty good! You can play."

"I mean, I have a piano at home I fiddle around on... but I don't know Beethoven or anything."

"Meh, who cares? Nor do I. Music should be fun. It should come from your soul, not charts. Written music is great, but I chase inspiration—improvising is the true joy of music for me. You know, your grandpa used to play piano."

"Really?" said Derik. "I didn't know that."

"Yeah, he used to play everything. He was in charge of the Bella Bella band—taught them to play their instruments, even got them uniforms, like a real James Brown."

"Huh… I knew he played saxophone, but I didn't know he led a band. Maybe that's why I care about music so much." He readies his hands, then launches into "Saria's Song."

"Hey, how do you know that? That's from *Ocarina of Time*."

"I looked it up online."

"But I grew up with that game. That's one of the greatest games of all time."

"I played it on the N64 you brought into the pawnshop."

"I'm impressed."

George steps up to the stage. "OK, you guys ready?"

"Yup."

George zips up his leather jacket. They mosey back to the boat. It's time to fish.

🌿 🌿 🌿

George shows sonny how to man the downrigger aboard Louis's boat. "Make sure you grip this handle tight, or else once that cannonball drops the line is going to run and you won't be able to grab it; it'll sink right to the bottom."

"Will it break? Maybe we can cannonball the fish."

George shakes his head. "No. If that happens, whatever you do, don't try and grab it, or else you're gonna break your arm."

"What am I supposed to do if it drops?"

"Just don't let it happen; hold on tight and make sure you lock it before you ever let go." He shows the uninitiated the locked position. The downrigger has a sturdy plastic handle that you crank to reel in or out, and the line is attached to a cannonball that drops the hook to a desired depth, shown on a gauge; it works in tandem with the fish finder, which uses sonar to show where to find schools of fish. George mimics his hand being contorted by the crank—the worst of positions for such a fragile joint. "I saw a guy do it: he broke his wrist and fell overboard trying to relieve himself of the pain. So make sure you hold on to this handle here," he repeats sternly (pun not intended, friends, but appreciated). Derik grabs hold as shown, feeling the weight of the cannonball threatening to plummet. George shows him how to lower and drop the hook, which he does well enough. "Now crank it!" Derik attempts feebly. "No! Like this." George retakes control. "You have to spin it fast, otherwise we're going to be here all day. Try again." Derik does his best. "You gotta do it faster." George evokes Henry.

"Just let me figure it out!" Derik snaps. "You always get so mad trying to explain things. Just let me figure it out, OK? I can't do it if you're standing there yelling at me 'Faster, faster,' like an idiot."

George steps back; he leaves Derik be, intensity reciprocated. He sucks on his vape. Derik channels his focus to the downrigger, understanding its function, its mechanics, meshing on a cellular level. He performs better in vengeance.

"Oh," says Louis, in that long arc of melancholic surprise. "There's a bunch of fish at sixty." He traces with his finger on the fish finder.

"So I reel it down till it shows sixty on the gauge, right?"

"Uh-huh."

Derik does so without hesitation. Like a hurricane, he gathers and releases. He's in terminator mode, just like when that kid kicked him upside the head while sparring—*Headshots are illegal, but it was a kick!*—and Derik repaid him with a flurry of body shots and leg kicks until the kid was backed against the wall, and Sensei said, "Stop!" with a smile, because she was proud—it was a real scrap!

He sets the depth to sixty, makes sure it's locked, then steps back, watching the end of the rod, nulling unnecessary thought. *Watch the rod. Watch the rod.*

How do I know when there's a bite?

It'll bend and bobble. Who cares, just watch the rod. He no longer asks questions or makes eye contact; he pours all focus toward finally catching a fish, even if the downrigger is the easy way.

George takes out a plastic bag of crisp joints from his coat pocket. "Want a puff?" he asks Louis.

Louis nods and softly says, "Yeah."

George sparks the joint and takes a hit before passing it to Louis who, wide-eyed, takes a hit, and immediately starts coughing. George chuckles. "Sure is good stuff, isn't it?"

"Yeah," Louis eventually manages to scrape out. He offers the joint to Raven, who refuses.

"No, thanks," says Raven. "I get too paranoid. I only smoke alone. I don't like doing it in public anymore."

George reclaims the joint and takes another hit. He holds in the smoke, then lets it out, coughing slightly. "Doesn't do much for me anymore," he says, passing it back to Louis. "My tolerance is so high." He and Louis share the joint until it smoulders to a roach.

Dad's smoking again.

As long as he's not driving.

Better than pills.

I wonder what it would be like to get high. He did it at my age. I'd probably think aliens are talking to me, like he does.

"I used to be able to smoke and do anything I wanted," says Raven, "but as I got older, I felt like I had a responsibility to act respectable in public... though I can't say I've improved at all in that regard. I guess that's the evolution of responsibility, isn't it?"

"It's hot out. Good thing we're in the shade a bit here." George changes the subject.

"It's thirty-four already," relays Louis from the thermometer.

The fog has cleared since morning.

"Thirty-four already? Jesus."

"Supposed to be a heat wave."

The downriggers are down, the boat's in position and everything is stocked: joints, sunscreen, snacks, water and ice—lots of ice to store the fish in coolers, lots of ice for the tea, lots of ice to rub on their burning skin if need be. George kicks back in his seat and puts his feet up, beneath the shade of the boat's blue awning, while Louis stands at the wheel and Raven hunches over, perched on the cooler, wavering in and out of deep thought as the wake from a passing boat rocks them. All the while, Derik stands defiant, with only his white cap and minimal sunscreen to protect him from the glaring sun; he suffers for cred, but also wants a tan like Louis's.

"Ahh. This is the life," says George.

"You should visit more often," Louis responds.

"I've been busy running the business back home. It's a lot of work running a pawnshop, having to buy and sell, manage pawns, worry about payroll. We got the boy working there now."

Louis turns and gives him a side-glance, pouting, nodding in approval. "Good—start him young."

"Yup. We have him organizing boxes in the back and taking care of display cases in the front. He sold his first watch the other day."

"Hey, how's Betty doing? Haven't seen her for *years*."

"She's doing good. She's still working at Norsat. She's happy as long as she has work to do. She's always running around town doing chores, keeping the kids busy."

Is it bending?

I don't want to ask.

Just check. "Is there a bite?" he says, eyeing the rod.

Everyone looks.

"Maybe," says George. "It's usually pretty obvious when you get a bite."

"Probably just jellyfish or kelp," clarifies Louis.

Derik churns words, the cogs spin. *No action needed.*

"We were looking at some places on the Island," George continues, "'cause we're thinking of investing in a house we can rent out and vacation at. Our mortgage is paid off, and we got some money saved up. I told her we're entitled to a house here, and a plot of land, but it's too remote for her."

"It sucks because there aren't a lot of houses here," says Raven. "At least when I asked, they said there weren't any available. There's a high demand for them, isn't that right?" he asks Louis.

Louis doesn't speak in haste; he thinks before he speaks. "There aren't enough houses for *our* people."

"I know... I could go on a wait-list to get one eventually—probably take a few years—but I'd feel bad taking it from someone who really needs it."

"Yeah, we don't need any more people living here—have enough troubles to deal with."

"More people means more people to help the community," says Raven. "I think the future is people moving to rural areas, working remotely, while respecting nature to help restore the land. Look at all these forest fires, heat waves and floods—they're all symptoms of climate change, and humanity could help remedy them if they were more integrated with the land instead of taking photos of their poutine."

"We don't need more outsiders," says Louis, adamant. "Just let us govern ourselves for once. White people are always trying to move in and change things. Things were just fine before they messed them up."

"I mean, yeah... but..."

"Yeah, everything's going to hell," says George. "You know, I convinced the wife to let us get a boat so we can always stay afloat in case Vancouver goes under."

An eagle calls from atop a cedar, opening the floodgates of joy within Derik, though he restrains the smile. This slight reprieve is met with a nodding of the rod, so Derik does proclaim, "I have a bite! ... I think. What do I do? What do I do?"

"Unlock it and reel it in," says Louis. And our hero does exactly that. He reels in, channelling fury from the thousand demons watching him with superfluous eyes. He reels in with the blood of ancestors coursing through him—broiling aptitude. And friends, he reels in a medium-sized rock cod (technically a rockfish, though they call them rock cod).

They're disappointed you're not excited.

I am excited.

No you're not, you're forcing it.

No, really, I am. I'm a man now. Look.

"It's a rock cod," Louis tells him, swinging it aboard with a flick of the line. Derik locks the downrigger in place. The spiny fish flips and jolts on deck. Louis grabs the pliers from the tackle, then shakes the hook loose from its mouth. "Gimme the club." He points near Derik's foot. Derik picks it up.

"I can do it," Derik says. Then, with great accuracy, force and mercy (let us not forget, friends, in some parts the club is known as a *priest*, for it's by that very device the last rites of the fish are administered) Derik knocks the fish on the noggin, effectively killing it.

"Nice job," says George. "You caught your first fish!"

Derik gently places the fish atop the ice in the cooler. He can't help but smile and say, "That was too easy," resuming his post. The downrigger proves to be an effective tool for culling rock cod, bombarding their subaqueous lair with cannonball after cannonball. They quickly fill one cooler, both lines hitting over and over.

"Look at this one!" says Derik. This time it's a brown rock cod with bulging eyes. "How come its eyes are like that?"

"Their eyes pop out when you bring them up so quick," says George, "because they're used to being so deep. It's like when divers have to use decompression tanks when they return to the surface." It isn't at all, really, but some wisdom of the deep is conveyed.

Derik beholds the horror in the fish's eyes as it spasms at his feet.

"I think we've caught enough rock cod. You can throw that one over."

"Throw it over? I don't want to waste it."

"It's the ocean—nothing goes to waste. Something will eat it."

I'm sorry. Derik picks it up and throws it overboard. He watches its scales glitter among the ruffled water as the boat drifts by. But he's not the only one: an eagle, aloft a distant tree, spies it and dives down. It swoops in with perfect form and grasps the flailing fish, stoked— *Thanks!* It knows the way, as it was watching our crew for some time, just waiting for one to be thrown back, as this is the way it has always been between people and eagles. The eagle takes the fish back to shore to eat, while Derik jumps up and down, saying, "Wow! That was *amazing*! How did it see the fish from so far?"

"They've got good eyesight," says Louis with a smile.

"Did you know it would do that?" Derik asks his dad.

"Yeah," he says, nonchalant.

"Wow! That was *so* cool. I want to do it again."

"Well, let's try and catch a salmon," says George. "We've got enough rock cod."

"How do we do that?"

"I'll take us to where I caught three sockeye the other day," says Louis. "We should be able to get some there." He returns to the helm as they secure the downriggers. They fly across the water, the sun beating down upon them.

Arriving at the new spot, they promptly drop the cannonballs and hooks. Louis takes them slowly forward, searching for a school on the fish finder. He passes over the crowds, the damned souls below, reaching up with their mercurial hands. The fish live happily their basic existence, though existence be the simplest of all things, and from which all things stem. Humans run around with their lopsided minds, complicating life, detracting from it. To preach the critical is to forgo the natural; i.e. "This steak is overcooked," or, "Billy, sit down and quit playing with your pencil before I belittle you in front of the class!"—forgo the reality of the steak, that it is indeed a perfect steak by definition, and Billy, that curiosity and wonder are phases of being, not distractions, or else, dear curmudgeons, curiosity and wonder they are not by definition. Hence, to say one thing is to depart from essence.

"We're passing over a school now," says Louis. "Down around fifty-five."

"That's not that low," says Derik, warpath waning. He unlocks the downrigger, lowers it and drops the cannonball—but he doesn't hold the handle tight enough, so it runs away from him; the cannonball plummets, ripping past the vexed salmon (brows furrowed in the local display) scattering them every which way. The crank spins out of control like Taz. Everyone stares in disbelief. Louis steps forth to grab it. Then Derik, with a firm stance, clenches his fist and holds his arm close to the crank as the numbers roll and time slows. With confidence, he punches in his fist, sacrificing limb again, and tenses for impact—a firm block. He doesn't try and grab the handle, as he imagines what would happen: the force would snap his index finger; his hand would get caught and contorted, stopping the mad crank but breaking his wrist; he would get spun into a different dimension; he sees the possibilities in a flash. Thus, he lets the crank collide with his forearm, like Achilles, shield raised, halting the blows of Hector. The numbers stop rolling; the cannonball rests like a hanged man— the crank is stopped. Before the others notice his heroic effort, Derik grabs a hold of the handle like nothing happened, and reels up slowly to fifty-five.

"My bad," he says. "I got it now, don't worry."

Everyone is wary, but impressed. They won't applaud him though, because it was his fault.

Minutes pass. They figure he must have damaged himself. Surely those skinny arms couldn't have absorbed such force as the free-whirling crank! Yet, there is nothing but a rose mark on his arm. In fact, Derik enjoys the pain; the slight burn of his forearm is his reward.

"How's your arm after catching that one?" asks George, insinuating.

Derik inspects his arm as a formality, because he knows it's nothing. He's only embarrassed for having let it slip. "Fine," he says. "I've blocked kicks harder than that." He smiles with his back turned.

"He's tougher than he looks," says Raven.

"Make sure you have a good grip on the handle next time," says Louis. "I don't want you losing a cannonball or wrecking my boat."

"Yeah, don't let that happen again," says George.

"I won't," says Derik, serious. He doesn't let on that he enjoys the rush.

George takes a consolidating puff from his vape.

Derik locks the downrigger, steps back and takes a deep breath.

Raven breaks the silence. "So did you hear the Pope is going to meet with Indigenous leaders? He invited them to the Vatican, though; he's not going to meet them on Canadian soil."

"They should hang him," says George. "It's the only way to make things right." He takes another hit. "Once a pedophile, always a pedophile."

"It's a start, I think … but yeah, he needs to apologize on our soil, not bring them to the place where it all started."

"I don't want that crook on our land."

"Nah," Louis adds to the fire, "me either."

"He can stay in his stupid church eating spaghetti for all I care."

Raven chuckles at such audacity.

"They should be looking for more graves, 'cause I know they're out there; there's probably thousands more." He takes another puff. "Trudeau should be helping dig up those graves, that's what I want to see."

Raven says, "That'd be pretty funny, actually."

"Oh, and another thing—"

The rod bends. "I got something!" says Derik. Louis starts the engine and slowly moves the boat forward. Derik reels in. "It feels heavier than the other bites." He keeps reeling. Lo and behold, there is no orange, pink or brown shining back at them, but a sleek, metallic blue that emerges, winding this way, then that. He's hooked a salmon! "Get the net! It's a salmon!"

George, stunned, pockets his vape and hops up from his seat. He grabs the net.

"OK, what do I do?" Derik asks.

"Calm down. Try to pull the line closer to me."

Derik grabs the line, but it cuts into his hand. He grabs it again, wraps the line around his hand, and directs the salmon behind stern like a barge from a tug. He reels in more, and the fish leaps out of the water. George leans over stern and submerges the net. The salmon darts left, then right, but soon it centres with the boat. It glides into the net, and George lifts it from the water. Its iridescence and blue-silver scales shine in the sun as drops of water cascade like diamonds. George brings it aboard. He puts down the net. The salmon flips and flops on deck.

"There ya go, your first salmon!" He pats Derik on the back heartily, purging the bad spirits that linger.

"That's a nice-sized sockeye," says Louis.

Derik marvels at the beauty: its skin of jewels and eyes full of life. Windows to soul, the eyes are, and it continues to amaze Derik how bright they are, as if he's been lied to his whole life about fish (or birds) not having souls. But the more he looks, the more he realizes how sublime and how similar are the creatures of Earth. *It's beautiful.*

"OK, you going to club it or what?"

"One second! Look how beautiful it is."

"It's a beautiful fish," says Raven, shades on. "Beautiful to eat as well."

Derik eventually does the deed—*Thank you, salmon, for giving me your life. I will make sure you don't go to waste*—and gives it a right whacking. George tosses it in the cooler, next to the rock cod with a gaping mouth. Then the second downrigger hits, bobbing, telling them, "Yea, verily—there is a creature that tugs me." George jumps to, reeling it in. Louis starts the ship forth once more. Sure enough, another salmon breaks the water. This time Derik mans the net, and as easily as the first, they capture their second communal salmon. It is duly reaped, bopped and tossed in the cooler.

"Wow this is easy," says Derik, torn. ... *Too easy.*

"I told you the downriggers work like a charm. Isn't this awesome?"

"It is and it isn't."

"Whaddaya mean?"

"It's nice that we're catching all these salmon ... but it doesn't *feel* the same as catching them by hand—you know, with a simple rod and reel. Like you said, I keep thinking about all their little eyes looking back up at me. It's like we're murdering their families."

"We're not *murdering* their families, Derik; there's plenty of fish out there for us to catch. It's our birthright to catch salmon on *our* land from *our* water."

"I know, but I feel like there's more honour in catching them by hand, instead of using the downrigger. It's too cheap, you know? It's like beating someone who's short at basketball. It's more rewarding when they're the same height, or taller even, 'cause then it's actually *fair*."

"You're just never satisfied, huh? We bring you all the way out here to Bella Bella—to some of the best fishing spots in the world—and you complain that it's *too easy*?"

"Never mind," says Derik, exhausted, like his teacher, Mrs. Crosschuk, when she tries to teach algebra. "It's good that we're catching all these fish. It's just that..." *I'll catch one on my own by hand.* "Never mind."

"I get what you mean," says Raven. "It's like we should be using our bare hands, or spears even. That's the test of a *true* fisherman."

They resume their pillage of the underwater villages. They haul aboard salmon after salmon, until—within a few hours, the sun peaking overhead—they've packed the coolers full, and are burnt. George closes the lid.

"Quite the haul, if I do say so myself." He stretches to the sky while groaning like a bear. "You think we should call it a day?"

Louis smiles, quite high. "We can head back if you want."

"Yeah. I think we'll be fried eggs if we stay out in this heat any longer."

Already their faces are red, noses Rudolphian—except Louis's, as he's already tanned from so much time on the water. "I'll take us back. Then we can break down the fish and freeze them."

"Sounds like a plan."

Raven sits in the shade, legs kicked up. "Nice."

They bring up the downriggers, keeping them erect, and store the flashy spoons. Louis guns it across the water, chopping as he goes.

6. Harder, Father

They moor the boat, then return to the Tanner household. There, they have a meal of staples—fresh-caught salmon, cut into fillets and broiled, seaweed, boiled potatoes, rice, ooligan grease and soy sauce—washed down with plenty of iced tea.

"Redbird, what are you having for dinner?" asks Coyote.

Me? Just worms in a nice beurre blanc.

It is indeed a heat wave, shattering some hundred records by several degrees across the province. People are dropping dead, deprived of water, crawling through the sandy streets to the supermarket aflame. Although more metaphor than singular occasion, the summer is off to a ferocious start, with the sun cackling and shooting his blazing darts upon the people of British Columbia.

What can be done? What *can* be done when the gods rear their heads after centuries of slumber and abidance? They cast their lot with the humans, with their grandeur and self-importance, that have all peaked—Yes, the acts of humans have peaked, dear friends!—and now must fall down to the dust, or burn in the eternal flash of the cosmos. Believe me, peaks come and go (bird here, after all), and perhaps this is not the last, but luxury is fleeting and only appreciated as it goes away. It is hard to accept, I guess, but let us move on, and savour the present, what we have now, for surely you humans do not care of the future, having brought yourselves to this junction; a spectator does not taunt the prisoner upon the chair.

Derik, in dinosaur pyjamas, folds back the covers, fluffs his pillow and hops into bed, letting the sheets wash over him. George plops on the edge, bouncing the mattress like a boat in a wake.

"Thanks for bringing me here, Dad," says Derik. "I'm really having a good time."

"You're welcome," George responds. He groans, then lies back, straight as a dead man. Derik twists his legs around, settling on the best flow.

"I can't believe how easy it was to catch all those salmon."

"Yup. I told you it'd be easy. Those downriggers work great."

"I keep thinking about what you said, how all those fish were staring back at you. Is that when you quit fishing?"

"No, I had to keep working—Mom would've killed me if I didn't. I stopped fishing when the industry started to collapse."

"I don't think it's fair to use those downriggers. I don't think it's fair to use any of the equipment actually—the seiners, the trawlers— they kill way too many fish too quickly; I doubt they have time to repopulate. What would the ocean be without fish? We need to use hooks instead of nets that rip up the ocean floor. That's why I want to catch one with a simple fishing rod—it's personal. If everyone had to kill their own cow, they'd realize how precious a life is, then hopefully not be so wasteful."

"Yeah, it's not sustainable. I wouldn't worry about that here, though; there's lots of fish here for everyone. It's when others come here and take our fish that we should worry. You know, before there were any white people here, we had a way with nature—to preserve. When we'd take a tree to make a canoe, we used to pray, and thank the tree for letting us cut it down. If we needed the bark, we'd peel it in such a way that the tree didn't die and could keep giving us more bark. Industrialization is what decimated the fish populations, 'cause everyone just took what they wanted. It was never like that before. Before, we had an abundance 'cause we worked with Mother Nature and made sure to use everything we took so nothing went to waste."

"I think it's getting to be that way again. For class, we planted a tree in the field at school. Mrs. Crosschuk taught us about using the land properly and respecting the environment. White people are beginning to realize how they killed the Earth."

"We can never go back to the way things were… No. We'll just have to adapt with the times, 'cause the times are a-changin.'" He smiles, turns, and rubs Derik's head. "It'll be all right. Quit worrying so much. You worry too much; it's not good for you." George turns off the lamp on his side. He rolls over toward the wall like a walrus. "Goodnight, son."

"Goodnight, Dad. Love you."

"I love you too."

George drifts off to sleep in minutes, while Derik stares at the ceiling, imagining all the stars that must be above. *Somewhere, somehow, there's a planet much closer to its sun than Earth. Maybe there, the fish rule and the humans are dying off.* Slowly he forgets where he is, the walls dissolve as his mind wanders the lost corridors; Derik falls asleep.

ψ ψ ψ

A loud bang wakes Derik at 3:14 a.m. *What was that? Was there a bang? Did I hear someone?*

Maybe it was Raven.

It was probably just the house settling. He probes through the white noise of the fan and George's snoring, searching for dissonance, listening for noise made by a human, or a wild animal perhaps. *It was probably just the house; it makes noises when it gets cold.* His eyes droop again as he falls asleep.

Then he hears snickering and whispering. *Raven?*

Woman.

Rena? He strains his ears, investigating the aural world. A plate shatters. A woman giggles, hardly trying to contain her laughter, then a large-sounding man tells her to hush, in that dumb tone lovers use when silly acts are excused by their attraction—because everything is fair in love!

Derik hears the couple stumble down the hall, bumping into walls, falling into each other and snickering, not caring who hears or who is trying to sleep, because everyone should behold the merriment of their union. *It's OK! It's OK. You don't need sleep! You'd miss* out on this show, which you know must be better than anything you've got. Derik's eyes are wide, and ears perked like a deer's.

"Watch out," says Sophie. "You're going to knock down the pictures."

"Mm, I don't care," says Richard, kissing her neck, latching onto her as she tries to walk down the hall. *The killer awoke before dawn. He put his boots on.* Then, with a loud shriek, they tumble, intertwined, into the room where George and Derik lie; bashing on the lights, they fall atop the bed themselves, her giggling and him still kissing her neck. Sophie lands on George's legs, waking him as if from a nightmare.

"What the hell!" George exclaims.

Sophie turns to see Derik staring back at her, equally as startled as her. "Ew," she says, her display of love spoiled. "Who are you? And why are you in my bed?" She stands, and Rich puffs his chest.

"Uh." Derik fumbles for words, tongue lashing around his closed mouth. "Auntie Rena said we could sleep here."

"Who *are* you?"

"I'm your uncle George," George groans.

"Oh. Why are you staying in *my* room though? I didn't say you could; this is *my* room." She hastens to confront her sleeping parents. Unfortunately for her, Rena has been awake this whole time, listening (as best she can) from the end of the hall in the master bedroom. Rich gives Derik an intimidating look, squinting. He says, "Hey."

Derik says, "Hey."

Rich leaves the room and George rolls over to sleep.

"They're our guests," Derik hears Rena say down the hall. "I told them they could."

"That's *my* room though!" says Sophie. "I don't want them sleeping in *my* bed. That's *my* bed. I told you I was coming home."

"It's not your room anymore—that's our guest room. You said you were staying at Richard's parents' house."

"Uh, no I didn't. I told you I was coming home. I sent you a text."

"... Sophie, it says you sent that an hour ago. We were all asleep."

"I don't care, I want them out of my room, *now*."

"No, it's too late for that. You should've said something earlier! You know I go to bed around nine."

"Sorry," she says, and all is forgiven. "But that's my room. They can sleep on the couches."

"There's no room for them on the couches—there's three of them and only two couches. You do the math."

"Excuse me? You're telling me I have to give up my bed to strangers?"

"They're not strangers, they're your relatives!" But before Rena can finish, Sophie is already squawking down the hall, like Lucy when I don't properly cover the eggs. (I mean, do we really need all six?)

Derik and George have no choice but to relocate before the whole town is stirred.

"Get out!" Sophie points out the door.

Derik hustles. George lumbers to his feet. "You couldn't wait till morning, huh? I think that's rather rude."

"It's *my* room! Get out!"

"Sophie, don't talk to your uncle like that," says Rena, tying her robe. "Show some respect."

"Please get out of my room. I spent all day getting here on a boat, and now I want to sleep. It's weird that you're in here anyway."

George says, "We're tired too. We also travelled by boat to get here."

"*Sorry.*"

"What a brat," George mutters as he walks by, pillow under his arm.

"What are you doing? That's my pillow!"

"Fine!" he says, chucking it back into the room. "What am I supposed to use, then, a phonebook?"

"I'll get you a pillow," Rena reassures him.

Derik scuttles for his toothbrush and stray clothes, notifying them to avoid further misunderstanding. He brushes Rich by accident. "Watch where you're going," says Dick.

"Sorry," says Derik.

With the father and son expelled, Sophie makes to close the door.

"You know you could've handled that better," says Rena. "Waking up the whole house like that."

"Goodnight," says Sophie, dainty as a flower. She shuts the door, then wraps her arms about Rich and giggles sweet nothings.

George plops onto the grey couch in the grey night. Raven smirks, his hands behind his head. "What a treat," he says.

George raises his hands in frustration. "God, you'd think we'd get some peace and quiet here at three in the morning. Now where am I supposed to sleep? On this couch?"

Rena brings them a foamy, blankets and pillows.

"Did you know she was coming home this late?" George asks her.

"No, I had no idea. You think I'd let you sleep in her old room knowing that? Of course not."

"Well, what are we supposed to do now? I can't sleep on the floor, and this couch hurts my back."

"I'll sleep on the floor," says Derik, imagining camping. "I don't mind."

George lays back into the couch, bending his knees to fit. Derik tries the foamy. *I don't mind this. I could be homeless if I wanted.*

Rena drapes the blanket over him. "Comfy?" Derik nods. She chucks George a blanket and pillow.

"Thanks," he says, making his nest.

"I'm sorry about her," says Rena. "She gets like that sometimes."

"Yeah, well, great," says George, already rolling into the couch to sleep.

"I'll get up early to make you breakfast."

Derik looks at the clock. *It already is early.*

"Goodnight." She heads back to bed.

"Goodnight," they reply.

Raven tells Derik, "Let me know if you get too uncomfortable. I don't mind swapping."

Derik, eager to suffer, says, "I'm fine. Thanks though."

Derik lays staring out to the moonlit backyard, hoping the giggles go away—that mad laughing in the walls—but all night he imagines an imp taunting him, juggling fire, cackling with eyes aflame. A hearty pounding continues for an hour upon the bed of space, flying freely past Venus and Saturn, the globe of stars wallpaper. Once the fields are tilled and the seed buried, the pleas cease, and Derik, at last, sleeps—for all of two hours.

The early summer sun wakes our fellows of couch and foam. Rena prepares breakfast with the grace of an angel. She waits till they're all awake, stretching away the remnants of sleep, before asking if they're hungry. "I got some bacon in the oven. How do you want your eggs?"

No one is quick to answer. Raven says, "Sure. I'll take them scrambled."

George rubs his back against the tree. "Sunny-side up for me, please."

"Whatever's easiest," says Derik.

"All right."

She prepares a hearty breakfast of eggs, crisp bacon, orange juice, black coffee and white toast with margarine. She puts peanut butter and raspberry jam on the table before them.

"I'm allergic to peanuts," says Derik, as Uncle Lou spreads some across his toast. "I'll go into shock if I have any."

"OK, well stay away from me then." Louis bites.

"Just don't kiss me and I'll be fine," Derik says, like a comic whose bit deteriorates instead of improving.

"So how did you sleep?" asks Rena "I hope you weren't too uncomfortable."

"Horrible," grumbles George. "That couch really hurts my back."

"I'm sorry she came in and woke you up in the middle of the night," she says, already putting food away. "She didn't tell me till late she'd be staying here."

They eat breakfast, trying to forget.

So that's who I'm related to. Sophie's not anything like me. I wouldn't do that in my parents' house. House—Grandpa's house. Dad said it was haunted; they all saw a ghost and ran out. "Who gets Grandpa's old house?" he asks.

"Aunt Lizzy is staying there right now, with her two sons," says George.

"So they own it?" asks Derik.

"We all own it: Rena, Lizzy and Me," says George.

"Is it worth a lot?"

"Probably not. Aunt Lizzy would never agree to sell it."

"Can we go see it?"

"No!"

"Why not? I want to see where you grew up. I think that'd be cool."

"I don't want to go back there. I have nothing but bad memories of that place. Plus, I don't want to go while Aunt Lizzy's there."

"Oh... Damn."

They finish breakfast.

"We should probably get moving if we want to lay down the long-line," says Louis. "It takes a while to set. Then we gotta let it soak."

"True enough."

They take turns showering, because lord knows they need a shower after riding the high seas, still smelling of fish guts and slime. They get dressed, then head out, taking the truck to the pier, while Sophie and Rich sleep.

Walking down the pier, with the sun risen over the water, they come to Louis's boat. George pats Derik on the back. "Today, son, you become a true fisherman; you're gonna learn how to cast a longline."

"Nice. What does that entail?"

There's a tangle of thick hooks on the deck, all attached to one line with separate short lines. "First, we gotta bait all these hooks." He pulls from a bucket a slimy old salmon with murky eyes. "This is what we use for bait."

"Is that a sockeye?"

"No, it's a chum."

"It smells." Derik recoils.

"Good—halibut like smelly fish."

"So halibut eat other fish?"

"Yup, that's right. So now I'll cut the bait into pieces, and you can attach it to the hooks." George makes short work of the salmon, filleting and cutting it into big chunks. Derik takes a piece and pierces it on the first hook.

"Like that?" He holds up his accomplishment.

"Yup. Now you just got to do that about ninety-nine more times."

"Oh boy."

There are actually three hundred.

"Lemme help out," says Raven. "I'll help bait. Let the master work the knife." George chuckles.

Louis, with rectangular shades, starts the motor and backs out of the pier, while the three prep all three hundred hooks.

⚜ ⚜ ⚜

Nothing beats a wild morning: often it is the case that a rough night and nonroutine morning lead to spectacular things. Hear how they help one another; hear how they band together against the common plight. The fog is dashed against the rocks. Sun holds dominion from his azure throne. The water sings below, black and white.

Derik stands on the bow, looking at the water as it breaks over and over into ripples, into waves, into sparkling crystals. He hears them speak. He listens. The world unfolds before him—why stop it? Why stop the world? *There is nothing left for us. All the keen hosts have passed.*

Louis pilots the boat from one side of the pass to the other as George, Raven and Derik start letting out the longline. The halibut look with dumb eyes. Lethargy wins the popular vote. Down go the hooks, one by one, to the bottom.

"Is there any special way to do this?" asks Derik.

"Just make sure you don't get between the line and the water," says George. "Never do that, or it'll drag you right over. I saw it happen to a guy: it dragged him over, right down to his death. Took them three weeks to find his body."

"Wow. What a horrible way to go."

Careful Derik does it, friends, just as he would hold a knife, or tread warily by potential explosives, like truck tires—as his dad once told him about a guy who was killed when an overinflated truck tire exploded right beside him. Or, for that matter, just as he would check that all the doors are locked, or, around water, subconsciously fear he might drown, see the world shrink all around him and hear the white light call his name. (He did almost drown once, has flashbacks.) His mind plays out every conceivable death, imagination with feedback from his father's. *My hand will get pulled in by the winch, then my shoulder; but my neck won't fit, so it'll choke me until I turn blue as they scurry for the off switch, and it'll break my neck and I'll die; the rope will wrap around my ankle and pull me over, just like Dad said, and drag me to the seabed, to the lost ones with eyes and mouths glowing orange; I'll fall in and a great white will get me...* You get the idea. *A whale will fall from the sky and there's not a thing we can do!*

"Watch your foot!" says George.

A hook catches Derik's pant leg and pulls it up, but he quickly shakes it free. He didn't feel much danger.

"Watch what you're doing!" says George. "I told you what can happen. You gotta pay attention before you get hurt."

"All right, Dad. I'm not going to die. It hardly got me."

"You have no idea how dangerous these lines are. Once they get you, it's too late. So pay attention!"

Harsh love from harsh men. But their focus pays off, as over goes the orange buoy, the caboose marking the end of the line. Three hundred hooks sing below.

"Now what do we do?" asks Derik.

"We wait," says George. "We have to let them soak so the halibut have time to take the bait."

88

"How do we know when they've taken the bait?"

"It doesn't matter," interjects Louis. "We'll pull everything up before nightfall. I don't leave anything out overnight anymore, ever since someone jacked my crab pots."

"Well, all right." Derik takes off his orange gloves. Water pours out. His hands are pruned and white, saturated with water. "Ew, look at my hands. It's like I've been swimming."

"We might want to get you some better gloves for when we pull up the longline," says George, "'cause the rope is going to eat right through them."

"It'll be fine," says Louis. "The winch makes it easy."

"OK," says Derik.

"Do you guys want to go on a bit of a tour?" says Louis. "You didn't get to see much yesterday."

"Sure!" says Derik. "That'd be sweet."

"Yeah, why don't we do that," says George. "Kill some time."

"Let me show you around."

Raven checks his texts. "Actually," he says, shady as Stanley Park, "can you drop me off on this island over here? I'm supposed to meet a friend." Who's to say spirits can't be friends, friends? "You don't have to wait for me. I'll call you if I need a lift."

"OK," says Louis, sounding suspicious.

"Who are you supposed to meet on a random island?" says Derik.

"It's not a random island. Levi said there's a cabin there for troublemakers who need a meditation retreat."

That sounds cool. I want to learn how to meditate.

I don't think you learn it. It's just something you do. "Can I come?"

"No. It's going to be really boring, I swear."

"Come on, I want to go!"

"Maybe later. We're only talking business, and he's going to show me the—presumably empty—cabin. I'll be back soon."

"All right," George interjects. "See you in a bit."

And that's all that's discussed. They pull close to shore, nigh the barnacles, and the striated rock formed in the volcanism all those millions of years ago—every grain of the hourglass a planet in its own right. Raven leaps to the rainbow-flecked moss and fades away into the alder and fern.

Derik is disappointed to lose the company of his friend, but they continue the voyage, finally admiring the surroundings, no more reapers of the corn. Through the magmatic dike swarm they go, isles crafted below ground, revealed to the surface like Aphrodite upon the universal clam, or a UFO with little grey humanoids walking down the ramp, dazzling lights behind them. They tour the waterways, with new island after new island appearing, until Louis lands in a shore of rocks.

"There are some rock carvings here," he says.

"Like, petroglyphs?" asks Derik.

"Yeah." Louis heads to stern and unzips his pants, pissing into the water.

Derik, thinking he should give him space, hops onto the rocks and scales the boulders, tying the boat. He admires all the different rocks: grey ones, white ones, black porous ones, white ones with bits of red or blue or yellow—all colours of rock, with different textures and patterns, whether formed plutonic, or cooled quickly in the air post-eruption, or layered slowly by years and years of sediment compressed by the Earth spinning round.

"Hey, look—some clams!" Derik reaches into the clear, cool water, and hoists one up.

"That's a cockle," says George.

"Can you eat it?"

"Yeah, they're good to eat. Have to rinse 'em really well or else you'll get a mouthful of sand—but they're good eating."

Should I take it?

Nah, too much work.

You're lazy. Derik scopes and finds more cockles. He brings them aboard. Louis gives him a plastic container to put them in.

George reminisces. "I used to go digging for cockles and clams with my mom every Sunday. We'd take them home and steam them, then serve them with warm butter." He licks his lips. "They were *so* good."

"All right, well let's do that," says Derik.

Louis thumbs his phone. "Sophie wants a ride to Shearwater to meet up with some friends. Do you mind if we head back to pick her up? It shouldn't take long."

"That's fine," says George.

"OK." Thumbs phone. "I'll tell her." He does that. "I'll show you that rock carving now." He leads them up some boulders to a dark rock. "There it is." He points out the faint indents.

"That's the rock carving?" says Derik. *I don't see anything.*

"Yeah. There's the hands; that's the face. It's a human."

"Huh." Derik chuckles. "I would've never noticed it if you didn't point it out."

"Check this out, too." He shows them an ancient ammonite encased in stone. "It's a fossil."

"Wow, that's cool. How old do you think it is?"

"It's gotta be at least a few thousand years old."

Probably millions. "Yeah... must be."

George sparks another joint. Louis partakes. "So how's it been going with Rich and Sophie? They just start dating?"

"He's a good guy. His dad is Lyonel Spence. You remember him, don't you?"

"Didn't he go to jail for beating his wife?"

"He was never convicted of anything."

"Yeah, I remember him. He worked for my dad before he fired him for drinking on the job."

"I thought all fishermen were drunks," says Derik. He can feel George's heat.

"You can't be drunk on the job; it's too dangerous," says George. "I've known men who were drunk and fell overboard and never made it back up; their gear weighed them down. You can't mess around like that."

"Oh," says Derik. He wanders about, poking at purple starfish, while they finish the joint, talking about how much Henry had disliked Lyonel, how they'd continued to fight over fishing spots.

"He said he'd kill him if he ever caught him pulling up his longline, but I guess he never did catch him doing it." George laughs. "Or else he would've done it."

"Rich is a pretty good kid. He's been real good to Sophie."

"Uh-huh."

"The other day he bought her flowers and made her dinner."

"Oh yeah, and another thing Lyonel did—"

Quick, drop the curtain!

Louis takes them to one last location before heading to pick up Sophie: an island with no beach, but mud, tall grass and more barnacled rocks. Farther in is the usual overgrowth—of fern and vine between dripping cedars—but for once there is a faint path, a parting of the lush green that time has not yet reclaimed. Black currants bob with the breeze over the path and broad leaves—hands grasp for their ankles. Over yon, they see the startled countenances of short totem poles about the size of Derik. He frolics among the tombs of his ancestors.

"Wow, what is this place?" he asks.

"This is called Grave Island," says Louis. "Many of your relatives were buried here."

The graves are marked with carved stone or totems of their respective clan, animals abstracted, boldly painted black, blue, red and white. He reads their names. *Agnus Day. May she finally have peace in the afterlife. Thomas Sparrow. A great father, husband, fisherman and role model. David Tanner. Here lies a great leader, who always helped others before helping himself. Violet Reid. She was taken too early. We'll always remember her for her grace and pure heart.* As Derik ventures further, reading names, gathering spirits, he finds the graves only get more disorganized, less ornate and certainly more weathered, the totems chipped, paint faded and fissures running with the grain.

"Was everyone buried here, or just the chiefs?" he asks.

"No, not just chiefs. Many people were buried here," says Louis.

"Some of these tombstones are new. Do people still get buried here?"

"Oh yeah."

"Will my grandpa be buried here?"

"No, his request was to have his ashes spread on the water."

"There's no way we're having him cremated," says George. "It goes against everything our people believed in: we knew not to burn the body or else it couldn't get to the afterlife."

Louis rubs his head. "They already had him cremated, I think."

"Fuck, they better not have! I specifically told them *not* to have him cremated."

Louis is quiet.

"Why is it such a big deal if they cremate him?" asks Derik.

"Because he needs his body to move on to the afterlife—I just told you! Otherwise he's doomed to wander as a ghost forever. That's why people are buried in coffins; burning them destroys their body and spirit."

Spirit, too?

I don't know about that. I don't think Heiltsuk had coffins, did they?

No, but they sure didn't cremate people. He knows George is getting worked up, like when he talks about sasquatches or hikers disappearing into portals. "How come Grandma Julia wasn't buried here? I remember you made us get baptized before we saw her grave in Vancouver 'cause you said she'd harm us if we didn't." *Gave her blue flowers.*

"When she died, my dad had her buried at the closest cemetery. It's not like I had any say in it—they didn't even tell me when she died."

"Do you think she would've wanted to be buried here?"

George thinks it over for a minute before responding. "Probably not... She's the one that moved us away from Bella Bella. I don't think it would have been fair to bring her back."

"Why'd she want to leave Bella Bella?"

"She wanted us to have a better life. That's why we moved to Vancouver when I was a kid, so we could go to better schools. Didn't matter, though, we got the strap wherever we went. If we stepped out of line they'd smack us with a ruler right across the knuckles."

"Was that 'cause you were a bad student?"

"They were just looking for an excuse to punish us. That's why I ended up not showing up much in high school."

"Sometimes my teachers are mean. I got yelled at the other day for running in the hall, even though other kids were doing it too."

"You're so lucky, you have no idea. I used to get beaten by my teachers. Other kids would always try and start fights with me. Everyone was trying to start something with me. I remember one time, this kid in my grade eight class said he was gonna beat me up after school after calling me a stupid chug."

"What? That's crazy. What did you do?"

"I went outside to confront him, but he was there with all his friends. First thing they did was throw dirt in my eyes. I started throwing punches, but I couldn't see them. Then they jumped on me, tackled me to the ground. Their punches didn't hurt, though. I was used to getting hit by my dad. I managed to trip one and climb on top of him. I just kept beating on him until they backed away and left me alone. They called me all sorts of names, but from then on, I knew they could never hurt me. They said, 'This isn't over. You're going to get into so much trouble.' I didn't care. I was mostly scared what my dad would say."

"What *did* he say?"

"Nothing, really. I was surprised. I think he was more worried what the principal would say."

"Did those kids ever try to beat you up again?"

"Nope. They realized I wasn't to be messed around with. I ended up getting suspended for a week; the principal was really mad. He said, 'You ever set hands on one of my boys again, and I'll make sure you never step foot in this school ever again.' That was the last time I ever got into a fight at that school. I had to apologize to those kids, too."

"Wow, really?"

"Yeah. That's why you have to be careful who you tell you're Native—you never know what they might do."

Well, no one's tried to fight me for being Native yet. He says nothing further on the matter. He realizes he'll never know what it's like to grow up in such a lawless, racist land, yet the experience—the tension and lessons—trickles through in the telling.

The birds sing. George takes a puff of his vape.

They embark solemnly, as if this were the funeral procession, as if they themselves were the last Danish knights, finely dressed and set upon Karves bedecked with garlands and blades. They head back toward the pier to pick up Sophie and Rich, with Derik transfixed by the glitter of the water.

A sound so pure and ethereal rings through his ears, blooms in his head—a warble of yearning, a clarion of lament. "What was that?" he asks the others. Again comes the call, resonating in Derik like a new favourite song, one in which the voice and the lyrics echo over and over. Derik scans for the source, the clearest crystal, and finds it, there, floating upon the water, its slender neck quivering as it calls to Derik in chilling trem.

"That's a loon," says Louis, smiling at Derik's unbridled inspiration.

It calls once more, the fair maid of "John Riley."

"That's the most beautiful sound I've ever heard," says Derik. O, the loon! A dollar there, yet ever so much more here.

For the better part of their journey back to the pier, Derik beholds the fleeting majesty of the loon calling upon the water, of an ancient time we may only visit via its icy call. Some say they rejuvenated the world post-deluge as they dove down for food; some say they call for a lost lover, one whom they'll never meet; and some (including yours truly) simply admire their beauty.

Hecate herself graces us with her presence on the dock; Sophie and Rich wait, side by side, the adept and the charmed—yet, it is he who believes she takes any form he desires. Louis pulls up, with George and Derik at the ready to starboard. They flip over the fenders, hop off and pull in the boat with ropes, which they then tie to the cleats. Derik stumbles, but manages to stop his fall with his right foot.

Sophie jests, "I think I know who isn't the fisherman."

"Yeah." Rich enables.

Derik ignores them.

"What's up, man?" says Dick. "Did you have a good time out on the boat?"

Shut up. Stop speaking. I wish he stopped at "What's up." "Yup, it was good."

Rich clears his throat and postures up. Enter Louis.

"So did you set the longline?" Sophie asks.

"Yup, the hooks are soaking," says Louis.

"Good." She holds out her open hand. "Gimme the keys then."

"Why? I'll drop you off at Shearwater."

"No, I want to go on a picnic with my friends. You said you were just setting out the longline. So let us have the boat for a while."

"No, Sophie—we're still using it."

"For what? You said you were only fishing for halibut."

"We're going salmon fishing, too."

"I already told my friends we could have the boat!" She raises her voice.

"I'm taking our guests out fishing for the day. They came a long way for this!"

"So did we! And my friends are guests too on our boat."

"It's not our boat, it's *my* boat. We'll drop you off at Shearwater and you can have a picnic there."

"Uh, no you won't. There's nowhere we can have a picnic there."

"Sure there is. There's picnic tables."

"Dad, just give me the keys, they're waiting for us. Mom said we could use the boat."

"I don't care, it's *my* boat—" Now he raises *his* voice.

"You said we could use the boat while we're here, and you used it all day yesterday!" She almost shouts. "It's not fair! Let us use it for a few hours."

"It's not a problem with us," says George, "if she wants to take the boat out for a few hours. We got lots of time to catch salmon while we're here."

"Yeah. Give us the boat for a few hours."

Louis rubs his neck. "Fine." He gives her the keys. "It needs fuel though."

"What? Why didn't you refuel it?"

"'Cause you told me you needed a lift!"

"You refuel it then. I don't know how."

Louis shakes his head. "Unbelievable."

"I know how to fuel it," says Richard. "I'll take care of it."

"Good. Thanks," Louis grunts.

She holds out her hand again. "Give me your card then."

"What for?"

"To pay for fuel. I don't have any money."

"Oh my God," he says, pulling out his wallet. He gives her his card. "Don't you dare buy anything else with it."

"Thank you," she says, entitled. Her and Rich board.

"No partying aboard the boat, OK?"

"Yup. Don't worry," she says, singsongy.

"Bring it back by seven at the latest. We need to bring in the long-line."

"All right, bye! See you later."

"See you, Lou," says Rich.

"Bye."

The engine starts. Off they go, as our three head back to the truck.

"May as well hit up the band store while we're nearby," George says, even though they're stocked to the gills on chips, candy and pop aboard *Wild Thing*. (They've got Cool Ranch, Nacho Cheese and Sweet Chili Heat Doritos; two packs each of Skittles, Mike and Ikes, and sour keys; stacks of Mars, Twix, Crunchie, Hershey's Cookies 'n' Creme and Big Turk; dozens of cans of cola, root beer, orange pop and Mountain Dew.) Louis starts the truck.

"But Dad, we got tons of snacks already. Do we really need more?"

"I want to see if they got any Hickory Sticks."

"What are we going to do after?"

"We can head back to the house and see what's on TV," suggests Louis.

Doesn't he have a job? "Why don't we just take out *Wild Thing*?"

"It doesn't have a winch to pull up the longline, and the downriggers aren't set up," says George. "*Relax.*"

Derik slips into depression as his world erodes around him.

7. Call Him Lucky

Derik looks down from the precipice with the sunlight glaring on his face, not yet heeding the abyss. "Uncle Louis, what do you do for work?"

Louis smirks on Derik's left, sensing the boy's feebleness. "I fix windows."

"...So you don't have a real job?"

The two men shift, agitated.

"I mean, you don't work nine to five every day?"

"Sometimes I do, sometimes I don't. It depends who needs a window replaced." *You idiot.*

That's weird. That's probably why Mom hates this place; no one's ever working.

That's not true, they fish.

Yeah, but is that work to them?

Goddammit, I don't want to watch TV. *They only get like three channels here.* "Is there anywhere we can go fishing around here, like with a fishing pole? I still want to catch a salmon by hand."

"You can fish off the pier by the old ferry, but we'd have to drive there," says Louis.

"Can we do that then?"

"If you pay for gas."

What?

"Yeah, Derik," says George, "it's too much work to go out there. We'll go back to the house so Uncle Lou and I can get some rest." *We didn't sleep well.*

"Can I go out on my own, then? I don't want to sit and watch TV."

"No, you can't."

"Why not?"

"A bear might get you," says Uncle Lou. "They're fattening up for winter."

It's June. "I won't go in the forest. I just want to see if there are any good fishing spots around."

George says, "I don't want you wandering out alone. Just wait till we go back on the boat, then you can catch all the fish you want. You were just complaining that we caught too many fish anyway."

"Yeah, but I still haven't caught a salmon by hand, with a fishing pole, from start to finish."

"What's it matter if you catch it by hand or not? You're still using a fishing pole—our people didn't have fishing poles."

"I want the sense of accomplishment."

"Well, forget that; a salmon's a salmon. You're starting to get on my nerves."

Derik recoils in his seat. Louis and George feel it—they endorse it—his commune with the Spirit of Vengeance. *They don't care about me, they only care when I'm sad.*

Why would they care if you were happy? If it's not broke, don't fix it.

And so it begins—descent into the deep. Derik pouts.

They drive into town. Derik traces his scars, feeling every bump in the road. Louis lets out a purging cough like the bark of a dog. Derik is too young to care about the nuances of such base intimidation; any reprieve is dismissed; the very hand that offers to help him up, he dismisses with indifference. *Got him.* Their insinuations usurp the mundane.

Everyone they pass stares. *Yeah, ignore the kid in the back, he's just a wimp, and his mom is white.* At the end of the day, you either act and look miserable or put on a strong face and accept that, yes, people really say the darnedest things—because there comes a time when these people all go away, and you're left with their lingering spirits, chatting however you experience it. Don't worry, though, they aren't you. You are only you.

"Dad, do you ever hear voices?"

"What's that?"

"Do you ever hear voices in your head, or are those all just your thoughts?"

"...Sometimes I get a thought in my head that sounds like someone else speaking. I remember one time I was with my pal Ken. We had drunk a lot and were stumbling out of the bar. He told me to get in the truck, but I knew he was drunk so I didn't want to. Then a voice told me, 'Get in the truck now, or Ken will die.' So I listened to the voice and got in the truck. Ken was speeding, going 120 down a mountain road." George mimics Ken at the wheel, frantically shifting his weight left and right. "He was going like that. Then he didn't see the turn in the road, so I yanked the wheel to the left, and we skidded down the road before flipping over. The car flipped *twice*. Luckily there wasn't anyone else on the road. Ken was knocked unconscious. And I think that's why I have such bad back pain, 'cause my head smashed against the roof, which compressed my spine. Somehow we didn't break any bones though. We were so lucky. And if I didn't listen to that voice, Ken would've died; he would've sped right off that cliff."

"Hm," says Derik. "How do you know that was a voice talking to you, and not just your own mind?"

George thinks about it. "Because it sounded like someone else's voice. I know when I have a thought in my head, and that wasn't it—it sounded different."

"So do you have schizophrenia, then? Schizophrenics hear voices."

"I don't think I am."

"You just said you hear voices in your head. How can that not be schizophrenia?"

George coughs, attempting to neutralize the intrusion, which is actually a behaviour associated with schizophrenia: making noises to try and clear the bad thoughts, the bad voices.

"I mean, it's never been a problem for me. Maybe usually they're just my thoughts, but I know for a *fact* that time it was a voice that told me to get in the truck."

"Weird." *I guess he has schizophrenia then.* "Hey, aren't we supposed to pick up Raven from that island?" Derik yearns for his mentor to help him articulate his feelings. *They don't know what I'm talking about.*

They think you're crazy.

You're ashamed of who you are.

The spirits flock; he discerns them not—even the bad are given audience before the royal court.

"No," says George. "He said he'd call us if he needed a lift. His friend probably has a boat."

Derik sighs. *They don't like you, they never will.*

I am the Lord of Darkness, when you blink or sleep, since the day you were born, circling you in the sweat lodge.

You are a separate entity; this really isn't me. Your voice is different, these thoughts are tinged by it.

I know which one isn't a real fisherman.

And then I just keep thinking about her, but then that's not me, it's her. This is me, my voice, it sounds like me—then why do I keep thinking about that?

It must be her spirit that is with me, then, because that's not my voice that keeps repeating itself telling me what I did wrong; I'm not doing anything wrong. I was just being me. I'm just possessed by her evil spirit—and so on.

Derik opens his mouth to start a conversation on the matter, but his intuition tells him his words will not be reciprocated. He keeps to himself. The boy reserves himself for sympathetic company.

They park and hop out of the truck, Derik holding his head low, avoiding eye contact. He does not burden anyone else with the burden he carries, and they resent him for it; they feel they can never reach him. They hate it because they can help, but their help is nullified, which is ultimately insulting—a vagrant who does not beg? "Why are we even here?" he says. "I don't want anything. We got lots of snacks already."

"You said you wanted to come here," says George.

"No, it was *your* idea."

"Come on, we're already here."

Derik begins to resent this small town, with its incessant onlookers making all business their own. He misses being able to run down the street past the rich and the poor shouting whatever pops into his head without being hassled about his intentions. (Is it for peace you run? Is someone chasing you? Why run in such a way?)

As they walk by a house on stilts, Derik hears a feeble meowing. Curious, he checks beneath in the shade and finds a cute silver kitten—a British shorthair, but not pure—looking back. "Hello," he says. He kneels before the kitten, and massages its neck with one finger ever so delicately. The kitten meows. *I always wanted a cat. Mom won't let us have one 'cause I'm allergic.* And—call it a sign, call it obtuse depiction of character motivation as per the narrator—Derik's spirits lighten, and bad times are banished to the shadow realm by the pure sun, the archetypal sun, spinning like a wheel in the sky, its rays cast ever onward. Derik has love.

"Derik!" calls George. "What are you doing?"

"There's a kitten here!" he calls back. He notices the still mass of fur and bone behind it, an emaciated corpse of a sibling of this here sole survivor, as Derik sees no mother or father tending this nest of rags and refuse. The kitten is all alone. A deep parental instinct engages within Derik, causing him distress over the mewling of this orphan. *Shadow.* He must protect him, he must feed him, he must take care of him. "You just wait here and I'll be right back, OK?"

"Meow."

He hates to leave him, even if for a second. He runs to George, who holds the door open. "There's a kitten under that house," says Derik "I think he needs water."

"You shouldn't feed stray cats or dogs around here. There are too many to take care of."

"Well, I can't just leave him there."

"Someone will help him. He probably belongs to whoever's house that is."

"Can we buy him some water… please?"

"No, just leave him *alone.*"

"There's a dead one right beside him—I think it might be his brother or sister. I don't think there's anyone taking care of him."

They acclimate to the air-conditioning. The only white girl there stares at Derik like he's Moby Dick. Shadows rise from the floor like mist from a swamp. The shelves swoon and billow like trees saying, "How do you do?" There's no bakery in the store, but there's one chocolate cake, with *Congratulations* written across it, from the communal baker's house. Twenty-five dollars is a fair price.

They walk through the aisles, saying hi to everyone they pass, while Derik continues to avert his face, hide his glance. The older he gets, the shorter his grudges last, but there is no stopping his vindication—like Cyclops, de-visored, sweeping his ocular red beam across the world, or Shiva, third eye open, destroying everything in its gaze; all fragments of the cosmos are rearranged or deemed fair. Derik builds the universal tower, then smashes it to Lego, to rebuild as he deems fit.

Shadow had a seizure at the top of the stairs—he's dead he's dead he's dead. He was my brother; he was my best friend. They had to put him down. I cried cried cried cried.

Where do you go when hell surrounds you? Do you stand firm in the soil, beat your chest and defy their attempts to overtake you? Do you invite them closer, to hear your words of praise, as you try to corral the snakes?

No one will save you, no one comes to help; the forces of evil torment you day and night; every blink, every wandering thought, they tell your faults, they play your past with malign commentary—how bad you are, how you messed up this, messed up that—over and over, every waking second, as people peer through your window and knock, hoping you'll answer the door.

You never loved me, never will. I wish I was dead. I wish I was with Grandpa, away from all this pain.

You'll never understand. You'll never know the desolation of heart it takes, and it is with diligence I am to convince you otherwise, that, oh yes, your view is very much crucial, your interpretation is very much true.

Suffering is relevant? Then bring me the knife, and I will bring us the absolute. Yet, cut off my head, and I will still whisper. I will love you like you never loved me, you fiend. If I could wire it directly into your brain, I would. If I could pump words into your liver, it'd be a lot quicker. Yet, here we are, my appendages raw with toil, and brain consuming itself, just like a cannibal, mad with the whistle of Bax, dancing to the flute of Pan. If you remain devoted, God save you, for there is no returning.

But there is no God you say! I cursed God from my bedside, day in and day out, and nothing came of it. I stood stark bare before the mirror at night, cutting my chest and calling Bloody Mary repeatedly, until she stood before me, and then we laughed, and then kissed. It's whatever I make of it, 'cause I am God! As could you be if you weren't so negligent with such matters. Now piss off, or put pennies in your eyes, as over the river Styx I will push thy final trip, and back over the river Styx we do not go, but flow underneath, as all the twisting arms and maws and souls we are.

They walk down the aisles. George swipes junk off the shelf.

He might as well buy everything. Stupid Sophie and her dickhead boyfriend, taking the boat. Now we're stuck here buying stuff I don't even want. Do they think this is fun? What a waste of time. I could be at home, owning noobs in ARAM. *What did I do to deserve this?*

Why don't you take a good look at yourself and ask why? Don't worry my son, I am with you.

"How 'bout these?" says George, licking his lips. *You dumb pussy bitch.*

"Cool," says Derik.

You want a bag of those, fag?

No.

George moves farther down the aisle, waddling his ass like a penguin. Next are some pizza chips he prizes like caviar, holding them up, placing them on a pedestal glowing with golden light, a choir aahing behind. "Ooh, look at those!" he says, pointing to Derik's misery, poking him right in the chest. "Those look good, don't they?" *Maybe you should be sad all the time so I feel this happy. Pussy.*

"No thanks."

George puts down the bag of chips and looks around, wondering what got into the boy.

Derik looks over at his uncle. *Louis is happy to observe another father struggling, as if that makes it OK how dissolute his relationship with his daughter is.*

"Rena wants us to pick up something for dinner. Do you guys want a couple of steaks?" *I'm so proud you guys are fighting, because, to me, this is fighting, and it makes me so happy because now I don't feel like a failure.*

"Sure, I'd like a big juicy steak," George says, licking his lips. They all approach the cool counter with the overpriced steaks, because all men love steak.

"All right," says Louis. *I'm let down because I really thought this would cheer up your son, who I'm not talking to directly because he doesn't deserve it, because he's a spoiled brat who goes inward when upset instead of showing it to the world so we can all be happy that we're not like him, even though we look miserable and act miserable all the time until he's like that, so we're actually a bunch of hypocrites. You should really be happy that I'm offering you steaks, 'cause that's a big deal.*

"I'm not that hungry," says Derik.

"Look here," says George. *You wimp.* "We're offering you steak." *So cheer the fuck up and be happy. Everything we're doing, we're doing for you. You have no reason to be upset, 'cause this is really what you want to do—be here in Bella Bella. Fuck your friends and your stupid-ass games. We bought a boat and sailed all the way out here just so you can see your homeland. Now pick a fucking steak.* "You should be grateful."

"I'll take that one."

"A T-bone?"

"Sure."

"Are you sure you don't want a tenderloin or New York strip?" *Because they're more expensive, and then we'll feel like we did you a favour so you have nothing to hold over us.*

"No thanks. I don't even like steak."

"What are you talking about? All you talked about leading up to your birthday was going to Hy's Steakhouse and we took you and you said you loved it, but you didn't even seem that excited. You never seem that excited—in fact everything is a bore to you and you're really unappreciative of what we do for you—so I don't know how to please you anymore." *So I'm giving up.*

"Fine, get me a New York strip."

"Will you eat it though?"

"Yup... I will."

George gathers the steaks. "I don't know what his problem is."

You should've beat him up more, and put him to work on the fishing boat, so he'd learn to be a man and stop pouting like a woman.

He takes after his mom.

The worst part is Derik's delusions contain some truth. It doesn't matter he started working at the pawnshop at age eleven. It doesn't matter he has feelings they don't understand, and feels them and studies them as much as he desires. As long as he breathes, they'll come for him. As long as his heart beats and thoughts flow, spirits will seek him; the universe will speak, and nothing will be the same.

They fill their cart, but it's not as satisfying as George was hoping. He wants his boy to frolic and leap and bound like a deer at his purchases, radiating curiosity and inspiration; yet Derik weaves past a hedge here, and dives into the thicket there.

Then there is light; the sides of the aisle part—behold! The lavender hues of cat food tins are before them! They move on celestial cloud to bypass the tiny sepulchres of feline delight, the glory of ground royal lambs and noble carrots derived from the very seeds the founders of humanity cultivated ages ago. Any pretentious tramp who would raise its tail and scoff at such treasure of gastronomy deserves to be cleaved by Heimdall's axe—he who guardeth the rainbow bridge to high heaven, where all drink and sing—or be devoured by the foul giant at the edge of the world, Bax—from whom the Heiltsuk carved ritual—whistling, tempting their desire and indulgence until they run pell-mell into its belly.

What say you, slave of whim, when your stomach surely has its fill of this here portion of minced delight? The men walk on hot coals to avoid it.

Then a light flashes in the right eye of George as he catches his son glance up from bowed head to the pyramid of tins and a cardboard cut-out of a perfect tabby. A fire does light inside George, and spin on his heels does he, so as to ask the fading lad, "You want some cat food to give to your cat? Would that cheer you up?"

Derik would rather hold a grudge, yet he relents, and his haunches are the lighter for it; his plight, his virtuous load, has been given wings! And I grow; my red wings reach for the sky, for this bird—though inclined to the mockery and sarcasm of the finch—takes to the sky, and all is fire by my opalescent plumes, glittering down, as I call to the world, coax it; I soothe all your tomorrows, friends, by my call, the Firebird of Russia, with my stray feathers lighting even the darkest of ways; I am the Thunderbird, my lightnings sunder sky, while my thunders peel the Earth to the molten sphere of time primordial. But the kindness found sufficient, the deed done, I return to that prancing robin who bluffs the red breast and *chirp-chirp-chirp*, for Derik, I am guardian, and have been since before form, when the architects with spangled metallurgy (thus its equivalent, its absolute and refined aspects), agreed, "Yes, this soul is allotted here, and you ever watch," and I duly accepted, for—bah!—who would, if not I?

"Yeah," says Derik. "That'd be nice."

George grabs a tin. "How many, you think? Two should be good."

"How 'bout three? That's our lucky number."

And George smiles, happy to return to some semblance of normalcy, for he had feared his son would never return to that sweet kid they took advantage of. "All right, we'll get three." He puts them in the cart, along with bottled water and more snacks.

Ah, sweet humanity—too swift to use thy rod! Derik breaks frown like day breaks night, and smiles, though he realizes, any second now, that unearthly resonance may dissemble the fresh bridge cable by cable, slab by slab, then atom by atom. For the time being, the foot-less bridge sways upon sweet wind.

Three tins they get for the failing critter. They pay for their goods, and the white lady looks on again—turning her pallid cheek, pink lips sharp, curving—*I like you 'cause you feel like I do, 'cause you're white.*

I just want to feed the kitten.

First thing, upon breaking open the light of day, Derik runneth to the house where the kitten lay, and promptly cracks the tin of food, placing it near so its saliva-inducing aroma may waft to the kitten's petite nose; then he opens the bottled water, fills the white cap and surgically drops drip after drip over the drowsy kitten's mouth. It comes to like a mechanical ride animated by a quarter, meowing and twisting its feeble neck away from the frightening cool of the water, then realizing what it is, how precious this silver be; it laps up drip upon drip of that good Aquafina. Derik massages its head and chest with his finger.

"He can't be very old, he's still squinting with his eyes," says Derik. "Too bad about his sibling." George looks on, captivated, though wary.

Derik takes a crumb of cat food and tries to feed the kitten, as he doesn't have the energy to eat on his own. He meows as babies cry, and refuses the food. "Come on, you have to eat something," Derik tells him. He whines, he meows; he meows, he whines. Eventually, he gobbles up the offering, as if to be done with the whole mad affair. Then, upon realizing such a thing exists—this divine sustenance—he feebly rolls over, and drags himself to the tin, where he fails tremendously to procure any bit of this delicacy, but instead licks it over and over, ingratiating flavour and kindling his will once again. To live! To *will* is the surest of sures and first! They see the clockwork of his rejuvenation, like that of a water-starved peace lily, hunched over in despair, only to rise up and reach to the solar rays once watered. Our kitten rises from near death to meow another day. And the whole ceremony begets celebration; Derik jumps up and down.

"There you go, you fed the kitten. Feel better?" queries George (somewhat backhandedly).

"Yeah … But I feel bad we have to leave him now. No one else is going to feed him."

"I told you, there's nothing you can do. Someone's cat probably gave birth and they couldn't take care of all the babies. It happens all the time around here because no one neuters their pets."

Derik cracks open the other tins and arranges them on a tiny stone and charred piece of wood like pedestals above dirt. "Now he has to gain his strength and get up to be able to eat these ones, instead of eating them all at once." *I bet a raccoon will get him.*

George crouches beside his son, admiring his affection. "You know, when my mom died, that's when my dad got me my dog Joseph. He thought he would keep me company, because he knew I was sad."

Derik listens sympathetically, realizing the sorrow of his father outweighs his own.

"He used to follow me everywhere: hunting, fishing, through town, to friends' houses—there'd be Joseph. Then one day, I remember we had to leave for a while (we had to go back to Bella Bella), so we left Joseph behind and the neighbour agreed to check on him to see if he was OK. I knew something bad was going to happen, I just knew it. I remember crying on the ferry back, saying, 'He's gone, he's gone—I just know it.' When we got back, the back gate was open. Joseph had run away.

"I bet he was searching for me. I think my dad left the gate open on purpose because he was sick of me having him around and didn't want to keep having to pay for dog food. I loved Joseph. He was my best friend… my brother. I guess he did what he was sent here to do: to protect me, and comfort me after my mom passed away. I was so lost; I didn't know where to go, what to do, it was like I was a ghost… I just felt so alone.

"I know how much Shadow meant to you, and I know things haven't been the same since he passed. It makes me so proud to see you be so loving toward animals, 'cause they didn't choose this life, yet they still love unconditionally." He kisses Derik's head. "I love you, son."

"Thanks, Dad. I love you too. What are we going to do about this kitten, though? We can't leave him here or he'll die."

"There's nothing we can do; you did all you can."

Derik's chin trembles. He looks up with watery eyes.

"It's a cruel world, son... It's a cruel world."

Derik rubs the kitten one last time. It seems to meow his name! Then he stands bravely, lip quivering. They walk back to the truck, where Louis is on standby. Derik hangs his head, sinking again into the sea of sadness.

But the meowings continue and draw near. Derik turns to find the kitten hopping, with one leg limp, trailing after them, meowing incessantly as ever. What a miraculous sight; the critter walks! "Look, he's walking!" He bends forward. "You have to go back though; we can't keep you."

"We can bring him back to the house if you want," says Louis. And friends, if the merry tin did kindle a flame, this prospect makes it a roaring hearth. The soul of this kitten is that of a lion, and how invigorating his roar!

"Really? Can we?"

"Sure, if you want to take care of him while you're here."

"We can't take him home though; Mom won't let us 'cause I'm allergic."

"It's up to you. You can look after him until you're gone, then maybe he'll stand a fighting chance in the wild."

Derik looks to George. "So can I bring him back with us?"

"If Uncle Louis doesn't mind, then fine."

"You don't think the owners will get mad?"

"They can get mad all they want; they don't deserve to have him, leaving him to die under this house. Now let's go, pick him up."

Derik plucks up the grave-walker with haste, tucking him close to his chest. He climbs aboard with utmost caution, making baby noises, communicating with non-lexical whines and whistles, soothing the kitten, who shows nothing but appreciation and fascination at his first source of compassion; even after much abuse and depravity, he still embraces love. They drive off back to the house.

"I think I figured out his name," Derik says.

"Yeah? What is it?" asks George.

"Lucky... His name is Lucky."

"Lucky? I like that. That's a good name. Lucky."

8. All Three Hundred

They arrive at the house. George takes a seat on the couch in the living room, while Derik hustles to the backyard and searches for the perfect place to keep Lucky. *Not under the house again. It should be up high so no one can get him.* But as he rifles through the boxes of nails, and saws on nails, and stray nails, Rena takes notice.

"We found a starving kitten and bought it some food. Uncle Louis said I could bring him back here. I hope it's all right. He needs a safe place to stay."

And Rena, maternally warmed, says, "Bring him inside!"

"Really? I don't want him making a mess on your carpet or anything. He's probably not toilet trained."

"Sophie makes more of a mess than he'll ever make. Come on, I got an old shoebox you can put him in."

"Perfect!"

"Aw," she says as he brings him in. "He's so small. Where'd you find him?"

"Underneath someone's house. He can't really walk, but we gave him some food and water and now he seems OK."

"He's so cute." Friends, together they build Lucky a new home: she gets the old shoebox from the garage and lines it with some paper towel, making it nice and cozy. Derik eases Lucky down as he meows, he meows! He seems comfy enough, lying down, looking up at them.

"I think he likes it," says Derik.

"Yup. That should keep him nice and safe for now."

All the rest of his waiting hours, waiting to return to sea, waiting for the boat back, Derik sits cross-legged on the floor, playing with Lucky, giving him belly rubs with one finger, speaking to him like a baby. At the start, Lucky meows and meows at seemingly anything, but now he begins chasing that very finger that feeds him; he paws with soft paws, nibbling playfully. Time passes quickly. George changes the channel.

The phone rings. Rena answers it. "Hello... Oh... Yeah... OK... Yeah. Oh *no*, really? Wow. How'd she do that? ... Yeah... Oh no. That's terrible. Yes he's here... I'll let him know... Is she all right? ... Hmm... Yeah... All right, bye." Call ended. "That was the nurse from the hospital. She said Eliza is there."

"Huh," says George. "Did they say what for?"

"Not really. She's stable, but they think she might have had too much of something. They're watching her now."

"Damn." He reclines. "That's too bad."

"Too much of what?" asks Derik.

"She probably overdosed on something."

"You mean she did too many drugs?"

"Probably."

"Are we going to go see her?"

"I don't wanna see her," George says in earnest.

"That's our sister, George. We'll need to pay her a visit," says Rena

"I don't think we're allowed to visit, 'cause of COVID restrictions."

She ponders. "I'll phone the hospital and find out. If we're allowed to see her, you're coming."

"We'll see."

"What about the house?" asks Derik.

"What *about* the house?" says George.

"Does that mean we get to go see it, if she's not there?"

"I doubt there's even a house left, if she was living there. I can't imagine the state it's in now."

"We should go see it while we have the chance."

"That reminds me, Rena, did you have Dad cremated?" George asks.

Rena's pupils dilate. "He *wanted* to be cremated. His final request was to have his ashes spread over the sea."

George shakes his head, murder in his eyes. "I told you not to have him cremated! You know that goes against our beliefs."

"You're always on about that—our people's beliefs. He wanted to be cremated, and have his ashes spread on the water, where he spent most of his life. We gave him his final wish."

"How is he supposed to pass on to the afterlife without his body, Rena?"

"Just because you believe that, doesn't mean it's true. You never gave him what he wanted anyway; you were always going against his wishes."

"No I wasn't!"

"Where were you when he was in the hospital? I was there when he made the request. Now you're doing the same thing with Eliza, just ignoring her until she's dead."

George waves her off and sucks his vape.

"So…" says Derik. "Can we go see the house?"

"No," says George.

"Come on! We may never get the chance again."

"I'll take you to see our old house," says Rena.

"Yay!" Derik raises his arms in victory.

"Well, if you're going, then I'm going too," says George, his tactic collapsing. "I want to see what condition it's in in case we decide to sell it."

"All right, it's settled: tomorrow we go see the house," says Derik. *I bet Dad will change his mind. Who cares—Auntie Rena will take me.* He continues playing with Lucky.

They eat a light dinner, halibut this time, and then comes the fateful hour when they set forth to catch that very fish. And now he must say goodbye. Derik holds Lucky's home, the shoebox, before him, solemn as he who holds the funeral candle. He kisses Lucky on the head. Lucky meows. Derik places him on the living room floor, in the corner, by the sliding door, next to his foamy. He tells him, "I'll be back soon. Love you." *Meow.* "Make sure he doesn't go running around if he gets out of his box," he says to Rena.

"I'll watch him, don't worry."

"Make sure no one moves him."

"*All right.* Go have a good time fishing."

They arrive at the pier well before seven, hopeful Sophie will have the decency to show early so they aren't rushed to pull in the long-line before dark. But as the sun dips farther and farther toward the horizon, and the hours crawl, Sophie does not show. They watch the boats come in—like survivors of the flood returning to their homes, to expectant families, embracing and exchanging warm words; yet, some do not return, and their families collapse in grief and sorrow, lamenting the fallen, laying their welcome flowers upon the water to drift apart, petal by petal, until they rot and swirl down with converging currents—but still no Sophie. Finally, Louis calls her.

"Where are you?" he says, grovelling like Geodude. The sky begins its transition to night, adopting its evening cloak of purple, blue and green, cold and biting as ice cream; dark are the fringes, my mouth slowly devouring the sky we call day. The cold wind chases hot, cutting across the water, nuclear. Poseidon's horses breach the distance from there to here, charging over us, slicing to the bone. And the legion of the dead follow with their ethereal spears and shields from the abodes of day. The birds spin higher and higher to escape the decay.

"We're waiting for you," says Louis. "Just bring back the boat! …I don't care, he can wait. We need the boat back. We have to get the longline—What? *No*! I didn't say that… Go ahead and tell her. You're the one being unreasonable. You promised to have the boat back by seven, and it's already nine! …I don't care who's on board, just—Hello? Hello?" Dumbfounded, he looks at the phone, then up at the others. "She hung up." He tries to call her back, twitching over digits, but she doesn't answer. "I swear, sometimes I wonder if she's even my kid, disrespecting me like that."

"My daughter's the same way," says George. "Won't respect any authority and gets mad when I try to tell her to do anything. That's just how girls are at that age."

"I told her we *need* the boat back, and she doesn't care. Now we're going to have to hurry before it gets too dark out."

"We could wait till tomorrow to haul up the longline. We could go out first thing in the morning."

"No, I don't want to leave it out overnight. Every time I do, some-one steals it."

"Well, she must be on her way back, right?" asks Derik.

Louis ignores him. "Unbelievable the privilege kids have nowadays. They just do whatever they want. They don't care who they upset."

Night has her way as the sun sets. Louis paces the pier, steamy, to and fro. The evening lights come on, and the distant islands fade to darkness.

Derik throws rocks at a pylon, trying to land one on top, but they either miss, clank the wood, or hit the top, bouncing off, going *ker-plunk* into the water; the squid corrupts the sapphire black with ink before dragging them to the depths, its tentacles smothering their faces. *Man, this is boring. Where's Raven?*

Probably flying around on his broomstick.

He's still on that island.

Doing what though?

I don't know—casting spells. I wish I was with him instead of waiting for crazy Sophie.

"Who's going to pull the longline up then?" Derik says. "You can't do it, you have a bad back. And Louis has to pilot the ship, doesn't he?"

"You better roll up your sleeves there, Bucko." George chuckles.

"I'm going to pull it up?"

"It's easy with the winch," says Louis.

"All right… I hope it's not that hard."

Louis perks up, spotting something in the distance. "I think that's them." He squints, spying the outline of his boat. "Yeah, that must be them."

"How can you tell?" says Derik, seeing only a pair of red and green lights.

"I know my boat when I see it." He can tell by the silhouette and has seen many a boat in his day. In come Sophie and Rich—Circe and her pig—taking their sweet time. She is perfect, her every word turns to scripture; she gets just what she came for. They put not down the fenders, for she is royal. Even the pier is in the way, as they crash to berth.

"Hey, watch what you're doing!" says Louis Fumes.

"OK, *chill*. Jesus, you're bad energy." She flips over the fenders without care. Rich ties loosely about the cleat. The queen steps to the pier.

The beggar addresses. "What took you so long? You were supposed to be here hours ago!"

"Get off my case! We were having dinner with friends." Sophie staggers, her nervous system hijacked by cheap spirits. She is more satisfied than bothered. "You got your boat back, now get to work." She giggles, and hands Louis the keys.

"Hey, you listen to me. This isn't how you treat your dad or our guests. You made them wait too. Now we gotta go out and pick up the longline in the dark."

"You always used to go out night-fishing anyway, leaving Mom and me at home." She struts away. "Have a good time!"

Rich grins. "See you guys." The lowly are dismissed.

Louis reels from the confrontation. He shakes his head. He unties the black rope and throws it on deck. "God, she makes me so mad sometimes. And she just doesn't care. She doesn't care that she's late."

"Yeah," says George. "She needs to learn some respect."

"Unbelievable," Louis grumbles as he starts the engine. The boat coughs noxious black smoke that only Derik notices. *Not sure if that's normal. Louis must know about it.*

They take in the last fenders and rope. It's time to reap the halibut from their dark domain.

It's eerie work, fishing at night at sea. It's as if the water lulls you to fathomless sleep, calling you to step forth for the plunge, to hug and embrace it. It offers liberation. Give up smell and sight, and let the currents flow through you. Humans grow submerged in the womb. Return, then, to your true home.

On board they find greasy pizza boxes and takeout containers (from the only real restaurant around) along with can after can of beer, festered by sun. "God, what a bunch of pigs!" says Louis.

"Looks like they had a party," says George.

"I don't get *no* respect from her. I told her to have the boat back by seven, she doesn't do it. I said no parties, and she parties. I give her everything she wants, I do all I can for her, and she still doesn't listen."

"You should set some boundaries sometime, otherwise she's gonna walk all over you."

"I do! But she just complains to her mom, then *I* get in trouble."

"You gotta put your foot down, otherwise she'll keep taking advantage of you. You can't expect her not to if you let her. Just say, 'Hey, I don't think this is right: I don't get any respect, you don't listen to me, and you really hurt my feelings.' That's all. Tell her how you really feel."

"I tried doing that, but I just end up looking like the bad guy."

"Better than her being the bad guy all the time."

"Yeah... true."

Louis is like a big, bald baby.

He's not really bald, his hair is just short. "I've only seen one Native who was bald," Dad told me once. "It happened to him after he shot a bald eagle. You should never shoot a bald eagle." He shot it right through the chest, then his wife left him.

Man, that smoke smells bad.

Louis navigates from the pier, George stout beside him, as Derik peers into the darkness from stern, captivated by the stars' unveiling. There is Pisces, the dual fish, the psychic fish, ruled by the great Poseidon, king of the sea, Neptune by his planetary vestibule. Herein lies the soul, the hermit of the night sky on his watery throne, with his legion of oceanic beings gathering to his call to whichever end of the Earth he doth take. But what is this? What strange portent to eye a satellite along with Hercules himself, eternalized in night. Derik spies it, starts, half-convinced he's finally found it: a sign of life outside this centric globe, though, nay, illusory, for round Sol do the planets spin... and even yet, who he spins around, who he calls Maker, is reserved for the hermits of the lonely cave, by which their looking glasses peer now, just waking from slumber of day. Stars, I adore thee; thee I adore, stars; adore I, thee, stars; I thee stars adore. Use the last one.

Beauty slowly fades.

I just want to go home. I want to sleep in my own bed.

I have to see Grandpa. I have to see all my relatives.

I can't wait till it's over.

Then what? We gotta sail all the way back, it'll take days! I wish we could fly, but we got this stupid boat.

The Thunderbird could carry us. He puts his hat on backwards. It's rigging time now, time to dance on the sails, waving tambourine, knife between teeth; a monkey does a backflip into the water, dodging sharks. Hey! Hey! Hey!

They spy the floating sun; the little orange buoy tells them, *Press start.*

"You see the buoy, the Scotchman?" says George.

"Yeah," says Derik.

"Grab it when it comes by."

Derik reaches over, grabs the buoy, pulls it to the side, then grabs the brainstem—rope sub-aqua. Even whales kiss submarines sometimes; young leviathans tongue the eye of the telescope. "Got it," says our lad, pulling aboard the buoy and start (or is it the end, for Quetzalcoatl's sake?).

"OK, great. Now feed the line into the winch. Watch your fingers!"

"Sorry!" Derik feeds the line into the winch's mouth—it bites— and he is flooded by the vilest sights he ever beheld on the internet, of industrial incidents involving such rotating, contriving mechanics, such as numerous sausage-makings gone awry, with God knows what incentive (I am Quetzalcoatl you see), vouching not to use prong or stick, but force in feed by hand, only to get torqued in, rotated, separated into many channels, lubed by fat and pork (because chicken is no fun), and ground to sausage, bone and all, until someone finally hits *Stop*, or many a shop foreman giving the recruit a tour of the printing press, only for the foreman to lay their hand upon the dervish wheels, roller upon roller, and get promptly sucked in, in a flash, projecting out the other side, still intact (bodily!) but (for function's sake) a boneless, crumpled sack of mush and dying fibres—'tis not long before they turn blue! Or perhaps the most miraculous, certainly the most majestic: the lathe! Whereupon our noble worker catches limb or sleeve and is wound tight, seemingly escaping death, until the machine locks gear and carries them round, smashing legs and arms upon concrete and metal, round and round, like Hercules himself, manifest from stars, entertaining us with the reckoning of helpless mortals, smashing them upon the hard earth, hammering home—O, the cruelness of gravity and, O, centrifuge—until our hero is paste on the floor, and innards pink mist. Such countless atrocities green-lit by our merciless overlords—the lords of steel! Such elucidation for our metaphor of Derik and the winch.

With all the hesitation in the world, he feeds in more line. The first hooks jangle out of the water like chrome ribs, bearing no wares. "Nothing so far."

"Make sure nothing gets tangled. Coil the line around once it comes in."

The winch hisses, then stops eating line. "It stopped," says Derik. George inspects. Now Louis comes over and inspects too.

"Goddammit," Louis says.

"What happened? I was doing everything you told me to."

"Just be quiet!" says Louis. He opens the casing, fiddling with the exposed wires. It starts. Now it stops. It starts ... and it stops. "There's a bad connection here," says he. Tries holding the wires just right so the connection is established. The winch repeatedly starts and stops, pulling in only one hook over the duration. He gets the wires just right, then the winch starts again, but he has to hold them in place or else it stops. "Pass me the electrical tape."

Derik looks in the tool kit. "The black one, right?"

"Don't you know what electrical tape is?" Louis gestures *gimme*, just like his daughter.

Derik hands it him. Louis struggles to re-establish connection, then tapes the wires a plenty. But the connection doesn't hold, and now he has to take off all the tape. "Fucking thing. What were you doing when it stopped?"

"Nothing!" says Derik. "I fed the line in and coiled it as it came out like he told me to." He points to George.

"Well you must've done something. It's not working now and it was working fine before." He tries taping the wires into place again, but can't get a connection. "Stupid useless piece of shit."

Now, friends, logic may suggest that whomever last used the machine is to blame, like the last kid to wash their hands at school in the overflowing basin, with bits of used paper towel pasted to the floor, taps and counter, so as to be blamed by the teacher for making a mess. Surely it is their fault, as they were last. So here too, Derik feels the eye of wrath turn upon him.

Louis rages against the winch, casting several hard blows against its metal conformity. There remains only one option: "We're gonna have to reel it in by hand."

"What?" says Derik. "The whole thing?"

Louis tries one last time—no connection. "Yes, the whole thing; it's *one* line—a longline. We can't leave half of it in the water."

"How do we pull it up by hand? Isn't it dangerous?"

"It's not dangerous, you just pull it up! Use some muscle. I pulled up five hundred hooks once when I was your age."

That's not fair. He was probably a lot bigger.

You wanted to catch one by hand—have at it, bucko.

Just do what he says.

"All right. I'll try my best."

"Don't try—just do," says George. "Come on! You said you always wanted to be a fisherman, here's your chance."

I never said that. I just wanted to catch a salmon. Derik avoids saying anything to avoid undermining his father's authority... But we all know what happens when he abides his rage.

Enter the lion pit, bitch.

"OK," says Derik. He picks up the line, and instantly it is taut against the side of the boat, as if the entire sea pulls it (which, in a sense, is what's happening). His orange gloves fill with water. He struggles to grasp the rope, as his grip is still slimy from the viscera of last week's catch used for bait. He gives a big pull, with both giants, cast of iron, looming over him, judging with flaming eyes. There is much resistance, so the line sinks back into the water, returning to where he began.

"Come on, put some back into it!"

He pulls again, as the whip lashes across his bare back, and he howls, howls with the wind. They threaten another, so he pulls harder. Progress! Sweet, delicious, juicy progress! He ignores his tormentors, for our lad would sooner crush the Earth than give way to their torrential taunts. Smiling faces, smiling faces—sometimes they don't tell the truth. What is there left in the world but to burn out in passion? A whip, then another! *Crack-crack* it goes on his back, arching back, sprouting arms and heckling him, like Cuphead, saying (with total nasality), "Come on, put your back into it." He pulls, he pulls! But the whip cracks on, and he loses grip, letting all progress slip back to the sea.

Pull harder, dammit! Jesus didn't die for this.

Jesus groans and crawls, eviscerated, bowels hanging out, mushing with sand, like someone smashing an octopus on the rocks, tenderizing it oozy, then rolling it in the sand for a nice spice coating.

Whip-whip! Crack-crack!

Chief George rises.

You know what we did with boys like you? We ate them—alive.

His voice flips, dissonant and distant, along with his face.

We made them watch us rip out their hearts and drip blood into their mouths.

And they give Jesus a miniature cross to bear, but he just groans and collapses, letting it fall beside him.

Crack! Whip! Whip! Harder, boy! Row harder! How do you expect to cross the Pacific with a weak row like yours?

The Captain taunts us as the waves bat the boat. They all row alike, without faces, just smooth skin like printless thumbs. Row! Row! He cracks the whip. Or else the sea will swallow us whole!

Derik pulls up the line, little by little, millimetre by sliver. "I keep thinking there's gonna be a halibut 'cause the line is so heavy."

You're not here to think. Pull!

He sweats. He pulls! His arms are numb. The rope cuts into his hands through the gloves—stabbing pain, stabbing, stab stab stab stab—his fingers lose all feeling, his arms feel as though they'll fall off. Something has to give! Surely he can't go on! Surely the boy can't reel in 268 more! Yet, steady moves the Western front.

The soldier kicks off his shoes, foul as summer corpses, pouncing flies, having trenched, day and night, in the septic mud, soaked in the grey water of death that pervades nowhere.

The doctor looks up. We'll have to amputate.

Each hook they'll pierce in my back to hang me from the mast with.

Ha! Dumb half-breed. You think you're actually Heiltsuk? You will never be like us. You have your book smarts and urbane colloquialisms and attitude; we'll stomp you into the ground! We turn your whiteness to coal. We are the destroyers of dreams!

The harder he works, the more destructive his imagination, stimulated by his rendezvous with death.

Get down on your knees my child! Yes! Pray to God! Bow down and prostrate to God!

I see it in their eyes.

Yes, like that. Yes. Good. Good. Keep reciting Matthew. Yes my child. Yes! Now hold that position. Let me undo these.

This is why you'll never be like us!

Let me have thy hand child. Trust me! You shake. Must I correct thee? Good; I didn't want to. Here, grab hold of this!

Hook after bare hook comes up, going directly into my back: Ninety-nine. One hundred. One hundred one. One hundred two. Blood leaks and smears.

He's all skin and bone. He doesn't have enough back!

Don't worry, we'll use the front too.

It's only fair that I touch your rod, now that you've felt mine.

Glad it never happened to me! That's why they're so testy.

Row harder! Pull harder! Face windward; drive right into the heart of the gale.

I am with you night and day.

And the line gives way, Derik growing stronger and stronger, because there's no turning back. The scars in his arm glow red-hot.

I pull us closer and closer to the void. We swirl around the whirlpool. The storm clouds gather. Lightning cracks across sky!

Whip! Whip! Crack! Crack!

Go harder! Harder!

If you insist. I pull us into the vortex.

The stars shatter. One by three the lights go out. I flap my wings and all is sundered. I ascend and morph. I grow so large I block out the moon, the sun if it were day, for I am Emperor of Cloud: I am the Thunderbird. These lightnings are mine—I send them across the sky by flapping my wings. Be not blind to the dance of light!

"What's that up there?" says Louis.

"Pull harder, boy!" says George. "We have to get that halibut!"

Derik pulls them closer and closer to the end: *One hundred ninety-one. One hundred ninety-two. One hundred ninety-three. One hundred ninety-four.*

My eyes water with lightning; it courses through my bones! On no ground I stand; every boat I will sink! Rainbows are my plumes. With my talons I crush mountains. Without me you are dirt, a corpse, bare flesh and bones, for I am *life*. And I burn the night as a star.

The winds riffle our clothes. The rains slice in sheets. Lightnings strike near and far.

The water parts—we're close enough to see the exposed floor—made to whirl all around, carrying the boat like a toy, pinning us to its walls. And one halibut flips in the eye of the whirlpool, revealing its white underside, then its dark top, flipping like a coin, the last hook stuck in its mouth.

Stop! Stop! We'll be sucked in! Let go! Let go!

There it is, son: a halibut! Pull it in, pull it in!

The waters spin faster and faster.

I think my arms are gonna break!

Carry on child; I am with thee!

Derik is their tether to the dance. He pulls! He pulls! His arms quiver with the strain. His whole body shakes. His teeth will soon shatter. Yet, he pulls! He pulls! "It's so close!"

Let go! Let go of the line! Louis hugs the bulwark, about to be sucked into the void. We're gonna die!

"Go, son! You got it! Just one more big pull! One more!"

I reach for the halibut—it's so close!

Go, my child! Have faith!

He gives one last pull with all his effort: Sisyphus pushes the boulder to the peak; Achilles dies off-screen; Gandalf clashes with the Balrog; the shaman manifests from nought.

I pull the boat close. My fingers graze the halibut as it flips. The whole universe stops—the stars, the planets, the waves—and the white light emanates from the world. The vortex spits us out with a blinding flash, and the boat flies like a boat should never fly, crashing into the distant water, shaking us like seeds of a rattle. Water spills from the sky, shot up by the cessation of force.

I fade my thundery wings and array of cloud. The stars return, one by one. Derik holds up the end of the line, no halibut to be found. "Three hundred," he gasps, then collapses onto the flooded deck.

Dang, not one? I'm out.

The boat's engine shuts off. Louis, startled, jostles to the wheel and tries the ignition. It won't start. "*Now* what the hell is going on?" he says. He tries each switch: the pump aft, the wipers, the radio—they all work. Finally, it starts, farting the most hideous black smoke from stern. It sounds as if it'll go at any second, and it does, throttling down at will. Louis pushes up the throttle, but it pulls itself back down. "I think it's dieselling. We'll have to head back slow. Goddammit, this is all *your* fault," he says, pointing at Derik.

"How is it my fault? It was farting black smoke before we left!"

"Then why didn't you say anything? Everything was working fine until you wrecked the winch. Now everything's screwed!" He accelerates, but the boat throttles down, forcing him to leave it at low RPM. Louis swears profusely, trying this and that.

"Maybe Sophie and her friends did something to it," says George. "They did crash it into the dock."

"That wouldn't have done it. The engine won't fail just 'cause of that."

"Well, I doubt Derik had anything to do with it. There was obviously something wrong with the engine beforehand."

Louis mutters as he putters them back to Bella Bella. "You should have more respect for someone else's boat," he says. "I took you out fishing, to the *best* spots."

I don't know what he's talking about. I did exactly what you told me to do. Did I look at him weird? Maybe it was when I grimaced when he said I'd have to pull up all the hooks by hand.

He wants you dead.

Should've just used Wild Thing, *winch didn't work anyway.*

George rolls his eyes and smiles at Derik. But now that the adrenaline fades with the pursuit, Derik starts to realize just how much pain he is in. His shoulders and back are stiff with shooting pains. His arms cramp with the littlest of movements. And the horror that is his hands just starts to manifest, as it lurks behind the orange gloves.

He is shaking. He raises his numb hands and water pours from the gloves. His hands tremble as he removes the left glove; he can barely use his fingers, let alone feel them. He pulls lightly on the tips of the glove, but it doesn't give, so he pulls harder, and they make a sucking sound as they come free. More water pours out—if the lighting was better, he could see it tinged pink. Now the pain surges as the nerves awaken, like peeling off Band-Aids. "Ugh," he moans, then he goes for it: he tears off the glove. His hand is bone white, shrivelled and saturated by water, and open-blisters are all over, streaming blood. The streams meet at the wrist and pour down his arm, the volume of which is made all the more appalling by the flowing water. He realizes the pain is only going to get worse the longer the wounds are exposed to air, so he tears off the other glove quickly, revealing even more blisters and flowing blood as it is his dominant hand.

He holds out his bloody hands, raising them to the sky in (some would say) lament, though to him it is more nuanced—complicated by pride, as if his gesture conveyed that, yes, "I will suffer most. I will work till I die," like the pious of Gulag.

You'd think someone would help, that someone would get the first aid kit (if there was one) but no; it's like jealousy has staved them off from all of the above, as they too realize what an honour it is to suffer before one's maker.

"Look at my hands!" says Derik. "I can't even move them." He can barely wiggle a finger, not because of pain, but because function is compromised.

"That's pretty bad," says George.

"What do I do?" he shouts.

"Wash them in water; salt water is good for cleansing wounds."

He washes them in the sea, the cold, briny sea, grimacing with each swish. He returns to his seat, raising his hands again. "Now what? They're still bleeding."

"Huh, I've never seen that before," says Louis. "Two guys pulled up seven hundred hooks by hand last week. They didn't get any blisters."

Does he think I'm a wimp? He didn't do shit! He just sat behind his wheel and complained! Fortunately for Derik (depending on your definition of *fortune*), all pains and sufferings are compared to his near-death experiences, which dwarf them in comparison. It's a matter of principle: back at home, any friend or motherly figure would surely gasp and salve his wounds with Polysporin, then wrap them in bandages, but here, after such heroic deeds, he is shamed for desiring any such aid—rather, he is shamed for bleeding, or showing any pain at all. If he took a knife and slit his wrists, they'd offer the same indifference, eager to half feign surprise, as if they willed it.

"You should see what it's like working herring season, working fourteen hours a day," says Louis. "No one complains there."

I didn't even complain; I just showed him my hands. Derik still has his hands raised, in shock at their indifference, though mostly because they desire it (or so his rage indicates).

"Yeah, that's weird—to bleed like that," says George. "Do you have a towel or anything so he can dry his hands?" he asks Louis.

Louis keeps his eyes straight ahead. "I got this towel," he says, grasping an oily rag.

"No, he can't use that—they'll get infected."

"Quit getting blood all over my boat."

"Sorry…" Derik holds his hands over the gunwale, feeding his blood to the fish. He inspects his wounds, fascinated but alarmed.

"You don't got anything, huh?" George finds a white cloth. "What about this?"

"That's a *good* rag—I don't want his blood all over it."

"I'll buy you a new rag." He wraps it around Derik's hands, sopping up blood. Derik winces. They lock eyes. George has seen this look before: it's only a matter of time before Derik snaps. "We're heading back, right?" he asks Louis.

"Yeah."

"OK, good."

Louis looks back at the tangled line. "Can you untangle the line?"

If he asks me to do it, I'm gonna stick my thumbs in his eyes.

"I think we should just head back," says George. "I'll help you with the line tomorrow. I think we've done enough for today."

It's true, friends: Derik has been pushed enough. His limits have been reached. His eyes turn homeward, as he would run into his mother's arms all those times George taught him to tuck his chin while giving him one too many taps to the head while teaching him to box. This is the end, and nothing but death will stop Derik from preserving the little sense of self he has left. George inspects his wounds again.

They putter back without a catch.

9. Showdown

They return to the Tanner residence well after midnight. They drive with the windows down, Derik huddling close, enjoying the white noise, black air streaming through his hair. He likes the sound of tires running over gravel, broken occasionally by an owl cooing, raven croaking or bullfrog clucking. The grasshoppers play violin.

George Shotgun says, "Yeah that sucks when it starts dieselling like that—could be a number of issues."

Louis turns sharply.

"I remember one time, we were aboard the *Marge Valence* and our power went out. We were sitting ducks in this *huge* storm; we were rolling and bobbing on the waves without power. It was insane." George hits his vape. "Oh yeah, we were just putting out the seine too. Jesus Christ. Waves were coming over the side." He acts it out. "Somehow the mechanic got the engine running again and we were able to make it back to Port Hardy. It was a miracle we didn't capsize."

"At least you got it running again. I'll have to have Jay take a look at it now."

George rambles on.

Look at my stigmata!

Louis coughs.

"I'm sure it's nothing major," says George.

At least I get to see Lucky again. I can't believe I have a cat now. I shouldn't get too attached though—I doubt I'll be able to keep him.

They get to the house, the truck lights spearing the windows. They gather their jackets and boots. They close their doors, which always seem louder at night—during the day, noise collapses into noise (an excuse to make more noise), but at night, noise seems noisier because the noise of noise is not noise but quiet, as all the noise-makers are at rest. Somewhere, a star is screaming.

They enter the house. Derik expects to find Raven sleeping on his rented couch, or perhaps reading articles in the phone light, but he is nowhere to be found. Instead, they find all the lights on, and Sophie and Rich at the kitchen table, her giggling, and him smirking. She churns instantly from pleasure to disgust as their midnight seance is ruined.

"Did you catch any fish?" she says.

Louis puts down the red cooler. "No."

She turns back to Rich and chuckles. "That's too bad. I guess you didn't need the boat after all." Clearly she doesn't gamble.

"Hey, did you notice anything wrong with the boat?" Louis asks her.

"Something's always wrong with your boat. I told you to invest in a new one; that one's too old."

"A boat will last a lifetime if well taken care of. I worked on boats older than me."

"Gross. Your boat smells. I think you should get a new one."

"I can't *afford* a new one… There's something wrong with the engine, and the winch wasn't working. You didn't notice any of that when you were using it?"

"No." She shrugs, somehow looking more pissed. "We never touched the winch."

"You didn't notice anything weird going on with the engine?" Louis asks Rich.

"Nope. Ran fine for us."

"Why are you asking him?" says Sophie. "You don't trust me or something?"

Louis clears his throat and looks away, rinsing his Thermos. "The engine broke down. It took us forever to get back."

"Not our problem," says Sophie. "It's *your* boat, remember?"

"It was working fine till you used it."

"Are you blaming us?" Her voice rises. Rena stirs from sleep in the bedroom. "It's your boat, Dad—you should be maintaining it better so it doesn't break down. All we did was take it to Shearwater and back. If it can't handle that, then it's a garbage boat. You should get a new one."

He grovels, dismantled, and makes himself some tea of valerian.

Derik takes a seat on the couch. He inspects his hands, gauges healing, searches for meaning. *Does anyone care that I'm injured?* His hands remain mangled, rent, pruned and white, but the bleeding has mostly stopped. He shakes with pain that throbs worse the more feeling returns. They say Thich Quang Duc felt little pain once fully aflame. Although perhaps he was aided by his fortitude and focus sustained by years of discipline and meditation (and what a vision: one ignited in prayer), nerves are destroyed by fire. It's only in recovery that pain catches up. Such delayed suffering Quang Duc never reached, fortunately, as he was bestowed the sweet mercy of death.

Derik searches for Lucky. He checks where he left the box by his foamy—nothing. He searches behind the couch—nothing. Heart now sprinting, he searches behind and under *both* couches—nothing. Not on the mantelpiece, not under the table, not in either of the rooms does he find Lucky. Sophie's smirk curls to the right.

"All right, I'm going to bed," says Louis. "I have to get up early to see Jay about the boat."

"Goodnight Dad," says Sophie, as she normally would never. She quickly sparks conversation with Rich, expressing her joy watching this eager boy look for what he loves, because, you know, if she can't have it, no one will.

The last person on Earth he wants to talk to is her, but he must. "Where's Lucky? Did you see my kitten?"

"You have a kitten?" she says without hesitation.

"Yeah, we found an abandoned kitten under a house and brought him back here to take care of—your parents said I could. He was in an old shoebox."

"Yeah, we saw it. We put it outside 'cause it had mange, and probably fleas."

Derik looks into the black night, the glass door mocking him with reflection. He cups his hands around his eyes, against the glass, to block out light and better see out. He notices a shoebox on the wood patio, but he can't see if Lucky's in it. His heart takes off. He unlocks the door and gives it a pull, but it doesn't open. He notices the second lock at the bottom, reaches down, fumbles unlocking it, and finally slides it open, jumping out onto the patio, falling to his knees before the shoebox to see that—no! It really is empty. Nothing but some crumpled paper towel and crumbs of cat food. Lucky is gone.

No, no, no. There's no way. There's no way she got rid of him.

Friends—oh, dear friends—it's not due to faulty narrative you don't understand the vengeance Derik is capable of, it just hasn't yet reached the precipice! He scours the tool shed, he stamps around the backyard calling, "Lucky? Lucky?! Where are you?! Lucky? *Lucky*?!" checking under the deck, in the thornbushes, and all around the house... but Lucky he does not find; no meows do his doe ears trace. And then it dawns on him, the entire universe zooms into play from deep, black space: Lucky is really gone.

The kitten you saved is gone.

Maybe it's a good thing, maybe he's strong enough to survive on his own.

He can't even walk! Standing there, in the dead of morning, in foreign land, with his hands throbbing, stinging with every touch, holding the empty home of his lost friend Lucky, something gives way; Derik snaps.

You should fight her.

No, no, calm down.

I mean it! This is it! No more being nice and getting taken advantage of. All I've done since I got here is get taken advantage of: by Dad, by Louis, by Rich and Sophie! Fuck this place! Damn it all to hell!

He must be around here somewhere if he can't walk.

I bet a raccoon got it. Squawk! I bet a raccoon got it. Shadow. Shadow. Shadow. Shadow. He pulls at his hair, laughing maniacally, rocking himself back and forth. *I should've taken him with me. Why did I leave him here with her?*

Rena said she'd take care of him, she said she'd watch him.

They don't care, they let Sophie do whatever she wants!

That's not true. Rena promised to make sure no one moved him. She said he was cute!

She can't watch him while she's asleep, idiot. Sophie took advantage of her going to bed early, just like last night. He storms into the house, teeth clenched, eyes glaring red. He holds the empty shoebox before him. "You really left my kitten outside?"

"Yeah," she says. "It was dirty and probably had fleas. Why are you so mad?"

"You put him outside even though you *knew* I was taking care of him?"

She cackles. "Yeah. I did. Whose kitten was that, anyway? You stole it from someone's house."

"Yeah, yeah, yeah. Something *always* belongs to someone when it benefits you. *It's my room. It's my boat,*" he mocks. "I guess I should have just let him die in neglect like the others."

"What's wrong with you?" she scoffs.

"What's wrong with *you*?! All you do is claim what isn't yours and take advantage of your parents. Must be easy being a single child, huh, *always* getting your way, never having to deal with opposition."

Sophie says, "Aw, what's the matter little boy? You sad 'cause you don't have your Pokémon cards to play with?"

"Ha, yeah. You know, I bet you'll abuse your kids the same way."

"Excuse me?"

"That's right. You'll be a horrible parent, just like you're a horrible daughter—"

"Don't talk to me like that, you don't know—"

"—constantly faulting others for your own insecurities."

"—what I've been through!"

"Aw, I'm sure it's rough, getting whatever you want. You know what I just did? I pulled up three hundred hooks, by *hand*." He throws the box against the fireplace, revealing his hands. "Now look at them! They're fucked!"

"All right, all right." George finally intervenes. "That's enough." He grabs Derik's shoulders lightly, guiding him to the backyard. "Go cool off outside."

Derik brushes him off. "Don't touch me." He points with wagging finger. "You're just as bad. Did you help me at all with pulling up the longline? No. 'Aw, my back hurts. I can't sleep on a couch.' *You* made me suffer. Now I'm just supposed to sit here and accept all this while my hands *throb* with pain. Piss off, *all* of you!" He sweeps his finger across the room. "I have nothing. Nothing! My dog died last year, I have to go to a new school, with *no* friends, and look where I am: a dumb, primitive land, for dumb, primitive people. You can all die for all I care, and know what? Take me with you while you're at it, 'cause I'll be a hell of a lot better off than I would being here any longer."

"All right!" says George. "Go!"

Derik steps outside and slams the door shut.

George turns to Sophie. "You shouldn't have touched his kitten. He was really attached to it."

"Shut up," she says. "Come on," she ushers Rich to her room. "Let's go." They leave George on the couch. He puffs his vape in vexation. Derik weeps on the steps of the deck, quivering from the ordeal.

The door handle turns—it's Raven. He enters, smiling. "Hey, you're still up."

George sighs. "Yup."

Raven takes his shoes off. "How'd the halibut fishing go? Did you catch any?"

"No, we didn't catch any." He looks to Derik outside, but sees only his own reflection. "Derik's upset." He explains how Lucky was acquired, then subsequently abandoned.

"Did you check around the shed? He probably didn't go far."

"Yup." He holds his breath. "He was looking all over. It's too dark to go looking for him now, we'll just have to wait till morning."

"He must be around here somewhere, unless a raccoon got him ... Though I've never seen a trash panda here before."

They hear the muffled arguing of Sophie and Rich.

Raven strips to his briefs and spreads out on his couch, tucking himself in, ready for sleep.

Outside, Derik retraces the day: the argument, the halibut, finding Lucky—all the days he spent with Shadow: the way he would follow them, their shadow, to the park, along the seawall, around the neighbourhood, humble, protective, appreciative, and eager, as if any minute someone would call "Shoot!" and a mallard would drop from the sky and he'd be the one to retrieve it. Madness turns to sorrow; tears fill his eyes. *Sure, I can act tough and keep fighting, but what's the point when everything I love goes away? What of all these harsh words and violence?*

For love? To return the devotion of the Creator's creations, who love you unconditionally, even if they get taken advantage of?

We don't deserve such selfless love. None of it matters. He looks to the stars, cursing life, cursing all hatred poured upon him (nay, it was more of a drip—an incessant drip that overflowed his cup). He kneels, he supplicates himself to the heavens, to the gods, raising his hands, then letting them fall to the ground. He weeps; he weeps. He covers his face, sniffling, diaphragm quivering, tears streaming onto his ravaged hands.

Eventually he heads back inside (though contemplates running off—*Where would I go?*) and lies on his foamy, fully clothed, taking no comforts, continuing to cry quietly.

"You know," starts George, having only feigned sleep, "you shouldn't get so upset when people do things that hurt you, or else you're going to have a very sad life, Derik."

"Maybe I want to be sad," says Derik, face muffled. *Sniffle.* "Everyone wants me to be sad anyway."

"That's not true," says George, resolute. "You know I don't like when you say that. I had a friend once, named Freddy—you remind me a lot of him. He used to let everything get to him; he would get so sad. Then I remember one day we found him at the cemetery. He was walking around the graves... and he was talking to himself—talking to people that weren't there. So we asked him, 'Freddy, who are you talking to?' And he said, 'Oh, isn't it *beautiful*, George?' He was looking at the sky, like a child, like he saw something that wasn't there. 'It's so *beautiful* up there, isn't it?' he said. 'It's like they're calling me—calling me to go home.' And I told him, 'Freddy, no one's calling you.' He said, 'But I hear them, George. They're so beautiful... the *light* is so beautiful.' And I told him, 'Freddy, whatever you do, *don't* go into that light—'cause it's *not* good.' 'But it's *beautiful*, it's beautiful,' he kept saying. And he kept walking around the cemetery, talking to no one...

"They found him a few months later, in his mom's basement—he had hung himself. He hung himself on a doorknob with a tie wrapped around his neck... I don't want that to happen to you, Derik." George's voice wavers. His eyes tear. "And sometimes, I look at you, and I see Freddy: how you act, the things you say, how you take everything so personally—like the world is against you. It's not right; it's not healthy to burden yourself with everything people do and say. It'll only make you go insane, like it did Freddy." A few tears stream down his face. Derik sees without looking.

Derik stops his crying because he knows he'll never experience such suffering as his dad—it'd be selfish to pretend. A son for a kitten? "I'm not gonna kill myself, Dad, that'd be stupid. If God wanted me dead, it would've happened a long time ago."

"The way you worry about everything, and bottle it up inside—quit it, Derik. You're only going to bring yourself to ruin. Everyone has problems! Just let them go. Look at Jesus. He tried to solve everyone's problems and they killed him for it."

"Well..."

"It's too much to bear for anyone, my son. Just let it go. Live your life, and move on... Or else you're gonna be miserable *all* the *time*."

Derik sighs. "Fine."

Something stirs in Sophie's room. There's a mumbling. The door swings open, pouring out yellow light, then out bolts a shade into the washroom quickly closing the door. The fan starts. They hear Sophie retch and vomit.

And friends, I cannot say Derik disapproves. "I just always wanted a kitten, so I did my best to take care of him. I *hate* seeing animals suffer. It's so annoying how people go out of their way to mess with me when all I want to do is be left alone."

"Well, just ignore them," George says firmly. "Don't let them get to you, or else they've won. There's always going to be someone who's trying to ruin your day or tell you how bad you are at something. You don't know what they've been through, how bad their lives are, so that they feel the need to project their hatred onto you, so just let it go. Be *happy.* You're very wise for your age. You're good looking, you're hardworking; all the girls will like you. You have so much to be proud of, and you have a family that loves you."

"I know, I know... I love you, Dad. I am truly very lucky to have you in my life."

George smiles, relieved. He leans from his couch, and kisses Derik on the forehead. "I love you too... so much. Goodnight, son."

"Goodnight, Dad."

George rolls into his blanket and falls asleep. Derik, now free of his burden, slowly drifts toward dream.

🌵 🌵 🌵

Derik awakes to the sun pouring in like honey through the blinds. Derik stretches out and reaches to the sky. George is still snoring, but Raven sits, admiring the rising. Derik looks around, startled to find him looking back. "You scared me," he says.

"You scare easy. How'd you sleep?"

"Good..." He checks the time on the TV box: eight. "I was really tired."

Something sizzles in the oven. Rena shows herself, and unleashes the intoxicating fumes of bacon rendering its fat, concentrating that deep, smoky, sweet, porky goodness. The hot air from the oven makes

Rena squint. She closes the door. She puts a nonstick pan on the stove to cook eggs.

George starts, stopped mid-snore, as he too wakes.

"Did you all sleep all right?" says Rena.

"Yeah," says Derik. He doesn't even bother mentioning his hands, as the pain has dulled, and healing has begun.

George moans, as he does when stretching to the sky, and before finishing, says, "I had a decent sleep. It's hard on these couches with my back… I was thinking, maybe we should just sleep on the boat, then we can sleep in our comfy beds. I keep getting really bad cramps sleeping on this couch."

"You said you were going to stay till Saturday," says Rena, disappointed. "I was gonna cook you the steaks you bought from the band store."

Derik—excited at the prospect to sleep aboard *Wild Thing* again—now feels bad, as George probably made the suggestion for his comfort.

"We'll be back for dinner. I can't wait for those steaks." He slurps, licking his lips. "But I can't sleep on this couch anymore; it's too hard on my back."

"All right," says Rena. "If you'd rather sleep in your own beds then go ahead. I won't stop you."

"What do you think of that, guys? Or would you rather stay here for another night?"

Derik grapples with his pity for Rena. *She sounds so sad though. I don't want to hurt her feelings. It's not her fault her daughter's a psycho.*

As if you're a saint.

Yet, still, he takes the excuse to leave drama behind. "I think it's a good idea if it's better for your back… It might be better for everyone, to not have us around." He tries to save face.

"We like having you around," says Rena. "You're our guests. You're family."

"Yeah, I know… I kind of want to sleep in my own bed, though. That's all."

"Well, all right—if that's what you want, I understand."

She finishes preparing breakfast and places it on the table. Grumpy Louis joins them. Derik waits to be the last to dive in. He's returned to his ascetic ways to negate his guilt for snapping, you see. They eat scrambled eggs, toast and bacon, washing it down with orange juice.

PART TWO

At that very moment the water that was boiling in the coffee percolator made a loud perking sound.

"Hear that!" Don Juan exclaimed with a shine in his eyes. "The boiling water agrees with me."

—Carlos Castañeda, *Journey to Ixtlan: The Lessons of Don Juan*

10. Chief's Spot Pawn

That was rough. I purge the sky/mind by transforming into the Thunderbird—works like a charm. You see, thoughts aren't locked in your head, like caged birds; they permeate the air, flying free. Anyway, we're headed to the past now, to a time before our hero left home, even before he knew Henry was dead, when Derik began working for George in his pawnshop, Chief's Spot Pawn. Some may say he was too young, but it's about the same age George started working for Henry aboard the *Marge Valence*.

Entered Raven. He was no stranger to Chief's Spot: he had pawned a guitar, some dated electronics—like the N64, and a CRT TV he brought in on a little red wagon—obscure-sized rings he knew too much about, and books, such as *Dances of the Northwest Coast*, written by Nevar Patchwork, and *The Book of Thoth*, by Aleister Crowley, both of which Derik snuck home to read as they had little monetary value. He was intrigued by Raven's mystique, even though they hadn't officially met.

I wonder if Redbird is my holy guardian angel.

I'd ask that guy Raven if I met him.

Don't! They'll think you're crazy.

Why? It's in the book!

Redbird is just an imaginary friend; you'll get over it.

Never had Raven brought in the likes of which he carried in on that day. Derik couldn't help but listen to the conversation between Raven and George as he feigned cleaning bronze bracelets.

"What have you got there?" asked George.

"It's a moon mask," said Raven. "It was carved by a ... by a local *artist* who went on vacation and never came back. He gave it to me before he left." It was layered like a gobstopper, with dark wood around the edge, the outer rims painted blue, brown, black, then red, while the inner face itself was light maple—a pleasant face with red lips, big black eyes, and thick, Mormin-like brows.

"Wow, look at that," said George. "Derik!" Derik stopped his charade. "Come take a look at this."

"Wow," said Derik. "It's beautiful." They both admired the handiwork: the bird's-eye grain, the harnessing of nature's matrix, the lush paints that glowed like blood, and the admirable features of the moon which displayed no sense of the uncanny. It reminded Derik of the moon in *Majora's Mask*, approaching on its collision with Termina. *The moon represents emotions but also strange journeys.*

George flipped it over. "It's a very nice mask. What do you want to do with it, pawn it or sell it?"

Rippled, did Raven's brows. "I'd like to sell it. I's got to pay rent, you know."

George continued inspecting. "What were you looking to get for it?"

"I don't know, I'm pretty desperate. How 'bout three hundred?"

"No, you kidding? It's got to be worth at least two grand. I'll give you four hundred."

Raven looked Derik in the eyes.

Whoa, he looks badass.

"Hey. The name's Raven."

He's finally introducing himself! "Nice to meet you. You're the one that brought in those books the other day, right?"

"Which ones?"

"Dances of the Northwest Coast and *The Book of Thoth."*

You're not supposed to let Dad know!

Who cares? He didn't even price them, he just threw them in the back.

"They're really interesting."

"I'm glad you like them."

"Can I ask you what your zodiac sign is?"

"You just did! I'm on the cusp of Pisces and Aries—whatever suits me in the moment. What about you, what's yours?"

"I'm a Libra. I carry the sword of the magus."

Raven chuckled. "To balance the spheres of light and shade, I assume."

"Dad's a Leo," said Derik. "That's why he makes everything about himself."

George cleared his throat.

"So your dad's offering me four hundred for this mask. What do you think? You think that's a good deal?"

Dad said to never buy masks, they're cursed. "Dad said to never buy masks, they're cursed."

George and Raven smiled at each other in acknowledgement. "That's right," said Raven. "They're priceless. I wouldn't say they're necessarily cursed, but it's definitely bad mojo to put a price on one as old as this."

"You passed the test," said George.

"What test?" asked Derik.

"To see whether you're morally corrupt or not. You should never put a price on sacred artifacts like this, or they'll haunt you the rest of your life."

There he goes, rambling on about ghosts again. "I get it, it's like Pokémon cards: you're either an average collector, looking to flip them for a profit, or you're a Pokémon *enjoyer*, appreciating them for their art and sentimental value."

"That's a good comparison," said Raven. "I still have my first-edition Blastoise at home."

Derik's eyes brightened. "No way! Is it in good condition?"

"It's not mint, but it's pretty good. No, I was an *enjoyer*, so I handled it quite a bit."

"Dang. Still cool though." Derik turned his attention back to the mask. *Nice paint, tight flame, strong patina.* "How old is the mask?" he asked.

"How old do you think it is?" asked George. "You should know—I taught you what to look for."

"Eighty years?"

"Yeah," said Raven. "It was made around 1940. Good guess."

George rubbed Derik's head, messing up his hair. "Good work, son."

"The person who gave it to me said it should never be bought or sold," said Raven.

"If it was bought, doesn't that automatically mean it was sold?" asked Derik. "You can't have one without the other."

Raven chuckled. "That's true, but I guess it guilts both the buyer and seller, so neither commit to the transaction."

Derik thought about it. *He's right!*

"The idea is that it should reside with someone who will cherish it and take care of it, which is why I've come to give it to you."

"You're *giving* this mask to us?" asked Derik.

"I don't think *giving* is the right word: it's yours to borrow, just as it was mine, and the shaman's before me. It's the least I can do for your dad for all the sweet deals." He winked at George.

George nudged Derik. "See. If you give people a fair price, they'll repay you."

Fair price? You just tried to lowball him.

I think it was all an act, to test you.

Well, that's not fair.

That's life. Ridin' high in April, shot down in May.

Glad I answered right.

"Raven's the shaman in charge of the sweat I told you about," added George.

"You're a shaman?" Derik asked.

"Some may say."

"When's the next sweat?" asked George.

"There's one this Saturday. You're welcome to attend if you like. It starts around six."

"Awesome. How long does it last usually?"

"About three hours. The organizers put on a feast after, too, but

I don't stick around for that. We start lighting the fire to heat up the rocks that go inside the lodge around three, but the actual sweat starts at six. You're welcome to stop by anytime before that."

"Great! We'll be there."

George had been to sweats before, but not in the city. Derik had only experienced them through George's stories.

Raven looks like Ganondorf.

"What should we bring as offerings? Tobacco ties?"

"Yeah, that'd be perfect."

They exchanged a few final words, then bid farewell. George would buy extra coloured cloth and pouches of tobacco to give to Raven, as was custom. In the meantime, he hung the mask on the wall, in the centre display, then strictly told everyone it wasn't for sale. "Unless someone offers us a million dollars." Derik caught himself daydreaming, staring at it.

"What's a sweat lodge anyway?" he asked his dad, knowing sort of what it was, but certainly no expert.

"It's basically a hut. They heat up these rocks in a big fire, then they bring them inside, shut the door, and sprinkle water on them to create steam. All the steam gets trapped inside, so you sweat, then you sing songs and say prayers."

"That's cool." If his mom, Betty, were there, she'd have responded, "No, they're hot," to make him consider the meaning of his words and stop repeating such catchphrases.

"It's a Sioux tradition, or Ojibwe—goodnight Sarah, see ya tomorrow!—the shaman burns incense on the stones so you get this great smell. The rocks are so hot they glow in the dark."

"Sounds neat."

"We should go to that one; I think you'll really like it." His inflection proceeded his merit; George wanted Derik to enjoy the sweat. "You'll learn a lot about our people, too."

"But we're Heiltsuk; it's not our tradition."

George shook his head. "We're all Natives. White people took our land." He chuckles. "We all have *that* in common."

"I thought we never gave up our land. Mrs. Crosschuk said it's—"

"That's true."

"—unceded territory."

"Yeah, that's what they say, but look around: Do you think the Musqueam own any of this?"

"They own the land, don't they?"

Again, George shook his head. "It's a formality, really; Gino owns all *this* land … Anyway, don't go making any plans for this Saturday," he said, with a flash of disapproval. "We're going to that sweat."

"But I'm going to Watermania with my friends on Saturday."

George glared at him impetuously, like a lion. "You're *going* to that sweat. When do you ever get to go to a sweat? You can go to Watermania whenever you want."

"I asked you if I could go today, and you said no because I'd be working."

"You're *going*," he growled.

"They don't get too hot do they?" He was flooded with memories of George spraying eucalyptus water on the fake rocks in the gym sauna (which had a sign specifically saying not to do so). "I can barely last fifteen minutes in the sauna."

"They get pretty hot, but you should be OK. Just remember to put your towel over your head if it gets too hot, then bend your head down low to the ground where the air is cooler—the hot air rises."

Should be OK? Derik had his doubts. What was the worst that could happen? He'd pass out and Mercury would guide him, with winged boots and a caduceus, whispering to him the wisdom of the universe distilled. Yes, and fits of embarrassment would surely follow for the rest of his days.

"If it gets too hot," said George, "you can yell, 'Open the door!' and they'll open the door—all the heat and bad spirits will rush out."

"Bad spirits?"

George nodded. "I saw it happen to someone. She was sitting there with a towel over her head, then she started moaning—making really weird noises, like an animal being sacrificed. She was clearly possessed. Then she reached back like this—" He jolted back against the wall, with his jaw gaping to the ceiling, and arms up like *Ls*, "and I *swear* I saw a spirit come out of her mouth—it was black, and started whirling around the top of the lodge. She kept screaming and crying, and I *knew* it was evil. I *knew* it was bad, Derik, so I yelled, 'Open the door!' and they opened the door right away. That thing flew out of there so fast. It needed somewhere to go—it didn't want to be there. If they didn't open the door, it for sure would've possessed someone else. That's how it works, it's like a parasite; it needs a host to live."

Derik imagined it, then sighed and said, "Yeah right. Sounds like bullshit."

"It's true! I *saw* it happen to her, Derik. I *saw* the bad spirit come out of her with my *own* eyes."

Customers came and went, the doorbell jangling like birds of an oak. People walked by with pizza.

I'll think about going to the sweat. What do I have to lose?

Well… everything! Friends, screen time, time for Slurpees, time to play games, time to laugh and time to cry. In a sense, much ado about time. But nothing dissolved the guilt simmering beneath his skin, his knowledge that if he didn't go, his father would be thoroughly disappointed.

"You need to learn about your people," George said that evening at the dinner table, after Derik had insinuated he may still be going to Watermania. "You said you wanted to learn the ways of the Heiltsuk."

"What about the Romans?" said Derik. "They invented heated swimming pools."

George pointed right at Derik's heart. "Quit messing around."

At a different—but identical—dinner table Coyote asks me, "Redbird, how do we define what is truly Heiltsuk, Indigenous or white?" Well, friend, I'm glad you asked. Here we have our Mormins—who don't meet expectations of deviants of the pure inspecting—who

BEAUTIFUL BEAUTIFUL

perhaps ought to have feathers in their hair, pipes for peace and red skin. Our Mormins bear nothing of the sort. Yet, as Derik would proudly boast, they belong to the Heiltsuk First Nation (except, of course, for Betty, a redhead with English ancestry). Just check his status card.

11. To Be a Rock, and Not to Roll

Sometimes our thoughts are misgiven. I'm here sitting on these eggs, but if I leave for a second, a pesky squirrel may gobble them up, just as it happened to my ancestors and me. I realize squirrels need to eat, but if they stopped forgetting where they buried their nuts, maybe my children could see the light of day. I do enjoy a nice worm, though, so I suppose worms don't appreciate me either. You can say it's "survival of the fittest," a phrase originating in Darwinist evolutionist theory, but what's the line between what's food and what's a victim of tyranny?

Charles Darwin had a half-cousin named Francis Galton, a proponent of eugenics: the set of beliefs and practices with the goal of improving genes. He theorized artificial selection could be applied to humans as it had been done to plants. Take the seeds of a tall plant, and its spawn will grow tall. This is an example of *positive* eugenics, because you're preserving positive traits. *Negative* eugenics involves exterminating blue plants, because you don't like the colour of their skin, thus eliminating *negative* traits. If you want blondes driving your tanks, then simply let them do all the passing-on-the-genesing. The idea is far from outlandish to animals like you and me, as we compete to breed, ensuring the strongest males pass on their genes. It's clear in this instance that strength is generally considered positive—but it's not always so easy to determine what is *good* and what is *bad*.

The problem of evil is a classic theological example: if God is omnipotent and all good, and there is evil in the world, then God can't exist because, surely, they would stop evil things from occurring in the world. It's important to note that bad isn't always evil; evil requires a conscious act, like murder, which isn't necessarily the case with bad—you wouldn't call an earthquake evil, unless you think God did it on purpose, which may be true. Maybe God is inherently evil—who knows? I digress. My point is: Why is murder evil? Squirrels eat my eggs all the time. I wouldn't consider them evil; the squirrels are just following their primitive urge to kill my children, just like you do chickens. Chickens don't call you evil (I know, I've clucked), so why consider murder evil? Obviously, it strips someone of life. But perhaps murderers can't help it, like the determinist squirrels, heeding the murderous voices in their heads; or maybe the murderee gets to go on to the next life, living as a Ferris wheel, full of joy and wonder? From God's cold, logical system, you become the next effect along the long list of cause and effect set forth in the creation of the universe, so there really is no evil.

You can also dodge the above argument entirely by taking a more Indigenous perspective by ascribing God *solely* a creator, as we've already proved good and evil to be human perceptions. Some would say the Creator is just a life force that sparked all things into being; some may subscribe gender, but it seems agreed the Creator is what started *all*. You can argue from here that the Creator is the first cause in the chain aforementioned that brought you here, and thus impartial to our perceptions of good and evil; that God is all, and we are all a part, including sadistic squirrels; or that special right is reserved for God to be fully a part of everything, yet wholly separate as a paradox. Any of these avenues transcend good and evil, as all is just.

This is relevant because Nazis thought eugenics was necessary to preserve their population by eliminating *bad* races, ensuring enough land and resources for the *good* ones. To them, it was as cold, logical and unempathetic as the universe appears to be with cancer, murder or natural disasters. They were squirrels, who misplaced their nuts, then consumed bird eggs, then culled all squirrels who didn't look like them. Did Nazis need to resort to such drastic measures? Most certainly not! But they could, and it made their lives easier at the expense of those they deemed subhuman, so they felt justified in their actions.

Unfortunately, Canada also had its fair share of eugenical perpetrators in the medical, educational and political fields. Tommy Douglas—the founder of the New Democratic Party, and voted "The Greatest Canadian of All Time" as part of a CBC television series—was a supporter of sterilizing "mental defectives." Another prominent Canadian eugenicist, Helen MacMurchy—a pioneer in the medical field who helped prevent high infant mortality rates by standardizing such practices as the sterilization of bottles and handwashing—helped institutionalize and sterilize the "feeble minded," an archaic term for anyone with an intellectual disability. Douglas and MacMurchy weren't outliers, they were two of the leading minds in their respective fields at the time. Eventually, eugenics became legislation in Canada, to the point that those with intellectual disabilities, Indigenous women, and anyone else labelled inferior, were rounded up into camps and sterilized against their will, sometimes without their knowledge. One woman had her uterus carved as if someone took a dozen cords from a dozen different countries, tied them in a ball, dipped them in wax, buried them, then tried charging their Tesla, so she couldn't possibly breed and transfer her *negative* genes, which she only discovered when she went to a doctor, years later, curious as to why she couldn't get pregnant.

"But Redbird," says Coyote. "That must've happened in the 1930s. Those eugenicists must've learned the errors of their ways."

Of course, my friend... Except incidents like this occurred as recently as 2018.

Such eugenic practices weren't just limited to sterilization, blood quantum laws and residential schooling are eugenical in nature as well. If you don't know, blood quantum is the measuring of one's Indianness by analyzing one's ancestry. To qualify as a status Indian, one has to have a certain amount of Indian blood (right away, you see the problem: What should be considered *enough*?) to access benefits such as post-secondary funding, lax hunting and fishing rights, or tax exemptions on reserve. This process is still ongoing, but gaining status was an even *bigger* issue decades ago, as you couldn't live on a reserve unless you had status. Indigenous women were especially affected, as they lost status if they married white men. The intent was to assimilate Indigenous people into Canadian settler society, to solve the "Indian problem" and relinquish land so the government could claim it (some would argue they stole it anyway, which is fair). If a woman lost status, she had little choice but to move to the city and take whatever work she could, which is a reason we see Indigenous people overrepresented in Vancouver's Downtown Eastside, resorting to prostitution or other illicit activities often to fuel drug addictions inflicted by predators. This is just one legacy of Canadian eugenic practices. Sometimes they just straight-up killed children in residential schools, which is genocide.

Some Indigenous, like George, were careful who they revealed their status to, due to atrocities committed against their ancestors, systemic racism and racial prejudice. Genocide has occurred throughout history, and there's no reason to believe it won't arise again. Sometimes it's difficult to see what you're doing as bad, as words have two meanings; one's temptation may be another's undoing. All we can do is try and experience what the other is experiencing to prevent such atrocities from occurring under new guise; everyone is doing what they believe is best, even if completely ruthless. So let us pray to see with future eyes to gain the wisdom of retrospect in hopes of maintaining peace and goodness for all... Also, please don't put me in a cage for being 2 percent parakeet again.

12. Derik's Great Work

Raven entered the temple, where there was no sign, only slender stairs leading between buildings. He changed into his black robe, and approached the masters upon the stage. "I have introduced myself to the disciple, Derik. I invited both him and his dad to sweat."

Uniwon's beaked nose protruded from his hood, the candles flickering. "Good. The plan is in motion. River Bear will convince him to go. Does that satisfy you?"

Raven's face shifted in thought. "I'm not sure he'll be convinced to go; he is reluctant to follow his heritage."

Uniwon's shadow rose. "He is of his age. His dad will make him go. It is set."

"Do not concern yourself with what is out of control," interjected Arconis. "Your contribution is done. He will be indoctrinated into the ways of his forefathers."

"Will shall be law," said Raven.

"Love under will," said all.

Raven raised his head. "What else is required of me?"

"Go forth," said Uniwon, "and prepare the ritual of the sweat."

"Verily, it shall be done."

Raven left his AA meeting.

"Derik, can I see you outside for two secs?" said Mrs. Crosschuk.

Derik ogled her sexy glasses (you see, it was the glasses that made her attractive to Derik—otherwise, her face was just a face), and said, "Yeah." He followed her to the hall, the dissonant chattering of students whirling about him, mocking him. Many were listening, as flies are drawn to syrup stains, spies in the House of Tudor, figuring the Abo kid was finally going to get his long-overdue bollocking.

"Have you ever spoken to Mrs. Bosch?" she said.

Derik shook his head. "No. Isn't that the school psychologist?"

"Yes, it is. Could you do me a favour and bring this box of crayons to her? She needs them for some of her students."

All fortifications were raised. "Why do I have to do it? Can't Kelly, who goes to see Mrs. Bosch every day, take them to her?"

"No. Kelly's not seeing Mrs. Bosch today. That's why I'm asking you to take them to her. So, if you'd be so kind, please take them to her office. You know where that is, right? Just down the hall on the left." Her voice was a cheese grater.

He looked at the crayons, then at her, distorted. His mood was colouring the world. "I don't want to see her though. Her office scares me." He knew if he said the wrong thing, they'd force him to run like a rabbit in the ditch. *Compassion killed the Jedi.* Mrs. Crosschuk was offended, her authority subverted.

"Just take this to Mrs. Bosch, OK? Go and have a little chat with her about your *story*."

Ah, motive unveiled! Derik flushed. The odour of terror emanated. He shakily took the box of crayons and walked down the hall with his head down, vision clinging to the dirty footprints on the floor.

He had never spoken to a psychologist before. He didn't take it lightly, as it's OK until it isn't. He and his friends gazed many a time into the abyss of her office, even jokingly pushed each other inside en route to the gym. It was dark—or "calming." Mrs. Bosch would sit at her desk, the computer screen lending an eerie glow to her face. He had seen and heard her give lessons before in numerous classrooms on austerity measures. She often smiled, which made Derik uneasy. She instilled unreasonable fear for a fridge.

Derik approached the door of her office and knocked lightly. *I hope she doesn't hear me. Then I can just go back to class and say I tried. I want to draw Pokémon.* But the crayons rattled in his shaky hand, giving away his position. The coloured faces of emotional intelligence did melt.

"Derik! Come in, have a seat," she said. Derik's eyes fixed immediately on the copy of his story on her desk. He looked away, hoping she wouldn't notice.

"Am I in trouble because of what I wrote?"

She laughed. "No, you're not in trouble. Mrs. Crosschuk and I thought it'd be a good idea to ask you about some of the things you included in it, but, overall, I found your story quite intriguing. You write beyond your years, Derik."

The phantom hands massaged the plush, violet cushion of his ego. "Thanks," he said with ambivalence. His mettle twisted like a leaf in the drain. Gengar was in the window. The clouds were chalk, and the forest, crayons.

"Tell me, where *did* you get the inspiration to write a story like this?"

"Mrs. Crosschuk told us we could write about anything we wanted, as long as it was related to school. So I chose to write about residential schools."

"*OK...* So the characters travel back in time, correct, to these *residential schools?*"

"Yes."

"And, correct me if I'm wrong, but it's Mr. Con, the band teacher, who goes back in time to, shall we say, *do battle* with these priests?"

"Yup. Mr. Con goes back in time with Talking Coyote to fight priests."

"So, why did you choose Mr. Con, of all people, to be the main character in your story?"

"'Cause he's funny, and me and my friends always joke that he probably fights crime, like a superhero, in his spare time."

"I see."

"It's ironic because he's really a nice teacher, and not a *con* like his name would lead you to believe. He's the best. I remember I was struggling to keep time once, so he told me, 'Just repeat in your head:

Der-ik Mor-min, Der-ik Mor-min.' The entire class laughed. I'll never forget that."

"Good!" She made note. "The thing that concerned both me and Mrs. Crosschuk was the mature nature of what you wrote about. Do you think Mr. Con would be happy to know he was involved in such a story?"

Her perspective T-boned his. "No… Probably not."

"Well, I'm just letting you know: maybe using your teacher in such a way is not being very respectful, is it?"

"…I'm sorry."

"Are you from Bella Bella, Derik?"

"No, but my dad is."

"Have you ever been there?"

"No. I want to… but my dad won't let me."

"And why's that?"

"I don't know. He hasn't been home for years." Of course, *home* meant Bella Bella, yet, the words quivered from his lips.

"I'm sorry to hear that. So, do you live with your mother currently?"

"Yeah… and my dad. I mean my dad hasn't been home *to Bella Bella* in years—we all live together."

"OK." She chuckles. "Minor misunderstanding there." She flipped the pages, chugging right along. "One thing I really found… creative—and cute—was the talking coyote. Where did the idea for that come from?"

"It's traditional for Indigenous stories to have a talking, wise animal as the narrator. I was also inspired by my dead dog, Shadow." *Shadow…* Derik saw him in the yard, saw him prancing in the field with spring flowers sprouting from the grass. "He was my best friend." (Don't look at me like that! I'm cutting onions, OK?)

"I'm sorry to hear that. How does that make you feel?"

"It's fine."

"Yeah?"

Derik realized she wouldn't stop excavating his grief. He cried.

She placed the box of tissues before him. "Our family lost our cat a few years ago. My daughter still gets sad when we bring it up. It's difficult losing a pet, they're like family members to us."

He blows his nose. "I know."

"What kind of dog was he?"

"A chocolate Lab."

She took a deep breath. "So it sounds like you were drawing from many influences in your life when you wrote this story. Is that fair to say?"

"Yes… Correct."

She readjusted. "Now, what was most troubling, was when we got to the monastery on the mountain." His eyes were red and swollen. "I understand a lot of what you wrote is fantastical. For example, you wrote, 'Spider-Man swang across the sky.' Clearly, Spider-Man did not swing across the sky. So why did you choose to include that in your story?"

"'Cause it's fiction; it's all made up. It's not like there's a real talking coyote, either."

"What purpose does Spider-Man serve, though?"

"Well, I think superheroes are the new gods."

"What do you mean by that?"

"We treat superheroes like gods: we idolize them, we pay worship in darkened rooms (theatres), actors embody them, we make up stories about them—that's why Spider-Man is in the sky, above everyone."

His wisdom surprised her. She took off her glasses. "What's startling to me—and it was startling to Mrs. Crosschuk, too—was how you say such slanderous things about the United Church. You shouldn't really be talking about religion, or writing about religion, like you did, here at school. Whatever you believe in your personal life—at home, or if you go to church—is OK; that's your right to believe in whatever it is you believe in. But here at school, you shouldn't be saying these sorts of things. For instance, you wrote, 'They drank their semen from gilt chalices.' You also go on to say, 'And the priests sodomized the children with the rod of God.'"

She was concerned he was nonplussed. This brought major discomfort to Derik as he figured such words were committed to writing, not speech. *It's all right. All is fair for beauty's sake.* "Right."

She stared at him a *long* while. "Do you feel that is appropriate to write for an English assignment at school?"

He shrugged. "Well, that's what happened, isn't it?"

❦ ❦ ❦

George slammed the dinner table with his fist. "I didn't tell you that!"

"You told me they had sex with little boys!"

"You don't go around telling people that. What's wrong with you?!"

"What? It's a fiction story. They made us read a book about the Taliban raping girls and killing fathers; then the girls had to collect and sell their bones for a living. I write about priests butt-fucking boys and suddenly I'm the bad guy?"

"You don't write about that kind of thing in school. Boy, if I did that, they would've given me the strap and my dad would've *beat* me, and then I would've been expelled."

"All right, George, that's enough," said Betty.

"It's true!" he said, hands raised.

"You're exaggerating. He already spoke to the school psychologist and his teacher; he knows what he did wrong, now he's going to fix it."

"Yeah, Dad."

George tended his mashed potatoes.

"I think I was sexually molested," said Candace, apathetic, instantly generating a scowl from George.

"Why would you say such a stupid thing?" he said.

"I'm not *stupid*."

"Well why would you say that?"

"'Cause I think it happened when I was too young to remember."

"How do you know then?" asked Derik.

"Because I can't have a normal relationship with a guy without fighting them. They also make me really uncomfortable."

Probably because Dad's crazy. Whenever we ask him where he's going, he'll say, "Going crazy."

"That doesn't mean you were molested," George clarified. "It just means you're difficult to work with."

"Difficult to work with? It's all your fault I'm the way I am—you're the one that raised me."

George groaned. "You can't go around saying you were molested when you aren't even sure it happened."

"Don't tell me what I can and cannot say, I can say whatever I want. I bet Grandpa did it. He used to make us sit on his lap and shit. He was a freak."

"Santa makes you sit on his lap," said Derik.

"Ugh. Don't get me started," she said. "We should cancel Santa."

"You don't know what it means to be sexually molested," said George. "I've had friends who killed themselves because they were molested by priests."

"You don't remember anything about being molested?" Derik asked Candace, genuinely curious.

"Grandpa used to grope my back. One time, he made me kiss him on his cheek, but he turned at the last second so I ended up kissing him on the lips."

George nearly choked on his food.

"That *is* weird," said Betty.

"Joe Biden kisses his grandchildren on the lips," said Derik. "Maybe he's just old-fashioned?"

"Listen to yourself," said Candace. "It doesn't matter if he's old, it's *wrong*."

"I agree, I'm just trying to understand where Grandpa could've been coming from… Maybe you blocked out the rest. Some people block out traumatic events because they're too traumatic. I didn't realize I almost drowned when I was four when we went to Disneyland. Mom and Dad were watching you in the hot tub, so I snuck into the pool. I couldn't swim though; I sank right to the bottom. Apparently babies naturally exhibit swimming techniques, but can't succeed until experience sparks the innate. I remember getting tunnel vision, like the world was enveloping me in darkness, then this voice came to me and said, 'Swim! Swim like Shadow,' and I saw him dog-paddling at the beach, so I copied him and dog-paddled to the stairs where I managed to grab the rail and pull myself out. I gasped for air. I didn't understand what had happened, though. That's why I was scared the rest of the trip, because my senses were hypersensitive. I was terrified of the Haunted Mansion 'cause I was hearing things."

"You've always been a worrywart," said George. "Are you sure you're not just making that up?"

Derik pondered. "I'm convinced my memory is correct, even if foggy."

"Speaking of Disneyland," said Candace, mischief in her eyes.

Derik looked to her and then to Betty, who hid her smirk. "What? What about Disneyland?"

"Oh, nothing," said Candace.

"You can't bring it up and not tell me. Do we get to go to Disneyland again? That'd be awesome. I want to see the new Star Wars ride."

"Mom and I are going to Disneyland," she said, "but you're not."

Derik dropped his fork. "What? You're kidding, right?"

Betty clicked her tongue in disapproval. "You weren't supposed to say anything."

"They have to know at *some* point," said Candace.

"I promised I'd take her if she did well in soccer this year," said Betty. "You'll get to go on your *own* trip. She wants to go, just the two of us."

"That's *so* not fair," said Derik. "I won a gold medal in karate and you took me to Dairy Queen. How come she gets to go to Disneyland?"

"We're going to go shopping in Beverly Hills, and she wants a manicure. You don't want to do any of that. Plus, it's too expensive for all of us to go. You and Dad can go on an adventure you'll actually enjoy."

"Don't worry, son," said George. "We'll have our fun."

"I want to go to Disneyland! I have all this money saved up; I'd like to go shopping, too."

"Oh, maybe another time," said Betty. She scowled at the beaming Candace. "So what happened after Mrs. Crosschuk talked to you?"

Derik heaped his rice, then sighed. "She probably thought Mrs. Bosch would give me pills or something, 'cause I'm crazy."

Betty frowned. "Don't be like that. What did she really say?"

"Mrs. Bosch thought I was *fine!*" Derik shrugged. "*Boys will be boys.* After class, when everyone was dismissed, Mrs. Crosschuk pulled me aside. She said, 'You can't write stuff like this—you can't swear in your story, you shouldn't say such terrible things about Jesus and the United Church—and you have to pay more respect to Indigenous culture and their traditional narratives, 'cause this is blasphemy.' She asked me if I knew what blasphemy was, and I said, 'Yes: it's offensive, and untrue.' But then I told her that I am Indigenous, and that it was a fictional story—she told me I could swear. Which she did! But she thought I meant *ass* or, at the worst, *bastard*—like in that story we read about the Apache girl who went home to Texas. See, everything I put in the story we had already learned and talked about: residential schools, the smallpox epidemic, swearing, cannibalism and what the priests did to kids! We discussed all that stuff."

"So what did she say in the end? Do you have to redo the assignment?"

"Yes… which is fine; I like writing. I'm just glad she didn't send me down to the principal's office, or worse! I suppose I could've gotten the strap."

George cleared his throat.

"Got him," said Candace. They made light of abuse.

"You better go right upstairs after dinner and rewrite your story, OK?"

"Got it."

"And make sure you meet *all* the criteria this time—no swearing, no talking about what the priests did to kids—right?"

"Yeah, I *will*."

"Good."

✿ ✿ ✿

Derik finished dinner, then went to his room to rewrite his story. No, he couldn't write about talking, time-travelling coyotes who back-talk the ironic teacher, or how Jesus descended from the sky, turned into Satan and choked out Archbishop Panfart in front of the entire town before feeding him to Leviathan. Nope, no more creativity; artistic freedom could no longer be his excuse. He had to write a proper assignment.

I'm just going to write about basketball, screw it. And that was that! He wrote on through the night, much to the ire of Candace who heard him typing like a madman. She unlocked his door from the outside.

"Go to bed!" she berated him.

"I can't, I have to finish my assignment."

"Who cares? It doesn't matter, you're graduating from elementary school in a few weeks."

"You think I want to do this? I'd rather play *Heroes of the Storm*."

"Quit typing so loud."

"They're red switches—that's as quiet as they get."

Candace woke Betty to complain. "He has to finish his assignment," said Betty, eyes still closed.

"I don't care, I can hear him from my room. He's been typing all night."

"Oh well! Just put in your earplugs."

"I can't 'cause you didn't buy me any."

Derik closed his door, put on his headphones and completed his assignment. He handed it in the next day. Mrs. Crosschuk marked it and returned it the day after. He got sixty-seven out of one hundred, about a C+, which was good enough for him.

"I passed," he said at the dinner table that evening.

"That's good, son," said George. "I'm proud of you. Now you're definitely going to that sweat."

"But Dad, I don't *want* to. I don't even like saunas! It's going to be too hot."

"You're going, and that's final. This is an opportunity for you to connect with your people."

"They're not *my people*, you keep *saying* that. My people are Canadians. My relatives are from Bella Bella *and* England."

"You can't go around saying all these crazy things about Natives when you don't even bother to get to know them. That's extremely disrespectful."

"Well, what am I supposed to do? I have no one to teach me what they do or what they believe in except you."

"There you go again. I bet if you went to this sweat, you'd meet someone who could tell you about the Heiltsuk. Talk to Raven! He'll teach you everything you need to know. You won't know until you try. You have to go out and make connections. You can't just sit in your room all day and play video games. This sweat is a perfect way to meet someone who can educate you on our culture."

"*Fine*, I'll go to the stupid sweat!" Derik rose from his seat to leave. "I'll just tell my friends Watermania will have to wait." He took his dish to the sink.

"Good." George stared at Betty with his big, brown, approval-seeking eyes. "It's settled then."

🌵 🌵 🌵

It was a beautiful, blue Saturday morning, the day of the sweat. George and Derik took Highway 99 south through the George Massey Tunnel to get some cheap tobacco at the gas station on the reserve to make prayer ties as an offering to the ancestors. They stopped at Tim Hortons along the way, getting themselves some Iced Capps and crullers.

"Dad, do you pay taxes?" Derik said.

"Yes, of course I pay taxes."

"I thought Indians didn't pay taxes... That's what my friends think, at least."

"Some things are tax exempt on reserve land. Like if I bought a TV on Native land, I wouldn't have to pay tax on it."

"I thought Vancouver was Musqueam land though. So how come we still have to pay taxes?"

"Because we don't live on the Musqueam reserve, that's why."

"So it's Musqueam land, everyone admits that, but because it's not actually the reserve, we still have to pay taxes?"

"*Yes,*" George said.

"What reserve are we going to now?"

"Tsawwassen."

"Oh, so it's officially called the Tsawwassen reserve?"

"Yes, Tsawwassen is the name of the First Nation. Doesn't it sound like a Native name?"

"I guess so—like Saskatchewan."

"Right."

They took the 17 turnoff, and followed it all the way to the jettison that led to the ferry terminal, where the gas station was. George filled up the tank. He knocked on Derik's window. Derik cracked open the door. "Why don't you go inside and see what kind of ice cream they've got?"

"Mom said you're not supposed to eat junk, your blood pressure's too high."

"I'll be all right. We'll sweat it off." The thought of future pleasure from sweet, sweet ice cream resonated within him, and cast his face glad, so Derik went inside to scope out the Ben & Jerry's which, truth be revealed, he desired much as well. Inside was a large lady who Derik thought was depressed, though she just needed a jovial spirit to counter.

George screwed the gas cap on, then sauntered inside.

"All they got is drumsticks and things," said Derik. George licked his lips and made his slurping sound.

"Let's get a couple." He picked up an ice cream sandwich and a red fruit pop. "Ice cream sandwiches, these are good."

"They're all right," said Derik, and followed suit, picking out some favourites. They carried the goods to the counter. The cashier smiled.

"Oo, they got Slim Jims too," said George, picking out a couple, then three, like he'd done with the cat tails: "You can eat the end." He had shown Derik along the dike weeks prior. He'd peeled away, with the cat tail flopping about, its cotton carried on the breeze. He had cut away the rough stalk with a pocketknife, revealing a white root, almost like a leek. "There you go. You can eat that now." He'd given it a chew, then handed it to Derik. Derik had taken a bite as well, eager to forage. It was crunchy and fibrous.

"Not bad, huh?"

Derik held disdain. He took a few more chews, then spat it out. "Gross," he said.

"Kind of tastes like cucumber."

"Not really."

"Mm." George took back the plant and had another bite to prove his point.

At one time, a time they thought they yearned for, foraging was necessary for survival. These days, however, they foraged supermarkets, where the fruit was always available and ripe.

"And fifty dollars for the gas," George told the cashier.

"OK," said she.

"Oh, and two lottery tickets as well."

"Do you want to pick your numbers?"

"Yes: three, twenty-two, eight, thirteen, forty-five and twenty-six. I don't care for the others, just make them random. Also, we're here to buy tobacco. Do you still have those tubs of Canadian Classic?"

She produced one from the locked cabinet.

"Awesome. We're going to a sweat later today. We're from Vancouver. This is my son, Derik." Finally she and Derik acknowledged one another. But Derik (as usual) felt like he wasn't well received because he sneered instinctively—which she noticed and kept framed in her mind—as both he and George had ferocity within them. He abhorred his beast, but that's what it did, so he lived with it as best he could. "Do you know anything about the sweats around here?"

"There's a guy named John who runs them. Usually hosts them every Saturday."

"Oh, John—I remember him. I used to come to the sweats out here, but it's just too far usually, now, with the kids. How's he doing these days?"

"He's doing good. They have a sweat going on now, I think, over at Liam's house."

"Oh yeah, that's where they used to have them. We should go to that one too, maybe next week. What do you think, Derik? I'm trying to get the boy interested in our culture; we're both Heiltsuk, by the way."

She smiled, acknowledging the common plight. That's how George talked to anyone remotely resembling a Native.

This is so awkward. Why would she care what First Nation we are?
"Yeah, maybe," said Derik, apprehensive. "Let's see how this one goes first."

"I don't know if I have their number anymore, could you write it down for me? I'd like to give John a call."

"Sure." She ripped out a blank receipt and jotted down his digits.

The two returned to the car. "See, that's how you build connections: you just ask them a few questions and have a sense of humour. You can smile once in a while, you know, Derik; people will like you more if you smile."

Derik was offended, so continued not smiling in protest. "Hey, look!" he said, pointing to the sky. George looked up. "Some eagles."

"Oh yeah." He started the car. "That's a good sign. The ancestors must be watching over us."

They took the scenic route through the Tsawwassen reserve: past the frames of condos, totems and basketball hoops, to the train yard, and back onto the highway, spying the eagles perched atop trees and utility poles with the currents coursing through their talons. "They're probably here for salmon season—which reminds me, I was going to call up Uncle Lou and see if he'll be in town anytime soon. Maybe he can take us out fishing on his boat."

🌵 🌵 🌵

Back at home—with the tobacco, red cloth and twine gathered—they began making prayer ties. George showed Derik the way.

"Take some cloth," he said. He had cut the broad red into little squares. "Now you take a pinch of tobacco, and put it inside." He watched Derik like a hawk as he did the same. "Good. Now close it like that. Take the string and tie it around like this." He tied the bindle for the flame.

Derik held up his. "Good?"

"Yup." George held his high, closing his eyes. "Thank you, Creator. Thank you, ancestors. Thank you for allowing us to attend a sweat together. Thank you so much." He brought it to his heart. "All my relations." He opened his eyes and placed it in the middle of the table. "It's important to thank the ancestors—we're making these for them."

"How many do we have to make?"

"Sixteen; four for each direction. Don't cut the string! They all have to be connected."

Derik put down the steel shears. "Oh," he said, slightly embarrassed. "What do we do with them at the actual sweat?"

"They hang them outside the door. Once the sweat is over, we toss them in the fire as an offering."

"Like a sacrifice?"

"It's an offering to the ancestors and Creator."

"Oh. So it's kind of like a donation at church?"

"Well, they're just taking your money at church."

"No they're not—it's a donation, so they can buy cookies and things."

"Nah, the priest takes all the money and goes on a shopping spree."

They both chuckled. "How come we stopped going to church?" asked Derik.

"Because they were a bunch of racist assholes. You don't remember what the priest said about Natives?"

"... Sort of."

"He said we *deserved* to go to residential school."

"Well, maybe some of the kids liked going to residential school."

"No Derik—that's *so* wrong. Most of them were horribly abused, including my mom and me."

"I read that the Heiltsuk invited the first missionaries to Bella Bella because they wanted to learn about the missionaries' spiritual endeavours."

"Yeah, where did you read that?"

"*Dances of the Northwest Coast* by Nevar Patchwork—that book Raven brought in that I was telling you about." The book was too academic for him to comprehend fully, but he retained the evocative bits.

"Do you really think that we'd invite them here to molest and torture us? That's basically what they did, Derik: they tortured us, beat us and took our children and everything we had. Do you really think we'd ask for that?"

"I didn't say that's what we asked for, but that we were intrigued by their beliefs. Of course we didn't ask for genocide."

George tied another tie.

"OK, do we have everything?"

"Towels?"

Towels around their necks. "Check."

"Prayer ties?"

"Check."

"Cloth and tobacco for Raven?"

"Check."

They indeed had everything, including their sandals (which was always an occasion). "OK, bye Tweety." George gave Betty a peck.

"Bye. Drive safe! Don't go too fast now."

Derik hugged her. "Love you."

"Have fun," she said.

She stood by the door—watching them leave, waving—then tended her garden.

ψ ψ ψ

They arrived at the house, which was only a few blocks from the pawnshop. The sun declined, peeking over the buildings, pale yellow as new steel. A blue haze covered the walls. People crowded the streets. Took them a long time to find parking.

"Hey," George said to someone. "Is this where the sweat is happening?" He looked down and up from the directions Betty had prepared for him.

"Yeah, it is."

George made small talk like only George could make small talk while Derik performed his best nod and listen. Derik was usually well behaved, because he thought he was ill-behaved, so he'd overcompensate. They met them from all over: Musqueam, Squamish, even Tlingit. It may not seem like a big deal to you, but it's quite like a Brit dealing with an Italian: they're both proud of their differences, however subtle, even if both are (usually) considered white. Everyone was uneasy around the Haida, like being wary of a German in case of another blitz.

George jostled and Derik shimmied through the crowd, finding their way to the backyards of four houses, a medicine wheel of territories, with the sweat lodge over the merge.

"*Wow*, look at that! That's the biggest sweat lodge I've ever seen," said George. Beside it, of course, was a roaring fire. That was their first stop. They moved to the flames that several fellow sapiens were tending, feeding in sticks, prodding with pitchforks and fanning, beckoning higher. It was indeed a fat fire, well fed with the souls of air so that it rose from its lowly pit, licking level with the roofs of houses. "You see those rocks down there?" George pointed.

"Yeah," said Derik.

"Those are the grandfathers. They get them red-hot before they bring them inside." It, indeed, was quite a hellish scene: the fire keeper, the fire, the pitchfork, the lodge a mound of skins and bones, with all souls soon to be sealed in darkness. Lo, the grandfathers, their ancestors, would be the light!

"I get it: they call them grandfathers because we all came from the Earth, right?"

"Right."

"But they should be called grandmothers, 'cause Earth is feminine—like Virgo, Taurus and Capricorn. Earth is redeemed by fire to restart the cycle."

George scratched his head. "I don't know. That's just what our people always called them." He turned to the fire keeper. Derik figured he was asking too many questions, so went a-wandering. *I should ask Raven about that. I want to know his birth time so I can cast his natal chart.* He watched the helpers drape plastic tablecloths over the picnic tables.

It was half past six when the official ceremony began. Raven revealed himself, making the rounds, greeting the travellers, and took his position by the entrance to the lodge. Structurally, the lodge was a frame of saplings, bent over one another to form a dome, then draped with blankets. It was not much different than the tents and makeshift shelters one could find nearby along Hastings, which wasn't ironic if you thought about it (as they're both sensible shelters and mostly house Indigenous people). Overtop was placed the buffalo skin, the spiritual chimney, symbolic of the eastern First Nations whose traditions they borrowed. Inside, the floor was made of cedar branches with a pit in the middle for the grandfathers.

Everyone formed a circle around the fire, stripped down to their bathing suits with towels over their shoulders. Several helpers smudged the goers with sage smouldering in abalone shells, casting purifying smoke with eagle feathers. Once cleansed, they bowed and offered gifts to Raven and the ancestors which he raised to the skies, thanking the spirits, thanking the ancestors, thanking God—the Creator. One by one they crawled inside. Raven set the gifts on the altar.

13. The Sweat

Derik, you take over. Break a leg. (All right, but it's often insufficient detailing the spirit world with language.) You see how serious he gets?

❦ ❦ ❦

It sure is going to be crowded in here.

"Scoot over a bit," says Dad. "Is that as far as you can go?"

"No," I tell him, and scoot.

I can't believe they fit everyone in. I wasn't sure we were going to make it—then we could've gone home… I like being here though, now that I'm here. Sure smells nice. There's the guy with the bucket—white bucket, full of water. Hands it to Raven. He has a cedar branch, that's what Dad said they use to splash water on the rocks to generate steam; that's what makes it so hot. What a dilemma: cool the grandfathers, or keep us cool? Smells like Christmas. Raven sure is skinny, like me, but old-man skinny; I'm just kid skinny. Does that guy have a tattoo? I should get one, like Candace. Maybe I'll hit puberty if I do. I'd get a lion over my heart, or maybe an eagle over my shoulder to flow with my arm.

The Devil brings the rocks with his pitchfork. I like the grating sound. The fire is dissected—the grandfathers, the organs. They should be called grandmothers.

Don't say that, you'll just upset them by breaking tradition. Just call them grandfathers.

It's not correct though!

Maybe they have a good reason, you don't know. Ask Raven.

I will later.

The guy hands in the fork with the glowing rock on the prongs. It looks like a modern lamp, without any buttons, just pure glow. A helper takes the pitchfork and begins to pile the rocks. They roll and clack against each other and the shallow walls of the pit, casting sparks and igniting the shadows red. Luckily, I'm at the back, so people in front of me take most of the heat (ha). The last rock is brought in and they close the door. It sure is dark in here; I get only glimpses of faces.

Raven shouts a drawn-out "*Whoa*," and the helpers copy him. He splashes water on the rocks; they splatter and hiss, filling the lodge with steam. People stir and whisper to one another. The few who speak, speak out loud, as their voices are amplified by the lodge—that's how a speaker works, they amplify sound. Here we are, in the middle of sound; we are sound, vibrations contained in time and space, as Mr. Con put it. *It's dark as a dungeon, damp as the dew*—Johnny Cash, the man in black; singing helps, my heart is rushing.

Keep the towel over your head.

No, I don't want to be a coward.

Wait then, just hang your head low, behind this person, like that. There, it's cool enough. Sure is hot though. Raven lashes on more water, gathering steam clouds that fall onto us. The rocks are still so hot I can feel them from here, along with the steam against my ears. Tomorrow I have nothing to do, I can sleep and play video games all day. The women gasp and the men groan.

Just don't ask for the door, or Dad will be pissed. I'll pass out if I have to.

"*Whoa*," bellows Raven. He lashes the rocks with more water. "Thank you, Creator; thank you, Great Spirit, for being here with us. Thank you everyone for coming. This is the lodge of healing. This is the lodge of ceremony. All are welcome; we are all united here. Thank you, Creator, for allowing us to be together." I can sense where Raven is, but I can't see him—only when he lashes the rocks with water, through the people. "Great Spirit, join us! I ask for your guidance during this celebration of ours. Please educate us how to improve ourselves, to be the best we can be, so that we may go out into the world and accomplish our work. Oh Great One, oh Great Spirit, thank you. All my relations. *Heh!*" Sounds like *yay*. And the helpers all say, "*Heh!*" like birds, singing of their land, expressing their gratitude. Raven throws more water on the stones. It evaporates instantly. "Good spirits are welcome, bad spirits must leave," he says angrily. You gotta be serious with the spirits, or they won't be serious with you—at least that's what Dad told me. "Please, join us in celebrating life. Join us, guide us, help us. Let us heal ourselves the best we can; let us be enlightened to the ways we do not yet know. Be at peace, ancestors, for your children are before you with good spirits and hearts. Thank you for all you have done. Thank you for giving us life. All my relations!"

"All my relations," they say.

"All my relations," I say late, but quiet. I don't think anyone noticed.

"*Yo*," says Raven, and the rattles rattle. A flurry of drums beat. "All right—let's begin with a song."

"*Heh*," the helpers say, and a gentle response from the crowd emerges; they're starting to get involved. I always want a crowd to get involved but they never do as much as I want (to get involved fully myself). Raven begins singing quite loud. That's good, I can stop holding in now. Sounds like a lot of *Heh*s. I don't know what he's singing. I wish I knew what he's singing, I feel so stupid for not knowing Heiltsuk.

It's not Heiltsuk it's... something else.

Dad doesn't know Heiltsuk either, only maybe a few words. I know *ooligan*, and *qqs* is eyes... I think. So many languages to learn: Heiltsuk, English, French, Musqueam, Spanish even! Nevar Patchwork wrote that *Bella Bella* is Spanish for beautiful beautiful. Grandpa knows the language—wish I could ask him, but we never see him anymore. Raven continues singing, the helpers join in, a chorus of wailing voices. A few people are humming (I hope it's because they don't know the words). Grandpa can't even read. He can speak Heiltsuk, though. Maybe that's why his voice is so deep. He looks like the

Godfather. Mom loves that movie. It's a classic film. Don Corleone came from Sicily, didn't he, like Gino? I think so, but I'm not sure.

Dad said he saw a guy turn into a wolf once and start howling during a sweat. Yeah right; that's insane. Imagine turning into Redbird right now (oh, I was going to ask Raven about that too!), and flying out of here, screeching, "Open the door!" circling the ceiling until they let you out, then soaring to the stratosphere with the spirits, all the way to heaven. *Stairway to Heaven* is such a great song, I love Led Zeppelin. Can't wait to listen to that on the way home. Maybe I'll fall asleep again with the streetlights going by. "You'll sleep good tonight," Dad said.

A woman groans—a zombie. Something bad is about to happen. Chow about to attack. She does it again, but louder. She screams... Now she's crying. Shadow goes bye-bye. I miss Shadow, he was my brother.

Why did he fall down the stairs?

'Cause he had a seizure. We had to put him down, Dad said. Shadow leapt out the door, chasing the dog that would bite me. He knew that chow was bad.

She keeps screaming and crying about something. A lot of these women are from the Downtown Eastside—troubled, perhaps addicts (like Aunt Lizzy), prostitutes or homeless. Dad never talks to Aunt Lizzy anymore. Imagine having a sister and not seeing her anymore; that'd be pretty mean... yet good.

The song stops with a final "*Wah*" from Raven and his backing band.

She's still crying. I can faintly see her head down in her hands and someone comforting her.

"Open the door," someone says.

"Open the door!" commands Raven. The fire keeper outside opens the door. All the heat I was loving leaves. She crawls on her hands and knees the short way round, widdershins, which is offensive, but they want her out so don't mind. I see the fire flicker outside. The door is closed again as the round isn't over. Raven sprinkles tobacco on the stones. It smells spicy and fragrant, like Grandma's house, plus some other herbs I don't know.

"*Yo,*" calls Raven. "Creator, thank you for the heat, thank you for the grandfathers."

"*Heh,*" call the helpers.

"May this lodge be filled with good spirits who will help us heal and not hinder us along our way to finding true sanctuary and peace in our lives, oh Creator."

"*Heh.*"

"This is the time for healing and thanking the Creator, for none of us would be here without them. I thank them for allowing us to be here, together." He keeps saying his prayers. I don't pray. Not since I left church. I don't want to pray. I don't even believe in God. The Creator is God. I cursed God; what did he do for me? My dog died. I got mauled by a dog. I don't have any armpit hair when all my friends do. I get teased at school. I have to go to a different school than all my friends. Life sucks. What proof do I have that God exists? I've never seen him, and no one can prove they have. They're all crazy who say they've seen God. I hope I don't have to say a prayer. I don't want to speak to these people.

"Thank you, Creator. All my relations."

"All my relations."

"We will now pass the talking stick, so that everyone may share why they are here. Only they who have the talking stick may speak, while all else listen. If you don't wish to speak, you may pass it on to the next person. Thank you."

Dammit, this is what I was scared of. They pass the talking stick around. We share why we're here. People are from all over, for many different reasons, mostly boring or sad. I hate when tanks hide in the brush. Just stay in the lane, let me clear the creeps, then get the orbs. It's that easy. I finally get the stick.

"I'm here because I want to learn the traditions of our people." That should please them.

You sound stupid.

"*Woah,*" goes Raven. Moans of approval and judgment.

"I'm also here 'cause my dad made me." Everyone laughs.

"Good, good."

"Thank you, and all my relations." I pass the stick.

Once everyone shares (which takes forever), they pour a bunch of water on the rocks. "This song is called 'Thank You Song.' Feel free to join in. This is where we thank the grandfathers."

"*Heh,*" they say. They start singing.

It sounds similar to the first, but the tempo is lower, less intense. They beat their drums and shake their rattles. Some begin to lash out as counterpoint, like wolves howling and crows cawing. This is pretty exciting. Pretty crazy. I wish I had an instrument. I wish I had my flute, though I don't think it would work well in here. It'd probably get so hot it would burn my lips. Raven lashes on more water, more water on the glow, generating more and more steam. I cover my head with my towel, hold it low. I can't even see Dad beside me, but I know he's there. It's so hot in here. I hope it doesn't get any hotter; my ears, face and nose burn. The sauna is nothing compared to this.

You should keep breathing.

I take in deep breaths while covering my mouth with the towel, trapping the cool air near my face and chest. I don't know how much more of this I can take. Their voices are getting louder; they're getting more primal, like a jungle rich with wild sounds. I hold my breath, hold it, hold it, then let it out. They can't hear me, it's so loud in here now. I do it again—hold it in, hold it in, let it out—again and again.

Focus on your heart beating with the drums.

"*Ay! Oh,*" says Raven. "Thank you, Grandfathers, all my relations."

"All my relations!"

"OK." He sounds so happy. "Open the door!"

"Open the door!" The door is opened. The hot air rushes out. The sword is quenched. We all crawl out, one after the other. Steam rises from us into the cool night.

"You know, you shouldn't say that. That I *made* you come here," says Dad.

"Oh, sorry. They thought it was funny."

"*Woo.*" He looks around. "Man, it was starting to get hot in there, then that crazy woman called for the door." He's so embarrassing sometimes. "So what did you think?"

"It was fun. It wasn't as hot as I thought it'd be."

"Don't worry, it only gets hotter."

"Great."

There's that woman who was crying, I think. Be nice. Another woman holds her to her breast. See the suffering in her eyes—she wants it. Dad turns sharply away from her. "Oh my God," he says, subduing his surprise. He asks if I see her.

"Yeah."

"That's my sister, Lizzy."

"Really?"

He looks over his shoulder, then turns back to me. "Yeah—that's her all right. Man, she looks terrible."

So that's Aunt Lizzy: the drug addict, the witch, the villain… She looks so sad though. She has pockmarks all over her face. "Should we say hello?"

"No! Let's just leave her alone," he says like a child.

Why not though? She's your sister.

Just leave it.

"Here, let's go," says Dad. "I want to ask Raven something."

I follow him. Raven seems busy, talking to so many different people. I wish I knew him better. Dad says to him, "Hey, I really liked that last song you sang. It was very powerful."

"Thank you," he says, sincere.

"Is there anywhere I can find the lyrics for it?" Dad chuckles. "I'm not exactly sure what you were saying."

"Sure. I can get you a translation, if you want."

"That'd be great, 'cause I'd really like to learn the words."

"Not a problem. I have your email. I'll send them to you."

"Thanks. Everything is going really great so far. I really like what you said about the grandfathers and how we all originated from them."

"Nice. It's true, isn't it? We all originated from the Earth."

"Then why aren't they called grandmothers?" I ask him. "Isn't Earth considered feminine, like Mother Earth?"

He smiles. "You know, I wondered that too, but no one ever mentioned it, so I just follow tradition. I think, maybe because the rocks are hot, they resemble fire—they were once molten, remember—which is masculine."

"Oh… That makes sense."

"I suppose grandparents would be more appropriate, but I try to stick to tradition when possible. We're already breaking the rules a bit by having everyone in one lodge. I was… No, I better not say."

"Why?" I ask. "What were you going to say?"

"It's just, some sweat lodges are kept secret, so I don't want to reveal too much. Sometimes you're not even allowed to post a photo on Facebook. I went to one sweat where they had two lodges, one for women and the other for men. I try to bring everyone together, so that's why we just have the one lodge."

"I see."

Ask him about Redbird; ask him about me.

No, not now. He'll think you're cringe.

"I've never been to a sweat this big before," says Dad. "Usually it's just seven or eight people."

"We only started with a few, then more and more came as word got out. We keep having to make it bigger and bigger."

"It's amazing you can fit them all inside."

"Yeah."

"Really adds to the experience, with everyone chanting together. My whole body was vibrating."

"Yeah, that's the idea: vibrations heal the body, along with the heat and sweat… Good vibrations, that is."

"You know, I was watching a show on the History Channel, where they said Stonehenge was meant to reflect vibrations to heal whoever was inside."

"Right."

"Same thing with the Great Pyramids. Apparently inside they have hidden chambers made of quartz that attune you to a certain frequency."

Not as cringe as Dad, though. I was thinking about speakers; the lodge is an amphitheatre.

"Yes, I've heard that," says Raven.

"I really think it's just a hidden alien base where they can talk to aliens. It's also supposed to be a generator, but they haven't figured out how to use it yet because that knowledge was lost thousands of years ago."

"He always makes it about aliens," I say.

"That's interesting. Did you two bring any instruments with you?"

"*No.* the boy likes playing the flute at home, but he can't play a thing like that in there." You don't bring white instruments to Native events.

"You should look into getting him a wood flute. That'd be really cool. Everyone either has a rattle or drum, but I've heard lots of Indigenous recordings with a flute. I think it's more of a South American thing, but whatever."

"That's not a bad idea."

"Yeah, that'd be sweet," I say. "But I was reading *The Book of Thoth,* and they said the flute is associated with Pan, and Pan is the Devil—I drew that card the other day. Does that mean I'm evil?"

Raven smirks. "No! Don't think of it like that; there are pros and cons to every card. The Devil is your urge to assert your will, it's a part of everyone's psyche. You just gotta roll with it. Concern yourself with what you *can* control, and let fate do the rest, is what I say."

Damn, that's true. I never thought of it that way.

"In the meantime, here." He hands Dad the rattle. "Use my rattle. I brought two."

"Oh, no, give it to him." Dad thumbs to me. "I can't use a thing like that, I don't have any rhythm." Raven gives me the rattle instead.

Wow! That's pretty cool. Belongs in a tourist shop. No, this is legit: that's real horn and leather. "Thanks! What's it made of?"

"That's a deer antler, and the bulb is made of hide from the same deer—it's important to use the whole animal."

There are strips of hide hanging from where the two pieces meet, with beads of yellow, red, black and white like the medicine wheel.

"That's a great honour you know, using a shaman's rattle," Dad says.

Raven smiles.

Show your appreciation.

"Thank you," say I. Unconvinced. "I feel very privileged."

"You're welcome." He looks around. "All right everyone," he announces. "The second round is about to begin." ·

We line up, and one by one, crawl back in. They bring in fresh rocks, piling them on the old ones, which are now grey, though still warm. Raven announces this is the men's round. "This is the round where we thank the male aspect in all of us. In our culture, everyone has a masculine side to them; this round isn't just for the men, but for everyone. We believe the male side represents willpower, philosophy and fire. So, Great Spirit, join us, and show us the way to enlightenment and appreciation of everything masculine in our lives and inside each and every one of us. *Yo!*"

"*Yo!*"

"All my relations."

"All my relations."

He lashes the rocks with water, creating more steam than ever. Already it's hotter than before, steam stinging every part of me. They start singing, fast and intense. The round begins.

I am inside you. I am the first: alpha, aleph, Adam, the ox head. From the dirt, I came, from the Great Sea, I swam; I am the male in all of you. Bow down before us. You will do what we say. We give you will, and will to act—the power and energy to go forth—bow down to no other. No fault is of your own, but due to false connections, because we are the will and the will is life; without us, you are naught. I go freely in and through your mind; I tell you all I am, which is perfect. Listen to me—listen to me!—I am yours and you are mine—there is no difference.

I rode the backs of snakes, I scaled mountains. I began your chain and kissed you when you were born. I slept beside you while you cooed and sucked your thumb, gazing up to the mobile, moving through stars, finding yourself, realizing how it began, and there I was, carrying you to and fro, invisible—not what you thought, yet you soared, free as a bird.

You are inoculated. (Gotcha!) Dance with your thoughts.

What a weird thing to think. It's like, where do thoughts come from? They seem to come out of thin air.

That guy sounds like a horse, and Raven does sound like a raven, cawing, raspy. I hope it gets hotter, honestly; it's not that hot. I'm not that hot. I could use some more water on the rocks, and he does it; Raven lashes more water on the rocks. Steam rises with my thoughts. What a silly thing to think. I must be a genius. *No one I think is in my tree.* I mean, I'm either really smart or really stupid—depends on the day I guess.

The dog attacked me, ripped open my arm (I needed fifty stitches—counted them every day). I kicked it and rolled over, then it went for my balls; that hurt the most! Everything else was just numb. I was in shock. Then my neighbour, the blonde-haired angel, hit the dog with the wagon and yelled until it scurried back into the house with its tail between its legs. It must have eaten my flesh though, because they wanted to reattach it but couldn't find it. Son of a bitch. That's why my left arm is shorter than the right.

No, it's not. Don't be stupid.

Now it's hot in here. If I went through that, I can endure a sweat. Dad sprays so much eucalyptus water on the rocks at the sauna anyway; it feels like this. This heat is more radiant 'cause all the people are hot, so it's a more persistent heat than the sauna.

The song ends.

"Thank you, Creator. All my relations."

"All my relations!"

"Now we will take time to say thanks, and show appreciation for the male aspect in all of us (and for the males in our lives) by passing around the talking stick. Remember, if you don't wish to speak, just say thanks, and pass the stick to your left. Thank you."

They pass around the talking stick. People thank their fathers, grandfathers, *the* grandfathers, the will to act, brothers, uncles, cousins, friends—everything male. Lady crying, trying to speak—Aunt Lizzy again? Sounds like it.

Baying tears. "…I'm thankful for my Dad… He was the greatest man I ever knew."

Was?

"I'm sorry… He passed away last week… from a heart *attack*." She breaks down.

Grandpa's dead? Is that actually Aunt Lizzy? She keeps crying and crying.

"I'm sorry… I shouldn't be here right now."

Someone calls for the door. They all call for the door. The door is opened and she crawls out. It's Aunt Lizzy—I see the fire flicker on half her face.

"*Ay!*" they chant.

Someone whispers too loudly to Raven, "We can't keep letting her back in here; she has bad spirits with her and we keep having to let all the hot air out."

"I know, I know. I'll talk to her once the round is over. Everyone, it is very sad to see one of us experience such grief and sadness—that is why we're here together, to *heal* through our sorrows. Unless someone else wishes to speak, we will continue with a song to purge the negative spirits that have followed some of us here. Speak now. Don't hold it in."

They pass the talking stick. A few more people speak about their dead relatives or friends. This is a sad place to be; I can feel the negativity.

"All right," says Raven. "Thank you for sharing. This song is for the male aspects. *Lo!* Let it be sung!"

"*Lo!*"

He lashes the rocks with water. I thought they were dead; they are still hot. Steam burns my face. Wait, so Grandpa's dead? Good; I never knew him.

That's not nice to think.

Raven sings aggressively. I'm scared.

You have to wait.

🌵 🌵 🌵

The round ends. They open the door. All the spirits rush out. Where's Aunt Lizzy? No point in hurrying. I wait for everyone to crawl by, feeling the cool air rush in. My shorts are soaked.

Dad leans toward me. "Holy cow, Derik, that round I saw an eagle covering you with its wings. I swear to God." He shakes his head. "It had its wings wrapped around you like a shield." He shows me; his arms are wings.

He's being crazy again, but I think they endorse it. "Nice," I say. "That's pretty cool."

"Yup. That must be your guardian then—an eagle. It was watching over you, Derik." If he only knew.

"So is Grandpa dead? That was Aunt Lizzy, right, the lady who was crying?"

"I don't think that was her. Someone would've told me if Grandpa was dead."

"I'm pretty sure that was her."

"No, must've been someone else."

"Are you sure?"

"Yeah, I'm sure," he says, mad. He crawls to the entrance.

It was dark, he didn't see her.

He's in denial.

I mean, it could've been someone else, I'm not sure. I follow him out.

I look for Aunt Lizzy but can't find her. She must've gone inside, or left. Is there a shower here, or do we just go home soaked in sweat?

Round three is for the female aspect in all of us. Raven lashes the grandfathers. I don't think it can get much hotter, but I was proven wrong the last time.

"We all have women in our lives, we all have a feminine side to us, *despite* our gender," Raven says. "Nurture, our emotions and feelings, the waves of the Great Sea—these are all feminine aspects. We care for one another; we take care of ourselves. We all floated in the sea of the womb within our mothers. Long, long ago, millions of years ago, our ancestors, the first to walk the land, ventured forth from the ocean, the water. Water gave birth to us as a species. Now we pay homage to the feminine. This round we give thanks to the females inside and around all of us. Thank you, Great Mother, Mother Earth, for nurturing us and giving us life. This round is for you. All my relations."

"All my relations!" The women are more vocal and intense. "*Heh!*" they say, then more.

Raven starts the song, sonorous and sweet. There are many yips and hollers. The tempo is more relaxed this time, and the rhythm sparser. If only I could tell what he was saying—sounds important.

I think I'm pretty feminine, but not *gay*. Chris has a girlfriend already—he's going out with Sylvia; they were holding hands when we were walking back from McDonald's. I wish I had a girlfriend—no, I don't, why would I have a girlfriend now? I have too much homework, a job and friends to hang out with.

A girlfriend is a friend though. It's just a friend who's a girl.

Yeah, but it implies more than that; you hug and kiss them and stuff.

You can hang out with them with your friends.

I don't think I'm attractive enough to have a girlfriend; they all think I'm ugly. I'm good at things, though: I can play sports, make art, work, pay for their food, do their math homework. They just say I'm cute, and that's it; they never think I'm hot or anything. Well, there was that one girl at Watermania who said I was hot but she was just being weird. I'm certainly not like Chris who can ask girls out all the time and they accept... I'll never be that way. I don't think I'll ever have children—I don't think anyone *would* with me. I shouldn't bring another Mormin into this world; they'd have to deal with too much racism and drama like me.

They'll only get status if you marry another Native.

I don't want to marry another Native. Candace is crazy. She threatened me with a knife once, then kicked me in the balls. It's getting hot in here.

I fly with silver wings. I am before you. I am the beacon of light all cherish; hope and peace are my tenements. I am come! Love me! Love me! Be not ashamed! Embrace me beneath my stars. To take your fill and be adored is the greatest act. All have done and gone since the beginning; all are nothing without me. I am Aphrodite, love is a middle name! I carry myself upon the celestial dew, to you, to you—do you dare refuse? Woe to whoever would refuse beauty so adorned at their door, ringing the bell, calling, calling, "I am here for you!"

I am the gentle poet, who tickles your ear; your skin tingles as I trace veins down to your hand. Touch me! Feel me! Let pleasure bloom throughout you. I love you; love me—love me—and be not ashamed.

The spirits all show up to play; yet, to them, you ascribe such seriousness. Freely they go through your porous mind, mingling with thought. Make them not precious! You will see people turn to animals, while we pass over in an instant. But thoughts keep flowing, each as good as the last, as the world keeps turning and the universe returns to the beginning. Bathe in the stars, let them wash over you! Transient glimpses into the realm of spirit and soul are constant. Do not discern, only observe! Appreciate the inner workings of God!

They pass around the talking stick.

"I want to thank my mom. She's the best mom I could've asked for. She takes care of me, drives me to school, buys me new clothes. I'd be nothing without her. Thank you, Mom." That was easy. Easy speaking the truth. Met with some cheers and confirmations. I pass the stick to Dad.

"I'm so grateful for my wife. We've been through hard times together, and she's always been there for me. I can't wait to spend the rest of my life with her. I'd also like to thank my mom, who died when I was young. I never got to say goodbye. I love you, Mom. I know you're out there." He tears up. So sad.

I'd probably join a gang if I lost my mom.

No you wouldn't, you're such a mama's boy.

I could be mean! Especially if the world owed me money.

No you couldn't.

I mean it!

This round's for the moms. (Mine's the best.)

🌱 🌱 🌱

Outside is Aunt Lizzy, hunched in her lawn chair with her towel around her back. The other lady is comforting her.

"I still think that was Aunt Lizzy who said her dad died," I tell Dad. "Should we go ask her?"

"No," he says, shaking his head. "I don't want to talk to her."

"But what if Grandpa's *dead*? Wouldn't you want to know?"

"He's not dead, Derik. Now quit bothering me; you're really starting to piss me off."

"Fine, I'll ask her." I go over to her. She's scared of something. "Hello… I'm sorry to hear that your dad died."

Her sadness lessens. She seems angry. "Nice to see you, Derik." Oh, she remembers me. How though? I was just a baby when she last saw me. Probably recognized Dad.

"Hello Aunt Lizzy. I wasn't sure if you'd remember me."

"I know who you are. Tell your *dad* our dad is dead. He died of a heart attack last week."

"Oh, OK. I'll tell him. I'm sorry to hear that."

"You know, he wanted to see you before he died... but your dad kept rejecting his calls."

I didn't know that. "They didn't get along too well."

"Well, he's gone now." Her chin quivers. "You'll never see him again." She sobs, her face in her hands. The other lady rubs her back, comforting her. I don't know what to say or do.

Should I hug her? No, I don't know her well enough. Should I say anything? What though, I love you? No, that'd be weird.

Correct your posture. Should I leave now? No, they'll think I'm mean.

They already think you're a creep.

I say, "I'm sorry," and pat her on the back. She cries harder. That didn't help anything. I return to Dad.

Don't tell him, he'll only freak out. She wasn't very nice.

She's grieving. How would you feel if your dad died?

I'd be very sad.

Didn't seem as mean as Dad made her out to be. Remember that action figure she got you for Christmas?

The final round is starting. We line up to enter.

With the sweat finished, we say our goodbyes—lots of hugs—then find our car.

"Man, that was great," says Dad. "Did you see how they tossed all the prayer ties in the fire at the end?"

"Yeah."

"That's them offering them to the ancestors... There, aren't you glad you went? You'll sleep well tonight, boy."

"Yeah. It was an interesting experience."

"Next time we'll bring our own instruments. Raven said he can get me a drum made with real elk skin." He looks at me with wide eyes, nodding, then a thumbs-up. "Pretty groovy, man. And, *and*, he said he'll give you one of his own rattles. Cool, huh?"

"*Yeah* ... That's pretty cool."

Lots of people out—Saturday night. I wait till we get home to break the news so he doesn't rage in a cage.

"So how was it?" Mom asks when we get home.

"Good—" He tells her all about it.

"Did you have fun?" she asks me.

"Yeah ... So Grandpa's dead."

"What?"

"Grandpa's dead. We saw Aunt Lizzy there, and she told me, personally, to tell Dad that Grandpa's dead. So here I am."

"Was she really there?" she asks Dad.

Dad nods. "Yeah. I didn't speak to her, though."

"So she told you Grandpa was dead?"

"Yeah. She was crying the whole time, and kept asking for the door. Then I went up to her and told her, 'Sorry to hear about your dad.' Then she confirmed that Grandpa's really dead."

"She was always a liar," Dad says. He empties his Thermos in the sink.

"She wouldn't lie about that, George. You should phone one of your relatives up north to see."

"I *am* going to," he says.

"OK."

"Why did you stop talking to Grandpa?" I ask. "She said he tried to call you."

"Because he was a terrible father and grandfather. He was so abusive to me and Auntie Sammy. I thought *maybe* he could be a better grandfather by coming to visit you and Candace, but he never did. The only time he showed up for Candace's birthday, he gave her a twenty and told her not to complain when he didn't show up again. He was an asshole. That's why I stopped taking his calls. Any more questions?"

Careful, he's mad.

"You know, I worked for him my entire life, and not *once* did he say thanks, or that he loved me. He promised to give us the herring licence—'cause he figured the money would make up for his actions—but you know who he ended up giving it to?"

Don't say anything.

I shake my head. "No."

"He gave it to Aunt Lizzy's kids: Blair and Anton. That was hundreds of thousands of dollars that was supposed to be *our* inheritance that I worked my entire life for."

"Maybe they need it more than us?"

That was stupid. Why'd you say that? Now he's really mad.

He straightens up, eyes of onyx. "He promised us the licence, Derik. He lied to me my *whole* life with hollow promises. He's not a good person." His tone drops. "You have no idea what he did to me when I was a kid, all the abuse I suffered to get to where I am now, so that you can have a good life." He goes upstairs to make some phone calls (I think).

"He always gets so mad when I bring up Grandpa," I tell Mom.

She rolls her eyes and shakes her head. "They've always been that way—such a dysfunctional family."

I watch her clean his Thermos and tell her what else happened.

14. Glory Days

Raven entered the temple in black robes. He stood before the masters with bowed head.

"It is done: the boy has been initiated into the beautiful, brave and free."

"Excellent," said Uniwon. "Have the boy and his father heard the news of Talking Eagle?"

"Yes, but they still deny his death. I'm unsure they'll attend his celebration."

"They won't deny fact," said Arconis. "They will be convinced to go."

"Very good," said Raven.

"Verily."

Up he looked. "Am I to go with them?"

"Of course—it is your mission to restore order by upholding the bargain of their ancestors."

"What made it a bargain?"

"Talking Eagle worked tirelessly to preserve history and tradition up and down the coast. We now repay him down the line, life after life."

"Yea. I understand. I will return north."

"When you go, we will put you in contact with Herxhlt," said Uniwon. "He will show you potential locations for a hermitage where you may meditate upon your great work in peace."

"Thank you. I am forever grateful. Will shall be law."

"Love under will."

Raven bowed in the candle's flame.

"Where's Candace?" Derik asked over dinner.

"At soccer practice," said Betty.

"That's cool."

"No, it's warm."

"If you had any respect for me, you'd come and see your dead grandpa with me," said George.

"Quit bugging me about that. You didn't even like him!"

"It doesn't matter whether I liked him or not, he was my dad. I *have* to go. If I don't, everyone in Bella Bella will be mad at me."

"Who cares? It doesn't sound like a nice place." *That's not true.* "There are ghosts and bears and smallpox."

"There isn't smallpox there anymore," said Betty. "Don't be silly."

"Why are they on lockdown then, while the rest of the world reopens?"

"Because Indigenous people are more protective of who they let in. They've suffered enough."

"What if I get possessed? You wouldn't let us visit Grandma Julia's grave until we were baptized. What makes you think I'll be safe in Bella Bella?"

"You'll be fine," said George. "I'll protect you. Nothing can harm you there."

"There's no way Mrs. Crosschuk will let me miss school. She already hates me."

"No she doesn't," said Betty. "She's just looking out for you."

Derik shook his head. "I don't think so; she's evil."

"Yeah, if she can't let you miss a few days of school to attend your grandpa's funeral, then she's evil," said George.

"OK!" Betty glared. "That's enough. She's a good teacher. Candace liked her a lot."

"It's not fair Candace gets to miss school to play soccer if I don't get to go see my grandpa one last time."

"You can't go to Bella Bella anyway," said Betty. "They're not letting anyone in."

"Even a status card–carrying Indian like myself?"

"No, Derik."

"They'll let us in," said George. "They can't stop us from attending my dad's funeral over a *cold*. I'm going no matter what—even if it means chartering my own boat because the damn ferries won't take us."

"Isn't there someone who can take you? I thought all your relatives had boats," said Derik. *Grandpa was never there for me. Why see his corpse?*

You should go.

Why?

Respect thy father and thy mother.

He was my grandpa though, that doesn't count.

You'd get to miss school.

"I'll phone up my cousin Benny. He mentioned he was heading up north for some seaweed and ooligan grease. I bet he's going to the funeral."

"No, George, they're not letting *anyone* in."

"I don't *care*, Betty. They can't stop me from attending my own dad's funeral."

"Fine. Whatever. You leave Derik out of this, though. He has to finish his assignments and graduate." Betty never wanted anything to do with Bella Bella, as it was a strange, foreign land to her, full of wackos like George. "Plus he has to go to his high school orientation."

God, I don't want to go to that orientation. Everyone's going to a different high school than me. I'll be a loner all over again. "I could ask Mrs. Crosschuk if I could get my final assignments early so I can finish them before we go—that way I'm not missing much, just the orientation. They just show you around the school, then give you hot dogs."

"No, you should go to that—it's important," said Betty. "Then you can find out where your classes will be, and maybe make new friends. You also get to meet your teachers for the first time."

Derik tried not to look frightened. "But Mom, I won't know anyone! It's going to be so awkward, me just sitting there while everyone else talks to their friends."

"Introduce yourself! Who knows, maybe you'll meet someone you really like."

"I've never been to Bella Bella, though. This might be my only chance to go."

"You've been there. We brought you there when you were a baby."

Derik riffled through memories. "I don't remember that."

"You were too young to remember."

"I think that's a good idea," said George. "Ask your teacher if you can get the assignments to finish them early."

"But he's graduating soon. He only has a few weeks of school left, then he's done. His education is more important than going to Bella Bella."

"Mom, school is boring. It's such a waste of time."

"No it's not."

"Yes, it *is*. The assignments are a joke. Why do I have to learn to draw ovoids? They're just pandering to Indigenous people 'cause they feel guilty for what their ancestors did to us in residential schools. They don't actually care about me."

They ruminated a dinner of rice, dried seaweed, canned salmon and ooligan grease.

"Fine. But you make sure you ask her for *everything* you're going to miss, and tell her where you're going and how long you'll be gone for, OK? You have to make sure everything is handed in and completed before you go, if you even *can* go." She turned to George. "You don't even know how you'll be getting there."

"Oh, we're going all right," said George. "Even if it's the last thing I do."

Derik asked Mrs. Crosschuk the next day.

"You couldn't have picked a worse time to leave, Derik," she said. "You have to complete your final social studies project, which is a group project, but you'd have to do it on your own, and then we're studying for the cumulative math test, which is on *everything* we've studied so far throughout the year, *plus* the algebra we'll be looking at this week."

"I'll do whatever it takes to see my grandpa one last time," said Derik. "My dad really wants me to go."

"All right, but I'm not sure you'll be able to complete all the work you have to do to graduate." She was, of course, motivating him with shame.

"I'll do it if it's the last thing I do."

"OK," she said. "I hope so."

She gave him the sheets.

Yes indeed, Derik had his work cut out for him. He had to present a PowerPoint on an ancient civilization of his choosing, and write a paper based on his thesis: the ancient Greeks were like the Heiltsuk. It was not a vague thesis for grade seven, as it allowed him to correlate how the Greeks and Heiltsuk both had an oral storytelling tradition, progressive women's rights and successful militaristic societies. You see, two of the oldest stories of Western civilization, the *Iliad* and the *Odyssey* (both by Homer), were originally spoken or sung. Yes, someone memorized (oh sweet mnemonics!) all fifteen thousand plus lines of the Trojan War, then some twelve thousand lines of Odysseus's homecoming, proving how sound instigates memory, like humming that ol' tune, or catching tigers by their toes. They *did* improvise to suit their audience—an advantage of oral storytelling. As for progressive women's rights, everyone knows the men went out killing (for hunt or war) leaving women to politic, as was the case with Spartan society (Sparta was a prominent city-state in Greece, though at times reluctant as any First Nation under the umbrella of Canada). Derik also related himself to the boy in *300* who staves off the wolf as part of his initiation.

Every waking minute not spent in school, eating or sleeping, Derik worked on his assignments, motivated by future adventures on a boat, travelling to the promised land of the Eagle, Raven, Orca and Wolf. He told all his friends and reminded himself over and over to remain determined. He worked and he worked through the week, chipping away at social studies, math, ADST, art, French and even PE, practising his stretches in the mirror. And you know what? It wasn't even a rush job, friends; no, he *excelled*.

"Derik, this is the best work you've done all year," said Mrs. Crosschuk, pulling him aside during work block.

"Really?" he said. "I worked every minute I could on them."

"*Yes*! It just goes to show what you're capable of when you actually put your mind to it."

"Yeah," said Derik, rubbing his neck. *I have to be inspired, otherwise I don't care and then everything is crap.* It certainly seemed to be the case. He knew he could bust out fractions whenever he needed to, even if he didn't want to, because he was highly intuitive. He simply couldn't be bothered with homework, as it was usually arbitrary. His mind rationalized lack of motivation as an excuse not to do something he didn't want to do.

Perhaps it was complacency that drove Derik to rebel intellectually against his overlords. He felt himself smarter than they, as if he knew something they didn't and would never. That something was quite difficult to define: perhaps it was the life of a dualist, merging the Western and Indigenous worlds, that not many understood or experienced, because to manifest a dualist as such required soloists as mother and father. Of course, it was possible to maintain dualism down the bloodline, though it tended to reconcile back to homogeny. Yes, perhaps that was that something, but environmental and societal factors were also at play. He did have three near-death experiences (at least, that's what he told people) in his formative years, when mind and being were most easily impressed. Then again, all visions and minds are unique, and none will comprehend the other for certain, so what he stumbled upon was universal.

The first time occurred when he nearly drowned, as previously mentioned, leaving him traumatized. He would scream uncontrollably when he couldn't stand in the pool, at the denunciation of his friend's mom, who'd taken them swimming one afternoon, forcing him to wear a life jacket and float in the deep end, both him and her oblivious to the source of fear.

"You're fine, look—Luke isn't screaming," she'd said. "You have a life jacket on," she'd said.

Yet he screamed!

The second time occurred after he'd traded rice crackers (which his mom often packed for him) for cookies. Little did he know, the cookies must've had peanuts in them, as his throat immediately began closing. He was only seven, so had no idea what was going on. He tried gargling, he tried eating cool melon, he even tried desperately hugging his chair to force open his lungs (which obviously didn't work). No one, including him, knew he was going into anaphylactic shock. He made it through the rest of the school day to his baby-sitter's; she noticed he was acting strange, but he was always acting strange, so she drank in her office. When his mom picked him up, his babysitter told her, "I don't get why he's blue." Just kidding—but it was pretty obvious. George ran reds racing him to the hospital, which Derik didn't remember, as he'd blacked out. His parents were cry-ing, thinking they were the worst parents in the world, until Derik, moments after the doctor administered epinephrine, rose, alert as can be, and started playing Lego.

"First-time parents, huh?" the doctor had said.

The third and final time (I hope) has been partially detailed by Derik already. A chow chow attacked him and ripped apart his arm (among other parts). Chow chows of course look cute and fluffy, with their purple tongues, but are notoriously territorial. Their thick manes and ferocity earned them the nickname Lions of the Chinese, as they were commonly used in warfare hundreds of years ago, mak-ing them one of the oldest known dog breeds.

Derik spent hours in plastic surgery, having his skin pulled, tucked and stitched back to form, leaving a dent where the flesh once was. He lost a lot of blood, and could've easily died if the dog had clamped down on his neck or severed an artery. Fortunately, his kar-ate training saved him, as he was able to block and kick the dog off, buying him time and protecting his vitals. His training, in fact, continued to benefit him post-surgery, as (after hours of physiotherapy, spent dunking his wounded arm in hot water and slowly extending it, little by little, to regain function) he regained strength by climbing pines and throwing punches in the dojo. He eventually won a gold medal for his Pinan Sono Ichi, competing in the National Kyokushin Championship for synchronized kata—despite facing adults with brown and black belts—making his sensei proud, and bringing a tear to George's eye.

He had also been shocked by sticking a paper clip in an outlet, fallen into a fish tank, climbed out the window (having decoded the locking mechanism), choked on ham and learned to tell time, all before the age of five.

Yes, he was quite the plutonian child, Derik, dancing with death so many times. Overall, these environmental factors, combined with his uncommon genes, did much to hone him into a person few could empathize with.

"You don't like TV?" they would say. "How come you no sit?"

He was capable of great focus and work when in the mood, which wasn't very often, because few things stimulated him as much as his prior experiences, or owning noobs in *Heroes of the Storm*. It was a curse, but also a gift, to be content not doing anything, living in colour.

Derik had completed his final assignments with passion and diligence, as he did with the comic book drawings he sold to peers for a few dollars each. Now that his schoolwork was taken care of, the question remained: How would they *actually* get to Bella Bella? Many First Nations had closed their borders mid-lockdown, with COVID as their excuse. They were finally free of tourists stealing their fish.

Jokes aside, even the weekly ferry stopped travelling to Bella Bella. The residents didn't seem to mind, as many had boats and got most of their food from the surrounding sea, but it affected the Mormins. They could no longer easily acquire their staple diet of sockeye, or roe on kelp (a specialty made by pickling herring eggs laid on kelp) due to living off reserve, dim relations and now lockdown. They could buy a bell pepper for cheap, and watch the Canucks lose, but it was proving quite the challenge finding transportation to Henry's funeral.

"I'd take you," said Cousin Benny to George over the phone, "if I was anywhere near Vancouver. But Alise won't let me. I was planning on going last week."

"Oh damn, eh? Sometimes I wish they'd stay out of our business," said George.

"Yeah, that's never gonna happen."

And they laughed. They laughed like babies laugh.

Relative after relative George called, but no one was near the city, so no one could take him to the promised land.

"I thought for *sure* someone would be able to give us a ride," he said Friday over dinner. Betty and Derik both figured this was it—the plan would fall through. The funeral was scheduled for July 1. Time was fading. Then he said something they'd never even considered: "I think I'm going to buy a boat."

"What?" said Betty. "Uh, no you're not."

"Mhm," he said as manically as anyone could utter those two syllables. "It's time I invested in a boat. There's no better time than now: we can go up to Bella Bella, we can go on vacation, we can go wherever we want. The government wants us to stay away from others, so we can picnic on some remote beach somewhere and go sportfishing!"

"You're *not* getting a boat," Betty said. Her guard was up.

"How are you going to get the money to buy a boat?" asked Derik, not thinking it was a bad idea, but, overall, respecting the common sense of his mother (as she was usually right).

"I have some money saved up. Don't worry about it. I sold the Boer rifle the other day. I have enough to afford a boat if I jolly well please. I've always wanted a boat, and now seems like the perfect time to buy one."

"How much does a boat cost?"

George vented steam. "I was looking at a thirty-foot Bayliner with twin Cummins diesel the other day, and the guy was asking seventy thousand for it."

"Seventy thousand? That's a lot of money for something we'll only use once," said Derik.

"What do you mean? We'll take it out every weekend. Quit being a smart-ass."

"Not when we go to the sweat lodge," Derik muttered.

"You have to get moorage for it and they're a ton of work to maintain," said Betty. "It's way too much, George. You're not getting a boat. We talked about this; it's a waste of money. And you think you're going to drive it up to Bella Bella? You haven't driven a boat in years."

"I can do it, it's like riding a bike! I have my captain's licence for Christ's sake; I'm more than qualified to pilot a boat that size."

"You're not getting a boat. Stop."

"Well, what if everything goes to hell, and we have to flee the city, then what? We won't be able to drive, the roads will all be backed up, *then* you'll wish we had a boat. Or what if there's a flood, or an earthquake and then a tsunami? We'll at least be able to float. It's the perfect time to get one."

"I said *no*." As usual, she quietly finished her food, then washed her plate. The matter was closed as far as she was concerned.

"He's got a good point," said Derik. "We could use it to get to Bella Bella, go fishing, and, if the world really *was* ending... I'm not sure Candace would fit aboard, though; she'd probably sink us."

"I'm not *fat*," Candace said.

"Yeah—there's no point in going fishing around here, all you'd catch is mudskippers. If we had a boat, we could go fishing for salmon, halibut, and cod!" George licked his lips. "How 'bout that, Betty—*cod*!"

"*No!*" she said. "You're not getting a boat. Get that out of your head."

George smiled at Derik with his eyes, as did Derik back, as if saying, "She'll crack. We'll get a boat soon."

"Can I go?" said Candace. "I want to go."

Derik prayed for this moment. "No," he said. "You're going to Disneyland."

"How come you never took us to Bella Bella?" she asked.

"You've been," said Betty. "We stayed in a cabin when you were little."

Derik imagined the cabin bedazzled by sun. *Maybe I do remember.* "We should go again."

"You don't want to go there," said Betty. "It's gloomy, and there are stray dogs everywhere."

"Well how come they're going?"

"'Cause we have to pay tribute to Grandpa," said Derik. "Even if he wasn't a good man."

"Why?"

"'Cause God wills it."

Candace sighed. "Whatever. None of that should matter when he was a creep."

15. Pleasure Craft

Precious days dropped one by one to oblivion. Their voyage, to visit the passed elder, seemed as though it wouldn't be. The funeral was already delayed—in the hope that more could attend if restrictions laxed—but how were they to travel without plane, ferry or boat? Charon shrugged from the opposite shore, his long limbs holding the oar. There was no way across.

Derik and George worked on in the shop, taking in jewellery (sometimes hot, handing it over to the police), last year's electronics and, once in a while, gold or silver. George weighed the ingots in his hand; they were always heavier than they looked. The history of cut-throat prospects, dubious undertakings and haunted quarries, all for that illusive sheen, burned a hole in his palm. "Seventy-three dollars on the dot," he said.

"Give me seventy-five and you have a deal."

"I said seventy-three; that's what it's worth. You can't haggle gold." He chuckled, magnanimous.

The man reluctantly took the money, went and bought himself a slice of pizza. George stored the gold for a rainy day (metaphorically, as it *was* actually raining out). "That'll be good when the banks collapse."

Derik rested his elbows on the counter. *Another boring Saturday.* "Is there *any* work I can do around here?"

George sighed. "It's pretty slow today."

Please let me go home. Please let me go home. "I already stacked all the boxes in the back and polished all the cases."

"You can be a real champ and polish all the jewellery. Remember, I told you it should be done once a week."

"I thought Vince did it already. It looks fine."

"No, I can see some fingerprints and smudges on the watches. Get to it!"

"Why, though? No one's gonna notice. As soon as I clean them, someone's going to come in here and smudge them anyway."

"Do you want a job or not?"

"I just don't get why I'm here during my weekend when there's nothing *really* to do."

"I need you here. It'll get busy soon, just watch. Everyone is out having breakfast. They'll start trickling in soon."

"Can I take my break now, then, before it starts getting busy?"

"Your break? You just started!"

"I started at seven. It's been two and a half hours."

"...You know what? If you want something to do, go and take this to Gino. You remember where Gino's deli is, right?"

"Hell yeah," said Derik. He couldn't get enough of their paninis with prosciutto, garlicky pesto, spinach, provolone, thin tomato slices and fresh-baked bread—he salivated just thinking about it. "I love that place."

George showed a ring to Derik in the back: silver, with an interlaced unicursal hexagram around a ruby flower, like the dawn sun encased in fog. Derik wanted it for himself. "This is Gino's special ring," George said with an air of ceremony. "I just had it verified for him. It's the real deal."

Derik recognized the symbol from the tarot. *The hexagram is macro, because it represents celestial bodies, while the flower is micro, because there are five petals.* "That's a magic ring, isn't it?"

"That's why Gino asked for it. He's into that sort of thing. If you check the maker's mark on the back—" George showed Derik. "—you can trace it to a jeweller from Cefalù, Italy. Gino had to have it once he found that out."

"Sure looks cool."

George embedded it in a velvet box. "It's better than *cool*—it's beautiful. Now take this to Gino at his deli, and *don't* lose it, or heads will roll."

Derik took the ring. "Oh, *don't* lose it! I was seriously contemplating it for a second there."

"I don't want anyone else holding it; it's worth thousands and thousands of dollars."

"All I have to do is give him the ring, right? I don't have to collect any money or anything?"

"Yes. If he tries to give you money for it, just refuse. Say, 'Thank you very much, but it's already taken care of.'" George slapped his hands together, done and dusted. "He's an extremely powerful client and landlord—he owns our building, technically—so don't go messing around when you get there, you understand?"

"What do you mean? How would I mess around in a deli?"

"Just act professional, all right? This is serious business. If you want to take over for me someday, you'll have to learn to interact with these big clients of mine."

Take over someday?

"Go in, ask for Gino, give him the ring, and tell him, 'Thank you for your business. Here's the ring you asked for.' Shake his hand, then *leave*, got it?"

Derik figured something was off by the way George revered Gino. *Did Gino pay for the ring? Who knows? Dad gives away stuff sometimes to regulars.* Derik had heard Gino sweet-talking customers before in his deli, including George.

"My *friend*, it's great to see you," Gino had said, putting one arm over George. "You're back for some mortadella, I can tell." He'd patted George's belly.

"You got the best sandwiches in town," said George. He basked in that kind of close affection, as did Gino. "Hey, I got this gold necklace in the other day, you should come take a look at it. It was made in Geneva in the eighteenth century; I just had it checked out."

And Gino had told him, "Send it my way," as if it were a sandwich.

He was one of George's best customers, and frequently purchased jewellery—though he would hardly ever be seen wearing the pieces, which ticked off George.

"I sell you all this jewellery but I never see you wearing it," he'd said.

"It's for special occasions!" Gino had said, directing the forces with his hands. "I don't wear such fine jewels when I'm fist deep in sausage meat, you know what I'm saying?"

They'd both laughed, living easy.

This was Derik's chance to perform a favour, and neither he nor George took it lightly; though clearly his heart was in two places at once. "Can I have some money to buy us some paninis after?"

And George, also salivating, caved. "Fine—but make sure you give him the ring first!" He gave Derik a twenty.

"He'll appreciate the business."

Derik walked down the street in his glossy shorts and T-shirt, somehow warm, as kids are, through the mosaic of culture that is Commercial: pho over there, poutine variations over here, ice cream over yonder, and a thrift store beside him—all the modes of Earth. There was a certain charming run-down quality to Commercial that kept it unpretentious with aged awnings, grimy signs and shops huddled close. Don't get me wrong, the millennials, rich and privileged had infiltrated, as they had most urban centres, but even then Commercial remained one with the dirt (so to speak), gentrification or no. It's difficult not to trash the rich because they stop the world for a feeling. They attach such self-importance to their rare glimpses at true emotion—great art, fights and literature come from struggle.

When Derik was born, back in 2008, Vancouver was still a tiny city on the periphery of Canada (Canada being a periphery of North America) where skiers landed on their way to Whistler for killer slopes. Then 2010 came, and with it, the Olympics. Suddenly the world realized: "Hm, Vancouver looks like a chill place to live." The wealthy flocked, buying up the Edwardian homes of East Van, the modern apartments downtown driving house prices into the millions.

Downtown Vancouver is now Canada's most densely populated city centre. Luckily, the Mormins were well into their mortgage and were still able to afford living in the city, while many were pushed into the sprawl, enjoying hours of commute from Maple Ridge, Coquitlam or Surrey. It was true, many Vancouverite neighbourhoods got torn down and rebuilt by the hour; yet, some still remained, including Little Italy, though I never knew dementors drank mimosas.

Gino was fortunate enough to own a lot before the flux, and hence was sitting on a gold mine (in more ways than one). Derik stood outside Gino's conjoined shops, admiring the beige awning and eclectic lettering: *Gino's Deli and Bakery*.

"But Redbird," says Coyote. "Why not call it something clever, like Il Cielo Dolce e Salato, or Happy Fortune Stuffed Face?"

Because, Gino doesn't mince words. He owns a deli and a bakery, hence the name.

"People will always need sandwiches," said Gino, chatting to a regular. "You know, good bread, good cheese and great meat—what's not to love?" He handed the customer a sub wrapped in butcher paper like the precious gift it was. "All right, you take care now."

"You too, Gino!"

Gino scanned the line. "Who's next?"

A lady stepped forward. "*Hi*, may I please have the vegetarian panini without cheese and bread, and the artichoke salad on the side as well?"

"OK," he said, and began assembling, enjoying the small talk they made.

Derik entered. The door chime rang. Gino probed him with Horus's eye, somehow both warm and controlling. There was a line six people deep, all hungrily awaiting their fix.

Derik admired the case of delectable meats and cheeses—whole, with their imported wrappers revealing their quality and origin—as well as the rows of jars of pickles, sun-dried tomatoes and olives; the cans of tuna in extra-virgin olive oil; and the packages of thin, crunchy breadsticks and crackers. The smells were foreign, yet so familiar—glory to the senses. And the smells and sounds of the bakery drifted over, creating the most blissful mélange anyone may experience.

He went right up to the counter and said to busy Gino, "Hello, I'm looking for Gino?" knowing full well it was him.

"You're looking for Gino, huh?" He was assembling the lady's order while his assistant sliced prosciutto cotto on the red slicer. "Wait one second. I have to take care of these customers first, OK?"

"Ah, sure." *Don't upset him,* he imagined his dad saying.

"You're George's kid, aren't you?"

"..." It took longer than usual to register. "Yes!"

"Good. Go get yourself a cannoli at the bakery; tell them I sent you. Enjoy it, stay awhile."

And Derik panicked, considering it payment, which George said not to accept. "OK." He didn't want to offend Gino, and it seemed harmless enough, so he went next door and got himself a cannoli— but bought it himself, never mentioning Gino. He ate it by the window. *Oh my God, this is so good!*

Gino must do something else besides make sandwiches all day; he couldn't have gotten this rich just making sandwiches, could he?

Maybe he bakes all the bread.

I bet he's a mobster—like Mom's favourite movie, The Godfather. *Part One was really good. I can't wait to watch Part Two. Gino reminds me of Don Corleone.*

That's racist though—just 'cause he's Italian? He's Italian, right?

Sounds like it. It smells so good in here. During Christmas break we'd always come here to buy panettone. It's delicious with butter—orange rind and raisins inside. We'd make the ultimate French toast with the leftovers.

"Hey, kid," called Gino. He was standing, drying his hands on his green towel, where the bakery met the deli. "You wanted to see me?"

Derik stood up from the stool by the window and stepped toward him.

"What's up?" said Gino.

Derik gave him the velvet case. "My dad, George Mormin, told me to give this to you. It's your special ring."

Gino opened it. The sun gathered in the rubies, dazzling his eyes. "Very nice." He looked at Derik. "Thanks, kid." He put a hand on his shoulder. "I appreciate it."

He never asked how much it was, but pulled out a roll of bills from his pocket and began riffling through them.

"No, no," said Derik, dismissing the gesture with a wave of his hand. "My dad said it's taken care of. He doesn't want *any* money for it."

"Wow," said Gino with a pout. "This is a beautiful ring. Tell your dad I'm truly grateful he's letting me have it, OK?"

"Yes, Mr. Gino."

He smiled. "Just call me Gino." Patting that shoulder. Derik was cautious, unsure how to act. "I like you; you're honest. You ever toss a pizza before?"

"Like, into the garbage?"

Gino smiled harder, more threatening. "Have you *ever* made a *pizza before*?" He added emphasis because he hated being misunderstood (as he'd yet to master English, his fourth language, after Italian, Latin and Hebrew).

"No, I've never made it before. Is it tough?"

"Not really," he said. "You just need good dough and a gentle touch; you need love in your heart." He thumped his chest with his fist. "We need some help in the back, making pizzas and breads. Your dad, he keep you busy?"

"Yes. I just started working at the shop."

"Good, good." He gripped Derik's shoulder with force and affection. "I started working for my father, too, when I was your age. It's good to start young; it teaches you a lot about life, to develop a good work ethic. You let me know if you ever need some more money. I'll teach you how to work in the back, making baked goods, all right?" He winked.

"Uh, all right, Gino. Thank you."

"Your dad, he doing all right? How's business?"

"Business is good. He's doing all right. We found out his dad died, which is sad. Now he wants a boat to be able to go back to Bella Bella to attend the funeral. It's the only way in, 'cause Indigenous closed borders to their reserves and no ferry goes there anymore."

"My apologies. I lost my father too, *years* ago. It was one of the saddest times of my life. You let him know that I have a boat he can look at—brand new—hardly been used."

"Really?"

"A customer gave it to me as payment, but I never use it. I don't even drive my own car, you know."

"That's awesome! I'll let him know as soon as I get back."

"*Bellissimo*! Good talking to you, kid. You got a bright future ahead of you. I got work to do now. Here, take some cookies, why don't you. Carrie! Box the kid up some cookies and cannoli."

"You got it," said Carrie.

Derik really wanted those sandwiches, but he didn't want to ruin a graceful exit.

"You take care now, huh? Send your dad my regards." Gino held his hand to the invisible wall as he strode back to the deli side.

"Thank you, Gino! I will." Derik accepted the box of treats, then left.

Chief's Spot was busy when he returned.

"What took you so long?" George said.

"I was talking to Mr. Gino. He offered me a job."

"You're not working for anyone but me." He was showing a customer watches.

"I could during the summer."

"No, I'll need you around here. There'll be lots of work to do this summer."

Derik realized his dad didn't want to hire anyone else (so as not to pay their wages); though time would tell George just wanted him around.

"I like this one," said the customer. "How much is it?"

"Twelve hundred."

"I'll give you nine hundred for it."

"It's worth fifteen," George bluffed. "Give me eleven fifty and it's yours—that's a good deal."

The man looked at the watch, validating his next offer. "OK, deal." They shook hands. "Thanks. I'll have someone polish it for you." He gave the watch to Derik. "Here, polish this." Derik got out the cloth. They went to the register.

"He said he has a boat you should look at. He got it as *payment* from one of his customers."

"What kind of boat is it?"

"I dunno. I told him you want to go to Bella Bella, then he told me he has a boat."

The customer got his watch, thanks were exchanged, then it was on to the next.

"He said it was brand new; he never drives it. He wants you to phone him."

"I don't wanna get caught up owing him anything. He's not the kind of guy you want to owe any money to."

"Why? He's so friendly. He gave me these cookies and cannoli for free."

"What did I tell you about accepting anything from him? I told you, don't do it."

"He insisted I take them; I didn't want to offend him. Besides, they're just cookies. He was going to give me money but I said no."

"He always does that; he wants you to owe him something so he can control you."

"...Is Gino a gangster?"

"Yes. He'll break your legs if you cross him."

"Really?"

George chuckles. "Probably."

"You're joking." Derik Gullible grinned. "Phone him! He'll probably give you a good deal on the boat."

214

"I will! Go help that lady over there looking at the trading cards."

And Derik did, friends. "It's a PSA nine, 'cause the centring is off. Needs to be perfect for a ten."

Weekend gazers grazed.

Once the morning rush faded, George called Gino.

"What did he say?" Derik asked him after.

"Said he's got a thirty-three-foot Bayliner, with twin Cummins diesel."

"Isn't that what you wanted?"

"It's exactly what I wanted! We had them aboard the *Marge Valence*. They're reliable *and* powerful."

"That's good. So are you going to buy it?"

"We'll see. I'm meeting him tomorrow at Granville Island Marina, and *you're* coming with me." He pointed, resolute.

"OK ... But we have to get doughnuts while we're there."

"Good thinking."

They ate the cookies.

At home, George told Betty he and Derik were going to Granville Island Market in the morning, which wasn't a lie, but deceptive.

"I have to go to the market," she said. "Let's all go together."

"No," said George. "I'm picking you up a gift."

Her brows twitched with suspicion. "You better not be looking at boats, George. I told you we can't afford one; they're not a good investment."

"We're not looking at boats. It's a surprise."

"Yeah, right." She was certain they were boat seeking, so remained upset.

Off they went to the market. First they would get gifts, as evidence there was no boat; then they would look at the boat.

"What are we going to get Mom?" said Derik, seat belt on.

"We'll get her some flowers. Then I want to check out this Native art shop; maybe they have something we can get her."

"She doesn't like flowers, though; she hates how they die."

What a metaphor for the Indigenous way. They made through the lines and heavy-traffic hustle and bustle at the gate, under the rainbow-lit sign beneath the bridge, to the colourful pipes that wrapped around shops where people killed for parking. It took them twenty minutes to find a spot.

"Sure is busy," said Derik.

"It's always busy on Sunday. Everyone and their grandma is out."

They moved through the fair. "Should we get her some handmade vodka?" said Derik. "She'll probably like that."

"No, she doesn't really drink."

"She made martinis when Carol and Hal were over."

"That was a special occasion. She only drinks once in a blue moon."

"Why was it special? You were just playing cards."

"It was special that we had friends over. Hal likes to drink."

"So what are we going to get her then?"

"You'll see. It's a secret."

"I hope it's expensive, or else she's going to be mad when you buy the boat."

"Everything's expensive here."

They stopped to watch the guy juggling frying pans. The shop smelt of cedar inside, finely polished, with lingering minerality. Derik inspected earrings and rings hanging from a spinnable transparent plastic column like fruit from a tree. "Hey Dad, Mom might like these." He showed George a pair of jade earrings. He checked the price tag. "Costs 120." He didn't want to say if they were pricey or not.

"She doesn't really wear earrings."

"What about bracelets? She wears them."

"She already has a nice bracelet made by a Native artist."

"OK, well, what are we going to get her then? A mini inukshuk?"

"No, our people didn't make inukshuks."

The people's voices modulated with the transition of consciousness. "What *did* our people make for art?"

"They made bentwood boxes, canoes, paddles; I remember, once, Grandpa took a tree branch and carved it down to a paddle in minutes—he just knew how to do it."

"I don't think Mom would like a paddle."

"Yeah, I *know*; I'm just telling you a story."

George went up to a series of framed prints, done in the traditional Northwest Coast style Heiltsuk is lumped in with. Northwest Coast style, you see, is more abstract, generally favouring symmetrical profiles that look to the viewer, emphasizing the head or face. The further south you go, the more realistic the depictions of humans, animals and shades between. One wouldn't typically depict landscapes in the great northwest.

The print George sought was a sun with four figures, one per quadrant, like an Aztec calendar, except with traditional colours of red, blue and black on bone white. Widdershins: the raven, wolf, orca, then eagle, all around the face of the sun.

"Check that one out." George pointed. "Cool, huh?"

Derik verified, "Looks nice."

"I think she'll like it."

"Yeah." Derik checked the price. "Eight hundred dollars?" He could no longer hide his thriftiness. "That's so expensive—for a print?"

"It'll be worth it if it makes Tweety happy and forget about the boat," George swindled.

"Yeah, but eight hundred dollars though? That's a lot of money."

"It's not that expensive. We buy art all the time at the shop for thousands of dollars—shouldn't we keep some for ourselves to display in our home?"

"Yeah, but you sell all that art—it's not *your* money."

They mulled it over, knowing what the other would say next. Derik looked for a mood to use to disagree with George, but it never washed up. "Where are you thinking of putting it?"

"Over the couch, in the living room. It'll look perfect there."

"I guess so… I *think* she'll like it… I'm just not sure she'll appreciate you spending eight hundred for it."

"We can always haggle; I think they'll come down to seven hundred." Some customers and an employee grumbled. "Let's go see the boat first. We'll settle on what to buy her after."

"Sounds like a plan."

And George thanked the cashiers, telling them, "We'll be back later."

Off to the market George and Derik went, stopping first at Lee's Donuts. You see, one could watch Lee and friends (because workers are friends, friends) making donuts fresh through the glass there, chopping dough into rings and frying them. You have to get them fresh for the full experience. That way, they're warm and supple, with crispy crags for contrast. The smell is intoxicating—that fried, yeasty, sweet aroma that convinces you there is no other. They got themselves two plain, a couple with sprinkles, then the rest chocolate. They washed them down with coffee and tea while strolling through the market.

They judged the fish first. They gawked at the price of halibut. "Thirty-five bucks a pound! Wow. I remember when it was ten dollars a pound."

Still feel good about overfishing?

Sorry, he's still like that.

"The thing I long for is roe on kelp; I miss having that as a snack."

"They might have some. It's probably not done the same way, and overpriced, but they might have it." He asked the fishmonger.

"You know what," they said, "let me check the freezer." And check they did, friends. They returned with a frozen square of roe on kelp. "I got this from a supplier from Haida Gwaii." He had a big smile; it was a special product.

"Nice. How much does it cost?"

"Fifty bucks."

Derik was quite shocked. *Fifty bucks for that? We used to get it for free.* Indeed, it was similar in price to other roes and cheap caviar.

George turned to him. "Think we should get it?"

Derik was nostalgic. "For fifty dollars?" He didn't want to offend the fishmonger, though his occupation demanded it.

"It'll be a treat. I want to try it again, too." George bought it. The fishmonger continued smiling in his blue hoodie and white apron.

"Thanks very much!"

They also bought some Indian candy (as it's known in colloquial circles)—salmon nuggets, marinated in soy sauce and maple syrup, then smoked till chewy, yet still tender inside. Smoke is a hallucinogen.

They got some fruit, and a couple pot pies for dinner. They were to meet Gino at the marina at eleven.

The knotty rope hit the navy water. The ripples were fringed silver. The water spoke in signs of the infinite tide. The boat was nice—or Gino wouldn't have had it—though suspicions were raised.

"She's a beaut. Where did you get her?" asked George.

Gino, adorned with jewels, a straw hat, short-sleeved open-collared shirt (the slightest blue)—which revealed a bed of curls for his gold necklace—and wide shades, chewed his gum and said, "I got it as a favour from a customer. He owed me some money, so he let me take his boat. It was kind of him."

"They must've owed you a lot if they gave you this as payment." And the two of them laughed madly, perplexing Derik, who smiled simply because he found them crazy.

"I held onto it for him, we can say—and he never came back!" Gallic shrug. "So the boat is mine." They boarded. "Come, let's have a look; be my guests."

It was everything you'd expect on a boat that size: stove, wash-room with shower, two separate quarters, spacious cabin and an upper deck, if you like piloting with the wind in your face.

"When was it made?" said George.

"2014. It's pretty much new, the guy hardly used it. I got it a few months back, but she just sits here; I never take her out."

"Why not? I'd be out on the water with her every day (if I didn't have business to worry about)."

"Business keeps us busy. You were a fisherman before?"

"Yup, that was my first gig."

"What did you catch?"

"Mostly herring, and salmon. I worked on a few seiners and gill-netters." He admired her side. "...*Artemis*..."

"Artemis was the ancient Greek goddess of the hunt," said Derik. "Analogous with Diana, and associated with the moon."

Gino gestured to Derik. "He gets it! He knows the significance."

George patted his belly and smiled.

"So what do you say?" centred Gino. "Do you want to have her?"

"How much you asking?"

Gino admired his rings—a rare sighting, him not fist-deep in gabagool. Wake collided with pilings. "I don't want any money; I have enough. Look at me! What else would I do with money? What do you have to trade? ...What about that black Mercedes?"

George had showed the car to him the other day. He'd just had it redone, hoping to resell it for sixty-five K for a ten K profit. "Hm," he said. "Let me think... That's a great car."

"Come on," Gino said, wings spread. "What's there to think about? That's a *fantastic* deal. I'm sure your family will appreciate having the boat. You can go back home for your father's funeral. I have to *fly* to get back to Italy."

It was a good deal; the boat was worth around one hundred thousand dollars. "You'd really trade it for the Mercedes?"

Gino bowed his head ever so slightly. "For you, I will."

A breeze rippled their clothes, whispered in their ears. "OK," said

George, holding out his hand. "The Mercedes for the boat."

Gino gave him the handshake. "It's a deal… But I also get your boy to help me at the bakery."

"Deal," said George.

Derik: "What?!"

They chuckled.

It's a good boat. I'm glad Dad finally got one.

"All right, who wants steaks Neptune?" said Gino. "I know a place."

❦ ❦ ❦

After lunch, Derik and George returned to their car, while Gino went sunbathing. "Say hi to Raven for me!" he called, and waved as they parted.

"How does he know Raven?"

"We go to AA together."

"Oh… So what are you going to get Mom? What about her gift?"

"I got an idea," said George. They stopped at the pawnshop on the way home. Employees promptly started cleaning. George took down the moon mask from the wall and had it wrapped.

"You're giving her the moon mask?"

"Yup. It deserves a good home. I think Tweety will like it."

"Where's she going to put it, though? Don't you think she'll find it a bit creepy?"

"No, she'll like it; it's a work of art! I'm sure she'll find a good place for it."

Derik imagined playing *Moonlight Sonata* on the piano, though he didn't know how, as his left would stutter the bass notes. He only ever knew Grandma Julia through her old piano. She, like Henry, was physically and mentally abusive toward George. She, on the other hand, actually went to residential school, where she adopted the Old Testament discipline. Why? Because it was the norm. She could've died a martyr, like many, or never had children, but for an Indigenous woman in the '60s such ambitions were wishful thinking. She did move the entire family, though, shortly before her death, which perhaps *was* her saving grace, but even the benefit of that was debatable—waves of music from the piano and moon.

🌵 🌵 🌵

Betty opened her gift back at home. "Oh," she said, holding the mask.

"That's a *real* moon mask. Someone brought it into the shop, and I thought, 'Tweety would love that!'"

"It's nice," she said. You could tell she liked it because she didn't say much. "I think I'll put it on the piano."

Derik nodded. "I was hoping you'd say that."

And on the piano it went.

Was Betty pissed George traded for a boat? You bet. Did it matter in the end? Probably, but everything worked out. She knew how much George wanted a boat and to return to Bella Bella for the celebration of Henry. George's fire burned bright; his inspiration endured Betty's practical criticism, so she could not deny his will to travel to Bella Bella. Derik and George were due north.

16. The First Voyage

George smashed the bottle of sparkling apple juice upon the bow, donning his mariner's cap. "I christen her *Wild Thing*," he said, holding the severed head as the fizzy apparition slid down the hull.

"Why *Wild Thing*?" asked Derik.

"'Cause she makes my *heart sing*."

Everything was set to begin the maiden voyage: arrangements were made to cover their urban duties; on board was two weeks' supply of food Betty had picked up from Costco—hot dogs (with buns), steaks, marinated chicken breasts, baby spinach, carrots, onions, celery, tomatoes, frozen blueberries, granola bars, flavoured sparkling water, dill pickle chips, potatoes, orange juice and gummy-bear vitamins, along with plastic cutlery; suitcases were packed, faces coated with sunscreen, water bottles filled, and George was strapped to the gills with that OG kush.

"There he is!" said George.

"There's who?" Derik turned to see.

Much to his surprise, Raven approached, wearing shades, carrying his luggage.

"No way!" Derik jumped up and down. "You're coming too?"

"Yes sirree!" He smiled. "How could I miss the opportunity to return to Bella Bella and pay my respects to the great Henry Mormin himself?" He stopped at the cleats. "Permission to come aboard, Captain?"

George nodded. "Permission granted."

Derik helped him with his luggage.

"Your dad also said he needed a deckhand pro bono."

"What's that mean?" asked Derik.

"It means I do all the work for free."

"There, now you have a friend to keep you company," George told Derik. "Happy?"

Derik nodded. "God won't sink us with a shaman aboard."

"Here's hoping," said Raven. "It's been a while since I've been on a boat."

Derik eagerly showed him around. George held his vape to the sky. "Thank you, Creator. Please bless us on our journey." The sky was blue with filaments of cloud. Waves were sweetly waking.

ᵜ ᵜ ᵜ

They performed their final check to make sure nothing was forgotten. "Fire extinguisher?" said George.

"Check," said Derik.

"Wallet." He patted his pockets. "Oh, did you bring the offerings?"

"Yup." Derik searched the bag holding tobacco, coloured broadcloth, sweet grass and weed. (There were no dispensaries in Bella Bella to meet the high demand, making weed a valuable commodity to trade for salmon and dried seaweed—the traditional fare. Also, weed *seemed* to be the lesser of evils compared to alcohol or prescription drugs, both of which continued to plague reserves.)

"Pass me that bag of joints," said George.

Derik passed him the bag of joints.

"Weed saved my life," said George. "It's way better for me to spark up a joint than rely on opiates for my bad back. It's probably even *better* at relieving my pain, *and* it doesn't give me constipation or make me super drowsy."

"That's good," said Raven. George offered him a joint. "No thanks. It only makes me paranoid... I did enough smoking in my day."

"Come on, you're a shaman; this is *medicine*."

"You don't need drugs to be a shaman. Maybe if it was a ceremony, like peyote or something, I'd have to partake... but not right now."

"I had peyote once. I was high for like three days."

"Yeah, it's an ordeal, that's for sure."

"I couldn't go to sleep, no matter how hard I tried. Every time I closed my eyes I would see these *crazy* visuals."

"Sounds about right. I danced for what felt like years."

George took another puff of the joint. "It turned me insane. I was frothing at the mouth. I was one step away from being a cannibal." He chuckled.

"Quit smoking, Dad," said Derik. "You have to drive the boat."

"Why? It doesn't really affect me."

"It's illegal to drive a boat high; remember what Mom said?"

"I don't give a *damn*. Most captains I knew were either high or drunk in the middle of forty-foot waves." He puffed away. "One little joint isn't going to do anything."

The dockmaster appeared from a piling. "Hey! Are you smoking marijuana aboard your vessel?"

George instinctively flicked the joint overboard. It fizzled on the water, and he coughed and coughed. "What do you want?"

"It's a violation under the Criminal Code, subsection 253, to operate a sea-faring vessel while impaired by cannabis."

"I wasn't smoking *cannabis*. Why don't you mind your own goddamn business."

The dockmaster wrote George a ticket. "I can smell it from here," said Face-Pad.

"You security people are always looking for something to complain about. I could drive this boat from here to Alaska, no problem. I'm not impaired at all."

But he wrote on. He ripped the ticket from the pad, then handed it to George without eye contact. "Check the rules next time. Maybe then you'll realize you're putting everyone else in danger. I'm calling the police if I see you piloting your vessel—it's the law."

"Screw you!" said George with fantastic emphasis. "Go get a real job." And the man walked away with a smirk. George shredded the ticket and tossed it in the water.

"See!" said Derik. "What did I tell you?"

George surveyed loyalty from his crew by the glint of their eyes. He waited till the dockmaster was well out of view, then started the engine. The propeller frothed the water; *Wild Thing* lurched forward.

The dockmaster ran back, shouting, "Hey! Turn off that engine, right now!"

George cackled. "Where we're going, there are no laws!"

Wild Thing pulled at her chains. Raven, without much hesitation, untied the lines.

We were jumping over ditches at school, then Zack tried, but couldn't jump to save his life, so hit his shins and fell in.

Help Raven! Derik untied the last rope, freeing them all. *Wild Thing* took off, lopping a heavy wake as George throttled, leaving the dockmaster behind in defeat.

Derik then realized what he was accomplice to, and yelled at George, "Why the hell did you do that for?! You just broke the law! Now we're all going to jail."

"We're Indigenous," said George. "We can do whatever we want on the water—it's our constitutional right!"

"He's gonna be waiting for us when we get back," said Derik.

"He can wait all he wants. All he's going to get is a boot up his ass if he comes anywhere close. Trying to give me a ticket for smoking some grass aboard my boat—to hell with him." George pushed further the throttle. "*Yeehaw!* We're free now, baby! *Free!*"

Derik sat at stern opposite Raven, and brooded, fretting his father's machismo. *They're going to send me to juvie.*

"It'll be fine," said Raven. "Don't worry. Weed's legal now anyway."

Derik didn't respond. He was reliving trauma. *The RCMP came and took all of Dad's guns. Didn't see him for three days. Came home from school, there he was, half-dead on the couch, face covered in stitches. He bought us stickers from the hospital.* The propeller span on, *Wild Thing* majestic as the clouds of space.

Indigenous folk tended to get lax treatment concerning their constitutional rights. This was demonstrated in the case *Regina v. Gladstone*. William and Donald Gladstone, Heiltsuk men with an abundance of roe on kelp, had decided to sail down to Vancouver to sell their stock. They were promptly charged, as it was illegal to sell herring spawn. They then appealed the charge on the basis that they, under section 35 of the Constitution Act of 1982, had the right to harvest, consume and trade roe on kelp as it was a traditional product of the Heiltsuk well before contact with explorers. The Supreme Court agreed, which set precedence for further, similar cases. It was a landmark victory for the Gladstones, Heiltsuk and First Nations across Canada. It's not at all clear what the herring thought of the situation.

That being chirped, the law certainly didn't favour Indigenous Peoples. One only had to look at the original purpose of the RCMP (to confiscate Indigenous children) to realize how unfairly Indigenous people were treated under Canadian law. As of this chirping, about 30 percent of prisoners are Indigenous, despite them constituting around 5 percent of the national population. It's six times more likely for an Indigenous person to land in jail than it is for whites. No, the law never has favoured the Indigenous at large. But George was another story—he knew how to push boundaries. He was *going* to that funeral, no matter what.

They were off to a strong start. There were mostly only tankers and tugs on the water—that is, until Derik spotted three speedboats approaching. "They're gaining on us, Dad! I think they're cops."

"They can't catch us," said George. "We're way ahead!" Lo, though, George couldn't see how quickly they advanced.

"Dad, they're right behind!"

George bade *Wild Thing* fly! Derik and Raven held the gunwale tight.

"Dad, stop! You can't outrun them."

Freedom was his priority, so freedom he'd find. They passed Stanley Park, with its old growth and all-encompassing seawall. They made haste to West Van. Raven and Derik could see POLICE clearly across the cabins of the pursuing vessels. The hounds were hot on their tail. Closer and closer they made, until: "Stop your boat now! This is the police! You're breaking the law! Stop right now!"

George continued his escape. His reputation was at stake. To end his first voyage so soon would only humiliate him before the world. They had almost cleared the lighthouse at the edge of the mainland where the highway climbed to sky; an eagle circled above, not the least bit bothered by the crows diving and feigning attack. George laughed maniacally.

"Are you crazy?" shouted Derik. He was furious with his father's recklessness. "Stop the boat, Dad! They're gonna arrest you!"

He cackled once more. "Why should I stop then?"

Derik could see their faces. He saw its spine rise and submerge, frothing the navy water like a glossy gear. The giant horned serpent towered, barring its rows of jagged teeth. It struck, and all was consumed.

"You want me to stop the boat?" said George. "OK." He killed the throttle. The boat glided to a stop, bobbing on the gentle waves. "What do you want?" he shouted, puffing his chest. "You come to take my freedom?"

"All right, settle down Tony Montana," said Raven. "No need to taunt the cops."

"Why would you try and outrun the cops, Dad? They could've shot you!"

"But they didn't, did they?"

"You're such an idiot!"

"Watch it." The fury of a thousand suns blared in his eyes, jaw like stone. "They won't do a *thing*. Watch."

The police stopped beside them, guns drawn. "Don't move!" said one. "We're coming aboard."

"Go ahead," said George.

They boarded. "Put your hands behind your back!" They cuffed George right away. "Have a seat." George sat. "So why were you running away from us, huh? You think you can outrun the law?"

George said, "I didn't break no law. I was just driving my new boat."

"We got a call from dock security that you were smoking cannabis, *before* you took off. You're not under the influence, are you?"

"Not at all. I could take this boat to China if I wanted."

"It's a criminal offence to pilot a boat while impaired."

"I know; I have my master's certificate."

"How come you didn't stop when we asked you to?"

"I couldn't hear you over the engine, it's loud. Go ahead and look me up—my name's George Mormin. We're headed to my dad's funeral."

"Just wait here. We're going to have a look around."

They searched the boat. "Found this," said one, holding the bag of weed. "Looks to be an ounce of marijuana."

"It's not illegal to have that aboard," piped George.

They radioed in the find. "You've been smoking, Mr. Mormin? Why don't you stand up for us."

"I told you, I'm sober as the day God made me."

"Go ahead and keep your eyes on my finger." He moved it from side to side. George followed. "Now lift your left foot and balance on your right."

George quivered as he tried, then lost balance, catching himself on the gunwale. "I couldn't do that whether I smoked or *not*."

"Try again." The cop mumbled to the one holding the bag of ice cream cake, "I can smell it on him." George trembled on one foot. The cop's radio scrambled. He turned to listen. "OK ... Are you sure?" He looked to the other. "All right." To George, "OK, you can stop now." George put down his foot. "So, you said you just came into possession of this boat?"

"Yeah. This is our first voyage."

"And you purchased her off a Mr. Ambrogino Galilei?"

"I traded him for it."

"All right ..." He turned to the other. "You can put that back." To George, "All right, Mr. Mormin, you're free to go. Best not be smoking any more of that local product while piloting your vessel in the future."

"No, I'll save it for when we dock." And they both chuckled. The cop slapped George's collegial arm. He said to Raven and Derik, "Sorry, fellas, didn't mean to ruin your morning."

Raven nodded. "No problem."

"Thank you, officer," said Derik.

"You take care now," he said to George, reboarding his boat.

"Hey, George!" The officer's superior waved.

George waved back. "Hey, Danis! Long time no see!" Derik noticed a certain sorrow in Danis's eyes.

"You behave now!"

"All right, I will!"

The police headed back toward the city.

"Wait," said Derik, stupefied. "Why the hell did they let you go?"

"I'll tell you later."

"No! You almost got us *arrested*. You tell me now."

"You're not old enough, Derik."

"I'm plenty old enough if you're going to drag me along like that. So tell me: why'd they just let you go? Tell me, or I tell Mom what happened."

George looked west with a smirk—the open vista of the Georgia Strait. "That was Aunt Sammy's former husband. He helped me stay out of prison once I stopped selling drugs."

Derik held mouth agape. "What?!"

Raven burst out laughing. "Sorry, I can't help but laugh."

"You were a drug dealer?"

"How do you think I got these scars?"

"When did you stop?"

"Long before you were born. They would've never stopped us if they knew it was me."

"What kind of drugs did you sell?"

George thought about it. "I'll tell you when you're older. Don't tell Mommy I told you that either."

"Does she know?"

"Of course she does. We don't keep secrets from each other."

"Just from me and Candace."

"We did our best to give you a good life so you don't have to deal with criminals like I did."

"I wish you woulda told us the truth."

"Why? It had nothing to do with you."

"What about those cops who raided our house and confiscated your guns?"

"They weren't looking for guns. They were there to protect you."

"Protect us from who?"

"The people who gave me these scars."

"Satan's Buds?"

George cleared his throat. "I've already told you enough. Just be happy you're safe. There's lots of things you don't know about me."

How could he do that to us? Did they try and kill him? Derik had many questions. (Wouldn't you?) But, like the Cannibal Dance, or rites of the adept, the revealing required maturation.

George puffed his vape. "You guys want to stop at Bowen Island for lunch?"

Derik looked to Raven, who just shrugged. "Yeah… I guess so."

"OK." George retook the helm.

I was raised by a drug dealer.

He said he stopped before you were born.

Yeah, but what about the scars? They must've done that to him.

Mom said he fell off a ladder.

Yeah, right. "Did you know anything about that?" he asked Raven.

"Heck no. You think he would've told me something like that? I had *no* idea."

Derik hung his head. "What does that make me then?"

Raven chuckled. "Look, plenty of Indigenous people get involved with illegal activity. I would be glad you're not, if I was you. Did you have any suspicions that was the case?"

"Besides the cop taking his guns? No… But I'll have to think about it!"

"Consider yourself blessed. Your dad did a good job ensuring you don't have the life he had."

"But what else is he hiding from me?"

"Everyone has secrets, Derik."

Derik ransacked his past for signs of George's nefariousness. *What about that time he brought home that suitcase of cash?*

No, he does that all the time at the pawnshop.

Maybe Satan's Buds own the pawnshop.

Gino owns the land. Gino's Satan's bud.

You'll never know; maybe it's all a hoax!

17. Thar She Blows?

Sailing is a delusionary existence, constantly mistaking waves for fins.

The fecundity of the Greater Vancouver region was a provision of plate tectonics. You see, friends, millions and millions of years ago, when giants monopolized the Earth, the Juan de Fuca Plate served its lush, tropical flora to the Northwest Coast of North America. The effects were twofold: mountains to the east—helping divide BC from the Prairies through the slow collision of plates, and the broad-leaved plants and ferns not found beyond. You see, the Prairies were flattened by miles of glaciers during the ice age, and before that, sea—a continent divided north to south—giving no home to trees.

Yea, verily, miles of ice covered the home of hotdish. Water levels remained low, locked in glaciers. If you want to get into it, oral stories were cyclically hip to it. From BC to Japan, people told of a catastrophic earthquake and ensuing tsunami akin to other flood tales. The Japanese marked it 1700, later *validated* by analysis of sediment deposits left by the tsunami and landslides in BC, as well as ghost forests (dead trees asphyxiated by seawater) and erosion of their footing. Just because it wasn't written down, or thought of being written down (one could suppose), didn't conjure it fiction—wise they were still to the word.

"I think there were giants," said George, chewing his bun of cheese, ham and mayo. They had anchored at Bowen Island. "I saw a show on the Discovery Channel where they proved that they were living here. I bet they're aliens—shape-shifters. That's why they have red hair."

"What are you even talking about?" said Derik.

"They proved that the giants had red hair—they found their bones, *and* hair samples—but they don't know where it came from, so I think the aliens brought it here—they proved it on the show. You should watch it sometime. They probably use portals, too—that's why it's so difficult to find one alive. Bigfoot is one of them; he's an alien. They're all leftover giants. They used to be a lot bigger, too."

Derik discerned the forest from the trees, panning for Bigfoot. A shadow shifted. *Was that Bigfoot?*

No, it wasn't. Maybe a bear?

No... Blastoise!

"That would explain the red hair," George rambled. (Long live the Defender of the Faith.) "The aliens probably came here, then were left behind. Then they started breeding with *Homo sapiens*, which gave them large frames. That's why Mommy has red hair."

Derik shook his head. "That makes *zero* sense."

"You know, Joseph had red hair," Raven said. "He was a ruddy-haired Syrian child—in Genesis, not Jesus's dad."

"Giants didn't roam the Earth," said Derik. "That's stupid; we would've found their bones already."

"But they *did* find their bones! I just *told* you."

"Yeah, but those must be old. I haven't heard of anyone finding Sasquatch or Bigfoot bones; they're always way older."

"They did! I'm telling you, you have to watch the show. They couldn't have been over a thousand years old they said."

"No... I think you're wrong."

George tried Raven. "Do you know anything about the giants?"

Raven thought about it. A rush of air entered his nose and saturated his lungs. "What kind of giants? Like dinosaurs, or Bigfoot?"

"The giants—they were like humans, but bigger."

"I've heard stories of giants that used to walk the Earth. They're mentioned in the *Poetic Edda*. But I read they represented communities, rather than singular beings—like a collective consciousness."

"No, no. These were real giants, not made-up ones. You never heard of them?"

"Yeah, I know what a giant is."

"They proved that they're still around, they're just hiding from us 'cause they know we'll capture them and torture them if we find them."

"Maybe," said Raven. "It's not impossible."

And Derik said, "I still think they would've found more evidence if they really existed."

"They found their *bones*," said George, arms splayed. "I told you. How much evidence do you need?"

"All right, Dad, you're just trying to be edgy, talking about giants and aliens."

George returned to his sandwich, eyes wide.

Derik looked to the forest. *Imagine seeing Bigfoot between the trees. That'd be sick. He must be really quiet if he's so good at hiding. He'd stop and wave at me.*

Hi Derik, I'm real!

Spider-Man swings across the sky.

If you believe in us, we'll believe in you.

Quit staring at the sun, your vision's going red.

"I saw Bigfoot once," said George. "I was about seven or eight. We were anchored nearby, Auntie Sammy, Grandpa and me. I ran into the forest to this stream to collect some water, because, you know, we didn't have clean drinking water back then. If you wanted clean water, you had to drink pop, 'cause all the water from taps was contaminated."

Raven said, "It's still like that for some First Nations."

"And when I came to this stream, I knew something was watching me—I could just feel it. Maybe I heard it breathing, but it didn't make a noise. I heard no broken branches, no footsteps, nothing. Then I looked up, and there it was: a sasquatch. It was at least eight feet tall, and it was just standing there, like this—" George jumped up abruptly, replicating the posture, putting Derik on edge. "It was watching me the entire time. It kept moving its head, like that, staring at me."

"Were you scared?" said Derik.

"I was startled at first, but I knew it wouldn't hurt me; it was friendly... It was curious. If it wanted to, it could've killed me at any moment, before I even knew it was there, but it didn't. But I just had this overwhelming feeling that it was *so* lonely." He shook his head. "It was communicating to me, telepathically, I just know it, 'cause it let me know not to be afraid. It told me it wouldn't hurt me. That's why I believe they must be aliens, 'cause they can communicate telepathically. Then it heard my sister coming. She broke a branch, and it took off through the forest, and it was gone in seconds."

"Did your sister see it?"

"She saw something run off, and believed my story, 'cause I was white as a ghost."

They chewed their sandwiches. "I *want* to see a sasquatch... but I don't think it's likely," said Derik. "I guess it's possible... but I doubt it. I doubt they'd be able to avoid detection for so long."

"But plenty of people have seen them; I saw one!"

"Yeah, yeah," said Derik, done with it. "Have you seen one?" he asked Raven.

"No, I can't say I've ever seen a sasquatch before," said Raven. "Though I've heard countless stories from people who have, and they're always pretty convinced it wasn't a bear or a—"

"Or an escaped gorilla."

"Yeah." He chuckled.

"My grandpa, Ronald Jack, used to give sasquatch tours to tourists," said George. "He said he saw one about once a month. He had plenty of witnesses with him, too, and they all agreed what they saw wasn't a bear."

"Really?" said Derik.

"Yeah. He wrote books on his encounters. He was a very famous hunter. Celebrities from California would pay him to take them out hunting."

"How come we never got to meet him?"

"I never really knew him. I just knew he was my mom's dad. I never really got to meet her side of the family, because they were all from Bella Coola."

"That's sad."

They finished their sandwiches. "Well, I guess we should start making our way up the strait here," said George.

"The Georgia Strait, right?" asked Derik.

"Right."

"Why is it called that, anyway? Did they name it after you?"

Raven said, "It was named after King George by George Vancouver—double George, or triple, I guess, with you here."

"No-good king—treated all our people like slaves," said George.

"*Yeah*! Damn English enslaved everyone and gave out diseased blankets, those bastards," echoed Derik.

Raven shrugged. "I like having a queen; I respect the monarchy. The explorers were just exploring. If they didn't do it, someone else would have. Like, whoever discovered which mushrooms were OK to eat? Thousands of people probably got sick or *died* in the process."

"I don't like the Queen. They're nothing but a bunch of inbred pedophiles," said George.

Derik looked out over the water. He envisioned King George in the sky, or, at least, what he thought he looked like as he had never seen a picture of him. He wore a gold crown with diamonds, rubies and amethysts, a red robe inlaid with white and black ermine, and many chains over his chest. He had a big dark-brown moustache with a monocle, and striped pants, all adorning his majestic girth from the epic feasts he had, day and night, and he was grinning, not moving, happy, pomp and, well, divine—'twas a fair image of the King in rule. *No, I should be thinking of chiefs, not English kings and queens,* Derik reprimanded himself. He actively altered the sight: he imagined a Heiltsuk chief with an eagle crown inlaid with square pieces of abalone shell, and a red and black robe with bone buttons and strips of cedar bark hanging down. That one danced, sauntered!, hopping up and down and rocking ever so slightly back and forth, like a bird. *That was the way it was.*

"Yup," sighed George with a mouthful of food. "We better get moving, or it'll be dark before you know it."

"What happens at night?" said Derik.

"It gets dark."

"Oh... Will it be too dark to see anything?"

"We won't be able to see any logs or debris before it's too late, unless we travel really slow with the spotlight on."

"I see."

They had plenty of time before night set in, as the sun was high overhead. They set sail once more.

"Do you think we'll see any killer whales?" asked Derik.

"Maybe," said George. "There are usually lots of them in the strait."

And friends, he was somewhat right. There were a few resident orcas nearby, as well as some passing through—transient. You could tell them apart by their fins: transients had sharper, taller dorsal fins than residents whose were curvier, like the fish-eating offshore whales. Also, the transients tended to carry more nicks and lashes from catching seals and other sea mammals that fought back. One thing that separated offshores from residents was their propensity for shark liver. It was too tempting not to dine on sleeper-shark liver, as it was particularly engorged with fat to aid buoyancy. Apparently, this could account for 80 percent of the shark's weight (absurd if you think about it) which would be foolish for any killer whale to refuse.

There are few things more ostentatious than whaling—reason being it's a messy, rough lot, that involves disgracing one of God's great creatures.

"But Redbird," asks Coyote, "what about lions, or cows? Are they not great animals?"

Assuming hunting is acceptable, as opposed to hunting plants, I would not hunt a lion or an elephant for that very same reason: they are all great, majestic, inspiring animals. On the other wing, cows (although not hunted, harvested just the same) are domestic beasts with stable populations. If all populations were stable, would fates be altered? For what purpose, though? Certainly not for their meat over that of cattle, who have been bred over millennia to have better, fattier, tastier meat. For ivory, oil or fur? Such things are not worth a life. Also, with finality, may a cow's song be heard halfway across the world? And yet, whales were nearly exterminated to grease your machines.

Humpback whales, with their resplendent songs of courtship and salutation, once swam right into Vancouver Harbour, feasting on nekton which grew abundantly under sun. Now no longer, except if lost, because whales don't bother asking for directions. Heavily on Ahab the blame falls, though Indigenous Peoples of the Northwest Coast whaled for thousands of years, especially along the Alaskan coast, as did the Inuit of Arctic Canada. For them, whales were a major source of sustenance; beluga skin contained vitamin C, for example. However, these First Nations used every part of the whale they could, which wasn't the case with most white whalers. Industry meant easy mode, which led to over-harvesting—spearing whales with guns, reeling them in, then boiling blubber on deck. Instead, some Indigenous performed an intimate ritual, bathing themselves, submerging four times, spouting water from their mouths like whales from their blowholes, then heading out in dugout canoes to hunt the largest creatures ever manifest. No, indeed, whaling differed in both respect and sustainability between cultures.

Raven continued professing his love of whales. "Orcas have different languages, too, from family to family—different dialects. I have a vinyl record of whale songs at home. Crows also have different dialects from family to family."

"I want to see one," said Derik. "I want to see a bear, and a deer and a—"

"There are bears sometimes in Bella Bella," said George. "Never seen a deer there, though."

The wind rushed past, saying, "We know you. Follow us."

Derik asked, "When can we start fishing? I want to try using the fishing rod. I've never used one before."

"Yeah, you have," said George "We took you fishing when you and Candace were both really little."

"Really? I don't remember."

"Yeah. We took you to Harrison Hot Springs. There's a lake there."

"Did we catch anything?"

"I caught a small fish. You don't remember? Man, you have a terrible memory."

"I have a great memory," said Derik. "It's just selective is all. I'm pretty sure I remember being born."

"Pfft," scoffed George. "Why, what do you think you remember?"

"I remember seeing this bright, shining, white light, and then some guy holding me while I screamed and cried."

George was silent.

"I also remember Great-Grandma holding me, even though I was only a month old. She held me on her knee, and then when she spoke, I thought she sounded like a great big bird. We have a photo of her holding me, so it's not like I made that up."

"Hm," said Raven. "I believe it's possible. They say you can't remember anything before two, but the world is so abstract then, it's probably just a matter of discerning impressions rather than concrete thoughts."

"Yeah," said Derik. He didn't quite understand what Raven was talking about, or how to articulate his experiences, but was still convinced his memories were intact. "Why, what's the earliest memory you have, Dad?"

George thought about it. "I remember my mom cooking while I watched her from the top of the stairs. She made these great big pies and stuck them on the windowsill to cool, like you see in cartoons." His lips he did lick. "I also remember looking at all the jars of pickled abalone and clams and cucumbers in the pantry. We had everything: tomatoes, plums, peaches, jams, homemade marmalade—oh, and stacks and stacks of canned salmon. It was so good. We didn't have refrigeration back then, so she had to jar or pickle everything, or else it would go bad."

"Right. And what's *your* earliest memory?" Derik asked Raven.

"I remember I was watching a montage of my life, but it played all at once—fourth dimension. Then an angel came and said to me, 'This is your mission. Will you accept it?' And I said yes, and they threw me into my mother's belly."

Derik didn't know what to make of that.

Another thing about whales: How could you keep them in captivity? They travel dozens of miles every day in the wild, yet someone figured it was OK to keep them in a swimming pool? No wonder they turned on their trainers, who forced them to perform for sardines. Imagine speaking, but all you hear is your voice played back on eleven. One orca was born in captivity then separated from its mother while she turned tricks. It was kept in a pen beside its biological father, who repeatedly rammed the partition with God knows what intention. The baby died soon after, and the park pulled all associated merchandise. It's so cruel it's almost funny.

"...So when are we going fishing?" asked Derik. "We should use our new rods, or else they were just a waste of money."

"Wait till we get close to Texada Island," said George. "There's no point in trying them around here, it's too deep. Those rods are better suited for lake or river fishing, where it's shallower."

"Ten-four," said Derik. "...Were the first explorers Spanish?"

"The first explorers were Spanish, yeah," said George

"Some were Russian!" added Raven.

"That's why you see a lot of Spanish names for islands and points."

"Do you think maybe *we're* part Spanish?"

"No," said George. "We don't have any Spanish blood in us."

"My friend's mom thought I was Spanish 'cause I have dark features."

"All Natives have dark features, and they tan really easily."

"Maybe it's 'cause we're all part Spanish. We should get one of those tests, where you spit in a vial and they tell you what genes you have. Then we'll know for sure."

"No. Those things are a total *scam*."

"Why? How are they a scam?"

"Because then they have all your DNA on file. Who knows what they'll do with it? They sell all that information, you know."

"What's it matter if someone has my DNA?"

"Maybe one day they'll decide to start rounding up Indians again, and putting them in camps. It wouldn't be the first time."

Derik scoffed. "That'll never happen."

"You never know. Maybe tomorrow we'll be on the menu again."

"They already know we're Indians anyway, we have status."

"It's expensive, that test. I think they charge you two hundred dollars to take it."

"That's not much to know where your ancestors came from; I have like a thousand dollars in the bank."

"You're *not* getting that test," said Stern George. "It's a waste of money. You should just keep saving for a new bike or something."

"All *right*. I won't get the test."

"You're Heiltsuk—that's all you need to know. They can't tell you much more than that anyway."

"I know quite a few people who took DNA tests," Raven said. "They were shocked to learn they were one twelfth African."

"We're all from Africa originally," said Derik. "That's what Mr. Jim said, my grade six teacher."

"That still doesn't explain the red hair," said George. "Some of us must have descended from giants."

"No giant talk please." Derik shoved the conversation back to George. "...That'd be so rad if I was part Spanish."

"You're *not* Spanish; they never landed in Bella Bella. Our people scared them off. They anchored off the coast, then sent some people ashore who never made it back 'cause we captured and ate them. That's why they called us cannibals." George grinned ear to ear, eyes wide. "We *liked* eating them, too."

"That's not quite true," said Raven. "Your dad and other Elders told me the Spanish traded and even played games with the Heiltsuk. They had rowing competitions, swimming competitions and even boating competitions (once they got hold of some). I asked him, thoroughly, during our interviews. Some groups *did* practise cannibalism, though—for real. The Cannibal Dance was the most prestigious of dances anyone could perform, as there were two categories of dance: one, which would be handed down based on title and family, and the other, which anyone was permitted to do, like the Cannibal Dance... unless you were female, I think. The Cannibal Dance was extremely important and sophisticated."

"That book you brought into the pawnshop mentioned no one was sure whether the Heiltsuk actually ate people or not," said Derik.

"Some people say yes, some people strongly deny it—for obvious reasons. The idea was that a young man was considered a cannibal, and unfit for civil life, until the masters of the secret society kidnapped him and took him away to some remote location where they initiated him slowly, and probably gave him hallucinogenic drugs so he really *did* act like a cannibal. He was tied to a pole, a 'cannibal pole,' and would dance for three days while men dressed as mythical birds—like Crooked Beak, who was said to deconstruct reality with its breath—danced around him, clacking their big wooden beaks. After that, they'd bring him back to town, where he'd begin life anew as a normal human being. They called it the Cannibal Dance in part because the initiate would consume himself in the process, kinda like a self-cannibalism, and basically resurrect as a transcendent individual, fit for subservience to society."

I wish I could do that dance.

Why? It sounds horrifying!

I'm sure it's not that bad.

I guess you would think you're really being kidnapped though, which would suck.

I would never eat a person. "Do you think they still do the dance somewhere?"

"Maybe. The thing is, it was always done in secret, by a secret society, in a secret location—so unless they announced it, we wouldn't know, would we?"

Yes, BC always was a murky, secluded place for most of the year, rich with secrets, attracting the worst of the worst. The first settlers (sorely lacking in space as of late) included outcasts and prospectors in search of gold and other precious resources. Travelling north, one may find many relics of their expeditions, now rusted and reclaimed by Gaia, or preserved for tourism—such as the boardwalks of Barkerville, or machines within Britannia Mine (where *House of the Dead* was filmed).

"They had a machine called the widowmaker," said Derik, recapping a recent field trip there. "Because whoever used it would be dead soon after. Then they would kick out their family."

Gold came and went, though (not so ironically) the Mormins built a business acquiring and selling it. It's how the Spanish got rich, after all, raiding the mythical El Dorado. For the Indigenous Peoples of BC, however, it served little purpose. Copper was more common and malleable, so more useful. Prospectors moved on from BC, while fringe types moved in, such as Malcolm Lowry and Brother XII. Even Crowley stopped by. "We never sighted the slightest suggestion of life all the way to Vancouver," he wrote, "...though there was a certain impressiveness in the very dreariness and desolation." The first Ordo Templi Orientis lodge in North America was established in Vancouver, also, lending to its mystique.

"Vancouver Island is full of Satanists," said George.

"Satanists—what do you mean?" asked Derik.

"Kids go missing there all the time. They kidnap them and sacrifice them to Satan, cutting out their hearts and drinking their blood."

"No way, that doesn't happen. You're joking, right?" Derik turned to Raven. "That doesn't happen, does it?"

"Not really."

"I'm serious!" said George. "I heard it on the news."

George was referencing the "satanic ritual abuse" panic that began upon publication of *Michelle Remembers* in 1980—a reportedly true story of a girl's imprisonment in a Satanic cult in Victoria—which has since been widely debunked.

"I think the Satanists are more in San Fran than here," said Raven.

"That's true," said George. "But I'm certain there are a lot on the Island."

❦ ❦ ❦

They sailed toward Texada Island, farther toward Vancouver Island, home of the Nanaimo bar.

"There are better stops along the way," said George. "There's nothing really north of here on Vancouver Island." It wasn't true—he just wanted to make haste in case the narrows turned against them. They skipped over the short, chopping waves that sparkled as they broke, turning to mist in the sun. The motions were repetitive, yet hypnotic.

If I fell overboard, they wouldn't even know. They wouldn't be able to hear me scream over the engine. They'd just keep going without me.

"Here—take the wheel." George let go. *Wild Thing* veered to the right. Derik, in static quiet, jumped to, grabbing hold.

"Don't do that!" Derik said. "—Let go of the wheel like that."

George laughed. "What? We're not going to hit anything out here!" He puffed his vape.

"What if we hit a big wave? The boat could roll over."

"No, not out here. The waves never get that big. In open ocean it could happen, but not out here; this is nothing. Make sure you keep her steady. Try and hit the waves at a bit of an angle."

"Like that?"

"Yeah, that's fine. Just keep her steady." George grabbed the wheel, demonstrating. "Like that."

Derik held the wheel with pride. "There's not much to it really. How do I turn on the autopilot?"

"No." George dismissed him quickly.

Onward they went on the treadmill of sparkling sea, until they reached Texada Island, where the first one got away.

18. Fire on the Beach

They spent the night in Comox after Derik failed to net the first salmon his dad hooked, Raven and George dipping into a sports bar to eat wings and burgers, and watch baseball, while Derik stayed aboard, pouting and feeling sorry for himself. *I just want to catch a fish; I want to prove I'm a real Native.*

That's ridiculous, not every Native knows how to fish.

Yeah they do, they all caught fish, that's what they ate.

Who cares? I just want to die—don't have a girlfriend, born to a drug dealer. My kids will just suffer the same fate (if I ever have any, which I won't).

George had asked him if he wanted to go with them, but he'd refused from behind the door. He hardly got any sleep, rocking on the water, bumping against the dock, fearing the boat would sink while they slept.

The next day, Derik sat hunched, with cap down, earbuds in, hardly moving at all. He didn't play any games, read any books, or watch YouTube videos. He dwelled on the salmon that escaped and every alternative outcome—everything he could've done different. He was in the sixth dimension, you see, where all possibilities occurred across past, present and future. Unfortunately, it had little bearing upon mundane circumstances. Raven and George ate scrambled eggs and took turns at the wheel.

They sailed to Campbell River, passing a beach packed with tourists, flocking for fish and chips, fried clams and oysters—a collage of flesh, neon swimwear, towels, folding chairs, parasols, shanties, circling gulls and children in the surf. Every parking spot was aggressively contested; it was a typical summer day. Even the morning air was warm (foreshadowing the inferno), our lads donning shorts—Raven blue, and George black nylon—except Derik, who wore dark track pants in protest of the bacchanal. *They're so crazy, jumping up and down in the sun.* George popped a lemon soda.

"Why so glum, chum?" he asked. Derik couldn't hear him over his Post Malone, so George stared. Derik reluctantly took out an earbud.

"What?" he said bluntly.

"You look upset. What's the matter?"

"Nothing… I'm fine." He was confrontational, but when asked how he felt, he began to relent; he felt his insolence morph.

"Don't get so upset just because one fish got away—sometimes you catch one, sometimes you don't. You'll get one soon."

"Thanks. Awesome." Derik was still upset, but the healing began like itchy wounds. *Stupid Dad didn't tell me what to do. Just expected me to know innately how to catch a fish.*

"You'll get the hang of it. I've been fishing my whole life—so has Raven."

"I know, but I didn't even get a *bite*. I thought I could get *one*."

"That was one tough fish; don't feel bad." George hugged Derik to his chest. Derik, reluctantly, let it happen. He required a threshold of affection to be passed before he could return to normal. George kissed him on the head. "I love you so much… I'm proud of you. You'll catch a fish—just keep trying and you'll get it eventually."

"I know… I love you too."

George drew away his face. "Let's have a good day, all right? Sun is shining. Waves are clear. We're stopping at Port Hardy; we can check and see if they have any Pokémon cards. How's that sound?"

"They won't have any; the new ones are sold out everywhere."

"Doesn't hurt to look! Probably less people buying them out here than in Vancouver."

George was right: island life wasn't city life. Rural living was much slower, laid back, unlike the kinetic urban with its infra-structure of power grids, compartment homes and waffle fries. On the Island, people owned large lots, merged with wilderness, drove freely on highways and back roads, and didn't raid stores for toilet paper, creating shortage and inflation. They approached the western fringe.

All around, names reflected colonialism: Desolation Sound for its complete lack of respectable prospects; Cape Caution, where one ought to pay attention!; and of course, Mount Baker, named after Joseph Baker, a lieutenant of George Vancouver. Yup, our old pal George gave out names like pins at a Pride convention. Even Haida Gwaii was called the Queen Charlotte Islands until 2010 (*Haida Gwaii*, of course, meaning "islands of the people," being the natural territory of the Haida First Nation).

❧ ❧ ❧

They reached Port Hardy in the evening. The pier was packed with fishers strolling after a full day of catching salmon. Many kicked back, with caps shadowing their eyes, gabbing under the falling sun. Our three docked, then walked the pier which rode the wake.

"If anyone asks, we have our tidal waters licence," said George, about as low as you'd expect.

"I thought we don't need a licence 'cause we're Indigenous?" said Derik.

"This is considered tidal water, so we're supposed to have special permits. If anyone asks, we have them."

"What if they ask to see them?"

"Then tell them you forgot it at home. No one's going to check. They should leave us alone."

"All right," Derik said, uneasy. *Probably get us in more trouble.* They took their rods, making sure *Wild Thing* was secure, and picked a spot on a floating dock. "Wow! Look at all the salmon!" Dozens of salmon darted through schools of herring, herding and eating them like wolves. With an aerial view from the pier, one could see the hordes of salmon circling the pilings, dividing ranks, but only fools would cast from such a height, as many tried, reeling their catch halfway up before it fell back. The successful took to the floating docks.

"If we don't catch a salmon here, then we can't call ourselves fishermen," said George.

"Aye," said Raven. "There's salmon aplenty."

Derik eagerly assembled his tackle, racing to first cast. An eagle in a tree nearby trilled. *I better catch a salmon. I'm not gonna stop until I do. Gotta make the ancestors proud.* They admired his tenacity.

"Whoa, he's ready this time," said Raven. Him and George chuckled, but Derik was serious. He'd hold back nothing this time.

I'll dive in and catch them with my bare hands if I have to. It meant everything to him: his livelihood, his maturation, his self-respect. His entire being was focused on this one goal. Nothing would stop him. No, even if Poseidon himself upturned the pier with a rogue wave, scattered all fish, sunk *Wild Thing* and sundered Vancouver Island, Derik would still catch that fish.

He stepped forward in reverence, the kelp made radiant by the sun. He drew his rod, cocked it over his shoulder, then cast with such force, such vigour and determination, he attracted the eyes of everyone remotely close to the pier—all who called it quits or strolled with ice cream in hand or gabbed subversively (especially the women). Derik hit his mark. The buzz bomb smacked the water, casting sparks, and sank to the world below.

The trick with the buzz bomb is to let it sink, reel it in till it's near the surface, then let it sink again, as it's the sinking that actually makes it buzz to attract the salmon. Otherwise, they have no impulse to swallow the lure, as their other senses indicate it is, indeed, artificial. Derik, though determined, did not know this, so let the lure rest on the bottom. *Just be patient.*

Raven and George cast and, like the other experienced fishers, used their buzz bombs properly.

"*Oh!* I got a bite," said George. He reeled in. "Never mind, it was snagged."

Raven persistently reeled in then let it fall. A salmon darted from the shadows of herring—like a UFO flying nigh jets, then blinking to the horizon—judging the lure and deeming it worthy: *This, I eat.* It charged and sucked in the buzz. Raven felt the tug, so flicked back to set. Instantly, the salmon routed, trying to free itself, to unhook the tether from hell, because would they call air heaven? *No! Get away! I don't want to die!* Both the salmon and Derik were equally determined in their efforts. It ran the line to the deep, blue water. Raven steered it left and right. It dove under the dock. Raven pulled up heavily; the rod arced to the surface. It eventually returned at full speed. They performed this ancient act for several minutes.

Meanwhile, Derik, losing patience, reeled in his buzz bomb: *Maybe I have a bite.* But he could not reel in; it was stuck... again. He broke into panic; his skin ignited. Everyone seemed to focus on him. Subtly (or so he figured) he tugged the line, but it would not come. *Oh no, oh no, not again. I can't be stuck again. No way. There's no way!*

"Derik, quick, get the net for Raven! He's got a bite!" George was too busy with his own line. "Derik!"

"One second!" *Try tugging right, like they do. Nothing. Try left! Nothing. Nothing is working. Nothing works.* He was still snagged despite his best efforts.

Raven had tired the salmon.

What, am I to see my maker? That's probably what it's thinking.

The fish gazed up to the shifting towers. Raven pulled it next to the dock, lifting its head out, and with one finger hooked behind its gills, gently raised it from the water and placed it at his feet. The fish flopped, traumatized.

"That's a nice coho you got there," said George.

"Yeah," said Raven. He grabbed the club and did the deed. He scanned the myriad colours in the sky as the sun dipped to the distant boats and mountains. "We should have a fire on the beach there and cook the salmon on one of those grills." The rusted-iron firepits had grills of thick, rectangular bars. "Then we can just gut 'em and throw the whole sides on—eat 'em caveman style, like the bunch of savages we are."

"Sounds good to me," said George. "Oh!" He tugged on the line. "I think I got a bite." He reeled in some. The line was taut. "Yup! Definitely got something. Derik, quick, get me the net! I got a bite!"

But Derik was still struggling to free his line on the lip of the dock, line wrapped around both hands, jerking madly.

"*Derik*, come quick! It's gonna get away!" George was as excited as a child. He did the dance immemorial with the fish, bargaining for its life—the right to claim a soul from the underworld. Derik tugged again and his hook popped free. *It's free!*

No way.

Yes, it is—look! He couldn't believe it. He reeled in the line, dropped his rod, then lunged for the net. He stood beside George, sticking it underwater. *OK, no sudden movements, like the T. rex in Jurassic Park. Stay in position. Lift up slowly when it's completely inside.* Derik was vigilant while George tired the salmon. It came willing, eventually, exhausted, but not defeated—*What do you want?!* Derik anticipated its movements, like sparring an opponent: tracing their breath, noting their clench, then jabbing between their guard and throwing a left hook, followed by a calf kick before ducking out.

"OK, now!" said George. "Pull it up!"

But Derik was patient this time. He let the fish glide into the net, then slowly pulled up. It realized it was caught, so flailed, so Derik hastened. Diamonds fell, glowing in the fading sun. The salmon thrashed in the net, but it was too late. Derik placed it on the dock. He had netted his first salmon.

"Nice work," said George. "We're going to eat well tonight!" He licked his lips.

Is it a coho? He didn't ask. He picked up his rod and began casting again. *They're all jigging; try jigging.* He adjusted, triggering the buzz of the bomb. All he wanted was a bite—at least a nibble. The silvery salmon repeatedly inspected the lure, but left it, swimming away.

Nah, it's a trap. I'm not hungry.

No, I don't want that; that thing is death.

Yup, I saw Bill get caught last week—dragged out by his mouth. Never saw him again.

The salmon weren't having it. Over and over he cast and jigged but found no takers. "They're right there! Why won't they take the lure!" He was frustrated. All around him was success: over there another father-son duo caught a flounder; on the opposite dock a sun-weathered old man with golden stubble, worn black cap and crooked teeth pulled up a trap full of Dungeness crab. *I'm the only one not catching anything. I could literally dive in and grab a salmon. They're right there.* And right there they were, friends, swimming back and forth, taunting him.

Raven caught another. A seal reared its head in the distance, ready to steal a bite. George stepped beside Derik. "You should aim beside the schools of herring—the salmon are always herding them there."

Derik observed the herring shift like a cluster of starlings, while the salmon, the wolves of this particular sea, swam parallel the dock, right in front of him. He dropped the lure before one, feet away. It hardly sank before the salmon eyed it, charged it, then swallowed it. He got his first bite! Off it took the line.

"I got one!" said Derik. "I got a bite!"

"Good," said George. "Just be patient. Let it tire itself out."

But Derik knew what to do, having dissected past failures and absorbed influence about him. He tired that fish out and then some, preventing it from going under the dock or worse!—wrapping the line around a piling. It was stronger than he figured, though he knew it would be a fight. The salmon passed once, giving evil eye, cursing Derik for having hooked it. It passed twice, then thrice, before tiring; Derik sapped its energy. "It's tired now. Get the net! I'm gonna pull it in."

George got the net, kneeled and dipped it in the water.

"OK," said Derik. "Here it comes."

Everything was perfect: the fish was tired, it swam close from a good distance, straight, parallel with the dock, and George was in position with the net; destiny and skill converged. *Should be closer, it's going to miss the net.*

Pull it closer.

But I don't want to scare it by yanking it, it might come off.

Here it goes! The salmon, again, was half in the net, then George lifted at the most awkward of angles. It was like he wanted the fish to go free at the last second, and failure to set in again, because that's exactly what happened. The fish hit the rim, thrashed for its life, unhooked itself, fell safely back in the sea, then swam off, free. All the spectators were elated; they wouldn't have to top Derik's effort. The energy of the travail dissipated.

But Derik was getting used to failure by now; he was not upset, nor mad at himself, but disappointed with his father. George messed up the catch that time. Although Derik didn't pull the fish close enough, it was ultimately the proper use of the net that facilitated the most embarrassment. He had hooked it, he had tired the fish, he had reeled it in; using the net was a fraction of the work. So the blame fell heavy on George.

"Aw," said Derik. "You had it! Why'd you let it go?"

"I didn't mean to, it slipped out!" George stood, wide eyed. Derik put him on the ropes.

"We're even now, OK? We both lost one."

"*You* had it too far out!" said George Flung-Hands. "You're supposed to bring it in close so I can grab it with the net."

Derik shook his head, seeing the purples, yellows, oranges, blues and greens rising from the horizon. "We were so close," he mocked. He was, of course, serious, also, criticizing his dad, but his tone was jest. They were competitive: Derik always wanted to be better at everything than George, and when he couldn't, he'd feign indifference till he could. George's greatest fear and joy was the day his son would best him. A father's curse—to be surpassed by his children, everywhere, anyhow, until his bones turn brittle, and hair turns grey—is also a gift—to pass on his talents to someone he loves, who aspires to be like him, and improve his legacy, accomplishing what he meant to do.

Raven reeled in another. "Bring me the net," he said. George dipped down the net, and the fish swam right in.

"See Derik," said George. "That's how you do it."

"You messed up with the net," Derik said. "Get over yourself."

Raven took the pliers and unhooked the hook with a yank. The fish flipped and flopped, but George kept it imprisoned in the water, holding the net at an angle. A spurt of blood drifted from the salmon's mouth.

"Nice one, isn't she?" said Raven.

"How do you know it's a female?" asked Derik.

"You can see the eggs in her belly."

I can't see any.

"OK, you can let her go now."

"You're not going to keep it?" said Derik.

"No… We got plenty already."

George submerged the net slowly. The salmon was disoriented, having accepted its fate. It swam away, shocked more than offended, and was instantly eaten by a seal.

The sun set, concluding feeding time (fish being most volatile at dusk or dawn). The cool wind rippled the water—solar wake. They were all chilled, wearing shorts, with their sunburnt legs. They forgot to wear sunscreen, as they weren't used to being exposed to the sun for so long. Raven reached up, making a *V* with his arms, as if (from Derik's angle, kneeled beside the fish with dead eyes) holding the sky.

Sun seekers walked the boardwalk of the quaint town similar to other industrial towns along the coast, with European-style shops of toys, cafes, fishing supplies and art. But in the park was no statue of green-tarnished copper, but a totem pole. Thick, chipped and pocked with wisdom, the red and blue paint still grabbed the eye. On the beach our heroes hauled their bounty. Raven sat on the log before the rusted firepit while George and Derik gathered firewood.

"Get something that's dry," said George. "Like this."

"OK. Calm down."

Derik gathered driftwood that had dried in the sun in his arms and dumped it beside the pit. George gathered sticks of cedar he cracked into pieces. "I wish we had the axe," he said. "Then I could make proper kindling."

He shredded a paper bag as tinder, then piled it in the pit. He set it with precision, nudging till perfect. Then he constructed a tipi of kindling overtop to direct the fire to the sky. He took some dry grass that grew among the sand and bundled it before the pile. He kneeled, then lit the dry grass, blowing it till aflame, then surely slid it into the pile. The tinder ignited, then claws of flame grasped the sticks with slow, steady breaths from George. A great fire was formed that sanitized the grill, and glowed orange and yellow in the blue dusk.

"We made fire!" said Raven. He laid out the fish, which George had gutted and scaled on the pier, tossing the guts to the seals, the dogs of the sea (although, if the salmon were wolves, in comparison, seals would be lions… and I suppose sharks would be tigers, and whales, elephants), who were thankful. "Do you want *me* to cut the sides off, or do you want to do it? You said you worked in a fish-processing plant."

George looked around. He found what he was looking for. "Let's cook one whole, on the grill, then you fillet one." He went and grabbed a pole of cedar, and began whittling.

"What are you doing?" said Derik. Raven filleted the fish, covering his hands with pink, sticky fluid—you can never get the smell out.

"You'll see." George whittled the bottom to a blunt point, then stuck it in the ground to test. "That's not going anywhere."

"What are you making?!" said Derik.

"Hold your horses! You'll see." He split the top lengthwise, two-thirds down, then scoured the beach for the final piece. He searched and he searched, a star already in the sky. At last, he found it: he took the shoelace from the old shoe, and tied shut the split top.

"What is it?"

"It's to cook the fish."

Derik wasn't impressed, as he didn't understand how it'd work. *Won't the fish just fall out? Looks dumb to me.*

"I just need two sticks to hold the fish, then we place it in front of the fire, and we got ourselves a rotisserie."

"Huh," said Derik. George crafted himself some thick cedar skewers, then stuck them through the fillets Raven prepared (with grocery bags for a cutting board). Derik poked the eye. "Gross," he said.

"The eyes are good!" said Raven. "You ever try one?"

"No! I'll never eat an eyeball."

"They'll help you see better."

"Are you *actually* cooking the head?"

"Of course! Some of the best eating is in the head. The cheeks are the best part."

Really? Derik's curiosity was peaked by Raven's enthusiasm. *I mean, if he likes them, they must be pretty good.* Raven washed off his stinky hands, while George dipped his carving in the sea.

"Why'd you do that?" said Derik.

"So it doesn't catch fire. I don't want it to burn while the salmon's cooking."

The fire burned steadily. George skewered the salmon to the cross, then stuck the cross in the sand. Right away the fillets sizzled faintly. Raven placed the whole salmon on the grill after coating it lightly with canola oil.

"This is going to be *so* good," said George. "Smoke's the best seasoning." They had journeyed far for this.

"This makes it all worth the effort," said Raven.

I cannot say they were jovial. Derik, especially, had mixed feelings, beginning his descent precipitated by George's change from goofy pawnshop owner to deranged fisherman. The open ocean was waiting, filling Derik with dread. *We're not even in Bella Bella yet.* They sat before the fire, watching flames dance. It was supposed to be a special occasion, as it was for their ancestors. Yet, Derik was already missing home—his room, his bed, his friends and mother. *I still have so far to go.*

Raven flipped the salmon and George rotated the cross.

"How much longer?" asked Derik.

"A few more minutes." George slurped. "I hope you're hungry!"

"Starving," said Raven, as Derik got up to grab mustard, buns, salad greens, paper plates and plastic forks from the boat. He carried it all in a yellow-striped picnic container with some citrus sodas. He took his time walking back. George was taking down the cross when he returned.

Raven poked the whole salmon. "This one needs a few more minutes."

George untied the shoelace and took off the steaming fillets encrusted with white fat and pink flesh. He took an overcooked end with crispy skin and tossed it in his mouth. It sizzled as he manoeuvred it around, trying not to burn himself. "*Wow* that's good!" he said, puffing steam. The whole salmon was done soon after. They laid them on clean plastic bags.

"All right, let's tuck in," said George. They loaded their plates. Derik took a cheek. The crucified salmon was well done—smoky and charred for more flavour—while the whole fish was moist, even underdone in parts. They picked their preferred bits, like a buffet, with a squirt of mustard, some salad greens and a soda. "This is fantastic." George devoured his, followed by Raven, while Derik preferred to chew his. They were all content in their own way.

"Great job on the rotisserie there, George," Raven said. "I've only ever seen my grandpa make one of those before."

"Thanks. Yup, the old man taught me how to make it. He was a master carver. I'm glad it turned out well."

"The cheeks are good," said Derik.

"Told you!" said Raven. "It's all that smiling they do."

Derik chuckled meekly. *This is my new favourite part.*

You're just saying that 'cause he likes them.

No, I mean it. They're so tender and flavourful! His spirit flickered.

They ate their bounty, reminiscing about old friends, even joking about the one that got away. Eating fresh-caught salmon cooked over a wood fire was an experience that couldn't be beat.

A couple, a gal and a guy, approached the fire, eyes of intrigue. The dude had a Modelo in his hand and wore a dark cap. The woman was short and heavy, squat, like a squash. They couldn't resist the allure of the fire. "How's it going?" the guy said.

"Good," said George. "Just eating the salmon we caught."

"That's a nice fire you got there." They introduced themselves as Dan and Laura.

"We're from Vancouver," said George. "Heading up to Bella Bella for my dad's funeral."

"Oh. We're Nuu-Chah-Nulth—from Duncan."

"Mm," she said.

"So what brings you here?" asked George.

"We came to look at a truck—a 2018 Silverado. But the guy jacked up the price by five grand once we got here, so we told him to take a hike." He pointed his thumb over his shoulder. "Now we're just staying the night before we head back tomorrow."

"Must've been white."

They both burst out laughing. "Who else would do a thing like that?" Instantly, they were friends. Dan kept eyeing the fish.

"You want some salmon? We got lots. Freshly caught and cooked."

"*Yeah*, that'd be great."

"Please," said Laura.

"Get them some plates," George told Derik.

What am I, a slave? Who the hell are these guys, taking our salmon? Whatever, it'll just go to waste. Derik got them plates, and spooned some salmon onto the plates, and then sprayed some mustard on the plates, but he didn't put mixed greens on the plates, because he figured they didn't want salad. They got their plates and were happy.

"Thanks, bud," said Dan; and the girl, "Thanks."

They think you're cringe.

"So you have a boat?" said George.

"Yup. We came here on our boat." He scarfed his salmon and washed it down with beer. "Who was your dad? I know a few people from Bella Bella."

"Henry Mormin was his name."

He held his fork in suspense. "You're kidding."

George inhaled sharply. "Nope. That was his name all right. Why, d'you know him?"

"He gave me my first job as a deckhand—taught me how to bait hooks and set a longline. He was the greatest fisherman I ever saw—always knew where the fish were. Holy cow, man. He died?"

"Yup."

"Damn, last time I saw him was in 2009 I think. When's the funeral?"

"Next Thursday."

Dan looked to Laura. "Should we go?"

"I can't," she said. "I have a *job*."

"Well I'm going. Who knows where I'd be without him. I'd probably be in prison. I used to tag buildings all over Nanaimo, but I didn't have time for that when I started working for your dad." He belched. "God, Henry Mormin! I can't believe that."

"That's life," said George. "We come and we go."

"Well, I'll follow you to Bella Bella, I haven't been there since I worked for him, I think. We would stop there for supplies, and to stock up on beer." He chuckled. "I remember it was my birthday, and he came out with the biggest bottle of Jack Daniels I ever saw. It was a magnum. Man, did we get drunk that night."

"Uh-huh."

"Sounds like a cool guy," said Derik, failing to fit in.

Dan snorted. "God, what a great guy. Sorry to hear he died."

"Yeah... It's sad to see him go." Derik saw the shifting sands within George.

The tide was coming in, lapping, dark, mysterious and foamy onto the beach. For a while, that was all they heard. Then the neighbouring voices of partygoers returned like baying hounds.

George fed sticks to the flame.

Laura and Dan finished the last of their salmon before departing. Derik and George left Raven to put out the fire. He filled a sandy, sun-worn bucket with water from the sea, then extinguished the last embers. They hissed and splattered; droplets danced on the red eyes, refusing to become steam.

Derik was ready to forgive his dad, but he wasn't in the most amiable of moods. "Do you think Grandpa is still around?"

George puffed his vape. "I think so, yeah."

"Does that make you happy, that he's still around?"

"No," he said, unsure. "I don't think he can pass on to heaven, that's why he's still around. He's probably too burdened by his possessions and everyone he's hurt. He has to make amends for his wrongs before God will allow him to."

"So you think Grandpa's going to hell?"

"No, I don't think Grandpa's going to hell. How can you say that?"

"Well if he's not going to heaven, doesn't that mean he's going to hell?"

"Derik, you have to think before you speak. I just *told* you, he has to make up for all the bad things he did."

"Like what? Dan seemed to like him, so did that guy who saw him play guitar."

"He was a terrible father to me; he used to beat my sisters and me. Those people that liked him never saw what he was like at home."

"Why are we going to his funeral, then, if he wasn't a good person?"

"Because you should respect your father and your mother. I *have* to go see him."

"You don't *have* to if he was a bad person."

"I *have* to!" George shot daggers.

Derik recognized the look: he was one step from being chewed out. *Why does he have to get so upset when I bring up Grandpa?*

You know how he is. Derik submitted by looking away. "How is he supposed to make amends when he's dead? Isn't he just a ghost now?"

"I don't want to talk about it."

"You can't just say you don't want to talk about it when it's the main reason why we're travelling to Bella Bella. Just like *you* brought up selling drugs, then stopped answering my questions."

"I told you all I can, Derik. The truth will only hurt you."

"Yeah, well, truth hurts sometimes. It's better I know than be left in the dark all the time."

"You have no idea what you're talking about."

"How? You're the one that dropped out of school to catch fish and sell drugs."

George charged Derik, thrusting his finger in his face. "I did what it took to survive, you ungrateful turd! So don't ever talk to me like that *again*. You don't know what I'm capable of."

Derik's chin quivered, his whole being shaking with adrenaline. *OK, that's enough. Drop it.* "…I guess I never will."

George kept his eyes locked as he slowly lowered his finger. He walked toward *Wild Thing*, his sway not seeming so strange with the waves beneath his feet.

Raven caught up to Derik. "Hey, what are you waiting for?"

Derik was still reeling from the confrontation. "Nothing. I was just admiring the view… Can I ask you something?"

"You know you can."

"Do you believe in heaven?"

Raven pondered, gazing at the silver breakers passing like static on an old TV. "What do you mean *believe* in—do I think heaven's real?"

"Yeah."

"Uh, sure—heaven *is* real. Whatever you think is real is real. So if you think heaven is real, then heaven is real."

"But do *you* think heaven's real?"

"Yeah, heaven is real. Why, why do you ask?"

"'Cause I thought Native people don't believe in heaven; heaven is a white person belief."

"That's not really true. Heaven is a Christian… destination. It's how they define the afterlife. All our energy, our spirit, all that we are that isn't physical (uh, to dualists, I suppose) goes somewhere once we die, and that *somewhere* is what they call heaven, basically. They probably wouldn't say that, though. They'd say you have your body, or a duplicate of your body, and your friends and loved ones will be there for all of eternity (which is a bit too much, if you ask me). No one knows for sure what it's *actually* like. Maybe we just float around as light bulbs. I don't think we can comprehend what it is until we get there."

And Derik was more confused than ever: was his grandpa still with him, somehow, in some form? He envisioned him with a full head of white hair, large stature, a true giant at six foot three, a warrior! He saw him dressed in dark slacks and a tucked-in Peru-brown button-up shirt (respectable for an elder), and his bass voice—a voice not made from English, a voice from the past, another time.

"I think my grandpa's still around… Do you believe that?"

"*Sure,*" said Raven, eager to confirm. "I *know* he's still around. His spirit lives on."

Indeed, his spirit lived on. But what is meant by such a statement? Henry Mormin lived on in many forms. In the most rudimentary sense, indicated by Newton's first law of thermodynamics—energy can be transformed from one form to another, but can neither be created nor destroyed—death released the energy that animated the body we called Henry Mormin. This questionable narrator would propose some sense of romance, however (for what is life without it?), and argue Henry's consciousness lived on.

How may one validate the continuance of consciousness? Certainly one wouldn't ask dear Henry. Perhaps, then, we can deduce what became of his consciousness, as it seems agreed it did not reside in the body; otherwise (a) he would've still been alive, or (b) what a restricted consciousness that'd be—"I'm slowly sinking into the ground!" or, "I never took care of it anyway." The mind wanders unrestrained. This possibility aside—because what else to prove, and how?—we can argue consciousness consists of a continuation of thought, personality or perception. Thus, one ought to study the passing of these constituents post-mortem. A person is most remembered after passing, after all. Any celebrity death instantly generates attention, affection and appreciation of their work. People tweet their condolences, they binge their films and they romanticize. In this sense, then, the dead live on in the thoughts and memories of the people *more so* than the living. Therefore, consciousness continues. To George and Raven, so did spirit. "Their spirit lives on," they would say. "They live on."

Of course, you could take your filth and throw it at the wall, dis-agreeing with the above. Only you can decide, and you get there by believing.

❦ ❦ ❦

Back on the boat, tensions were still high between Derik and George. *It won't last long. The worst is exposed. Now the healing can begin.* It was usually Derik's responsibility to forgive. George put away some cups, then entered his stateroom.

Raven laid his pillows on the booth (which was also his bed), then reclined, putting his feet up. "*Ah,*" he sighed. "This is nice." They were all tired. Rest was much welcomed. Derik put away the condiments, paper plates and leftover mixed greens.

"Not everyone has the patience to study their beliefs like you do," Raven said, reading the room. The moon made the air blue. "They're usually biased toward their own emotions rather than being reasonable."

"I know… It's just annoying trying to figure out anything when everything keeps changing."

Raven winked, silver illuminating his left face, and shadow, his right. "I know what you mean… Try not to overthink things. Sometimes you just have to accept fate, and let the world take you away on this crazy journey called *life.*"

He's right. There's nothing else you can do. "I try and appreciate the journey, but sometimes it's difficult."

Raven sighed. "It is until you let what will be, be. There's no point in getting upset over what's beyond your control."

"You're right," Derik said, resigned. He went for his room, then stopped. "Can I ask you one more thing?"

"Of course."

"In *The Book of Thoth,* Crowley mentions conversation with one's holy guardian angel as being the most supreme act one can perform. Sometimes, I feel like I'm talking to someone else, in my head, called

Redbird. He tells me to do things, ways to keep me safe and how to be a better person. Do you think that's my holy guardian angel?"

Raven tensed with the gravity of the moment. "Could be. I've often thought maybe I've finally conversed with my HGA, but it's difficult to tell for certain. How to attain that conversation is a secret only you can figure out... You equated angels with birds because they both have wings?"

"Maybe... I don't know."

Raven smiled, then sat back. "A guardian's a guardian. Maybe they're beings of light, and depictions of angels are more symbolic rather than physical representations. If Redbird means that much to you, then they're probably worth listening to."

"I started thinking that way after I got attacked by the dog."

"That makes sense. Maybe he is your guardian, if he protected you. Does he ever mess with you, like try and get you to do stupid things?"

"All the time! Usually it's pretty funny, though."

Raven chuckled. "Sounds like a trickster to me. The trickster is a part of all our psyches. They force us to question our perception of reality to keep us rooted. That's impressive you notice that—most people don't."

Derik was unsure how to receive the compliment.

"You're young, Derik. Only time will tell whether Redbird endures as your guardian. Perhaps it's a passing influence. I would treat him like a friend, but don't think you've *solved* your mind. The mind will always find a way to reinvent itself, and maybe that process is what we call the trickster. To put it another way: you will fall many a time in life—what matters is how you pick yourself back up."

"Thank you for the advice... I really appreciate it."

"You're always welcome, Derik. Stay gold."

He didn't get the reference. He closed the door, caught in the past. The wind and the water flooded the room with white noise, furthering the corporeal abandonment. He tucked himself under the covers. *I wonder what we're doing tomorrow.*

Sailing over the open ocean. I hope Dad isn't upset at me.

Why? He lied to you!

He didn't lie, he just withheld the truth, like good dads do if it'll hurt you.

He's just sensitive because he has to go home and Grandpa's dead.

I understand.

The last thing he needs is you asking him to reveal his entire past.

I know, I know.

Chirp. He contemplated what to say in the morning.

❦ ❦ ❦

The morning was calm with a pink dawn. Sound carries easier over water, so Derik was awoken by the kids running on the pier like a rushed knock at the door. They were frenetic. Something serious was occurring.

Derik opened the door, entered the world. Raven was sitting at the table, sipping piping-hot tea. He was distracted by the gathering, looking out over stern. "What's going on outside?" Derik said.

"Oh, you're up! I was just watching the people drumming on the beach. They're having some kind of ceremony."

Derik stepped onto stern and leaned over the pier. On the beach were seven drummers, beating traditional drums with painted elks, bears, eagles and ravens, formline, and they were singing solemn songs. But they were turning to the sea, to which spectators pointed and aimed their phones. He couldn't see what they were looking at. Derik stepped onto the pier, and found an unobstructed view where he could see far over the water. Someone recorded what they saw.

"Hello," Derik said. "What's everyone looking at?"

"They were honouring the kids they found at those residential schools, then these killer whales showed up."

Derik saw the telltale dorsal fin of an orca slice the water. "Cool!"

Raven joined him. Two fins rose from the sea, then three, then four.

"Four's an important number," said Raven. "You can build a house with four. There are also four directions."

Orcas always appear to be smiling, and maybe they are, friends. They swam for a long time near the surface, looking to the beach, intrigued by the people's songs, as if remembering by blood the benevolence of song, but also lamenting with the people, recalling all lost to past wrongs.

"What does it mean if there's four of them?"

Raven chose his words carefully. "They're paying their respects." He nodded, and smiled. "You know, they say chiefs are reincarnated as orcas."

"So they're all chiefs?"

Raven shrugged. "Perhaps."

Derik smiled. *I finally saw a whale.* "Do you think one of them is my grandpa?"

"...You know what? I wouldn't doubt it."

PART THREE

This is the end,
beautiful friend...

—The Doors

19. Grandpa's Ashes

In before: Orcas aren't technically whales.

The end is the only constant; you can always give it all away to begin again. The snake swallows its tail, the blue bus takes you to the next stop, you redeem your coins. The end is a friend, just like me, or Bax, the Great-Cannibal-to-the-North.

Let's finish what we started. We resume where Part One left off, which we make present, we who keep the flame.

George and Rena take Derik to visit their childhood home.

Look. The stairs climb to the right. The hallway goes to the kitchen. On the left is the living room with a fireplace. On the mantle is an urn. Besides that, there's a couch and junk.

Tears fill George's eyes. He approaches the urn. He holds it. "...Is this Dad?"

"Yes," says Rena. "Those are his ashes."

He hugs it. He sniffles. He cries, bowing his head. "I'm so sorry, Dad... I'm sorry they did this to you. I love you... Even if you never loved me." He puts back the urn, his eyes red with tears.

"He loved all his children," says Rena. She squeezes Derik close. "He just had difficulty showing it."

George's back tenses. "I want to spread his ashes on Grave Island, with our ancestors, where he belongs."

"He told us to spread his ashes on the water," says Rena. "It was all he asked."

George grabs a rock from the mantle and throws it across the room. It ricochets off the wall and bounces off the floor, coming to a rest at his feet. "We're taking him to Grave Island!" Looks can kill.

"We can do both: we'll spread his ashes on Grave Island and on the water. I think he'd want that."

George turns away and sobs uncontrollably. Derik, though intimidated, rubs his dad's back. George embraces him, yearning for affection, all his machismo a guise. "It's OK, Dad. Grandpa will be reborn no matter what."

George pulls away, wiping his tears. "It matters to *me*, and it mattered to *our* people. There's a reason they didn't burn their dead, or how else is the Creator supposed to find them without their body?"

"It doesn't matter. God will find them no matter what. His spirit lives on, either way, just like you said."

"His spirit needs his body until the Creator says it's time to go. Otherwise he's stuck here, forever." *Grandpa places his hand on Dad's shoulder.* "Our people knew that. I told them specifically, '*Don't* have him cremated,' and what do they go ahead and do? They cremate him … That was my *only* request."

"He wanted to be cremated," says Rena. "I know you may not like it, but that's what *he* wanted."

"Hey Dad, you know what I learned from Raven?" says Derik.

"What?" says George.

"That you shouldn't get upset over things out of your control. Grandpa lived the life he lived; if his final request was to be cremated, so be it. Just let it be. It was his decision."

"He's right, you know," says Rena.

"You told me not to get upset over what people say and do, or my life would be miserable. Why, then, get upset over Grandpa's final decision? *Que sera, sera.*" *Grandpa fades like time.*

George's tears abate in the face of reason. "Fine," he stammers. "We'll spread his ashes on Grave Island and the water… A fisherman always returns to the sea."

Our three embrace. "Fine," says Rena, muffled. "I think that's best."

The house is flooded with memories, though not all bad. George regales of the feasts his mom would prepare in the kitchen. "Canned peaches, plums, cherries, apricots… apple pies… blueberry pies! On Sundays, we'd have a big roast for dinner. The whole house would smell *so* good." But his nostalgia is stunted when his eyes behold the filthy dishes and overflowing garbage. Dust is thick on the counters and walls. He wipes sporadic tears. Derik looks into the pantry, but something stops him from entering. All he sees are empty shelves, cobwebs and darkness. He stares a long while; he shivers, and his hair stands. He imagines his grandma at residential school, locked in the basement with the sinners, crying for help that never comes, crying with lost talk.

"Yup—this doesn't do me any good, being here," George says. "I went to a therapist once who tried to hypnotize me. They put me to sleep, then I just started *screaming*. They had me pinned down when I woke up because they said I tried to jump out the window of the office there. They told me, 'Wherever you just were, don't ever go back there again. It'll do you no good going there.' All I remember thinking about was here, and all the messed-up things they did to me, those who were meant to protect and watch over me."

Derik says, "At least you loved me. You could've turned out like him, but you didn't; you're a good dad. You should be proud of that."

Rena hugs Derik, with tears in her eyes. "He turned out better than we did," she tells George.

They feel what each other feels.

✤ ✤ ✤

They check out the backyard. There isn't much to see. George lifts the hatchet from the stump, then chops it back down. They head back to the entryway. "All right; let's get out of here," says George.

"We haven't been upstairs yet," Derik says. "Can I see your old room?"

"I don't want to. You can go if you want. I'll meet you outside." George heads outside. Rena takes Derik upstairs. It stinks of spent beer cans and death. One room is speckled with blood. They pinch their noses.

"Something must've died up here," says Rena. "I wish they'd take better care of the place."

They peek into the rooms, avoiding the horrors within. "This was your dad's old room. He shared it with Auntie Sammy. They were really close, you know. We called them twins."

"Were they actually twins?"

"No. But they might as well have been. They were inseparable until our mom passed away."

"Then what happened?"

"Your dad started working for Grandpa. We hardly saw him anymore, 'cause he was always out fishing."

It's just a room... I'm not sure what I expected. The floorboards creak. One window faces the water from its lofty position on the hill. Derik stands in the centre, waiting for a sign—a crow cawing a certain number, or a ghost telling him what went wrong... but nothing.

They head outside. "Is that it?" says Derik. "Did we see everything?"

"That's all I'm seeing," says George. "I don't want to come back here again."

"So what do we do now?"

"We wait for them to sell the house and give us our share—the sooner the better," says George.

"I don't think Eliza wants to sell it," says Rena.

"Well, that's all I want to do with it. That house is haunted."

A black sedan with tinted windows approaches, scrunching gravel. "Who's that?" says Derik. Some shady figures get out. Some nod, some walk straight to the house, some light cigarettes.

"Ooh," says Rena. "They're your cousins."

Is that Blair and Anton? They sure look older. I remember Dad had to watch them once. We traded Pokémon cards.

"Hey, it's Squirtle," says Blair. "How's it going, cuz?"

"Hey. Good." *He doesn't remember your name.*

That's fine. I like nicknames.

"What's up Uncle George? Been a long time since we've seen you."

"We just finished checking out the house," George says. "How are things with you?"

"We just finished seeing our mom at the hospital." Anton looks around, sniffing the air, though his nose is clogged. "They think she probably had heat stroke. It was so fucking hot out." He snickers. "I was walking around with a fan taped to my chest."

"Yeah, it was pretty hot," says George.

"I thought she ODed," says Derik. *Not sure if serious, though reprehensible. Hope he doesn't hit me.*

"Nah." Anton brushes off his shoulder. "Doctor said she had heat stroke. She needs to drink more water." He hawks a loogie.

"*Mm*," says Rena. "That's good news. Did you speak to her?"

"No. She was sleeping."

"Hm."

"So you keeping busy Uncle George?" asks Blair. "We heard you own a 7-Eleven."

"I own a pawnshop—Chief's Spot Pawn, on Commercial."

Blair laughs mockingly, while Anton smirks. "My bad. How's business?"

"*Yeah*. Business is good. We're staying afloat during the pandemic. It's all I can ask for."

"We got some fishing equipment we were looking to sell. We'll have to stop by sometime."

"Great. I look forward to it."

They never will.

You never know.

"So what's up Squirt? You haven't grown at all since the last time we saw you," says Anton.

"Yeah," affirms Blair.

"I've grown a little! I'm Wartortle now."

Anton hacks at his juvenile conjecture. "You need to eat more salmon." He laughs.

"Yeah," says Blair.

The leaners stir, having spent their cigarettes. They grind them into the ground, then swagger to the house. Blair fist-bumps one, telling them, "We'll be in in a minute."

"Hey Auntie, you got any salmon for us?" asks Anton. "We've been living off fry bread the last few days."

"Sure, we got lots. I'll get Uncle Lou to drop some off."

"You're the best."

"Well," says George. "We better get going. We have a lot to do before the funeral."

"All right, see ya buddy," says Anton. "We'll see you there."

"Bye."

"Make sure your mom gets lots of water!" says Derik over his shoulder, as they enter the truck.

Blair clears his throat. They enter the house, leaving the door open.

Rena drives away. "Why were you so *mean* to them?" she says to George.

"Who, me? I wasn't being mean."

"Yes you were. You were being standoffish."

"No I wasn't. They're the ones who thought I worked at a 7-Eleven."

"They thought you *owned* one."

"Well, I don't. That's *so* insulting—a 7-Eleven. They're the ones still living off welfare cheques."

"George, those are your nephews!"

"What? They are, aren't they?"

"You should be more caring toward family. It's not like you see them very often."

"That's Lizzy's fault. I wanted to be there for them, but she never let me."

"Don't blame them for what *she* did."

"I'm not blaming them for what she did."

"They're starving, weren't you listening?"

"Is that my fault? They have a whole house to themselves *and* they have the herring licence. They could go to the store and buy whatever they want, if they didn't blow it on booze and drugs. You shouldn't encourage that kind of behaviour, giving them *your* hard-earned food. You earned that—they didn't."

"I'll always help family in need."

"Where was Lizzy when we needed her? You know she manipulated Dad to get money and the house. She doesn't deserve any of it, yet you bend over backwards to support her."

"No, I don't. I take care of family—unlike you."

As if Dad was such a saint. "Does that mean Aunt Lizzy won't be at the funeral?"

Rena sighs, looking out the window to her left.

George says, "I hope not. I don't want to see her."

"That's a horrible thing to say," says Rena. "You know how sick she's been since Dad passed. She took it the worst."

"She's getting what she deserves. It's long overdue."

"Don't be so petty. Remember all those times we went door to door, *begging* for food so neighbours would feed us?" She turns the wheel. "Not everyone has the courage to ask for help when they need it."

"Just take us to the pier."

They pick up Raven, then return to *Wild Thing* to spend the rest of their days in Bella Bella in peace. Our three take their baggage, with the sun overhead, and walk the ramp to the boat.

"Bye Auntie Rena!" says Derik. She doesn't hear. The truck's tires peel. "Is she mad at me?"

"Probably," says George. "She's always mad about something."

"Why are you always fighting family? You said you're supposed to respect them. I know Candace and I fight sometimes, but I still respect her... even if I don't want to be around her all the time."

"You don't know what my sisters are like, Derik. They're manipulative; they turned Grandpa against me—*especially* Aunt Lizzy. You saw how her kids talked to me—like I was nothing—that's because all she told them about me was lies."

"Then shouldn't you be the bigger person and forgive them? They're family after all. It's what Grandpa would've wanted."

"Grandpa had his whole *life* to bring the family together again, and to help me, and what did he do? He gambled away his life savings."

"Well, you don't have to burn bridges. We're only here for a few more days, might as well make the most of it. Otherwise you'll look back with regret."

George opens the door and throws his bag on the booth. "You're probably right."

Derik smiles. "Just treat them like strangers, and be nice—that's what I do when I don't like someone."

"They may as well be strangers." He puts the kettle on the stove for tea.

🌵 🌵 🌵

They spend the rest of the day eating snacks and drinking soda, idling about, watching downloaded videos on the laptop. Raven comes and goes, performing reconnaissance. Derik eventually stows away in his room; he loves being alone. Some would say he's an introvert; though, really, he appreciates both worlds, public and private. He likes being with friends, going to the movies, biking through the streets, or playing video games at someone's house.

But then you're alone, and you must heed its call.

There comes a time when you open the door and let everyone explore what you thought you were.

It's no longer private once you let them in.

No, now it is public, and all the affairs you had built, all the thoughts you fostered, clear of yesterday's relations, fade like ghosts from the lens.

You see, reality alone is not reality in company; some hate being alone, some thrive. Let us look to Plato's *Allegory of the Cave*, where people were chained in a cave, forced all their lives to stare at a wall upon which were silhouettes of puppets. The chained named and contemplated that shadow theatre, but, once freed, realized what they believed was an illusion. From shadows, they made science— logic with little input. Thus, one makes sense of their environment, whether adorned with public knowledge or not. The chained had belief, even if knowledge was illusory. Belief in public may not be belief alone, and vice versa, but both are belief, and belief moves mountains.

So there sits Derik, alone in his room, reflecting on the past: their first voyage, the stops on Vancouver Island, seeing his first whale!, the storm that could've sank them, and the dream splinters, dispersed by the waves; and then he came *home*, learned of his people, spoke their vernacular and fished, fished like his fathers before. He now sees the light at the end of the tunnel. Sure, here is family; sure, his genes stem from this very water and soil—but here is not the home he knows.

ψ ψ ψ

Knock knock. It's George.

"What?" says Derik.

"It's me."

"I know it's you, you're the only one on board." The walls are thin. "What do you want?"

"So that was Auntie Rena on the phone. She wants to have us over for dinner."

"Yeah, so what? I thought you two were mad at each other."

"Yeah… She wants us over for a barbecue. She said she'll cook those steaks we bought."

Derik gets up and opens the door, which folds like the door of a closet. "So you wanna go to her house for dinner? I don't want to go if you don't want to."

Guilt is writ across his face. "Well, we came all the way up here to show you where your family came from. I think we should have dinner with them."

This is how he gets after too many vapes alone. Derik, too, feels somewhat, sort of guilty, a little bit. "I'm pretty tired," he says. "I think we've seen them enough. Maybe we should just leave them alone. We'll see them tomorrow at Grandpa's celebration of life anyway."

"Yeah… That's true."

You're being domineering. Look away. He messes with his phone.

"So apparently Sophie is pregnant… Auntie Rena just found out."

"Oh… Awesome." *That's why she was so crazy.*

"Yeah. That's why I think it might be a good idea for us to go and pay them a visit."

The decision drags his conscience. *You need to rest, for tomorrow. Just tell him no.* "You know, I've been through enough over the past few days: I went through hell trying to catch a halibut; I saved a kitten, then lost it; we're far away from home; we don't have internet or cable—I hardly even have phone reception to text Mom or my friends. This whole time I've been far outside my comfort zone, and I was already stressed enough as it is over school. Just let me have a night of rest before the funeral, so I can actually *enjoy* my experience tomorrow, all right?"

"They're expecting us, though. Auntie Rena said she's baking a chocolate cake." Licks lips. "Your favourite!"

"Tell her to save it for the celebration. I'm sure it'd make a lot of people happy. I think we all need some alone time before we gather tomorrow at the longhouse."

"OK," George says.

He's feeling sorry for himself. Go keep him company. "Do you want to watch *The Avengers*?"

"Yeah… That's not a bad idea."

"Let's do that then. Then we can make popcorn, and relax until the big day tomorrow."

"OK. Sounds good." He goes to leave, but hesitates. "Hey, son?"

"Yes Dad?"
"I love you."
"I love you too."

20. Vision of Bax

Get your things, let's go.

All right, Redbird. I grab the tackle, put on my tan bucket hat. Dad eating breakfast.

"Where are you going?" he says. It's so obvious.

"I want to fish on my own, to try and catch a salmon."

"Well, wait; I'll go with you. Just let me finish eating my breakfast."

"No, it's OK. I'm just gonna cast off the dock here."

"Fine. Don't go wandering off though."

He always thinks I'll get lost, like Shadow. Shadow always came home eventually, like that time he ran off into the forest, when we were walking near our house. I thought he was gone, but Dad assured me he'd be back. He literally knocked at the door (well, he scratched) and Dad let him in while we were sleeping. "I won't, don't worry."

I hop the gunwale. Is that it? Am I out of sight? Yeah. OK. I walk the pier, past mumblings of boats, straight to the beach. (Who was I kidding when I said I'd stay at the dock?) I don't think you can call it a beach with all these rocks. Water's black without sun, can't see any fish. Of course not, you'll have to cast far out. Can't really do it here, climb rocks to the other side. I balance the gear, soft and sturdy over the barnacled rocks. No one can see me in the fog, just silhouettes.

I reach the grey sand. Wonder what bird made those prints. An eagle? No, too small. Seagull? No, these aren't webbed. Could be a crow, I guess. I sit on the sand.

Take off your sandals.

OK—I do. Feels so good between my toes. I prepare the hooks how Dad showed me. The birds flock.

"What are you doing?" says the crow.

Just fishing.

"Is that what it is?"

"You'll share your catch with us, right?" says the seagull.

You can have what I don't need.

Communicating with them only works when people aren't around, or else they're reserved. Ravens and eagles are the most reluctant. Hook's ready. I close the tackle box, stand to cast. Release bail arm, hold line with index, cock back rod, aim right... there! I cast among the silver rippling.

"Nice one," says the eagle.

Thank you.

"I'll take your bycatch."

Yeah, I know, I know. I won't forget.

"Aw, nice man," says the raven. "You bet there's fish there, huh?"

Why else would I cast there?

"Cheeky... I am sun."

The red and white bobber bobs on the waves. So many crazy things happened the last few weeks. Nice to just sit here and relax.

What do you think Raven's doing?

Probably just being Raven. He wasn't there when I woke up. He's probably searching for gold. Remember what he said about the Cannibal Dance, that they'll kidnap you?

Yeah. That'd be scary. I wonder what it would be like, though. Would I actually be scared? Maybe I'd want to do it. Maybe I've had enough of this life anyway.

Don't think that, you're only twelve.

It was more fun when I was eleven.

No, it wasn't. That's when Shadow died.

The boats will come for you, sliding on glass—canoes, painted formline, blue, red and black. The dancers wear masks, like ones I've seen in dream: there's the clam, from whence all came, à la Bill Reid, then the crow, with black beak and eyes. They caw just like the real thing. Who can forget the moon mask, soft and pleasant, glowing light blue, I hear it humming, too. They shake their masks and cedar fringe like leaves of the wind.

But what about the rowers? They'll all be dressed black, like *kuroko*, void of features, only black and masks. People walking around without mouths.

That's good, keep going. What else would happen?

Rattles and drums and chants. They sing of something.

What would it be?

I'm not sure, I'm just an idiot who doesn't know Heiltsuk. I don't know how I can consider myself a real Indian.

Be quiet.

How do you know it's even Heiltsuk if you don't speak it?

The words will come to you in time.

Raven flocks. He's the one in charge. Shadow walking through the field. He'll come down in bird form, then morph human, with his Thunderbird staff upraised, wearing the yellow blanket, grid with faces, like Grandpa had in the photo. Man, he looked so cool. I couldn't believe it, like—Is that really you?

"Yes, sonny, it's me."

That's so cool. Raven has a frontlet, inlaid with abalone for eyes and border. Batman clone Aunt Lizzy gave me.

"Ahoy there," Raven says, all glad. "A boy fishing all alone? What kind of world is this?"

I just want to catch a fish on my own… What are you up to?

"We're about to dance the greatest dance of them all: the Cannibal Dance. Care to join us? You are a cannibal after all."

No I'm not! I would *never* eat a human.

"Time will tell. Come, dance with us."

I don't want to—I'm scared.

"Scared of what? You have nothing to fear if of good spirit. Join us!"

The bobber bobs. You have a bite! Reel it in, reel it in! … Nothing.

I'm never gonna catch a salmon on my own.

Patience—you have to have patience.

I cast again, even farther. Let it sink. Think of the dance. OK…
I mean, I would never eat a human (I don't think). Why would I?
That's gross.

Your people did it.

Why though?

Good question. To scare themselves. You like being scared.

That's (sort of) true. I doubt it would taste good.

Don't think that.

Why not? We're on the topic. I bet it tastes like negligence and
animosity.

That's funny.

I don't know how to dance!

"Of course you do," says Raven. "Even *babies* know how to dance."

You dance in your room all the time to Harry Styles.

Candace caught me and made fun of me.

So what? You're just doing what feels good. Who cares what you
do alone to feel good, as long it doesn't make you crazy.

Breathe me in. Breathe me out.

"Let us celebrate!" says Raven. "We've been waiting too long not
to. You know, we've been waiting for you, Derik, to join us."

Why am I deserving?

"Because it is your time to mature, like a butterfly."

A butterfly? That's pretty lame.

"A flap here is a hurricane there. You are to *evolve*, just like Haunter.
The whole point of the dance is to transcend self. All the greats have
done it, and through it were saved. Yea, you are very special to us
indeed. So it would be our honour to initiate you into the true and
right. We will guide you to the next stage."

The dancers are looking at me with crooked glances. My dad will
be worried, though. I told him I was just going fishing.

"Know, wholeheartedly, we will return with the sun no higher. He
won't even realize you left the dock."

Aren't you supposed to kidnap me and force me to dance against
my will?

"Do you want us to kidnap you? It is enough you are here."

No… not really.

"Derik, my lad, not everything is what it seems. Doubt the chatter of your mind! Trust instinct. You know this is the way, otherwise we wouldn't be here."

You mean I knew there'd be a dance today?

"Fate has brought us together, happiness is appreciating fate, so dance, and be free! Shed your lowly husk and unite with rhythm, for *life* is rhythm. We don't wait forever."

I don't know anyone. Have to go to a new school, be a loner. Why can't I just stay with my friends?

"Surely you recognize the spirits, gods and figures that have been with you all your life. They are your friends, as am I. How can you consider yourself alone when you have companions all around you, who want you to dance, who want you to rejoice? What better, then, to celebrate with them? Do not be afraid, I will let no harm befall you. Leave your rod and tackle behind on this timeless shore. I will protect you, just like your guardian, Redbird."

You see him, too?

"All I see is *you*."

I'm not sure Redbird's separate, but it certainly seems to be the case. I am and I'm not, just like God.

I think he's my holy guardian angel. He came to me after the dog attack.

No, it's just the bicameral mind, like God was to Moses, or anyone he *spoke* to.

I'm not Moses.

I know, I'm just saying—he was found in a stream. Imagine being found in a stream. Logic is a nagging parent—let it nag. I don't even know the lyrics to the song.

They come to you, listen: We are going, we are going to the house on the mountain. We are going, we are all going, to the house on the mountain. There we will dance—there we will celebrate—tomorrow will wait, while we dance on the mountain all night.

That makes sense. Fine. I will go. But I don't want to eat anyone. I just want to dance the dance of my people.

"Verily, it is good."

My foot will sink in the saturated sand as I climb aboard. "Sit right in the middle," Raven will say. And I do.

"Comfy?"

Yes.

"Let us begin." He'll raise his staff to the sky and command the rowers row. We'll travel through the fog, entering a new world. Silver sun with white rays. The dancers dance, keeping perfect balance, like dervishes spinning atop minarets. The rattles shake and drums beat. The waves lap against the hulls and paddles. *Swoosh. Swoosh. Swish.*

I wonder if Dad would be jealous if I did the Cannibal Dance. I don't think I'd tell him, to be honest.

Why not?

He'd probably get jealous that I had an authentic Indigenous experience, and he didn't. I think he'd want to do it, just like he likes going to those sweats. The sweat was neat, but man, some bad mojo doing it in the city, I think. Fireballs rain from the sky, incinerating the dinosaurs. I need a rattle. One dancer will offer me theirs, and I'll gladly accept. Thanks!

Man, they sure are frightening with tunnels for eyes. I shake that rattle like my life depends on it, like the sun will never rise again, 'cause who knows, it might not—it's only likely. But what if they really *are* kidnapping me? Maybe this whole *celebration* was a means to get me to Bella Bella so they could eat me.

Seems unlikely.

It'd be a heck of a way to go! I hope I don't suffer.

Yes, there is day and night, but not like here, not the standard twenty-four-hour spin of the globe. The moon rises side by side the sun, going freely about the sky, sometimes back, sometimes forward, sometimes north, sometimes consuming the stars. Star Eater. I wish someone would call me that. Time is relative: a pot never boils observed, but look away, and talk to a friend, then return to find it rolling.

We are going, we are going, to the house on the mountain to dance all night.

They'll take me to the island, risen like jewel among fog. Gino's special ring. This is *the* island, just like here is *the* Raven—God over god. If I told you it was heaven, would you believe me? I want to get ahead of myself.

We land atop the grey sand. The music stops.

"Here we are," says Raven. "This is the island, and up there is the mountain of song. I'm afraid you must venture to the top alone, though."

My gut sinks, suspicions confirmed. I go to speak.

"But!" He stops me, with one finger raised. "Many companions you will find along the way, for life is truly always around you."

You said you were taking me to dance, now I have to climb a mountain?

"This is the tradition. Young men were taken to the remote, sacred locations of the forest. Think of the journey as part of the ritual."

I'm not allowed to go alone into the forest. My dad said there are bears and cougars that'll get me.

"Don't be a coward; you've already agreed to do the dance, now there is no turning back." I think it'd feel pretty sus at that point. Just make a lot of noise—sing!—and let them know you're coming. You'll be fine.

"There is no difference between your imagination and the waking realm—you have the power to see that; that is why we brought you here. We trust you, Derik. Do you trust us?"

I look around. Yeah, I guess so.

"Good. You like being alone, anyway." He knows me all too well. I disembark from the canoe.

What happens if I do die, though?

"You won't. I'll make sure of it."

But what if I do? What actually happens? I guess I just float around as a spirit, looking at my body. (Unless they have it cremated, then ashes.) What happened, Grandpa? Was it painful?

"No, sonny."

I guess there's no body to feel pain. I wouldn't care about any-thing, because I'd have no things to worry about, as suffering is rela-tive, just like time. Whatever, if God wanted me dead, he would've done it a long time ago. I have nothing to fear.

"There is one final thing you must do before you leave," says Raven. He pulls out a black potion in a crystal jar. "It's dangerous to go alone. Drink this."

You said I'd be fine, and not truly alone!

"I know, but it's a Zelda reference I had to fit in. Here, take it."

I take it. Looks like squid ink.

"It will help you see things you've only seen traces of."

I pop the cork and give it a whiff, then instantly recoil in horror.

"Don't smell it!"

Too late! God, that smells like death!

"I know. It gets worse the more you smell it. Fortunately, it doesn't taste nearly as bad as it smells."

I sniff again, and start dry-heaving. They all laugh at me. Just like they laughed at me at school for having a crush on Sylvia. It won't make me sick, will it?

"You'll probably feel nauseous, but it is normal—do not fret. It is best to drink it quick."

I'll have to take his word for it. Dad probably tried this. He said he did everything. Leave no stone unturned. I take Raven's word for it, and down the hatch! I finish every last drop. I start gagging immedi-ately, which makes them laugh even more. I guess it is pretty funny. That tastes *way* worse than it smells.

"I know, but if I said how bad it was, you'd never drink it." See! They're all liars.

It tastes like Buckley's.

"And it works."

It works. The rattlers rattle and drummers drum in crescendo.

"The preparations are complete. Go Derik! You may now begin your adventure. Travel to the house on the mountain! Lo, you will see many sights. The spirits and gods move through you; the world will reveal its secrets. You know the way of the shaman: your vision is truer than the elemental table. Behold the fabric of space apparent, as it always will be, for there is no going back." What has been seen, cannot be unseen. "You are well prepared." The music swells. "Go forth, and make your ancestors proud!"

They cheer as I follow the trail.

I should probably reel in; maybe I got something.

Who cares, if you catch something, you catch something, if you don't, you don't. What happens next?

Well… I climb from the overgrowth of fern and vine, to spacious cedars, as I can spy in the distance, under grey skies. What do I see? A ghost, a phantom? Nothing yet, just trees. Birds sing pentatonic. They're so selfless, singing all day for no one. I feel anxious, like a bear will get me. They don't sneak up on you, it's usually you sneaking up on them, then frightening them, which causes them to attack. They're usually pretty chill. You know, good vibes. Nerves are for studying patterns, discerning predators from the trees, determining what's irregular—that's why I'm so good at math. I'd be a good hunter. "Can't eat bear," Dad told me. "They'll give you parasites." Worms under my skin. Everyone has stuff living on them, they just can't see it. It's not my fault I'm anxious all the time, I just don't have the right environment. Teachers want me to sit still, like a mannequin. I just want to play and be free! God, Azmodan is so rigged, all you gotta do is roll your face across the keyboard to win.

I don't know where to go.

Follow your instincts, like Shadow.

I ride the rhythm, the heartbeat of Earth, like melody, step after step, playing my flute. I am the Magi following the star to Bethlehem of blue night, Nuit encompassing all around. What a lonely trek through the desert the camel makes. I will offer my gifts at his feet. Trees. What is that fleet of white I spy with my eye? That ought to be the one, the only, Pan Pan Pan! O great

goat god of the wild, fur crisp as the bramble, I sing my praises
to thee, to thee! Yo, Pan, *yo*! He prances through the forest, and
I follow.

"I am the god of all," says Pan. He shows me the way, for I was
blind, but now see. We come to a clearing, then he turns bright as
Jupiter. I shield my eyes, only to find him there no longer.

I sit on a stump, pulling needles from the pine. "May I have these?"
I'll ask it.

"I grow them for you," it'll reply.

This is like the Haunted Mansion at Disneyland, spirits dancing
all around. Why wouldn't they be here? Of course they're here. Just
'cause I can't see them, doesn't mean they're not. That'd be like saying
life doesn't exist because you can't put it in a test tube.

"Hey sonny. I'm proud of you," says Grandpa. "Always remember
that."

Thanks Grandpa, but I hardly knew you.

Maybe it's better you didn't know him, quite honestly.

I think I would've liked to see him more.

Not if he brings out the worst in Dad. Dad's more important—
hate to say it. He raised you, whether you like it or not.

I wouldn't want it any other way.

You sure?

Well, unless he was the Rock or something.

Here's Satan. Now *he* scares me.

No need to be scared, he's just Saturn, like in *The Book of Thoth*—
your ego. "Stay with me," he says.

This isn't hell, is it?

"Earth is my dominion. Attach to it and hurt. I fell as lightning. I
am the negative of Christ."

That's pretty badass. Who else is there? Spiderman swings across
the sky. Thor sunders the ground with his hammer. I restore it. The
birds sing my name!

"*Poo-tee-weet*," chirps Redbird. "Find your inner cannibal, Derik!"

What?

He flies away. He never stays in one place. As soon as I apply dogma, he'll undercut it till I stop. Classic trickster.

The creatures gather: fawns, birds, porcupines, even hamsters. (Why not?) Maybe bugs are the real aliens, 'cause if you can't watch your step, then what are you worth?

What's that sound?

Do you hear something?

Might be a boat or motor. Run! Run for your life! Chow. Shadow. No, it's too high, like a whistling. It doesn't stop, keeps getting louder and louder. Pan? Pan, is that you? O illustrious god! The whistling has come to reclaim the land. What have they done to the Earth?

"I am the monster of your nightmares, slithering my bulk through the dead leaves and dirty ground, wafting my noxious fumes in wake," I hear. Not sure who or what the voice belongs to.

The whistling continues. It scatters the animals and spirits and gods. Uh-oh. That can't be good—like the waves receding before a tsunami.

It calls to you. *Derik... Derik...*

I clasp my hands to my ears. I turn to find no one.

Please stop. You're hurting me.

"I would never hurt you, it'd only hurt me. We are one."

The whistling stops. Not a trace do I find. It continues inside my head. I had tympanostomy tubes when I was younger. I enjoy pain, it makes me feel alive. Witness me! Where to go next, but up?

I will climb the highest mountain, just to get to you. I begin my slow ascent.

There goes a squirrel, surfing through your hair!

I hear the chickadees with their sweet call, *Der-ik... Der-ik.*

Maybe it was just the birds.

No, I still hear the whistling, faint yet near.

What do I have to fear?

Don't be scared of what you can't control.

Have faith! Raven told me that, *and* Dad. Death is just a transition. There can't be no not-thing—it doesn't make any sense (unless everything is nothing). The sparrow shoots. All is forgiven.

They will mock you, they will cast you out, but with me you'll keep eternal company. Love, and be free!

I shall ascend mossy face and crooked limb to the top. I spy a brook, and a maiden the likes of which I cannot fathom. She's a born mystery.

"Come be with me forever," she whispers. Her words are waves. I lay down beside her, as she desires. "I've been waiting so long for you." And the days and nights I'll drift like dream. The sun winds down my spine as I extend into space. Supernovae are Lucky's roar.

I hope he's safe.

You did all you could.

Sophie, that wretch! How could she be so cruel?

I awake. Where is my woman, can I bring her home?

No, she is Nuit, destined for greater things. If you love something, set it free.

Go! Climb!

I rise, brushing off the burrs. I've got to find the house on the mountain.

Up the rocks I climb—rocks formed all those years ago in the deep, crystallizing from molten, the gargantuan plates inching from the equator, with tufts of flora for hair, upon the back of Mother Earth. *Chirp chirp, chirp chirp.* I reach ledge after ledge with no peak, no return in sight. The cliff is steep—the taunting shades below reaching with their fading hands and misty maws—but there goes Pan, without ledge to stand on. Go, Pan, go!

I am one with the birds. A crow darts, eye level. They wheel the sky, taunting the eagle who flies as lord, for I am their emperor. They always do that, but I never see them actually attack, or swift would be their undoing. I am so high, trees cannot root. The vista opens under silver sky. I catch my breath, so tired after climbing day and night.

Scan the horizon. What do you see?

There's nothing but the endless sea, and the desire to be, to *be*!

This is it: I've reached the precipice. My stitches glow burning-red. My hands are clammy, head aches. It's easier going up than down.

Don't hesitate, or you will doubt.

It's like getting out of bed in the morning: I don't typically want to go to school, but it's never as bad as I think it'll be (usually). I reach for the first nook, then the second. My hold is slim, but I've trained for this all my life, climbing trees in the park. I can hang by one finger!

Steady. Now bring up your foot. Good. Now the next.

I lift myself off the ground.

Can't go back now, no. You'll never get to watch Saturday morning cartoons again. You'll have to grow up and leave all that stuff behind.

All right, one step at a time.

I gain inch by inch on all that remains of the mountain. Ever so slowly, I climb. The entire Earth will shake, overdue with the quake that sends us back to the ice age. She will reclaim what was once hers. Nonsense, this is all hers. We could all perish, and she'll spin just the same. I feel my bones creak, my entire being trembles with the strain. I could just let go, and put an end to the cursed bloodline. Afterall, if there is only *to be*, the Creator won't mind. I would float like a spirit, leaving this prison behind… Nah—this is fun. I reach for the edge, pull myself up, then collapse, exhausted, finally earning my rest.

The sun will turn black as it consumes itself, dawning the new age. I command the sky to fall, it shatters like glass. Ra abides at the helm, reigning steeds, solar wake, while Thoth records from the prow all your trespasses before. Your heart is weighed against the feather of Maat, truth! So help you if found wanting, as the demon will devour you. I have spoken all to dust, and to dust it returns.

I hear the whistling again, rending my ears. How long have I suffered in this place, tormented by the trespasses of others? No longer. Bring the cure. But there is no autosave. I understand how a Sasquatch could hide here; no one will find me, nor hear me scream. Death is quick to reclaim. Mushrooms sprout overnight. You will have me eventually, but not now!

Maybe I should take them with me. I am an ape after all, the only beast capable of malice.

Bring the girl to me. The one who tormented me day and night...
No, not my sister—Sophie! How dare she release my kitten.

She only put it outside where it belongs.

Balderdash! I saved it from poverty. Surely it was I that was benevolent.

You prolonged its suffering.

How? I gave it food, water, love! How could anyone deny my love?

Because it knew not before, and thus was content in ignorance; happiness is relative.

True. It's like playing *Ocarina of Time*: yeah, the graphics and controls are dated, but your mind fills the gaps.

What's the point of inflicting your pain on others? You're only projecting; you only know others by how you know yourself.

Because they deserve it for what they did to me.

Who?

Candace: she tells on me, kicks me in the nuts, makes fun of me in front of her friends and my friends and the neighbours and even my teachers! She's my older sister, she's supposed to help me, not make life harder.

Adversity makes you more resilient.

Resilient for what? It never gets any easier. That's all a scam so others can take advantage of you and not have to discipline themselves.

All right, what would you do to her?

Throw her off the balcony.

OK, great—that won't solve anything, it's only one story.

I can go higher!

She'll probably brush it off, tell mom, then kick the shit out of you.

What about Dad? You love him, despite his inconsistent parenting. Mom you obviously love. What about Grandpa?

Well, he's dead, and doesn't deserve it 'cause he never personally did anything bad to me besides avoid me (it seems).

Louis?

Nah.

Rena?

Definitely not.

Sophie on the other hand, she deserves the hate. She mocked you, disposed of your kitten! She kept you up all night with her wanton ways.

You're just jealous because you're not getting any—quit being an incel.

I'm twelve! Maybe I'll wait till I'm married. Grandma did. Men only care 'cause they want to spread their seed.

So you'd eat her then?

If I had to eat someone to fit in, yeah, I suppose I would.

Raven appears in bird form upon the bough, with ghosts hanging in their collective trance. "The wheel of death continues to spin, as it has spun for me many a time. *So* many times!"

The *kuroko* drag Sophie by her hair. "Help!" she shouts. "Where are you taking me? Let me go! Let me *go!*" And I froth at the mouth like a dog with rabies. "Let go of me! Let *go!*"

Raven turns human in smoke floating down. He upholds the blade. "Thank you, Creator, for this sacrifice," he prays. "Please let Derik eat, so he may be healed of his sins. All my relations and amen." Then he cuts off her head, just like you do a chicken. The rattlers rattle and drummers drum in cheer.

I wouldn't be able to eat human flesh. Wouldn't it make you sick?

No, *our* people did it, so did many people. It only makes sense to consume your enemy to gain their power and ensure they can't cross to the afterlife. That's cold-blooded.

I grab her head and bite right into the cheek. I love salmon cheeks, it's the best part. I'll never be the same again, just like the dog attack. The ground will quake and spirits scatter with the dancers.

Raven says, "The deed is done," and flies away. I'm all alone... again—as I always have been. I hear the whistle, the knife stabs my ears. What is it? Where is it coming from?

It's music, listen. You have to listen very hard, but you can hear it. Anything is music if you listen hard enough; the universe is music!

This is different, this is something else. Bax—yes, it has to be! I have consumed the flesh of evil and now I will experience the devil, the Great Cannibal of the North, that runs my mind insane. There it will be, slithering its bulk like an engorged leech through the dark woods, leading me to the house on the mountain for which I came.

But who is Bax, really? What are its powers? Nevar Patchwork wrote that it's in charge of the Cannibal Dance, the most exalted dance of my people. Raven said cannibals were meant to consume themselves as a form of reincarnation.

That's the ticket! I'll turn over the headless body to find it's me! I was devouring myself all along, as I consumed myself in hatred. Hate, and hate yourself. I must choose to fill my world with hate or love!

I come to the longhouse. Raven appears on top. "Now, my boy, we must begin your enlightenment," he says. "You have done well to reach this point. But be prepared, the worst and best are yet to come." He throws down his staff, then turns to bird once more. He soars amid smoke and shade. The staff trembles, as the dancers, spirits, gods, rowers, *kuroko* and all else gather warily, as the ground shakes beneath their feet. Look up there! It's Redbird! He takes his ultimate form: the Thunderbird! He extends lightning across the darkening sky.

There are two odd-looking totem poles on either side of the entrance, which is decorated like a mouth. One has a crooked, swirling beak, while the other has a thick beak like an eagle and is crowned with feathers. Their bodies are tattooed formline, wings tucked in, and talons clasping the ground.

But as I approach, they blink.

Crooked Beak charges me, so I flee. But a tether wraps around my neck, extending from the longhouse, and chokes me to the ground. I cannot untie it, try as I might. It drags me to the entrance. Red smoke rises from the roof. Crooked Beak inspects me with beady eyes, cocking its head. I reach for its beak, just to see if it's real. (You know how they say to pinch yourself to see if you're dreaming?) It recoils, cawing, flapping its wings. I see the intelligence in its eyes. I'm mad, frothing at the mouth, cursing like a sailor, speaking in tongues.

"Lean into your hate."

There's that voice again—Bax it must be. I'll break off your beak and eat you alive!

This brings it great amusement, as it points its beak to the sky, and rattles its throat. Then Qulus moves, keeper of fog, sister to the Thunderbird. They judge me worthy.

All spectators watch from behind trees. Then the tether is yanked, and I'm drawn closer to the dark.

"You are my pet now, Cannibal," rumbles Bax from within. "I shall not refer to you by name, for you are useless—low as the dirt. These are my birds: Crooked Beak sunders reality with its horrid breath, and Qulus calls all rain to fall. They are of me, and I of you, because I am within you. I am all you hate. Hate, and be strong. No other shall say nay."

I grasp for the rope, but it is too late. I'm hooked. I speak, but no words do I make. All is lost.

I'm pulled inside, head scraping the knotted wood, and the door shuts, leaving me trapped in darkness.

21. The Cannibal Dance

I am within—the house on the mountain. I can hear the singers sing, rattlers rattle and drummers drum outside. I cough and nearly vomit. What could I have done to deserve such agony?

Lived. Like Lucky, I didn't choose this life, this life was chosen for me. Do you think I'd want to be born into a family where I hardly know my relatives? I'm either Indigenous and not white enough, or white and not Indigenous enough—it's never simple.

That's not true, there were many times when people appreciated you for you.

I was just a novelty, a token individual to check off the list. They never loved me for me, but what they wanted me to be.

Is not the point of the Cannibal Dance to evolve, and become better? No one can do anything to me if I let everything go.

I can't see my hand before me. The waves sweep through my mind. My neck is sore, just like when Dad yanked me by the scruff.

It wasn't that bad, it could've been worse, and he was just trying to discipline you.

A bit harsh, though.

Yeah, but he had it *way* worse; his Dad used to beat him.

I crawl, as have we all, searching for an exit that isn't there, or help that never comes (chow shaking me by his fortress of a head). I will rise, slowly, my vision flooded with stars like when I got kicked upside the head in karate. I trace the rope, and find it attached to the pole I've read about: the Cannibal Pole. Christmas tree. I could try and untie it, but why? What's the point? I brought myself here, whether I realized it or not. I deserve such a fate.

I hear Bax speak: "You cannot escape yourself. Don't be stupid." I hear it slither across the floor. I hear it groan. I can't restrain my madness, I reach for what I cannot see, trying to choke the beast. It must be my ego, incessantly enforcing its will. Dad always said to kill your ego. But how can you kill an essential part of you?

"It is good to give in to your urge," says Bax. "You have already eaten the flesh of your kind, cannibal—why think of yourself any higher?"

The whistling fills the room. I claw at my ears to make it stop.

"Hate, and be strong! Consume all opposition. Eat them alive." Its belly grumbles. It is near, I feel it, though where I cannot ascertain. It hisses from all directions, everywhere the centre. "Living is *easy* being a worm in dirt."

I am not a worm!

"Yes, you are! You are one with the dirt!"

My teeth gnash.

It feeds off your fear!

I am not scared of you.

Bax laughs. "You think you are clever. Fear me, and fear yourself. You cannot escape truth." Its voice is a congregation of laughs and heckles. "I brought you here, I spoke to you *first*. Forget that incessant guardian you call Redbird; the birds belong to *me*! Bow down before your true god!" The whistling slices through my brain, as its voices ricochet as waves of the storm. "You think you can escape me through death? You are nothing without me! I give you life."

What a sorry life it is.

Its laugh reverberates, the whistling brings me to my knees. I yearn for an end to this insanity. Isn't this normal?

As long as you deny your thoughts.

My eardrums rupture and teeth crack, as I resist the demands of Bax.

Why resist? Maybe it's right: listen, and relent!

I've been through too much: birth; falling down the stairs; fist-fighting the bully; being shoved down, stepped on; Dad yelling at me to sleep; Candace teasing me for being ugly; the dog ripping me apart; Shadow being put to sleep; the storm; stumbling in track, losing the race; scraping knees; losing the first five dollars I ever earned; not knowing the answer when Mrs. Crosschuk called on me; getting slapped by Sylvia, my crush; Mary abandoning me, my first friend; crying before the class; going to the principal's office and drawing the gates of heaven; bleeding for God; nearly drowning; anaphylaxis from peanuts; sleeping in the hospital, feeling the surgery, angels healing me in purple night; almost getting run over; choking on bread; electrocution; falling from the balcony; bashing my head open on the ice; nursing my wounds, watching the violet swells turn to scars as Mom changed the bandages; getting kicked, tripped, smacked and spat on—everything! Everything I've suffered follows me and will do so until I drop dead. What am I to do, then, but try and live a normal life? The whistling will never cease.

"Let your fears consume you. *Become* what you hate. You are useless, *so* useless. Taste the ash of what you once were. Submit to Death!"

And I will bow down before it, numb from the whistling and pain. The fire lights in the centre of the room, and for the first time I see the being that torments me—a mass of oozing, dark flesh with maws of sharp teeth all over, laughing, cackling, mocking, whispering independent as the suckers of an octopus. That's why they have faces in every part of our ancient art; there is intelligence in the heart.

Bax ripples closer. Even its eyes are mouths! Its hums shiver the walls. Finally, the whistling stops, as does all thought. "Behold your true self!" But before I know it, the fire dims, and Bax returns to the shade.

We're just getting started. A coo startles me; anything startles me now, at the edge of sanity. Standing atop the bluff affords no slips. The room morphs and twists to the sky as the flames lick high. Long, spindly legs I do see, stepping from the shadow. Down comes the black sword that is Great Heron's beak. It coos, clacking, inquisitive of this ant they call Derik.

That's crazy, referring to yourself in the third person.

Hush. What's it matter how I refer to myself? Great Heron prods me, and cocks its head. These aren't normal birds, however; these are the man-eaters of Bax! It retches, and strikes! Yes, it wants your brain; it wants to taste my mind.

I scurry behind the pole, unsure of what is real, unsure of what's fair to do. When can I dance? When can I sing and be free?

Just wait.

Who else sits around the fire? There's Qulus, probing me with her beady eyes, and Crooked Beak! It lunges its terrible visage. But they can't kill me… right?

"This is your reality." Bax is back. "Together, we make your mind, your emotions, your will and body. We are the pieces that make you whole."

I finally notice Raven, in his ultimate form, perched behind the fire, watching me with ebon eyes, his talons gripping the stage. Raven brought light from darkness. His wings are folded like a coat, and he too is tattooed formline like the rest—living, breathing totems for the ages. His gaze won't leave me.

"These are my birds," says Bax. "They can't wait to devour you, for what bird doesn't enjoy a little worm?"

Great Heron pecks from the shadows, drawing blood. I use the pole as cover as it tries for another. Yeah, well, do your worst! I'm not scared of you. I'm not scared of anything! You want to kill me, fine. What is death anyway, but a new beginning?

Bax cackles. "You *need* us, worm. You cannot live without us."

If you are me, and I you, then you can't live without me, either. What say you then, fat worm, if I end it myself?

"Do it, I care not. I have seen you lie to yourself time and time immemorial, lashing, foaming at the mouth, whining, 'Why am I cursed?'" Its voice sounds identical to mine. "'I just want to go home.' You are *weak*. At the threshold you stared, telling yourself, 'Tomorrow I will do the deed. Tomorrow I will change.' You utter nothing but *lies*."

To know lies is to know truth.

"So... What does it matter?"

You can not hurt me if I accept you, because to deny you would be to deny myself.

Bax and its birds stir, gauging each other's reactions. Bax groans, "Finally! He understands." It returns to hiding once more.

"You have passed the test," Raven says. "Now *dance.*"

Wack. The musicians hit the log worn from songs before—the smooth cedar, laid horizontal like a bench at the north end of the house—signalling the start. The fire shall grow soft and red, revealing the singers singing and dancers dancing about the edge of the room. They chant in chorus. *Wack.* Each hit is like thunder. I hear Redbird screeching in his ultimate form.

"Dance!" Raven's voice reaches me, like a thought. "Life depends upon it."

Doubtful and traumatized, I will still rise to my feet, just like all the times the world knocked me down before. I dance the celestial dance like no one's watching.

"Harder! Faster!"

I will look to the dancers, mimicking what they do, stamping around the pole like a bird for food.

"Faster! Harder! Dance for life, dance for the Creator; dance for your family, dance for everyone! Dance with your ancestors."

Move your hips and arms and legs with the rhythm. *Feel* the music. The longhouse vibrates to our fevered pitch, threatening to collapse. Faster and faster they play as we dance through the night into day. One way wraps the tether, the other unwinds it. Faster and faster—faster and faster! The drums beat the heart, rattles liberate the mind, as we wheel around the flame. I will dance until my feet bleed, only death may stop me! My head and ears pulse with the whistling of Bax, not showing the least sign of stopping. Together, we will dance forever!

Then Bax returns from the north, revealing the horrid profile of its nose, its hefty bulk, its all-consuming gut hanging to the floor. It lashes in hatred toward the dancers as they swing out of reach. Don't stop! Do not dare stop. Bax approaches, but the floor caves into the pit, revealing the grandfathers, the rocks of the sweat, below.

"Go now!" Raven says. "Bury Bax! Relegate it to where it belongs."

But why would I bury that which is me, which I have sworn to acknowledge?

"Because it belongs in the realm below—your subconscious!" says Raven. "Bury it along with your ancestry, as your foundation!"

Bax curses, it promise me powers I've only dreamt of! No... I must do this. This is right. I go to Bax, hanging on the edge of the pit.

I cannot get rid of you... but I can put you where you belong.

"No!" it shouts. "I make you strong! Don't be a *fool!*"

I've made up my mind. I stomp its final grip, sending it down, where it sears upon the rocks. But it doesn't burn, no, it *melts*. It melts and smothers the rocks, giving rise to the most toxic smoke. It screams and shouts in agony, wishing to torment me still. And from the pit rise thousands of mosquitoes, as the song stops, the spectators standing idle. I run to the pole, hoping it will protect me, but it does not. They swarm, and suck me dry of blood. The tether snaps without strain, the deed done, as I lie there, dying.

Light returns from the smoke hole in the ceiling. It feels so good to see the sun again. The *kuroko* scoop dirt over the pit. But I am still a cannibal. There's still one last stage.

Great Heron picks me up with its beak, as Crooked Beak rattles its call, destroying all spectators, destroying the house, turning all to white. Great Heron lays me down in empty space. There's no easy way to do this; I must suffer the final ordeal. Qulus slowly approaches my feet, looming over with beady eyes. She opens her beak, then spits acid all over, dissolving my clothes, dissolving my skin to the bone. Great Heron pecks open my skull, finally tasting my brain, savouring my thoughts. Then Raven hops forth, the last, the first. He pecks out my left eye, then the right, so I'm reborn anew.

22. Evolution

Guess who?

That was so cool. I wish I could do that for real.

No you don't, it'd be horrifying!

Come on, quit being a coward.

I'm not, it's just... I want to go back to that time when they did the Cannibal Dance, it seems so much more interesting.

It's all relative, you'd get bored and crave Heroes of the Storm *eventually.*

They grow up so fast. Yes, it's me again—Batman's sidekick.

Derik looks around, noticing the down of an eagle strewn behind him. *Was it there before? I can't remember.* The bobber gently rides the waves. *I don't think I'm going to catch anything... I might as well head back.* He reels in, collects his tackle, then climbs over the rocks.

He walks past the gulls, ravens and eagles, to the land of the beautiful, brave and free. George is standing on the dock, by *Wild Thing*, looking for him. He puffs his vape, eyeing Derik as he approaches.

"I'm late, aren't I? What time is it?"

"Almost ten."

"Oh... I thought I was gone a lot longer."

"Where'd you go? You said you were just fishing over here. I was looking all over for you."

"I was just behind the rocks, over there."

"Don't go running off like that. Remember what I said—a bear might get you."

"I'm fine. I can see a bear coming."

"They're faster than you think, then once they get you, you're doomed."

Derik passes over his tackle. "What's for breakfast?"

"Cereal."

"Again? Isn't there a place we can get some pancakes or something?"

"No. There'll be plenty of food at the celebration."

"What time is it at again?"

"Starts around six, but we have to go early to help set up."

"Nice. We have plenty of time."

Raven shows. "Hey. You going fishing?" he asks Derik.

"No, I just went."

"Oh. Did you catch anything?"

"Nope... Thanks for reminding me."

"Better luck next year." Raven boards, heading to the washroom.

"Hey, so Auntie Rena called this morning," says George

"OK."

"She posted signs all over town, letting everyone know we'll be meeting at the Big House tonight. She's also having programs printed."

"Great. That's good news. Did everyone only just find out it was tonight?"

"Guess so. They were lucky to book the Big House 'cause it was on such short notice."

"What would've happened if they couldn't book it?"

George puffs his vape. "We'd probably have it at the school or something. We're on Indian Time—we move when the Great Spirit moves us, don't worry about it. Auntie Rena mentioned that Sophie got in a fight with Rich last night."

"Oh yeah?"

"Yeah. Apparently they got in an argument, before he punched her in the face, then walked out—they haven't heard from him since."

"Wait, what? Really?"

"She's sitting at home with a black eye. So I said we'll be over for lunch to say hi."

"See! It was a good idea we didn't go and see them. We would've just gotten involved, then who knows what would've happened." *That explains why I was so hesitant to go; I could feel the tension in the air.*

"I suppose… So go get ready, then we'll head on over. Put on your nice sweater too, we have a lot to do before tonight."

"All right… Do you think Auntie Rena and Uncle Louis are still mad at me?"

"They're not mad at you. Why would they be mad at you?"

"I don't know… I can just tell when someone's mad at me."

"No, they *want* to see you. You overthink things too much. They're happy you're here, Derik. You make up things in your head that aren't true. You should really try and stay more grounded sometimes."

Derik smiles. "I know; I can't help it." He starts getting ready.

They walk, for it isn't far. Raven stays behind, playing cards with himself. He'll meet them at the Big House later.

Rena opens the door. She hugs George. "I'm glad you're here."

Louis smiles in the background. Sophie is on the couch, watching TV, facing away.

"Hello, Derik." Rena gives him a big hug. *She loves you.* "It's good to see you." She's already set the table with sliced steak, homemade bread, a tub of margarine and a pitcher of iced tea. Rena and George take a seat with Louis, while Derik stands by the door. *If you're late to the dojo, you have to kneel and wait for Sensei to invite you in.*

"What is it with these stray dogs walking around?" says George. "Four of them approached us on the way here. You'd think someone would open an animal shelter by now."

"They never get them neutered," says Rena. "Then when they have puppies, they just abandon them 'cause they can't take care of them. It's really bad."

I bet that's what happened to Lucky.

Don't mention him—it'll only stir the pot.

"They had no collars or tags, nothing! Someone's going to get really hurt one of these days."

"It used to be a lot worse," says Louis. "Now they know how to actually control it."

"Hm." George looks to Sophie. "Hello, Sophie. How are you doing?"

"Fine," she stays, staring at the TV.

George asks Rena, "So, will the programs be ready in time?"

"Yes. Here, start eating. We have to pick them up after this."

"All righty." George puts some steak on his plate.

"Derik, are you hungry?" asks Rena. "We got lots of steak for you."

"Not right now. Thank you, though. I'm saving room for the chocolate cake."

Rena smiles. "The printer's just down the road. I need your help carrying the cross, too."

"There's a cross?" says George.

"Mm. Wilson said he was making one with the family crest on it."

"Fantastic." George tells Derik, "You'll like Wilson—he's your cousin. He's a great carver."

"He's going to call me when we can pick it up," adds Rena.

"You know, I remember the time we—"

Derik's attention wanders from the conversation as he watches Sophie flip through the channels. She hesitates on Pokémon as Mew crosses the screen. She puts down the remote.

"Go and watch TV," Rena sincerely tells Derik. "Take off your shoes, make yourself comfortable."

"OK," he says. He approaches, but stands awkwardly at the edge of the carpet, not wanting to intrude on Sophie's space.

"So, I guess Rich won't be at the celebration tonight, will he?" George says.

"Have a seat," Sophie tells Derik, patting beside her on the couch. Derik obliges, but sits as far as possible, next to the sliding door.

"This is how Pichu evolves into Pikachu," he says with regret, having spoiled the episode. *I just wanted to say something.*

"I like Pikachu. She's so cute."

"It's a boy. Ash's Pikachu is male."

"Oh. I always assumed Pikachu was a girl."

"Not this one; they can be both genders... They look the same either way."

Sophie chuckles. "Right?"

Derik glances at her, but is repelled by her black eye. Sophie's lip quivers. She sniffles.

"He said, 'You won't be seeing me again,'" says Louis. "Then he picked up his things and left. Haven't heard from him since."

"What a jerk," says George.

"What's your favourite Pokémon?" Derik asks Sophie. He looks at her and sees her eyes tear.

"I don't know." Sniffle. "I guess Pikachu."

"Why? Because he's cute?"

"Yeah. He's the only one I know, really... Why, what's yours?"

Haunter. "...I guess Pikachu. He's loyal to Ash, and protects him. He's also super fast, which I like."

"Yeah." Sophie smiles.

"I like the electric types." Derik looks to the silver blur caught in the corner of his eye from the backyard. A cat struts the patio to a former dip container. "Is that Lucky?" He hops to his feet, putting face and hands to the glass.

"Yup," says Sophie. "He comes by every now and then. You can feed him, if you want. He's probably hungry." Derik opens the door mid-sentence. Lucky meows and approaches. Derik kneels, stroking Lucky's back with the back of his hand. Lucky purrs and rubs against him, circling. "You made it! I thought we lost you, and I was very sad," Derik says, baby voiced. Now tears fill his eyes, but he is so happy. *I want to squeeze him.*

Don't—it's not good for either of you. He's free now. Let him be. Lucky walks back to his makeshift bowl, meowing. Derik looks around for food and notices Sophie standing by the door. She points to the purple bag with the purr-fect tabby on it. "That's his food." Derik fills the container, then places it down. Lucky promptly dives in.

"I'm so glad he's all right," says Derik.

"He kept coming back. I think he was looking for you."

Yeah, right—he wouldn't remember me after one day. But it's true, friends. Derik denies the attachment to avoid getting hurt. "He looks healthy. He couldn't walk before, now he seems fine."

"Are you going to take him home with you?"

"No... I can't. This is his home. I couldn't do that to him. It's not meant to be."

"That's silly. He clearly likes you."

"I know... but most animals like me. He'll be better off here than in the city."

"That's sweet of you, but you should take him. You're clearly attached."

"I'm allergic to cats anyway."

"Suit yourself." She returns to the couch.

Derik pets him gently while he eats. "I'm so proud that you're nice and healthy, and thriving. I love you." Derik kisses Lucky's paw, then pets his head "I wish I could take you, but this is where you belong. I hope you grow up to be nice and big and have lots of friends." Lucky meows. He finishes eating. "I have to go now, OK?" Lucky purrs, and rubs against Derik. Derik massages Lucky's neck. "I'll miss you, but you promise me you'll be safe, OK? Be a good cat." Purring, Lucky walks away, across the deck, looking to the world, looking for what's next, as Derik proudly watches. He re-enters the house, hiding his face, and closes the sliding door. He sits beside Sophie again, this time a little closer.

"Hm." She pouts in admiration.

Rena is smiling. She gets the call. "That was Wilson. He said the cross is ready whenever we are."

"Well, we should get going then," says George. "We've only got a few hours before everyone starts showing up at the Big House."

"Yes, we have to start setting up as well."

George finishes his iced tea, then everyone puts on their shoes and heads out to the truck.

23. Celebration of Life

The Big House is something to behold. (I just stick sticks together till it works.) The front is flat, with formline red, blue and black over wood grain. Stepping inside, one is greeted with a sign explaining the symbology of the four totem poles and art within. The main hall contains fine sand in the middle around a fire pit, and tiers of benches on either side. The four totems are carved with whales, ravens, eagles and small faces. The raven pole in particular is covered with corroded copper plates, of external splendour and internal corruption. The whale's fin is jointed on—not one continuous piece. By the stage are blankets bearing the Mormin crest: me, carrying a whale, my sister (only half joking, friends). Over the drummer's log is the largest—white, with the face of the moon, akin to the mask Raven gave to George.

The signs around town say six o'clock. The clouds gather. Tonight, it will rain.

Rena sets up the PowerPoint to project pictures of Henry, while Louis unfolds tables backstage where the feast will be. George props up the cross by the screen.

"How many people do you think are going to show up?" asks Derik.

"I don't know, I'd be surprised if anyone shows up in this weather," jokes George.

"About a hundred or so," says Rena. "They'll show up. Just you watch."

And friends, even that is an underestimation. Dozens start to trickle in, carrying gifts and food! Platters of baby carrots and broccoli with ranch, homemade bars and muffins, salmon in its many forms, sheet pizzas, sandwiches and of course chocolate cake. They place it all in the back and help out where needed, arranging food beside napkins and cutlery, brewing coffee and setting up the last of the tables. The benches on one side fill quickly—the ones facing the angled screen. Rain or shine, the people come together.

Derik sticks with Raven, overwhelmed by so many distant relatives.

"What does this pole mean?" he asks him.

Raven shrugs. "It means whatever you want it to mean. There aren't any revelations here; it's an eagle above a whale. Why, what do you think it means?"

Derik rubs his chin in contemplation. "I think it means intelligence over emotion, 'cause the eagle is intelligence and the whale is emotion."

"Boom! There ya go—I think that sounds respectable. All that matters is you believe in what you believe."

"I want to know what our people thought it *originally* meant, though. They obviously designed it a certain way."

Raven shakes his head. "Hogwash. They don't mean what they meant back then, so form your own meaning. It's like the Bible: maybe back in the day when it was written, it was just pulp fiction. What matters now is how people interpret it and what it means to them—that's how we evolve as a society. We take stories, integrate them into our collective consciousness, and then we write more stories."

"Hey, Raven." Someone recognizes him. "Hope you're teaching him good!"

Raven meanders away. Derik takes the seat closest to the entrance, analyzing the pole, but also avoiding expectations to be near the stage. He doesn't want the burden most consider an honour. *This isn't my real family anyway; I never really knew Grandpa.* Nonetheless, he corrects his posture, sitting up straight, hands on his lap.

They finish setting up minutes after six. Rena finds him. "What are you doing sitting all the way over here? Come join your relatives."

"OK."

She takes him closer to the stage.

"There you are," says George. "I was looking all over for you."

"Sorry."

"There's some people I want you to meet." George introduces Derik to relatives he only knows through stories. "This is Jerry. He's the guy I was telling you about that had the GTO... This is the chief's son, Peter... Carla, I'd like you to meet my son. This is your cousin, Carla; her and I used to share a room together in Steveston... Alexander was the captain of the first boat I worked on besides my dad's." And then there's Ivan, who went to jail over a drug deal gone awry. There are many more friends, friends, whose names Derik struggles to retain, as he knows he won't see them for another decade, if ever. At last, he joins their ranks. Oh, this is your godfather who fought on Mars... and this is your great-grandma who crunched numbers for Caeser Augustus during the Mongol occupation of Rio de Janeiro—etc. It seems the entire town is here to honour Henry, all of whom Derik has some relation to.

The programs are passed around. Derik eagerly opens his. He's greeted with the picture he first saw at Rena's. *He kinda looks like Gandhi.* He notes the schedule. Spiderman swings across the sky.

The house is packed. Arnold Bower, the speaker, is another descendant of the Mormin clan. His mom changed her name upon marrying, a move that would've stripped her of status not too long ago.

"Hello, folks," says he. "It's great to be here with all of you this evening. I want to welcome you all here, tonight, to the Big House, so we can celebrate the life of Henry Mormin. He was an Elder... a father... a son... a brother... and a friend to many; but to all of us, he was family... I'd like to start by asking his son, his daughters and his grandkids to come down and join me." Derik's fear is manifest: he is ashamed of being an exile. He follows George to the sand, joining Rena and Sophie. Here are the legend's spawn.

"We'd like to honour his family by giving them these vests." One by one the vests are given: black, with a red Thunderbird holding a whale stitched to the back. Derik admires his dad's, then Arnold puts his own over his shoulders. He is proud, laden with shame. *We died for you. We suffered.* Derik hangs his head, but looks up out of respect. Sophie maintains her disdain.

Arnold covers the mic, asking Rena, "Is Eliza still in the hospital?"

"Yes."

"Where are her kids?"

She shakes her head. "They're late."

Arnold returns to the mic. "It is a great shame Eliza, Henry's daughter, and her children are not here with us, but we will make sure they get their vests. These vests bear our family crest, the mark of a true Mormin, along with a traditional name, which will be given at a later ceremony. The story goes that the Thunderbird would pick up whales with his talons, and wherever he dropped them, an island would rise from the sea. And that's why we have so many islands around us, now, because of the Thunderbird."

George growls, mumbling to Derik, "He's not really a true Mormin."

Arnold glances, mouth ajar, but the ceremony drags him along. "Thank you. You may now return to your seats." Derik bounds the steps.

"We will now have Henry's daughter, Rena, tell us about his life." Arnold hands Rena the mic, then stands to the side.

"Hello, everyone. I always looked up to my dad, both metaphorically and figuratively, for he was a tall man. He was a great fisherman who always worked hard to provide for his family, to give us shelter, even if he just about killed himself doing it. There were times when we had nothing on the table, if the fishing season was unkind to us, but, to me, we always had everything we needed. To me, we always had a feast. I'm the second oldest of his five children. It's a shame most of his children couldn't be here today: Eliza is in the hospital, Philip died in infancy, and we lost our sister Samantha to cancer, years ago. Henry loved all his children, and I'm sure he'd want us all to be here, together.

"Henry first met and courted my mom, Julia, when he was just sixteen. Together, they would travel to the city, to Vancouver, to go dancing and listen to music in the clubs there. They married in 1963, a time of rebirth and rejuvenation among our community here in Bella Bella. They immediately started a family. Eventually they decided to relocate by moving us all to Vancouver, the city they knew and loved, in hopes that one day we'd have better work and education. It was a tremendous shock to us all when Julia contracted hepatitis and was bound to a hospital bed. She passed shortly after, leaving Henry to care for four children, *all* on his own.

"It was difficult—" She tears up. "—*so* difficult—providing for all of us, but his love endured. That was his greatest accomplishment. He continued working as a fisherman and captain well into his sixties, piloting his boat, the *Marge Valence*, teaching generation after generation of fishermen where the best spots to fish were. Eventually (after much nagging from me and Eliza), he retired, and settled in Bella Bella to be close to his family. He lived here the rest of his days." Her chin quivers. "He was the best possible father I could have ever hoped for... Thank you, Dad. Thank you for all the good you did for us. I hope you have peace at last. I love you, and I will always hold you dear to my heart. Please—rest in peace."

There are sniffles and weeping among the gathered. Arnold takes the stage again. "Thank you, Rena, for those touching words for a great man. I am sure he is watching over all of us... and probably eyeing that chocolate cake." It's good to balance sorrows with laughs. "I'm going to read to you now the Fisherman's twenty-third psalm from the pamphlet, so please turn to that." The pages turn.

"This is a good one—Psalm Twenty-Three—pay attention to this one," George whispers to Derik.

"The Lord is my pilot; I shall not drift.

"He lighteth me across the darkest waters:

"In the deepest channels he steereth me.

"He keepeth my log:

"He guardeth me by the star of holiness

"For his name's sake..."

Derik recalls reciting the original in church, without the nautical tinge. Verily, he remembers his mom holding the Psalter between them, and reciting en masse, dressed up in their Sunday best, "The Lord is my shepherd; I shall not be in want..."

"Yea, though I said, amidst the thunder and tempests of life,

"I will feel no danger: for thou art with me;

"Thy love and thy care they shelter me.

"Thou preparest a harbour ahead

"In the heaven of eternity:

"Thou anointest the waves with oil;

"My boat rideth calmly…"

Derik sees Henry, crumpled in the middle of the street, clutching his chest, with rain pouring upon him. No one comes. For hours he lies there, dying, praying for the end.

"Surely sunlight and starlight

"Favour me on all voyages I take:

"And I shall rest in the port of my God

"Forever… Amen."

Spread are hushed *amens*.

"Thank you, Henry," Arnold adds. "May the Creator be kind to you… We're going to open the floor now to anyone who wishes to share a few words about Henry. Just raise your hand and I will come to you with the microphone."

They are hesitant to start; the hall is quiet. A man raises his hand. It's Dan, from the beach back in Port Hardy. "I'll start… I remember Henry was a great fisherman; he always knew where the fish were. Nowadays, there's all sorts of gadgets to tell you what's below, in the water, but he didn't need any of that. He would tell you where the fish were *going* to be. So we'd trust him, and place the nets where he said. Usually he was right, and we'd come home with a big catch." Eyes sparkle. "And then we'd party until the sun came up. Sometimes we'd celebrate a bit *too* much: I remember once we set the net, and left it to soak, but it was late, so we all ended up falling asleep. Well, I woke to him shouting, 'Get down the net! Get it down!' and my head hurt like you wouldn't believe. I got up and looked outside, and there was the net, in the same spot, but the tide had dropped fifteen feet, so it was just hanging there. He was so embarrassed. We had to cut the net down. It took forever for us to repair. But he never blamed anyone—only himself. He was a true captain; he took responsibility... I miss you, Henry. Thank you for teaching me what you knew."

"Thank you for sharing." Arnold steps back to the sand. Several hands are already up. He takes the mic to a man with a crew cut, big and round in his Rolling Stones hoodie. "Henry was the greatest guitarist I ever saw. I got to see him play in a bar downtown, in Victoria. I've never heard anyone that good before, or since. He'd make Jimi Hendrix sweat, he was that good. He could shred with the best of them, or he could play the sweetest, softest licks you've ever heard and make you weep, he was that damn good. He set that place on fire. We were dancing and shouting. They just don't play music like that anymore. He would always play the crowd favourites and take requests. He could play anything just by ear, just by listening. I bought him a beer once—many, actually—and got a chance to speak to him. For hours he told me about how much he loved the blues, and where it came from, and when he first heard it on the radio, and which records he owned. I'll never forget that. He was such an inspiration to me and my friends. We used to go and see him whenever he played on the Island. I got through many tough times in my life thinking about that music he played... Thank you, Henry. We'll miss you."

"Thank you," says Arnold. "Who else would like to share? How about a woman?" He finds Sophie.

"Go ahead."

"I loved my grandpa. I wouldn't be here if it wasn't for him... But he was a total adulterer." Some jeer. The commotion begins. "He tried to molest me, and I know for a *fact* he molested my friends!" The commotion boils. Arnold tries (politely as possible) to reclaim the mic, baring disbelief along with many others. Sophie turns, shielding the mic, pulling away from her father's hand on her shoulder. "The truth has to come out!" Her voice cracks with the final syllable. They wrestle the mic from her. Louis grabs her by the shoulders and guides her backstage, but she shakes him off, leaving on her own, saying, "Don't touch me! I know what I'm doing."

There are many upset faces calculating how to proceed. Is it true? Does it matter when he's dead?

They did that to us at school.

Good, she probably had it coming.

What a scumbag.

She's lying!

Why didn't anyone mention it before?

God, so many negative thoughts. Is it me, or is it this place?

Probably a bit of both.

"Sorry about that," says Arnold. "I know many of us are struggling to deal with the loss of our Elder, Henry—and it's difficult for some to express how they feel. Let's have one more person speak, because I think a lot of us are looking forward to the feast."

The crowd is rife with murmurs, confusion and apprehension. George raises his hand. Arnold hesitates, pretending not to notice, but the draw is too strong to be ignored; the mic is brought. George holds it to his mouth, head bowed. He waits for the audience to quiet.

Get a load of this guy. He thinks he's Chief.

What a freak.

Let him speak!

Come on, Dad, don't embarrass us.

I want to hear what he has to say.

"…My dad was many different things to many different people: he was a father, a brother, a great musician and fisherman. I remember every morning he would play my mom's old piano. He'd always play the same song: Yesterday… all my troubles seemed so far away! His fingers were so big, they'd cover *two* keys at once. Somehow he'd still manage to play whatever he wanted, whether it was jazz or classical music—he could play anything.

"Sometimes he would leave for days on end, and I'd have to go and retrieve him from hotels downtown. He loved to stay at the Balmoral—that was his home away from home. And I just remember getting *so* mad at him, 'cause he was killing himself slowly being there, living the way he did. But he was *always* ready to work. No matter what, he'd be there first, waiting aboard the *Marge Valence*. 'What took you so long?' he'd say. 'Let's go!' He was the hardest working man I ever knew.

"Once, we were caught in a storm, with waves forty feet high—couldn't see the shore. The winds were so strong, they uprooted trees all along the coast. It was a hurricane, basically. And somehow he managed to pilot the boat through all that and bring us to a harbour. When we went in to get our rooms at the hotel, they were shocked. 'You were out there in *that*?' they said. 'You must be insane! We lost power hours ago.' But it was nothing to him. He just shrugged, and asked if they had any coffee." Some chuckle.

"...He wasn't the nicest man; he did what it took to survive. He somehow managed to avoid the residential schools by working and doing what he knew, and I'm proud I got to learn that from him. Whatever you may think of him, however he touched you or influenced you, just look around: we're all here for *him*, to celebrate the good he brought to all of us... And that, to me, is the mark of a true Elder. If I can forgive him, so can you ..." The crowd is divided: some dab their tears, some bicker, some glare and some beam. "Thank you. Rest in peace, Dad. All my relations."

"All my relations," whispers Raven.

Thank you, son.

George returns the mic to Arnold. "Thank you, George, for your thoughtful words." He returns to the stage. "Thank you, everyone, for sharing. It's truly amazing how many people he influenced in so many different ways. I'm sure he is proud of you all. We'll close now with a poem from the program. Rena will read it for us whenever she's ready."

Rena takes the stage once again, bolstering against her tears and frustrations. She recites the poem:

"Don't think of me as dead and gone,
"I'm simply dancing to the land of song.
"Although I set like the evening sun,
"I've run my race, I had my fun.

"In the morning, find me shining bright,

"The summer water's sparkling light.

"I am the dew upon the flowers,

"The white underbellies of the flounders.

"And if to you I have been unkind,

"I pray in your heart love you'll find.

"Please embrace life in peace,

"Together rejoice, together feast,

"For I love you, and always will,

"You are forever my greatest thrill.

"Thank you, for all that you've done,

"Together, I know, we remain as one."

How true—how true indeed. The people are silent, heads bowed. They remember Henry. And in their memories, he lives. The Big House thunders. Rain rattles the roof.

Arnold concludes, "Thank you, Henry, for all you did for us. May the Creator give you a seat by his side." Smiles. "Now let's celebrate the life of a truly great man—let's eat!" There is much chatter, silence exhausted. "We ask that you let the Elders please eat first, then everyone may help themselves after. Please form a neat line. Thank you to everyone who brought food to share. Thank you, everyone, for joining us and coming together."

The Elders head backstage.

The people layer their plates and trade stories; lost relatives reunite. They feast, covering time lost. Sophie is nowhere to be seen. Derik gets himself a few sandwiches and a muffin. *There's the chocolate cake. Don't—just leave it for them. Leave it for Grandpa.* He eats with cousins he never knew he had. All in all, it's more celebration than mourning.

✤ ✤ ✤

One by one, the attendees trickle out into the stormy night, as it is still the week, so, yes, many have work in the morrow. Pretty soon only George, Rena, Louis, Derik, Raven and Arnold are left with a few devoted.

"I hope she gets the help she needs," George says. "Is she planning on keeping the baby?"

"I don't know. I haven't spoken to her about it," says Louis. "It's her decision what she wants to do. We'll be here to help her."

"That's good… Well, I guess we better go. So we'll meet you at the docks around ten tomorrow?"

"Yup, we'll see you then," says Rena.

They say their goodbyes, wave and hug. George and Derik step out into the familiar rain. George pulls his jacket over his head, shielding himself, while Derik lets it soak his hair.

"I can't imagine what winter is like," he says, "if it rains this much during the summer."

"It rains most of the year."

"Just like Vancouver, I guess."

A relative pulls up in their truck, offering them a ride, but they refuse. "Our boat's just down there! Thank you, though."

They make their way down the ramp, then, at last, board *Wild Thing*. George shivers, and promptly cranks the heat. He hangs up his coat to dry.

"So… What did you think of Grandpa's celebration?" asks Derik.

"I think it went really well, considering. Better than I thought it would."

"Was that because Aunt Lizzy didn't show up?"

"Aw, who cares. We wouldn't have spoken to each other anyway."

Enough's enough. "Even at your *dad's funeral*? How would you feel if I ignored Candace at *your* funeral? Wouldn't you want us to reconcile our differences for you?"

George contemplates. "Yes… of course."

"Well then, don't you think you should go and make amends with *your* sister? Remember what Auntie Rena said, that Grandpa would want all his children to be here together? Don't you think that's what he would want?"

"... I'm not so sure."

"Cut the crap. You know that's what he would want, and you know that's what you should do. I don't care what she's done to you. You may never see her again. All you have to do is go and see her. You don't even have to apologize—just say hi, that's it. Then you get to go home with a clean conscience. She wasn't even at the funeral!" *Maybe she didn't go 'cause Dad was there.*

"Mhm. I'm not going," he refuses, like a child.

"Quit being so immature. I made amends with Sophie even though she tried to dispose of Lucky. Then look what happened: Lucky turned out fine. Some good came of it. The least you can do is visit your sister who you may never see again."

"No, Derik. Get that out of your head. I'm *not* going to see her. We don't get along. She was a horrible person to me. I *don't* want to see her, so just drop the conversation."

Derik watches George take off his boots. "What did you think of Sophie calling Grandpa an adulterer?"

George stands. "She was probably right. They used to do that kind of stuff to us all the time at the Indian day school. Nowadays, they can't get away with it. So many times, too, I discovered him passed out in his room with different women."

"Doesn't that make you upset, that your father was that way?"

"Of course it does." He prepares tea. "But I'm not going to stand here and let it ruin my life. I try not to think about those things. There were lots of terrible things he did to me, and I told you that. He was a deeply flawed man *and* father. I'm sure glad I'm not him, as I'd have a lot of explaining to do once I met the man upstairs."

"You mean God?"

"*Yes*—the Creator."

"Do you think maybe that's why Sophie was upset all the time, because he tried to molest her?"

"Many of us were molested, Derik. It's what they did back in the day." *God, I'd be so pissed if someone molested me. I'd gouge their eyes out. Now I feel bad for how I treated Sophie.*

Meh, you were nice to her the last time you saw her—that's all you can do.

Raven appears. "Hey gents. Sorry, I was busy chatting with Arnold about the importance of the Hamatsa. You know they have all that information posted on the board there when you walk in? Guess it's not so secret anymore!"

"What did he tell you?" asks Derik.

"Nothing I didn't really know already, but it was a nice chat."

"He just wants power," says George. "You know he's taking Grandpa's name, right?"

"What do you mean?" says Derik. "Like, *Henry*?"

"No, his *traditional* name. Didn't you hear him mentioning they're having a naming ceremony later?"

"No…"

"Now that Grandpa's gone, Arnold will take his name for himself at that ceremony."

"Didn't you say his name was Talking Eagle?"

"Yes, but that's not his traditional name." Chirp. "His traditional name is in Heiltsuk."

"What is it? Do you know?"

George dismisses him with a wave of his hand. "I don't want to talk about it, it just makes me upset. I got in a big argument with them over that. Getting your name was one of the most important moments for our people. There would be a giant ceremony, and you would be given a name that fits you better than your birth name, because how are you supposed to know how someone is when they're just born? This name signalled you were an adult."

"Do you have a traditional name?"

"No, but a shaman came to me in a dream and told me my name was River Bear."

"River Bear? Is that 'cause you're big like a bear?"

"It's 'cause I know a good opportunity when I see one, like a bear by a river during spawning season." He takes his tea and heads to his room. "Anyway, I'm going to bed. It's been a long day."

"What about my name? When will I get a name?"

"The Creator will give it to you when you're ready."

Lame. That'll take forever. Raven, as if reading his thoughts, says, "Just be patient, and you'll get one eventually."

"All right."

"Goodnight," says George.

"Goodnight, Dad. Love you."

"Goodnight. Love you too."

"Goodnight," says Raven.

George shuts the door.

"Do you know what his traditional name was?" Derik asks Raven.

"Nope. Names were inherited, so it was probably passed down to him. Talking Eagle is just as good, really; what's it matter when you grow up speaking English?"

"I never thought of that. It's more authentic if it's Heiltsuk?"

"Authentic to what, being Indigenous? Indigeneity resides with the land. Where you came from, you spoke English. Thus English resonates more within you. It's cool to drop Heiltsuk, Latin or Enochian, but I can never remember the words unless I'm using the language on the regular. Otherwise, it just evaporates as it utilizes short-term memory."

"I don't really care, if Arnold wants Grandpa's name, he can have it. Our people are always fighting over who's more Indigenous. Derik's good enough for me… though I wish I had a nickname. What about Redbird Anon? Can I have that one?"

"You said that was your guardian, though."

"Maybe it's just me. I like birds: they fly wherever they want, like radio waves (which are red on the electromagnetic spectrum). *Anon* means near, but it's also short for *anonymous*, as I like to be secretive. Also, our family crest is the Thunderbird, which Redbird turns into when he's mad, excited, or just trolling—never quite clear which."

Raven smirks. "Sounds like you really thought that through."

Derik pours himself juice, trying to hide his pride. "I have a very active imagination." Rain taps the windows from the dark. "So, what did you think about the celebration?"

"I thought it was good... Yeah, I liked it a lot. It was great to be in the Big House, finally. It took a long time to build. I think they were still building it the *last* time I was here. They did a good job replicating the old architecture. Of course, not everyone agrees with me."

"What do you mean?"

"Well, a lot of people are upset they didn't get to work on it, 'cause they're carpenters, or they think it should've been done differently. Most were upset it was designed by white people, I think, which makes sense—even though they did some good things, like use local timber and collaborate with local artists, like Arnold... I think it's going to be a long time before everyone sees eye to eye on such matters, which is just how reconciliation, relationships work."

"Right."

"You can't please everyone, but you should try. At least the healing process has begun."

"That's true... That's true."

"It's difficult to describe, really. Some things are ruined by speaking, 'cause speech comes after thought, or instinct. All I know is that something good is happening after decades of bad. How long before it blooms, I cannot say—could be years, could be generations. Something good will come of it in the end. Of that, I'm sure... Could be wrong though! I'm usually wrong... But then maybe that's why I know what's right."

"Good point."

Raven lies on the booth, yawns and stretches. "*Man* I'm tired."

Derik heads for his room. "All right, I'm going to bed. Goodnight Raven."

"Goodnight! Don't let the bedbugs bite."

Derik closes the door. He turns off the lights. He sits, looking out the porthole, listening to the rain.

24. Aunt Lizzy

Derik wakes to George tapping his spoon on the kettle—*ding, ding, ding, ding*. He hears George approach, then knock. "Derik... Derik, are you awake?"

He was hoping he wouldn't ask twice. "...No."

"I want you to get up and get ready. We're going to the hospital."

"*Why?*"

"We're going to see Aunt Lizzy. Come on, hurry up and get dressed. Auntie Rena is waiting for us." George walks back to the kitchen.

Derik groans, stretching in bed. "I knew it."

Did you?

Whatever, I'm happy to just get this over with.

Let's go. Get ready.

🌵 🌵 🌵

They enter the hospital, carrying their relics. As you can imagine, the hospital is quite small.

"We can't accept visitors," says the nurse. "It's COVID protocol."

"Dang," feigns George. "Well, I guess we're going home then."

"No you're not," says Rena. "You're going to see your sister." She asks the nurse, "We're her family—aren't we allowed to see her?"

The nurse tilts her glasses to look beyond. "Most visitors are family. You can see her for a few minutes, but then I must ask you to leave. Is that all right?"

"Yes, that's fine."

"Her room is this way. Please follow me." They follow, and come to a dark room with four hospital beds, Lizzy in the closer left. She's pretending to sleep. The nurse shakes her gently. Her eyes open.

"You have visitors here to see you, only for a few minutes." She gives them their privacy.

"It's good to see you," Rena hugs her. She puts the Mormin vest over her shoulders, telling her what she missed.

Lizzy turns to George. "What are you doing here?"

"We wanted to see you before we spread Dad's ashes, so you can say goodbye to him."

She looks away, and scoffs. "What do you care? You're only here because he's dead. You never came to see him in the hospital; you never answered his calls when he was dying and wanted to see his grandkids. Now he's gone, and you pretend to care? Get lost."

"I did my best to love him when he was alive."

"Yeah George, I'm sure you really did your best," she says, sarcastic. "He did all he could to provide for us and make sure you had a job, and how do you repay him? You keep his grandchildren, who he loved, away from him."

Is that true? He loved all his children—I assume that includes you, Dad. Derik realizes he's finally getting the other side of the story. Both George and Lizzy's eyes swell with the passion in their voices. "All I wanted, my whole life, was for Dad to see and love my kids," says George. "So *don't* tell me I didn't try to make that happen. I tried."

"Why didn't you answer his calls then, huh? Why'd you ignore him, as he lay dying in this very hospital?"

"I don't know!" He points as if stabbing. "And now I have to live the rest of my life knowing I could've done more."

The silence is thick. A machine breathes for a patient.

Rena speaks. "I know it's asking a lot of both of you, to come together, but this is the last time we'll all be together with Dad." Her words resonate with her arguing siblings.

George wipes a tear. "You're right."

"This isn't about us, this is about him," she continues. "He would've wanted to see you come together because he loved us all equally, whether he made it obvious or not. Now quit fighting like kids, and say goodbye to him."

They don't look at each other, but turn the same toward the urn Rena holds. Quivering, tears streaming, Lizzy rests her palm upon it, then George. They whisper their goodbyes, hardly audible to themselves, as Derik watches, almost doubtful of the significance, having realized reconciliation was unfeasible before arriving.

I should be nicer to Candace. Things could be a lot worse.

They slowly release their hold on the man they love.

"I know he's proud of you both," says Rena. "Wherever he may be."

The atmosphere is awkward after, as George and Lizzy haven't expressed such feelings to each other since childhood. Time will reveal the good brought forth by relinquishing their complicated history, and starting anew.

"We're heading to Grave Island now," says Rena. "We're spreading his ashes there and in the sea."

"Fine," says Lizzy. "He would like that."

"Wilson made us a cross for him," she adds, "so we can visit him anytime we like."

"Good. He always liked carving."

"Exactly."

They say their goodbyes. It's been over a decade since they last did so, yet it sounds like it was just yesterday. As they're leaving, Derik stands by her bed, her staring into the dark room.

"Auntie Lizzy… I just want to say thank you for the action figure you got me for my first Christmas. I still have it at home… I'll never get rid of it. Sometimes I look at it, and it reminds me of the inside of an abalone shell, you know, the ones they use for smudges? I look at it, and I think of you, and I think of Grandpa, and Auntie Sammy— the last time we were all together—and it makes me happy." He tries not to cry, but doesn't conceal his emotion, proud to feel as strongly as her and George, proud of the passion welling in his throat. "I never got to tell you thank you till today… So thank you, Aunt Lizzy, for the memories." He hugs her. *She's so weak and skinny.*

Don't think that, hug her. Let her know you love her.

I don't know if I love her. It doesn't matter, just pretend—love is self-less. He lets go. "Buh-bye."

As he leaves, she says, "Thank you."

🌢 🌢 🌢

Derik finds George and Rena outside, waiting for him by the truck.

"Well," Derik can't help but inquire, "how do you think that went?"

They climb inside. "Fine," says George. "Better than I expected."

Rena smiles.

"You know, you never know when you might lose someone. Better that you forgive them than live the rest of your life wishing you had," says Derik like an old man, like a monk, like—well, Raven.

George sighs, gripping the handle above the window. "Yup."

"Well put," says Rena. "You know, you should listen to him," she joshes George. "He's wiser than you."

Derik chuckles. "Yeah Dad."

Rena punches George's shoulder in jest, causing him to put up his guard. "Watch it," he says, with a smile—a bear among eagles.

There's one last thing they must do.

25. Sparkling Sea

They head to Grave Island, where many a Mormin was buried long before that name was known to them. The sky is grey and sprinkling. Arnold takes them on his boat, while George regales stories of Henry, merry to banish his sorrow. Arnold stops halfway to the island. Rena spreads the first of the ashes.

"Thank you, Dad," she says. "I wish you peace in the afterlife."

The waves rock the boat gently while she disperses the ashes.

Arnold continues to Grave Island. It's small compared to its neighbours. Barnacled rocks form the shore, strewn with spent shells, kelp dark green and orange, ceramic shards and bits of rust. Derik picks up a cup covered in barnacles, along with fallen feathers of baby eagles and ravens. The path is overgrown with ferns and vine.

George bears the cross with the family crest on his shoulder. They enter the forest. The disturbed leaves pour water down Derik's neck, not used to visitors. Within are the graves: Western monoliths and crosses, carved granite, epitaphs and totems. Wherever they step, they contact a grave. Rena carries the urn. All is returning whence it came.

They reach the site where Henry will rest, as did his ancestors. What is left to say that hasn't been? "Creator, watch over him." George plants the cross. They hammer it down with a rock, but hit concrete, an unmarked grave, so try over there. There is no footing for wheeling wights, just moss and vine; yet, it stands, Arnold vowing to return in vigilance.

With the last of the ashes, come tears. George finally feels he is truly letting go. Derik rubs his back, encouraging him to feel what he feels. The deed is done—the final act. The forces take what remains.

They return to the boat, silent, until George hums the tune his mom used to sing to him: "Que sera, sera... Whatever will be, will be." The sun peeks through the clouds. Derik trails, as they board, saying, "Goodbye, Grandpa. I love you." The trees whisper with breeze.

Once back in town, they say their goodbyes. "Thank you, Uncle Louis, for helping me catch my first salmon."

"Oh," Louis says, surprised. "No problem. You did well."

"Thank you, Auntie Rena, for being such a loving host."

Rena embraces him, then kisses his forehead. "Keep being good," she says. "Don't take after your dad."

"OK." He chuckles.

"Visit sometime. We'll be here for you."

They promise to call. All is well and set. Derik and George return to *Wild Thing*.

🌵 🌵 🌵

"Well, time to head out," says George. "It was great coming back, but I miss being at home with Mommy."

"Yeah," says Derik. "It was quite the adventure."

"What did you feel, spreading your grandpa's ashes at last?" asks Raven.

"It was sad," says Derik. "...But it also felt right. He's finally free to be among his ancestors, instead of being in a jar in his old house."

"Yes, he can continue on to the next stage of his existence."

"So are we actually leaving now?" asks Derik.

"I think it's about time," says George. "I bet there's a million and one things to do at the shop."

"I think I'm going to head to Haida Gwaii," says Raven. "I'm supposed to scout for a location for a retreat. A friend told me they'd take me there."

"Uh-huh," says George.

"You don't need me, do you? Derik's a competent deckhand now, and navigator, having seen the land. I'll catch you back in Vancouver."

"We should be fine. Supposed to be nothing but clear skies ahead."

"Are you taking a boat?" asks Derik. "Why don't you let us drop you off? I want to see the Hecate Strait."

"Nah, it's fine; I'll fly." He flaps his arms, then winks. He slaps them each on the shoulder then goes to pack. "Don't worry about me, they got a nice boat."

"We should probably stock up at the band store before we leave," says George.

"But we have *tons* of food," says Derik. "We don't need more junk."

"Better safe than sorry." He pulls out his keys. "You coming, or you just gonna wait here?"

Derik admires the sun's rays piercing the clouds, sparking the water. "I'll wait here… There's something I want to do before we leave."

"Oh yeah, what's that?"

"It's a secret." He smirks.

"OK, well, don't go running off again. It's not safe, you know, being by yourself in the forest."

"I know." Derik imagines a wave crashing over him, then sucking him out to sea while the birds watch him drown, only for his dad to discover him later face-down on the rocks. "I'll be fine."

"He's a young man, George; he is well endowed—nothing bad will come of him."

"Just promise me you'll stay safe."

"I will. Don't worry."

George gives Raven the handshake and a mighty hug. "Thanks for tagging along, and helping the boy. See you back in Vancouver."

"You bet. Take care, George. Thank you for allowing me to join you both."

"Anytime."

They go their separate ways, for now, but together, remain united. Derik grabs his trusty rod and tackle, and heads out to the beach of rapture after saying goodbye to Raven.

He prepares the line, attaching a copper spoon, then scans the water for a sign.

Here, says the whistle, distant, yet so near.

Derik arches his back, aims and casts, hitting the mark. It takes only seconds for a bite.

Out goes the line; the reel spins. He remembers: *Let it run, let it tire.* The rod bends; the fish pulls. Left then right he steers, right then left he swings, keeping rhythm with the fish. Inch by inch he gains, until the telltale silver flashes—it's a salmon. His heart races, thudding here, now skipping. His clasp upon the cork handle starts to slip with his clammy hands. The fish isn't giving up. Minutes flee. His shoulders ache and his arms are tired, yet patience he demonstrates, and for patience, he is rewarded, as he senses the salmon give. He sees it swim left then right, right then left, in diminishing bursts. It's only a matter of time now.

He steps into the water, not caring to keep his shoes and pants dry. He has no net—he could only carry so much—but he won't need one. The salmon comes in close. He lowers himself slowly, and gently dips his hand in the water. He hooks the salmon behind its gills with one finger. It does not flop, nor does it flip. No, it does not struggle at all. Derik has caught his first fish, from start to finish.

He leaves it in the water, recalling the trauma caused. With compassion, he holds its belly, admiring its beauty. He pulls out the hook with confidence. A spurt of pink blood joins the current. "Thank you," he says. Derik looks to the sky. "Thank you, God. Thank you, Grandpa." He looks back to the fish, and slowly lets go. It stays, gazing up at him.

Then it swims away, as I return over the sparkling sea.

Acknowledgements

I'd like to thank all the people of Bella Bella, for preserving their culture and providing me with wisdom, aid and inspiration for this novel. I, of course, love and appreciate my mom, dad and sister for their enduring support toward my artistic pursuits. Thank you to all my family and ancestors. Thank you, Emma, for your commitment in bringing this novel to light. Thank you, Silas, for believing in me. Thank you to everyone I met through the Indigenous Teacher Education Program, the First Nations House of Learning, and X̱wi7x̱wa Library for enlightening me to all things Indigenous. Thank you to all my friends and acquaintances who have influenced my life. I am truly grateful for all of you.

About the Author

Brandon Reid holds a B.Ed. from UBC with a specialization in Indigenous education, and a journalism diploma from Langara College. His work has been published in the *Barely South Review*, the *Richmond Review* and *The Province*. He is a member of the Heiltsuk First Nation, with a mix of Indigenous and English ancestry. He resides in Richmond, BC, where he works as a TTOC. In his spare time, he enjoys cooking, playing music and listening to comedy podcasts.